OF DRAG KINGS &

THE WHEEL OF FATE

What Reviewers Say About Bold Strokes Authors

KIM BALDWIN

"'A riveting novel of suspense' seems to be a very overworked phrase. However, it is extremely apt when discussing Kim Baldwin's [*Hunter's Pursuit*]. An exciting page turner [features] Katarzyna Demetrious, a bounty hunter…with a million dollar price on her head. Look for this excellent novel of suspense…" – **R. Lynne Watson**, *MegaScene*

RONICA BLACK

"Black juggles the assorted elements of her first book, [*In Too Deep*], with assured pacing and estimable panache…[including]…the relative depth—for genre fiction—of the central characters: Erin, the married-but-separated detective who comes to her lesbian senses; loner Patricia, the policewoman-mentor who finds herself falling for Erin; and sultry club owner Elizabeth, the sexually predatory suspect who discards women like Kleenex…until she meets Erin."– **Richard Labonte**, *Book Marks, Q Syndicate, 2005*

ROSE BEECHAM

"…her characters seem fully capable of walking away from the particulars of whodunit and engaging the reader in other aspects of their lives." – *Lambda Book Report*

GUN BROOKE

"*Course of Action* is a romance…populated with a host of captivating and amiable characters. The glimpses into the lifestyles of the rich and beautiful people are rather like guilty pleasures.…[A] most satisfying and entertaining reading experience." – **Arlene Germain**, reviewer for the *Lambda Book Report* and the *Midwest Book Review*

JANE FLETCHER

"*The Walls of Westernfort* is not only a highly engaging and fast-paced adventure novel, it provides the reader with an interesting framework for examining the same questions of loyalty, faith, family and love that [the characters] must face." – **M. J. Lowe**, *Midwest Book Review*

RADCLY/FE

"…well-honed storytelling skills…solid prose and sure-handedness of the narrative…" – **Elizabeth Flynn**, *Lambda Book Report*

"…well-plotted…lovely romance...I couldn't turn the pages fast enough!" – **Ann Bannon**, author of *The Beebo Brinker Chronicles*

OF DRAG KINGS &
THE WHEEL OF FATE

by

Susan Smith

2006

OF DRAG KINGS & THE WHEEL OF FATE

ISBN 1-933110-5-11
THIS TRADE PAPERBACK IS PUBLISHED BY
BOLD STROKES BOOKS, INC.,
NEW YORK, USA

FIRST EDITION: JUSTICE HOUSE PUBLISHING 2001
SECOND EDITION: BOLD STROKES BOOKS, INC., AUGUST 2006

CREDITS
EDITORS: CINDY CRESAP AND SHELLEY THRASHER
PRODUCTION DESIGN: J. BARRE GREYSTONE
COVER ART: CHRISTINE BEETOW
COVER GRAPHIC: SHERI (GRAPHICARTIST2020@HOTMAIL.COM)

Acknowledgments

Thanks to Debra Butler of the Addicts for hooking it up, Radclyffe for taking a chance, Cindy Cresap for editing with style and grace.

DEDICATION

To Adrienne Lowik, Johnny Class—
you are the rest of the book.

CHAPTER ONE

It was in the cemetery that Rosalind Olchawski first received the word on love. She was walking in Forest Lawn, seeking beauty where it was rumored to be found. There weren't many places in Buffalo she'd found to be beautiful, but she'd only been a resident for a month. It was Rosalind's nature to try to be generous, with places and with people, and to find pleasing what was presented as pleasing. So she walked, and her accepting nature found the cemetery agreeable, the monuments somber and interesting, the trees stubbornly green against an early September sky.

Rosalind drew a hand through her hair, the strands mingling red and gold, the pale white of bleached bone, the yellow of saffron in a riot of color. Her eyes were a similar mingling—brown and gray and green—agate, like the edge of a mountain lake reflecting the changing leaves of autumn. Her face was that of an eternal youth, despite the fine lines that stress had started to carve near her mouth, around her eyes. At thirty-three, Rosalind Olchawski had the look of a perpetual teenager, with the weariness of the aged.

Walking was an addiction, a time to put her seething brain on hold and let her body move without direction, a Zen exercise for a woman who lived too long and often in her head. In her own estimation, walking had saved her sanity during the writing of her dissertation. Having completed a doctorate, she was now convinced that no one went through the process and remained sane. She'd seen friends and colleagues succumb to their own brands of madness—fits of temper, drunken bouts, marriages thrown up on the rocks. Rosalind smiled, just a little, at that.

Her marriage had already been shredded by the time she'd started writing and over before she was halfway done. Poor Paul, he didn't even get the satisfaction of suffering grandly through her dissertation, claiming all the neglected spouse's privileges and sympathy. He'd been neglected long before and taken his privileges elsewhere.

Rosalind sighed and put her hands in the pockets of her jacket. It was an ungenerous memory, one that she didn't like to revisit. There was too much unfinished, too much inexplicable about the unraveling of her marriage for her to be settled with how it happened. Maybe no memory was easy until it was digested and reformed.

A car passed her on the cemetery path, moving at a stately pace. She stepped aside, wondering if they were visiting relatives or were tourists. Rosalind ducked her head, to acknowledge their potential grief and hide her inappropriate thoughts. She didn't know anyone who was buried here, but she could try to maintain a respectful air. A cemetery was a place for reflection, for communing with the divine. Her mind refused to get caught up in the rhythm of celestial time and churned out thoughts that had no impression of eternity. She held on to a hope that the beauty of the setting might change that.

An arrow of black tore across her vision, low and to the left. It took her a moment to recognize the shape. Rosalind watched as the crow backwinged and landed on a headstone some fifteen feet off the path. It arranged its feathers with a full body shake and turned, feet shuffling on the blue stone. One bright black marble of an eye found her. She had the oddest sensation that the crow was about to speak when it opened its sooty beak, but no sound came out. The silence was unnerving, as if she couldn't hear what was being said to her. The crow cocked its head, glanced away, then was gone. The blue stone drew her eye. She walked off the path to get a better look.

It was unfinished. On the front was a patch smooth as glass, with writing inscribed. Not the name and date that Rosalind expected, but a quote.

> Love is the emblem
> of eternity; it confounds
> all notion of time,
> effaces all memory
> of a beginning, all fear
> of an end.

She reached in her pocket for a scrap of paper to copy it down. It was the kind of thing she'd love to recite, later, to a friend, to try to capture the moment of the crow and the gravestone. She wondered who slept under the stone, why they'd left no record of who they'd been and when they had lived. A feeling of ineffable sadness gripped her, the weight of a grief she didn't possess.

She interpreted the feeling as a stab of loneliness for Ithaca, for a familiar setting and familiar people. She was gentle with herself, letting the feeling pass. Loneliness was perfectly normal in a new town. She was starting a new job, which she had to admit she loved. She'd already made a friend.

Rosalind had had the impression, before she'd moved there, that Buffalo was a dying rust-belt town, forlorn after the close of the steel mills, known only for chicken wings and bad football. She'd expected to find many sports bars, the truth behind all those snow jokes, and a monochrome city against a monochrome sky on the edge of a Great Lake. She'd consoled herself with thoughts of the two-hour drive to Toronto and all the theater to be had in that splendid Canadian metropolis. Ellie had shown her the way.

It was one of those getting-to-know-you departmental functions, the kind with name tags and plastic cups of juice. A chance, Rosalind thought very privately, for her to start practicing kissing ass. She remembered the very moment she met Ellie.

She had to be from the theater department. Her entrance was too perfect, and too loud, for her to be in English. The woman who entered wore black in celebration of mortuary finery. Black silk shirt, black leather jacket, black jeans over narrow black boots, all set against a curling array of ash blond hair. She sashayed into the room blowing kisses, just adoring everyone she came near in a manner too exaggerated to be real. Suddenly everyone else in the room was beige and wan. The woman poured herself a glass of juice, laughing with a mouth scarlet and brilliant.

Rosalind felt like she was back in high school. She wanted this woman to come talk to her, to laugh at her jokes, to turn the light of her attention her way. When the woman glanced at her and smiled, she nearly dropped her cup of juice. When the woman excused herself from an unfinished conversation and strolled over to her, Rosalind struggled to keep herself from looking over her shoulder to see who she was approaching.

The woman stopped right next to her and leaned in as if they were the oldest of friends, sharing a secret. "You look like you have a sense of humor. It's my duty to preserve that." There was such amusement in her tone that Rosalind found herself smiling in return.

"I like to think that I do," she said. It was the start of a conversation that hadn't ended for hours.

Ellie would like the quote, she decided. The weight of grief she called loneliness shifted, she started walking faster. Maybe it was time to start unpacking her office.

❖

"Dr. Olchawski?" The voice called from the partially open door, half shielding the office of the newest addition to the English department at the University at Buffalo. The doctor in question, looking more like one of her students in faded jeans and a red T-shirt with a Shakespeare in Delaware Park logo, was lost behind a mountain of papers threatening to swamp her desk. She bravely held the suicidal mass at bay, bracing an arm against it as she reached out with her foot, edging the door open. "Incredible. I didn't think you were tall enough for that move, let alone limber enough. How can you have this much junk? The semester just started."

Ellie's voice was rimmed and threaded with amusement. She sank into the empty chair at the corner of the desk, watching as the stack of papers started to teeter. The papers were given a firm shove back onto the desk, then a warning look.

"I'm still moving in," Rosalind commented to her reclining friend.

Ellie looked up at the picture over the desk, of Rosalind in Renaissance Festival wench's garb, a tankard in each hand, bosom straining against the low-cut gown. "You should put that thing away, before your students start palpitating."

"This, from an actress. I thought you'd appreciate period costume," Rosalind said, sinking into her chair.

"Oh, I do. But you're lovely enough in your street drag. Put you in something low cut, and you're lethal," Ellie said, with an appreciative look. Rosalind turned her agate eyes on her friend and narrowed them shrewdly.

"Thou dost protest too much. What's all the flattery for?"

Ellie's mobile face became the picture of innocence, a cherub out of Caravaggio. "Can't I just appreciate my dear friend?"

"No."

"Oh. Well, Dr. Olchawski, I was wondering if I could trade sexual favors to get an A," Ellie said brightly.

"Well, sure. I haven't had a date in months," Rosalind said immediately, putting her glasses on.

Ellie proceeded to look shocked and saddened. "Not my favors, unfortunately. I only wish I were gay. There are no heterosexual men in theater. More's the pity. Ros, you're a catch. No, I was thinking of a double date. Bill has a friend in poetics. He'd be perfect for you."

Rosalind took her glasses back off, rubbing a hand across her eyes. "Oh, Ellie. No. School just started, I don't want to—"

"Ros. It's been nine months. You can stop mourning. It's the twenty-first century. People do get divorced," Ellie said, taking the glasses away from her friend.

The truth was that Rosalind was not mourning, at least not her failed marriage. That she had expected, from the moment Paul had proposed to her. There had been a warning voice in the back of her mind, saying, *Not a good idea.* She could never quite put her finger on why. He was a good man, pleasant to look at, good company, gentle in a fashion. They'd known one another forever, finally dating in their late twenties because everyone seemed to think they should. It wasn't regret she felt when he finally turned elsewhere to seek companionship, after she'd stopped sleeping with him. It was relief.

She hadn't even minded when he came home and told her about his affair. She'd accepted it with only a twinge of guilty pleasure, as if to say, *Finally. We can admit that this was a mistake all along.* She hadn't chastised him for his infidelity or turned down his offer of divorce.

It reduced him to tears that she didn't think enough of him to rage at him, strike out at him. *Why would I?* Rosalind wondered. She'd never hated him. That would require an intensity of emotion that didn't exist in her. She was a warm person, everyone said so, but hot, no. Not given to the fires of jealousy or rage, anger or revenge. Or, a small part of her admitted, love.

Paul had been good to her. She felt affection for his good heart, his simple masculine virtues and vanities, his dreams that seemed so manageable. She also felt a sense of superiority, a distance from the possessiveness he seemed to feel about her person. She really didn't care if he found someone else to make him happy; she just knew that she couldn't. It had broken his heart finally that she didn't love him enough to hate him.

"You're not normal, Ros. If I didn't know better, I'd say you were frigid. Or a dyke, but you never show any interest in girls either. You just don't get worked up over anybody."

She wanted to. In her heart, Rosalind yearned to be driven to distraction, to make every mistake a lover could, to lose herself in courtship's dance and retreat. To be out of control, to feel like there was nothing she wouldn't fight, wouldn't overcome to have...whoever.

That's where her imagination failed her. At thirty-three, nine months after her divorce from her old friend and erstwhile husband, she despaired of it ever happening. *I must be missing a piece of my heart, damaged in some way, because I've never felt it.* The poet, the lover, the madman are of imagination all compact...I'm not so sure.

"Oh, Ellie. A poet. A blind date with a poet. Just what I need," Rosalind finally said.

"Look, I promise you it'll be fun. There's a drag show downtown at Club Marcella. I want to go check it out before I send my students to review it. You love that stuff. Fits right in with that Gender in Shakespeare seminar you were telling me about. You look like you need to have some fun, baby. Come out and play."

Hours later, in Rosalind's car on the way to the club, Ellie was still exclaiming that it would be a grand evening. Rosalind had insisted on taking her car as an escape valve. If the date went awry, Ellie could go home with Bill, and she could slip away on her own.

"You remember my signal if he's boring the devil out of me?" she asked Ellie, not for the first time.

"You start choking on the little umbrella in your drink and fall off the chair. When you turn blue, I yell 'Man overboard!' and drag you clear." She turned the rearview mirror so she could regard herself. Rosalind turned the mirror back.

"That's for driving, not looking at yourself. No, if I go like this, you meet me at the pay phone and we invent a sick relative."

Ellie nodded in a parody of comprehension. "The eagle flies at midnight. The crow is on the gravestone."

Rosalind looked sharply at her friend. After Ellie had surprised her with news of the double date, she'd forgotten about the quote from the cemetery. "Did I tell you about the crow?"

"You make this gesture—" Ellie said, demonstrating.

"No, not that. I spent the afternoon in Forest Lawn. I found this quote I wanted to read to you, something carved on one of the stones. I only noticed it because a crow flew down and landed on the stone." Rosalind left one hand on the wheel and reached in her pocket for the scrap of paper. She pulled it out, feeling a small thrill of triumph. "Read that."

Ellie did, squinting over Rosalind's handwriting. "How very Gothic and morbid. It's gorgeous. I didn't know you liked Madame de Staël. What had you haunting the cemetery this afternoon?"

"Just walking. I wanted to see Red Jacket's monument and the pond with the swans." Rosalind took the scrap of paper back and folded it neatly in half. "Do you believe in it?" she asked, glancing at Ellie.

Ellie was fixing her lipstick, making obscene faces at herself in the mirror. "Red Jacket or the swans? I believe in swans, but they are a little suspect."

"Love." When Rosalind spoke the word, it took on the grandeur of Paris, the strangeness of Byzantium. She had added, without knowing it, a level of reverence that only those who had never visited could add to the name of a destination. "Love like that, that erases time."

Ellie stopped applying her makeup. "It's the blind date, isn't it? Look, I think he'll be a nice guy. Bill said he'd be perfect for you—"

"*Bill* said? You mean you haven't even met this guy?" Rosalind demanded, taking the corner sharply.

"I'm looking out for your best interests! Sweetie, you may not have noticed, but you are moping. I'm trying to get you out into the world."

"Ellie, I just moved here. I'm starting a new job, getting to know the area. I don't have to start dating immediately."

"Great excuse. I might even buy it, if I were an idiot," Ellie returned, smiling broadly.

It deflated Rosalind's small store of anger. She parked where Ellie indicated, sheepish. She picked up her purse, took a quick look at herself in the mirror, and saw the wary mix of despair and hope in her own eyes. She looked away, unable to face it. Life was much more bearable without the apparition of hope, whispering its sugared promises of paradise. That sort of thing happened to other people, people who were larger than life. Like Ellie. She could see Ellie getting consumed with passion.

Rosalind knew it was different for her. She'd been married to a man she'd known most of her life. And wasn't friendship what all women's magazines recommended as the basis for a lasting relationship? She and Paul had been great friends. There hadn't been the bodice-ripping lust, but surely that was fiction. Warm affection was the reality. "It's a crime that women grow up reading romance novels," Rosalind said, halfway to herself.

"It's a crime that love does exist, and we are reminded of its absence. If anybody ever told the truth about love, the pages would curl and burn."

"I should be so lucky."

Ellie linked her arm though Rosalind's.

"Your luck is changing. Trust me, I'm an actress. We're superstitious about these things. I see great change coming your way, starting tonight."

Ellie had included Marcella's on her tour of small theaters, coffeehouses, and gay bars. Rosalind knew that Marcella's was a drag bar downtown in the Theater District, firmly planted between the two largest regional houses, Studio Area and Shea's Buffalo.

Both theaters Ellie advised her to take in small doses. "They cater to the white suburban tourists from Orchard Park and Williamsville. They'll get touring companies doing *Phantom*, *Grease*, and, for a real big thrill, *Rent*. If you like your musicals white bread, go to Shea's. If you want to find some good stuff being done, hit the Ujima Company, Buffalo Ensemble, Paul Robeson. Any of the small houses. The tourists would drop dead of fright to see what's really being done in Buffalo," Ellie proclaimed like a priestess giving the mystery to an initiate.

The Theater District was largely a marketing ploy on behalf of a dying downtown, trying to lure new blood and money in from the suburbs. Businesses were expiring by the day, residents had long fled, but a small strip of bars and clubs aimed at young people was thriving on Chippewa Street. The Irish Classical Theater on Chippewa drew a mixed crowd—suits and hipsters, students and old guard, suburbanites who wanted to feel very adventuresome. The bars on Chippewa had started a minirevival, supporting a few restaurants, coffee shops, and fast-food joints, mingled with the older businesses. The old shoe store was still there, next to the new Atomic Café. The pizzeria still sat across from the porn shop that always had two huge cats sleeping in the window. Chippewa was alive with college students and yuppies.

An enterprising businessman from neighboring Rochester saw the market and found it good. He'd purchased the space next to Shea's box office, a club space that he transformed into Marcella's. He'd named the bar for his own drag queen persona and set about making a success of it. Local gay papers carried ads of buff, nearly naked men holding up text detailing drink specials. He held contests, special parties, events, and, finally, the first regular drag nights in Buffalo. Model searches encouraged the young to show off their assets for the chance at a calendar or poster of their own.

The front room of Marcella's had a long curved aluminum and glass bar, a dance floor with a DJ booth, and an impressive light system. Handsome young men with soap-star smiles and lifetime memberships to health clubs gyrated and enticed one another. Shined, oiled, sleek, and sexy dancers hired for their looks performed on the bar, on the dance floor, as bar backs and bouncers. Marcella had an eye for beautiful young men and included them in the decor.

The bar was quickly adopted by a contingent of straight girls in full makeup and tight dresses, enjoying the display of splendid male flesh, enjoying the chance to dance and flirt with the boys in an atmosphere oddly safe. They could dance salaciously with gorgeous men, who then went home with each other. When the crowd from Chippewa started drifting in, Marcella's became a gold mine.

Everyone had thought that Marcella's wouldn't last. A gay club, in the middle of the straightest, most touristy part of downtown? Madness. Yet a strange synergy took over. The Theater District embraced Marcella's; the crowds from Amherst and Williamsville, some of them at least, loved it. It was like visiting a foreign country, where friendly, colorful natives are eager to perform their folk dances for you, take your money, then disparage you behind your back.

Straight people brought cash, so Marcella's catered to them. The drag shows proved to be immensely popular and became a fixture. Ellie had told her about the drag shows, told her that the level of performance could be exceptional. She wanted to send her first-year acting students to see the show. "I'd send them to St. Catherine's to see the lap dancing if I could get away with it. Now that takes energy, working with enthusiasm night after night, but I don't think they're ready for that yet," Ellie said, breezing past the bouncer, a three-hundred-pound man in a security guard's uniform.

He nodded to Ellie affably, then held his arm up, blocking Rosalind from entering. Ellie turned around and frowned at the guard. "Tony, come on. You know me. Would I bring the unworthy here?"

"She with you? Okay, Ellie, but keep an eye on that one. She looks like trouble." He pointed to Rosalind, who promptly blushed.

Ellie led them past the dance floor, past the gorgeous men displaying themselves for one another. Rosalind did her best not to stare like a tourist on her first trip to a gay bar. Ellie was a performance in herself—moving across the floor, greeting other regulars, blowing air kisses to the dancing men. One of the men turned, saw Ellie pass by, and threw a smile of appreciation at Rosalind.

She realized that she was being congratulated and felt a flush of warmth at the assumption. That someone would think she could land Ellie was flattering. Rosalind stood up a little straighter and smiled back, enjoying the moment of notoriety. She was still smiling as she followed Ellie into the back room. She started looking around, checking to see if anyone else made the same assumption. It was like trying on another identity for the night. Her mind skipped off, picturing what the night might be like if it were just her and Ellie there to see the show. People would see them sitting together, alone, laughing. They'd assume they were lovers. Rosalind pictured Ellie ordering wine, narrating the finer points of the drag show…

The appearance of Ellie's boyfriend shattered her fantasy. Bill was almost colorless next to her—sandy hair receding, face as smooth as a boy's. He was quiet where Ellie was flamboyant, but Ellie found his presence comforting. He kissed Ellie demurely on the cheek and held out his hand to Rosalind. "I'd like you to meet Greg, my friend from the department. Greg, this is Rosalind." He stepped aside, and Rosalind got her first look at her date for the evening.

Whatever perverse hope that had lingered in the secret chambers of her heart died on the spot. He wasn't a bad-looking man, with his longish hair and his goatee and his glasses. It was the way he turned to Bill with a self-congratulatory smirk, as if she couldn't see the exchange. He'd been expecting the worst and seemed pleased with the sight of her. He stroked his goatee with one hand, a gesture she promptly hated. He took her hand, but managed not to say hello. Rosalind smiled graciously and silently promised to get back at Ellie.

The back room at Marcella's had cafe tables in front of a proscenium stage. It reminded Rosalind of a high school auditorium, despite the loud music from the front room. A good rigging and lighting system had been installed, and occasionally a runway would be rented for fashion shows and special events. The stage had created, in the regular Friday night shows, royalty of its own. The audience knew the performers, many of whom worked every week, and had their favorites.

Miz Understood, a buxom blonde, was the MC. Her routine had the snap of vicious stand-up, and the audience loved her. She would get them worked up between numbers, handle hecklers and intoxicated tourists, and keep the peace.

Ellie sat them down at Table 14, right in front of the stage. Bill held the chair for Ellie, and Greg sat himself, leaving Rosalind to select her own chair. Bill sat to Ellie's left; Rosalind chose the space where she could keep her friend in sight. To Rosalind's left was Greg, her poet blind date. Rosalind smoothed down her skirt, wondering if she should have dressed more dramatically.

She loved simple clothes, plums and russets, deep browns and oranges. She took a quick look at Greg and tried not to sigh. He was stroking his goatee again, a gesture so reminiscent of Errol Flynn movies that she wanted to scream. What was she doing here, anyway? *He looks like a poet*, with his nervous eyes and his acerbic commentary on the denizens of the club. This had all the earmarks of a colossal mistake.

The warning voice in the back of her head chided her for being unkind. She hadn't dated in months; how could she reject this man out of hand? Calmly, reasonably, she told herself to engage him in conversation, get to know him, to find pleasing what was presented as pleasing. She'd had enough practice at that. So Rosalind smiled, warmly, and put on her most interested face.

A beautiful boy with a Caesar haircut, wearing only leather shorts and a chest harness, appeared at the table to take their drink order. "I'll have a Glenlivet, neat," Ellie said grandly, accepting the role of psychopomp for the night. She ordered Bill a gin and tonic without asking, and Greg ordered a Bordeaux. Ellie looked at Rosalind, knowing that she usually drank white wine.

Something, maybe the setting, maybe the look on Ellie's face, the relaxation and self-knowledge, spurred her on. She resolved to make a real adventure of the night. "Glenlivet, neat," she said in a perfect imitation of Ellie's tone.

Her friend laughed, delighted.

The waiter left, sliding off between tables filled up with men in suits, women in cocktail dresses.

Rosalind looked around the room, at the difference in the back room crowd. Male/female pairings dominated, with an occasional table of only men. The doors to the front of the bar were shut, closing out the techno pulsing on the dance floor. "I thought this was a gay club," Rosalind said to Ellie.

"It is. This is the tourist room. Suburbanites just love coming to see the show. Makes them feel wicked."

"So, Rosalind, Bill tells me that you're from Ithaca," Greg said, looking her over very carefully.

It made Rosalind wonder what he saw. It was clear to her that he had a certain dislike for Ellie, his mouth pinched in mild discomfort when she burst forth in laughter, when she waved enthusiastically to a drag queen she knew. Ellie's spontaneous joy looked a little too brazen, seen through his eyes. Greg was smiling at her, so what did he see? Someone more acceptable, quiet, attractive in a distracted academic way, without Ellie's fire and verve. The thought of such a comparison made Rosalind feel resentful and ornery.

"I did my PhD at Cornell. But I'm originally from Poughkeepsie," Rosalind said, forcing herself to look directly at him. She noticed that he frowned when he glanced around the room and didn't bother to conceal his distaste.

"Po-what? Never heard of it. One of those made-up Indian names, right? Is that New York State?" he said, sipping at his Bordeaux. A drop of the dark red liquid spilled onto his shirt; he cursed and brushed at it with a napkin.

Lights in the room faded down and came up on stage. Miz Understood came out to the cheers of the regulars. She was a large queen in a short champagne skirt, a gold jacket, and bustier. Candles on the tables glowed, the light reflecting off the sequins on Miz Understood's jacket. In her right hand she held a mike with a display of dexterity that Rosalind found remarkable, considering her three-inch, fire-engine red nails. For that matter, Rosalind admired outright the queen's ability to walk in five-inch spike heels, something she had only attempted once and nearly broke her ankles.

"Good evening, ladies, gentlemen, and the other way around. You know me, I'm Miz Understood. My husband doesn't get me. But if you come back to my dressing room later on, honey, you'll get me." She picked out a tourist in a blue suit, sitting close to the stage, and pounced on him. She stopped dead, pointing. "Whoa! Lance, put the spot on him."

Miz Understood walked offstage, went right to the table, then sat down in the startled man's lap. "I'm the welcome wagon. Well, come on! Honey, she's not good enough for you. You need a lot of woman." Miz Understood indicated, with a wave of her red nails, the painfully thin woman sitting with the man. The man in the blue suit had the grace to laugh nervously, so Miz Understood let him off the hook. She rose and went back to the stage.

"He was a good sport. Send him a drink. And my room key. We have something different tonight for all of you. Egyptia has a Special Friend performing with her." The queen paused, holding the mike out to the audience. Everyone oohed and ahhed in anticipation, until Miz Understood took the mike back. "That's better. But before we bring out our own Queen of Denial—and I don't mean a river in Egypt, honey— I'd like to introduce my girlfriend, Diva Las Vegas, doing what she does so well."

Ellie and Bill relaxed, enjoying the show. Diva Las Vegas slid on stage and right into a rendition of "I am Woman." Greg rolled his eyes. "Something bothering you, Greg?" Ellie asked sweetly.

"Yes. The ridiculous insistence these people have on calling themselves 'she.' They've even got you doing it," Greg said, blotting at his beard with a napkin.

"There isn't enough royalty in the world, and not enough that we can disrespect it," Bill said.

Greg picked up his glass and found it empty. "The boy in the Daisy Dukes will never make it over here to take my order."

"Not during the show, no. You'll have to brave the bar," Bill said.

Greg grumbled and left the table without asking if anyone else wanted anything.

Ellie heaved a sigh of relief as soon as he was out of earshot. "I've got a treat for you," she leaned over and shouted into Rosalind's ear.

"Greg's going home?"

"No, not that. The something special they're doing tonight? I think I found your Ganymede."

They had been in Rosalind's office a few days after they'd met. Ellie was helping her move in, tossing books out of their cardboard boxes with abandon. She'd picked up Rosalind's *Unabridged Works of Shakespeare* and hefted it. "I feel the spirit moving me. Take this book, close your eyes, flip open to a page, and point to a word. That will tell your fortune."

"You're kidding, right?"

"You leave vibrations on your favorite book, it becomes attuned to you. You should try it with a dictionary, it's wild. Just close your eyes, clear your mind, and let the book tell you what you need."

So Rosalind closed her eyes, took the heavy book in both hands, and let it fall open to a page. She'd stabbed her finger down randomly, then opened her eyes. Ellie looked over her shoulder at where her finger had landed. "From *As You Like It*. Ganymede. The name Rosalind takes when she disguises herself as a young man."

"Great. I'm destined to cross-dress and hide in a forest." Rosalind put the book down. She didn't know why fortune-telling irked her, but it always had, from Tarot cards to horoscopes. There were far more interesting things the book could have told her, if it were divining. It was proof that fortune-telling didn't work for her.

"You have to interpret the signs. The book is telling you what you need. Something that's a part of you, under a different name. Maybe in a guise you wouldn't expect."

On stage, Diva Las Vegas was finishing her song. The lights dimmed down, the Diva made a grand exit. Egyptia entered, a six-foot-two queen in a stunning platinum wig. Bill whistled in admiration. Egyptia had flawless chocolate skin set against pale green eyes, slim arms, and legs that went on for days. She jumped into her signature number, "We are Family."

Men ran up to the stage and handed her dollar bills. Egyptia flirted with them, making her favorites tuck the money in her plunging neckline.

Rosalind asked Ellie, "Why are they bringing money to the stage?"

"Show of appreciation. You always tip your favorite queens."

Egyptia finished the number to loud cheers and hooting. A boy ran on stage with a chair; she favored him with a blinding smile. He grinned, before vanishing into the audience. The lights dimmed down, leaving a single brilliant spot on Egyptia as she draped herself into the chair, beautifully alone.

From the darkness a form started to emerge, walking slowly into the pool of light. Rosalind caught a glimpse of blue-black hair, slicked back; smooth skin stretched over perfect cheekbones; a slim, broad-shouldered frame in a sleek black suit with an amber tie. She felt her heart start beating faster, like a sprinter off the block. When this vision paused and swept electric blue eyes over the crowd, Rosalind swore that they looked right at her, into her. She could feel sparks jumping on her skin.

The illusion was perfect. Elvis gave a sleepy-eyed look at the audience, curled his lip, ran a hand through his black hair. Egyptia turned her head away, ignoring him. He moved closer to the chair, a sensual menace that Egyptia struggled to ignore. Music started, Elvis crooned in the background.

Are you lonesome tonight? The King sang, and the sex god in the black suit lip-synched to the sighing Egyptia. She tried to act aloof, but the sex god slid around the chair, easing a smile out of the pouting queen. Egyptia gave up the fight and melted, eyes adoring the handsome young man. He knew he'd charmed her, his smile grew, he added a shake to his hips as he sang.

"He's gorgeous," Rosalind breathed, unaware she was speaking aloud. Her heartbeat threatened to deafen her. Was this it? Finally she'd be killed by a stroke in the middle of this splendid creature's performance? *With my luck, someone that gorgeous just has to be gay. Mother Nature does not love me.*

Ellie smirked at her, drawing her eyes away from the stage for the barest minute.

"What?" Rosalind asked, her eyes drifting back to the King.

"Yes. He is gorgeous, isn't she? Your Ganymede."

Bill looked like he was salivating, too, so Rosalind didn't feel quite as bad. Then it registered, what Ellie had said. "She. You said she," Rosalind repeated, trying to grasp something vitally important, despite the pain in her chest from the coming attack.

"You should say 'he,' hon. He's a male impersonator, who just started performing with Egyptia. A drag king. I think they're friends," Bill said, watching the sex god stroke Egyptia's neck with long-fingered hands. Egyptia looked ready to faint.

Rosalind thought she might follow her. The sex god in the jet black suit was a woman.

That knowledge should have affected her, cooled her blood, brought a sheepish grin to her lips. The act had been perfect. She'd bought into it. There were plenty of sound reasons for enjoying the number, appreciating the levels of cultural meaning, academic ways to digest it. It wasn't her intellect that was engaged. Knowing that the performer in the black suit was a woman made Rosalind's heart go into overtime, long-distance running. She felt her breath catch, felt herself get wet.

Her arousal was a complete surprise, and she viewed it from a distant corner of her mind with amazement, as if aliens had taken over her body. *I'm not going to die of a stroke, I'm being invaded by the pod people.* She was not someone who got hot and bothered, so her body's undisputed response seemed to short-circuit her brain. Her mind couldn't produce an acceptable reason for the reaction; the sheer novelty of it overwhelmed her. There had to be a way to survive this with some dignity.

Rosalind's well-trained mind went to work, trying to offset her rioting body. She knew plenty of historical context for women dressing as men. Shakespeare was rife with cross-dressing and mistaken identity, and hadn't she read that women dressed as soldiers during the Civil War? That was a good bit of information to work into the conversation. It would give her back some of the distance her body was yearning to overcome. "She's incredible. Do we go up and give her money?" Rosalind asked, hoping that the enthusiasm she heard in her own voice would be taken as purely academic approval.

"I'm not sure with drag kings. They don't seem to," Bill said.

During the performance no one ran up with money for Egyptia, either. It was as if Egyptia and Elvis existed only for one another, their charisma crowding all other presence out of the room. Interrupting that courtship was unthinkable.

"We could always send her a drink," Ellie said.

Tell me, dear, are you lonesome tonight? The song ended, the lights faded down on Egyptia grabbing the sex god and pulling that dark head down for a kiss.

When the blackout came, Rosalind felt it like a slap in the face.

Greg came back from the bar as the last note of the song stilled. "You wouldn't believe the traffic at the bar. This big queen popped me in the eye with his shoulder pad."

Ellie lunged out and grabbed a passing bar back, a pretty boy in leather shorts. "Send Elvis a drink, on Table 14."

Rosalind, still savoring the last sight of those long-fingered hands, was shocked out of her reverie. "Ellie!" Rosalind, her face flaming, pushed the hair back behind her ears. It kept falling out of the loose braid she'd put it in, threatening to all come down any minute. Greg was talking about something, so she looked at him, watching his mouth move behind his beard. The thunk of a heavy glass on the table startled her, and she looked up into the bluest eyes she'd ever seen.

Lord, that color has to be illegal. One large hand grabbed the back of a chair and spun it around, then long legs straddled it, arms resting on the table. The sex god had landed. Up close the Elvis illusion evaporated, leaving in its place a remarkably handsome boy. Rosalind looked into her face in a kind of suspended wonder, feeling a recognition that couldn't be hers mingle with the desire she wasn't ready to reject. Rosalind looked into the face of the handsome girl, knowing that there must be a word for the feeling of relief when you find something you never knew was missing.

"Thanks for the drink." The voice was low and smoky.

Rosalind felt her eyes flutter closed on hearing it. She had a vision of that voice, like warm caramel, sliding over her skin, whispering in her ear...

"Our pleasure," Ellie said, and the blue eyes swiveled that way. Rosalind found it easier to breathe.

The blue-black hair was tousled, falling out of its grease, bangs spiking down over the girl's eyes.

Rosalind found her hand reaching out before she caught herself, as if she'd done that a thousand times. She found her face burning, again. *Get a grip, Ros, she's a child.* The girl had to be her students' age. Twenty, maybe twenty-one.

The gorgeous creature smiled crookedly at Ellie. "You liked the show?"

"It was fantastic! Diva, Kandy Kane, and Egyptia doing 'Mr. Postman' was inspired," Ellie said with an enthusiasm Rosalind was profoundly grateful for. She couldn't speak a word if she'd been shot.

Bill raised his glass. "To royalty, of all genders!"

The sex god—try as she might, Rosalind could not stop thinking of her as that—raised her glass in a mocking salute.

"What's your name?" Ellie asked.

Rosalind had been quiet as a snake in a mongoose's jaws ever since the girl sat down. She knew her face must be flushed; steam felt like it was escaping from under her collar. She wondered if she were coming down with something. Something abrupt and deadly. Mediterranean flu?

"I'm Taryn," the girl said, still performing, holding out her hand to Ellie. She extended it to Bill; then Rosalind was face to face with Taryn and lost all powers of coherent thought.

"This is Rosalind Olchawski," Ellie supplied. Rosalind felt her hand folded in the sex god's and a sense of rightness that shocked her back to herself. The room receded, and there was an echo like distant drums or hundreds of people chanting. The professor locked stares with the drag king. Rosalind saw the moment that recognition crept into her strangely familiar eyes.

Her lips opened to speak, a welcome poised on them. "You," Taryn said.

Rosalind didn't blink.

"You," she said in confirmation. Rosalind kept hold of the hand, not ever wanting to give it back. The hand felt exactly as she knew it would, powerful, strong, with a gentle touch, warm, magnetic, like everything else about the dark girl. Rosalind glanced down, marveling at how good her hand looked in the drag king's. Nor did its owner seem eager to have it back.

"Pleasure to meet you, Rosalind." Taryn said her name with delicious emphasis. The tip of her tongue slipped out and licked her upper lip in a gesture that could only be anticipation.

"Lovely to meet you, Taryn." *She actually closed her eyes when I said her name.*

The noise of the club fired up around them again; the night took on its accustomed rhythm. Greg thrust his hand across their line of sight, severing their contact. No one else seemed to notice the moment that had passed between them. Taryn glanced down at his hand, reluctantly releasing Rosalind's. She gave Greg's hand a cursory shake.

"Taryn's a beautiful name. Where's it from?" Ellie asked.

The dark girl smiled at her, seeming to enjoy smiling at everyone at the table, except for Greg. "It's Irish. From Tara, the Hill of the Kings. My mom was a Celtic nut."

"It suits you," Rosalind heard herself saying. *Lord, where did that come from? I am not drunk!* She was embarrassed, but the girl didn't seem at all put out. She turned back to Rosalind, nodding, as if her approval had been sought. Rosalind felt the world melting away again.

Ellie came to her rescue, asking Taryn how she started performing.

The girl shrugged, lifting broad shoulders in a gesture that did terrible things to Rosalind's imagination. The front of her suit coat fitted smoothly, no hint of breasts. Rosalind wondered how she bound them, then caught herself staring. She looked down into her drink and was surprised to find it empty.

"Egyptia's a friend of Rhea's. Egyptia needed somebody tall enough to balance her, and Rhea suggested me," Taryn said, offhand, glancing at Rosalind, then back to Ellie.

"Who's Rhea?" Rosalind found herself asking, then desperately wishing she could just bite her tongue off and get it over with. The girl looked at her again, with the hint of an amused grin.

"The witch I live with." Taryn sipped her whisky like a soldier in a WWII movie. She looked back up at Rosalind abruptly, her mouth opening. "Wait a minute. Rosalind. Rhea warned me about you, when I was leaving the house."

This was too good to let go, the way the drag king and her friend were staring into one another's eyes. Ellie asked, "Warned you, about Ros? How?"

Taryn smiled. "Rhea practices the Craft. She knows things. She said to me, 'Beware the Rose that is flung in your path.'"

"And you think she meant Ros?" Ellie persisted, enjoying this immensely.

"Maybe. I've learned to take her warnings seriously. You don't look dangerous, though. Are you?"

"No." Rosalind answered instantly, wanting Taryn to know she was safe; she'd never hurt her. The impulse made no sense to her, so she quietly smothered it.

"Want another drink?" Bill asked, seeing that Taryn had finished hers. Taryn looked at the glass, then at Bill.

She hesitated, so Ellie cut in. "I'd love to hear more about your friend Rhea."

It was a good direction to take, Rosalind saw. Taryn settled back into the chair at the mention of Rhea's name, a smile creeping across her face.

Rosalind caught herself staring and blushed. There was a drink in her hand. Good. That occupied her for several seconds, while she downed it in three gulps. She couldn't keep her eyes away from Taryn for more than a minute. It was terrible, the time ticking away between safe glances up. There was another drink in her hand. Ellie must have replaced it. Good. I feel like I'm starving to death in front of a banquet.

"One more drink," Taryn said with a small motion of her head toward Rosalind.

"So is Rhea your girlfriend?"

Rosalind choked on her drink. How could Ellie ask that? Yet Taryn didn't seem at all put out by the question.

"Used to be, a long time ago. She's my guardian angel. She gave me a place when I had nowhere else to go."

The way Taryn said it was both comforting and not comforting to Rosalind, the sudden, irrational jealousy surprising her. She felt a moment of relief that someone had been there for Taryn, that Rhea had offered her protection, then a wave of hot envy that swamped her. She wanted to be the one who Taryn spoke of in that tone of voice. She just had no idea why that was so important. What did it matter to her if some girl she'd known five minutes was involved?

"Come on, now. How long ago could it be? You can't be more than nineteen or twenty." Ellie laughed.

Taryn set the drink down and pulled a pack of cigarettes out of her coat, raising an eyebrow at Ellie.

"How old are you?" Bill asked. Taryn flicked open a silver lighter by striking it on her thigh, lighting it the same way. Rosalind nearly fainted.

"Old enough to know better," the girl commented, exhaling.

The bar back brought another round, and Ellie and Bill fought over paying for it. Rosalind found herself watching Taryn, silent, as Ellie plied her with questions. Greg sulked next to her, forgotten.

Taryn ate all her attention. The girl was charismatic, brash, powerful. She radiated something dark and dangerous, playing it off with a self-deprecating shrug and a devil's grin.

Ellie was flirting madly with her, and so was Bill. Taryn seemed to enjoy the attention and flirted back. Only Rosalind was silent, recording the scene. Every move of her lips, every flash of a smile, every lift of an eyebrow spoke to Rosalind in an ancient language, and she'd just been handed the Rosetta Stone. She wanted to know everything about the girl, but strangely felt like she already did and was just being reminded of the details.

The force of recognition hadn't faded. She forgot Greg completely until he chimed in to a conversation Ellie and Taryn were having about performance. "How can you say that gender is fluid? This circus act aside, men are men and women are women," Greg said, shocking Rosalind out of her enraptured haze.

She had to fight down the urge to smack him and defend Taryn. Somehow, she didn't think the girl would appreciate the rescue, not yet anyway.

Taryn sipped her whisky, her eyes locking on Greg. Her voice dropped down to a panther's purr. "It's not a circus act," Taryn said, spinning the ice cubes in her glass.

"How do you keep track? We should be calling you 'he,' I suppose. You're not a drag queen," Greg said, and was rewarded with Taryn's undivided attention.

"No, I'm not. But it is respectful to call queens 'she,'" Taryn said. Egyptia walked past the table and blew a kiss at Taryn. She smiled and raised her glass in a salute.

Greg snorted. "But you're a transvestite. You dress up as the opposite sex."

There was a moment of silence while Taryn sized Greg up. Her eyes traveled over him coolly as she finished her drink. "Greg, what are you dressed up as?"

He blinked, not expecting this. "I'm not dressed up as anything."

Taryn set the glass down. "Oxford shirt, blue, buttoned to the neck, no tie. Jacket, corduroy, leather patches on the elbows. Pressed jeans, argyle socks, boat shoes. Pierre Cardin frames on your glasses. Trimmed goatee that you keep stroking. Hair to the collar, conservative, but not corporate. An academic. You want to look like your students—youngish, sort of hip, but older than them as well. 'Words Count' button. You're an English prof or a writer. A '90s, Beat coffeehouse, open mike, jazz poet kinda guy. You smoke, but you don't eat meat. You think women should get equal pay, but the feminists have gone too far. Probably married once, no kids. You still feel around for the ring." Taryn paused at Greg's open-mouthed shock. "We all dress up as something. The queens just put more thought into it." She stood up abruptly, pushing the chair back under the table. "Thanks for the drinks," she said to no one in particular, then walked off into the crowd.

Rosalind felt her heart shatter when Taryn left. It was too soon. They hadn't—

Greg laughed nervously. "Whew. Junior Sherlock Holmes. Dykic Friends Network."

Rosalind stood up, moving before she grabbed him and hit him. "Greg, shut up."

To Ellie's surprise and delight, she took off after Taryn, pushing through the crowd.

Rosalind made her way to the front room, past the dance floor, looking around for Taryn. She couldn't let the girl go, not like this. She didn't want Taryn thinking that Greg spoke for her, that he had anything to do with her. She wanted to apologize, to continue the conversation. She stood near the dance floor, casting hopeless looks into the crowd of gyrating men. The black suit had vanished. Desperate, she turned to the bar and saw a familiar platinum wig. Egyptia, sitting on a bar stool.

Rosalind pushed her way to the bar and ended up at Egyptia's knee. The queen looked quizzically down at her from a great height, obviously thinking her a tourist. "Can I help you, honey?"

Rosalind nodded. "I'm looking for a friend of yours. The one who did the number with you? Taryn."

Egyptia folded her hands. "You looking for Taryn. Uh huh. Well, look behind you, girl."

Rosalind spun around so fast she nearly collided with the girl.

As it was, Taryn took a hop backward to avoid spilling the drinks she was carrying. "Whoa! Not the suit, it's my best one." She frowned, holding the drinks away from the front of her suit coat. She handed a drink to Egyptia, then set the other on the bar. "Something I can do for you?" Taryn asked, neutrally.

Rosalind crossed the space between them, putting her hand on the girl's arm. To her surprise, Taryn didn't shrug it off, or even acknowledge that it was there. "Taryn. I'm sorry about that," Rosalind said, wanting to reconnect with the girl. There was too much unfinished between them to end like this.

"About your boyfriend being a jerk? Not my problem."

"He's not my boyfriend," Rosalind said too quickly.

It seemed to help. Taryn's angry pose relaxed slightly. "He's not good enough for you," she said in a low voice.

Rosalind flushed with warmth at the statement, though it seemed to come from left field. Every word she and the girl had spoken to one another had that quality, like old friends renewing a familiar conversation. What should have been beyond awkward between them was shrugged off, accepted, and forgotten. She felt such a pull toward the girl that she didn't even question it. It just seemed right. "Can I buy you a drink? To apologize."

Taryn raised an eyebrow at her, nodding at the drink on the bar. "Already have one. Your friends have been buying me drinks all night. You trying to get me drunk?"

"No!" Rosalind said, again blurting it out before she could think about it. Something about the girl seemed to short-circuit her brain, making her babble like a teenager. It didn't help that the drag king seemed to be flirting with her and enjoying her discomfiture.

"Then what are you trying to do, Rosalind?" Taryn's voice was serious.

The question hit her square in the chest. She took her hand off the girl's arm, brushing the hair back behind her ears. What was she doing, Rosalind wondered, chasing a drag king at least ten years her junior around a gay club? She was an adult, a professor, for God's sake, and this phenomenal girl, who was currently driving her to distraction, was barely older than her students. She was indulging in the novelty of her own desire, without thinking about the consequences.

"I just want to know you." Her heart answered, before her brain could censor it.

Taryn was silent, still and cool as a stone behind the masklike beauty of her face. She was quiet so long that Rosalind felt her heart contract, felt shame wash over her in a tidal wave. She became suddenly aware of what she must sound like, what she must look like to this splendid youth, a fawning tourist chasing her around the bar. She thought about her plum skirt and jacket, the way her hair kept escaping from the braid, how suburban she must look. She ducked her head, absently pushing at her hair. Convinced the girl was mocking her with that cool, arrogant silence, she turned away, her soul in shreds.

"Sorry about that. I don't know where that came from. Nice meeting you," Rosalind mumbled, shoulders dropping. Maybe she could get Ellie to leave with her now, before the night got any worse. Maybe she could escape with the tatters of her dignity.

A strong hand closed on her arm, circling it around the bicep, halting her escape. She took a deep breath and faced her captor. Her eyes rose to meet the drag king's, and Rosalind was surprised to find them unfocused, swimming with an unreadable emotion.

"You drink coffee?" Taryn asked, her voice rough, conflicted.

Rosalind nodded, unable to speak.

Ellie looked up to find a very flushed Rosalind walking back to the table. She watched as Rosalind bumped into the chair, then noticed it and picked up her purse. "I wondered where you ran off to. Greg left. He sends his regrets."

Rosalind nodded absently, as if she had forgotten Greg entirely.

Ellie noticed the purse clutched in a death grip. "Where are you off to?"

Rosalind looked at her friend, surprise on her face. "I'm having coffee with Taryn," she said, too happy to be able to mask it.

Ellie's jaw dropped. "No way! You and Elvis? Ros, I didn't know you were into sexy butch girls. Don't let her break your heart."

Rosalind gave her a reproving look, trying to regain her professorial dignity. "Ellie, it's just coffee."

The look didn't work, or maybe her friend knew her too well. Ellie's grin widened, taking over her whole face. "It's never just coffee. I'll want the details tomorrow."

Taryn slipped away backstage, leaving her at the bar with Egyptia. The queen kept looking her up and down, knitting her eyebrows, occasionally smiling in an unnerving, Mona Lisa way.

Rosalind finally couldn't stand it and braved a question. "Have you known Taryn long?"

Egyptia smiled blindingly. "Since she moved in with Rhea. What you do for a living, honey? You a banker or something?"

"I teach at the local college," Rosalind said. There was that name again. No one seemed to be able to mention Taryn's name without linking Rhea's to it. It distracted her on a level she couldn't place.

"Buff State or UB?"

"UB. Just started, actually," Rosalind said, her neck craning to look up at the drag queen's impressive height. Egyptia seemed very amused by something, and Rosalind had a feeling it was her. "Something funny?"

The queen shook her platinum wig, patting Rosalind on the arm. "Just maybe. You ain't Taryn's type. She hasn't had a professor before."

This was useful information, despite the manner in which it was being delivered. Rosalind didn't stop to correct the queen's impression that Taryn "had" her. She focused on the clue that Egyptia had started with. "What is Taryn's type?" she asked, unable to help herself.

"Sweet little femme girls, all punked out and shaved heads and nose rings and all. Goes through them like tissues, sister. Not that an occasional tourist don't line up for her. That Taryn's a dog. Just last week she—" Egyptia leaned in conspiratorially, to be interrupted by a smoky voice right behind her.

"What did I do last week?" Taryn said, making both of them jump. She had traded her black suit for a charcoal T-shirt and a pair of jeans, combat boots, and a black leather belt. She'd unbound her breasts, and Rosalind found herself staring at them through the thin cotton shirt. Her hair looked like she'd run an impatient hand through it, sending black strands at all angles, falling over her eyes.

"Nothin', honey, just like the cereal commercial. You outta here, T?" Egyptia asked, smirking.

"None of your damned business," Taryn said, and punched the queen on the arm. She held out a hand to Rosalind, who took it automatically. "I know this great coffee joint."

CHAPTER TWO

Ellie had included Spot Coffee in her Buffalo crash course. Rosalind knew that it was walking distance from Marcella's, just down on the corner of Chippewa and Delaware Ave. It was the hangout of choice for those who didn't drink, or couldn't yet drink, but wanted to be a part of the Chippewa nightlife. Ellie had brought her here once or twice, but walking in with Taryn was very different.

Spot was staffed by three shaven-headed femme girls, to borrow Egyptia's phrase, all of whom seemed to drop what they were doing and come over and kiss Taryn. Rosalind felt invisible next to her, when the girls would pop up, greet Taryn, then send lingering looks her way after she passed. Taryn handled them all with aplomb, a devil's grin and a kiss on the cheek, just this close to their lips.

Rosalind tried to ignore them and studied the mural of Chippewa Street on the wall facing the door.

"T! Hey, girl!"

"T! When are you gonna call me?"

"T! I missed you last night."

This last was a voice Rosalind recognized, and it splintered her disinterested stance. She looked and saw one of her new students, hanging with her arms around Taryn's neck. From what Rosalind could see, which was admittedly only the back of her head, the student had metallic red hair, shaved down to a half inch, six earrings in each ear, and a spiderweb tattoo on the back of her neck. Her nose was pierced with a simple stud, and when she opened her mouth to kiss Taryn, Rosalind saw that her tongue was, as well. It took Rosalind a moment to retrieve a name; she was distracted by the way the girl was kissing Taryn.

Rosalind's mind produced the name with a flourish, *Colleen*, in a vain attempt to move her emotional response back from inappropriate.

The sight of her kissing Taryn made visual sense; this was the kind of girl Egyptia had described as Taryn's type. Rosalind thought that she could appreciate that, from an outside perspective. The urge toward murder was something she had never experienced before.

Taryn endured the kiss, then gently disengaged Colleen's arms from around her neck.

"I never said I'd be there," Taryn said.

Colleen pouted when Taryn slipped out of her arms. "You're normally anywhere Rhea is. You want your usual?" Colleen was heading back behind the register.

"Yeah. What about you?" Taryn asked, turning to Rosalind.

Colleen saw Taryn's companion for the first time and blanched. "Dr. Olchawski! I didn't know, I mean—"

Taryn slipped her hand under Rosalind's elbow, a gesture so intimate that Colleen's eyes bugged out. She leaned down and spoke next to Rosalind's ear, her breath sending chills down Rosalind's spine. Knowing that they had an audience only made her heart beat faster, something she never would have guessed about herself. Taryn was playing it like a scene, she could tell that, but she was enjoying it far too much to stop her. "Why don't you go get us a table? I'll get what you like," she purred, and Rosalind smiled agreement at her.

She sat down at a table in the back room, near the overstuffed chairs and couches full of college kids playing board games, reading, strumming on guitars. She slid in by the wall, where she could watch Taryn get the coffee and cross the floor to her. Taryn stood at the counter, flirting with anyone in reach. Rosalind didn't need this display to know that she was a demon. Every move she made was sinful. Even carrying hot coffee in a crowded room reeked of sex, of a sultry promise in the lope of her long legs, the careful balance of her hands.

Rosalind felt a shiver go up her spine. She knew that Colleen watched every move Taryn was making and knew that Taryn was playing it up for her. Rosalind recognized her own actions as impulsive, dangerously close to being one of the teenagers who surrounded her. She would probably pay for this, strolling in on her arm, in whatever performance Taryn was enacting.

There was still time for her to think about what she was doing before Taryn came back with their coffee. Rosalind glanced down at her purse, knowing that she could leave right now, call it a night, call the adventure over. She wasn't a teenager. She knew very well what her presence here spoke. Ellie was right. Coffee was never just coffee. There might be other times for her to explore why her body reacted the way it did around the drag king, why her normally steady and reliable heart started to make a virtue of broken rhythm.

When Taryn turned her head, laughing, and looked for her, there was a split second that Rosalind was convinced her smile of pleasure was genuine. That she looked up, found her in the room, and couldn't contain the joy at the recognition. It banished all thoughts of leaving. Rosalind smiled back, her heart aching. She admitted she didn't know what she was getting herself into, but she was doing it anyway. She took her hand off her purse.

Taryn slid in next to her, handing her a mug bigger than a soup bowl. "They seem to know you here," Rosalind said, fighting down jealousy at the number of pretty girls flinging themselves at her new friend. She had to remind herself that she'd known Taryn maybe an hour and had no claim on her. In fact, Taryn looked like someone that couldn't be claimed, from her performance in front of Colleen. Taryn took a sip of her coffee, black as her hair. "That answers one question," Rosalind commented. Taryn's eyebrow rose.

"What's that?"

Rosalind looked directly into her eyes, finding the hint of amusement there. "How you take your coffee."

The raised eyebrow and devil's grin were signs she'd begun to recognize, hints of a sense of humor under the posturing. They spoke of amusement, with a faint hint of menace. This wasn't safe, Rosalind had to remind herself, despite her feelings very much to the contrary. Taryn was looking like a classic bad boy, and Rosalind had never in her wildest imagination expected herself to be so charmed by a bad boy.

"Thanks for being cool in front of Colleen. She gets a little clingy sometimes."

Rosalind managed to remain calm, despite the amount of blood racing to her heart. "She a girlfriend of yours?"

"Nah. We just slept together a few times, you know? But she thinks that means we're going steady."

Someone from the front room shouted Taryn's name, and her head turned. Rosalind could see a tattoo on the back of her neck, below her hair. Half of it rose from the collar of the charcoal T-shirt, circular, the beginning of a wheel hidden by the cloth. Rosalind's eyes traced it lovingly, wondering if she could touch it.

The dark head turned back and caught her staring. Taryn's eyes held hers, dancing. She reached up and pulled the collar of her shirt down in the back, showing the rest of the tattoo to Rosalind without saying a word.

It was a black eagle rising to embrace the sun, contained in an elaborate circular border. It was an image that belonged on the wall of an ancient temple, worked in enameled tiles and precious stones. The flames of the sun licked over the edge of the circle, and the feathers of the eagle looked like they were starting to melt. *Like Icarus*, Rosalind thought, then looked again, thinking of Michelangelo's drawing of Zeus and Ganymede.

It was not hubris she saw in the arch of the black eagle's neck; it was joy. The eagle was abandoned in its passion, surrendering to the sun, transported in the moment of immolation. Rosalind could barely resist the urge to lay her palm against it, to see if the sun burned her. "It's magnificent. Very moving," Rosalind said, tucking her hand under her leg to keep from reaching for it.

"Thanks." Taryn's smile was genuine, pleased by her appreciation. "Rhea does all my work. She does tattoos and piercing for a living. That's her shop down on Elmwood—A Pound Of Flesh." The image sprang fully formed into Rosalind's mind of Taryn, like the eagle, splayed out on a table, with Rhea above her, needle in hand. It took great effort to push that image aside and tell her mind to go lie down as if it were a misbehaving dog.

"I've never seen anything like it. Did she design it?" Rosalind asked, to regain control of herself in the conversation. A disarmed smile came over Taryn's face, an expression that mesmerized and delighted Rosalind in its uniqueness. For a moment, Rosalind felt something old and stubborn shift; the mask Taryn wore showed a hairline crack. Taryn actually looked shy, enjoying praise where she didn't expect to find it.

"Nah. I did. I design all my own stuff." She rolled up the sleeve on the charcoal shirt, showing a defined bicep to Rosalind.

The muscle was impressive enough that it took Rosalind a moment to focus on the tattoo. Like the eagle, it had been lovingly drawn, the rendering an act of worship. It was a drawing of the head of a Greek statue, a beautiful young man with deep-set eyes and a rough-cut mane of hair. Every line captured the arrogance and vitality of youth, an unconquerable spirit burning out of the flesh that held it. His gaze carried across the centuries, a part of Taryn's skin. Rosalind read the Greek beneath it, *Phil Alexandros, Basileus.* "Friend of Alexander, the King. Why that?" Rosalind asked, and was rewarded with a blinding smile from the dark girl.

"You recognize him?" she asked, surprise and pleasure mingling in her voice.

Rosalind realized that she had done something incredibly right, without meaning to. It made her flush with warmth, the enthusiasm on Taryn's face. "Alexander the Great. I recognize the statue. From Pella, when he was a young man, I believe," Rosalind said, basking in the warmth radiating from Taryn.

"Most people don't have a clue. They wonder why I have a man's head on my arm." She rolled the sleeve back down gently, almost reverently. In the attentive silence that Rosalind offered, Taryn quickened.

She looked at Rosalind carefully, to see if the enthusiasm was genuine, before she started speaking. "He was the greatest general to ever walk the earth. And he was family—gay, you know? I read all of Mary Renault's stories about him when I was seventeen. Rhea made me. I fought her. I hated reading, it reminded me of school. She kept hammering away at me, ignoring my shit. I finally read it. I didn't want her thinking she was right. She thinks she's right all the time. But the idea that somebody who conquered the whole world when he was my age, who was never beaten in battle and was gay, you have to feel that. I always believed I was the descendant of a great warrior, but I don't know where I'm from. So I picked him."

Rosalind could see that she was being completely honest. Her conviction had Rosalind convinced. Taryn radiated charisma. She certainly had the power of persuasion. Rosalind looked into her eyes, lit with passion, at the broad sweep of her shoulders as she reclined against the wall, the dark hair tangled like a mane, careless and gorgeous as a young lion. Rosalind readily believed that this could be the descendant of a great warrior. The beloved Boy King of Macedonia didn't seem exactly right somehow, but Taryn's obvious attachment to him was too much to be questioned. If you don't know your own history, you take what you can from the rest.

"That makes perfect sense," she said quietly, simply.

Taryn rolled her head back against the wall, lazily eyeing Rosalind. "You say everything right. You've been practicing. Egyptia told you what to say."

"Nope. Just got it right on my own," Rosalind said, imitating her tone.

Taryn laughed, a rich, rolling sound that went right to the center of Rosalind's bones. She had a feeling of triumph, as if making this girl laugh, getting her to drop her arrogant stance, were the finest thing she'd ever done. "I'll show you the rest of my tattoos some time," Taryn said, with a wicked gleam in her eye.

"That'd be great," Rosalind answered, before realizing that she'd just been invited up to see Taryn's etchings. She blushed and sipped at her coffee.

"So I know your last name. Olchawski. Polish, right? And you are a doctor."

"A professor," Rosalind said, suddenly shy. She didn't want Taryn to think she was bragging. She didn't want the conversation to go down to that level. She wanted to find out everything about Taryn, not just the details. They would fall into place on their own. "Tell me what you love. What makes you wake up at night crying. What you can't live without. When you are happiest." The words came out in a rush. Rosalind let them fall from her lips, knowing them to be absolutely true, absolutely what she had to know about Taryn.

The blue eyes went wide. Taryn leaned forward on the table, dangerously close to Rosalind. "Be careful what you ask for." Taryn's voice had gone hoarse.

Rosalind felt a strength suffusing her, a certainty that balanced Taryn's misgiving. "I'm tired of being careful," she said, and put her hand on top of Taryn's where it rested on the table.

The drag king waited, looking for all the world like a cat about to bolt. She inhaled, settling back against the wall, but she didn't take her hand away from Rosalind's. "You're...something else. I'll give you that. Okay, where do you want to start?"

"With what you love," Rosalind said, her voice perfectly steady, unlike her insides.

"My people. Drawing. Performing. Rhea. Fighting for what's right. Women," Taryn said, a ghost of a smile playing about her lips.

The words made Rosalind's heart ache, like it was expanding to encompass them. "Rhea," Rosalind said, hearing the way Taryn lingered on the name.

"Yeah. I'm starting to see why she warned me about you. I live with her, Papa Joe, and a few others, depending on the week. Goblin, Laurel, and I have rooms, but lots of people stay. It's a big house. Old Victorian in Allentown, down on Mariner. Rhea's been fixing it up for years."

"Fighting for what's right?" Rosalind asked.

Taryn's head lifted, her eyes burning like they were lit from within by a supernatural glow. "I'm a soldier on the front lines of the gender wars."

Rosalind noticed, eventually, that their coffee mugs had been empty for some time. The sound of Taryn's voice had her mesmerized—the way the girl's lips moved; the guarded, angry pose vanishing with every minute. Taryn talked about drawing, about designing tattoos for Rhea's clients, about the people she lived with in the rundown Victorian in the Allentown district. What Rosalind heard was the affection Taryn had for them, the way her face grew soft and delighted when she spoke of them, particularly Rhea. Taryn was telling her a story of getting her first tattoo, of the endorphin high that came along with the constant pain.

"You get addicted to it. Once you have your first tattoo, you can't wait to get another one." Taryn stopped, her eyes focusing on Rosalind. Rosalind felt her skin start to heat just from that and glanced down. When Taryn stood up and walked around behind her, she felt her heart go into overdrive. The girl lifted her hair, holding the braid in her large hands.

"You keep fighting with your hair," Taryn said, unclasping the broach, combing out the strands with her fingers. Rosalind sighed and held very still, shivering from the feel of fingers in her hair. She felt Taryn settle the hair around her shoulders, stroking it. "There," Taryn said, her voice like a guest in Rosalind's ear. Her hand stayed on the back of Rosalind's neck, resting lightly.

Rosalind closed her eyes, unable to believe what an effect this girl was having on her. Paul had never affected her this way in all their years of marriage. Other women never affected her this way, though she found many of them very attractive. This was something primal, a question that Taryn's nearness asked her, and her body opened in welcome. She wondered if it was obvious, how weak she felt, how hungry. She felt the hands leave her neck and wanted to cry.

Taryn slid back down next to her, watching her face. The look on the drag king's face was knowing, clear as the sun at its zenith burning through the clouds. Rosalind felt like she couldn't hide anything from this girl. Their bodies were already speaking. With agonizing slowness, Taryn took her face in her hands, directing Rosalind's motion. She pulled gently and Rosalind leaned forward, following. She closed her eyes, trembling, knowing that Taryn was going to kiss her.

"You two want anything else?" The voice was cutting, meant to divide them. Colleen stood, hand on her hip, picking up their mugs. Rosalind almost answered that question, telling Colleen exactly what she did want, but Taryn's sudden laughter calmed her anger. She smiled, ruefully, seeing the humor in it. She started to laugh, too, sharing Taryn's mirth. Colleen rolled her eyes and snatched the mugs from the table.

"Oh, God, what a look. I'm in for a world of trouble in class," Rosalind said, watching Colleen walk away. It didn't matter to her right then, that she had been seen in public nearly kissing…She turned, to find Taryn's impossibly blue eyes watching her. Her heart trip-hammered all over again.

"Why don't you give me a lift home?" Taryn said, making Rosalind's bones melt.

She'd parked on Pearl Street, behind Marcella's. Taryn strolled casually to the car, keeping her hands in the pockets of her jeans, inhaling the warm September air with an enthusiasm Rosalind echoed. "Gorgeous night," Taryn said.

"I didn't know it'd be so warm. Somehow I expected it to be snowing in September, from the stories I've heard about Buffalo."

"You can't believe everything you hear. You know Allentown?" Taryn asked her when Rosalind stopped and unlocked the door on the Saturn.

"Some. I know Allen Street. You'll have to direct me from there."

Taryn walked around and held the door open for Rosalind, surprising the professor enough that she dropped her keys. Taryn bent and scooped them up smoothly, handing them back to her.

"I will. You're in good hands."

CHAPTER THREE

The house at 34 Mariner was a dark purple, shuttered and trimmed in green. The front walk had a small garden of flowers, still braving the weather of September. A few leaves had fallen, a storm had tilted the stalks at crazy angles, but the garden maintained. It was only a five-minute drive from downtown, a fact that Rosalind mightily regretted. She hadn't been able to work up a topic of conversation.

The closeness of being in the car, with Taryn at her side, had obliterated whatever mad confidence had been carrying her. Her mind was churning, trying to analyze possible scenarios: Taryn would expect her to just provide a ride home and wave goodbye, Taryn would say something slick and ask for her number, in which case she might offer it, kiss her, and faint. This was territory she had no map for, and she was getting very lost.

Rosalind parked one door down, a huge red boat of a convertible taking up the space in front of the house. "Papa Joe's beast. He refuses to spend more than five hundred dollars for a car. He buys these clunkers, then fixes them up so they run, then drives them into the ground. I think he's a frustrated performance artist," Taryn said as Rosalind shut off the engine.

Rosalind wracked her brain trying to think of something clever to say. The connection that had worked so well when there was a table between them was melting as their skin got closer, getting harder to define. Taryn seemed perfectly at ease, lounging in the seat, making no move toward the door handle. Taryn's nearness was making hash of her thoughts. The streetlight cast blue sparks from her black hair, highlighted the curve of her neck.

"Well. It looks like a lovely house. I love the Victorians in this area," Rosalind said, feeling like slapping herself. How could Taryn go on looking at her like that, so unerringly steady? *Doesn't she know that she was about to kill a professor with the blue of her eyes?* Rosalind thought desperately. A vision of the police finding her dead of a stroke in her car, with Taryn still sitting next to her smoking a cigarette, plagued Rosalind.

Taryn leaned forward and kissed her. There was no warning, no time to prepare herself, and Rosalind was drowning. Taryn's lips claimed hers, easing them open with a sure tongue, exploring the inside of her mouth. Rosalind put her hands on Taryn's shoulders and leaned in, pulling against her. She felt her whole body crave contact with Taryn, felt the kiss as a promise of a meeting. What started out as a slow tease became frenzied. She tangled her hands in Taryn's hair, trying to prolong the kiss forever. One strong arm wound around her waist, lifting her nearly into Taryn's lap. She felt Taryn's hands on her neck, her shoulders, sliding down to her breasts. She gasped against Taryn's mouth, then kissed her harder.

Taryn broke away, kissing her way down Rosalind's neck, down the exposed flesh above her shirt. She cupped Rosalind's breasts in her hands, feeling them through the thin barrier of silk. "Come upstairs with me," Taryn murmured against the skin of her throat. Rosalind closed her eyes.

The voice that answered was hers, but it was a tone she'd never heard before. "Yes."

Rosalind had a vague impression of a staircase, of climbing it wrapped around Taryn, seeming to climb Taryn at the same time. They paused on the top step, Rosalind falling back against the wall, Taryn still on the stairs. It gave Rosalind the height advantage to take Taryn's head in her hands and lean down, kissing the drag king. They were unwilling to be out of contact for a moment.

Taryn guided them down the hall, finding her way in the dark with impressive dexterity. She kicked the door open with the heel of her boot, while unbuttoning Rosalind's shirt. Her jacket was somewhere back on the stairs; her skirt was unzipped, ready to follow. The haze that kissing Taryn induced protected Rosalind from knowing exactly how she got undressed so quickly.

She was on her back on a mattress on the floor, protesting Taryn's movement away from her. The air was cold where Taryn had lain on top of her, like an arctic wind after the feverish touch of flesh. Taryn stood, silhouetted against the streetlight from the window, and pulled off her T-shirt. She kicked off her boots, crawling back down on top of Rosalind in her jeans. The weight of her body anchored the spinning professor. She needed Taryn to hold her down or she would spin right off the surface of the earth.

Hands were on her rib cage, holding her like a feather, raising her up. Her breast was in Taryn's mouth, ruining the efforts she'd made to be quiet. She didn't care anymore if there was anyone else in the house, on the block, in the city. Rosalind moaned out loud, nearly screaming when she felt Taryn's teeth close on her nipple.

Her arousal became painful, the ache between her thighs unbearable. This had never happened to her, not in all the fumbling sexual encounters during her marriage, not in the years preceding it. Rosalind's body became one coil of need, the wetness flowing from her, painting her thighs. If Taryn stopped touching her, she would die; she knew it. She felt herself falling, felt strong hands catch her, hold her in midair. She lay back down on the mattress, her muscles trembling too much to hold her up.

She felt long fingers reach between her thighs, stroking, teasing her. Rosalind's hands turned to steel, clamping down on Taryn's broad shoulders. Incoherent commands flowed from her lips, her head sprawled on the pillow. She thought she heard a low, rumbling laugh, felt Taryn take her fingertips away. She wanted to scream her frustration.

Rosalind felt weight leave her body. Taryn's hand parted her thighs, lifting her legs over broad shoulders. Rosalind opened her eyes and saw the dark head bend down. She could feel breath, a second before she felt her tongue. She inhaled sharply, trying not to scream. The sight of Taryn's black head bent lovingly between her thighs was almost too much for her. When the girl added her fingers, sliding smoothly into her aching wetness, Rosalind gave up the fight and screamed. After a lifetime of considering herself a warm person, but not a passionate one, Rosalind came face to face with the blast furnace in her heart. She came hard, muscles trapping the dark girl as if she would never let her go.

Rosalind took a deep, ragged breath, calling the air back into her lungs. Her throat was raw from calling out things she couldn't remember moments after, but she thought she'd heard herself invoking Taryn's name, like the secret name of God. The breath filled her lungs, awareness inched back. Rosalind's mind stopped careening, and she fell apart.

She started crying like her heart had been rent. She felt as vulnerable as if her skin had been stripped off. Tears ran down her cheeks, she choked on them, trying not to let them out, unable to stop them. *Great, this is sexy.*

Taryn didn't seem bothered or really even surprised. She climbed up Rosalind's body, kissing her stomach, her throat. She took the woman into her arms and gathered her, unresisting, to her chest. Rosalind put an arm around Taryn's narrow waist, ducked her head against the drag king's chest, and cried her heart out. There was something impossibly soothing about Taryn stroking her hair, crooning nonsense to her in a low voice. Rosalind felt a sense of freedom that made her giddy. At last the tears passed. She raised her head, still feeling shaky, as if a breeze could blow her apart. Taryn's eyes were inches from hers, regarding her. The look on her face was amazing, a waiting tenderness that Rosalind would never have expected from the arrogant girl. Rosalind started to tear up again. "Sorry," she said, gearing up to explain her weakness away.

Taryn leaned forward and kissed her, very softly, stopping her words. The kiss was comforting, gentle, but her nearness had the opposite effect on Rosalind. To her own complete surprise, she felt her desire flare up, the strength of it shocking. *I've turned into a sex maniac overnight*, Rosalind thought. She kissed Taryn back, exploring her lips, tasting herself on them. It sent a shiver through her.

Taryn lay quietly in her arms, letting her set the pace. Rosalind felt bold and started to trace the lines of Taryn's face—the firm jawline, the high cheekbones, the minute scar that divided her right eyebrow. Rosalind slid her hand behind her neck, feeling the heat of the sun on her palm, feeling the abandon of the eagle in the solar embrace.

"You said you'd let me see the rest of your tattoos," she heard herself say in a husky voice. Taryn grinned and rolled over. She stretched her arms above her head, letting Rosalind have an unrestricted view of her back. She saw the whole of the tattoo on her neck, familiar to her now. For a moment her eye stopped, imagining that the wheel design of the border had shifted minutely. She told herself that it must be the indirect light in the bedroom; lots of familiar things would look different to her now.

Her hands strayed down over the shoulder blades, feeling the muscles barely sheathed under smooth skin. On the left shoulder blade was a snake, coiled around a tree. An apple was set enticingly in the snake's mouth. Rosalind followed the lines, the scales, to get a sense for it. From the right shoulder, diagonal across the whole of the back, was a dagger.

It looked ancient, Egyptian perhaps, with a broadleaf blade and narrow, wrapped hilt. On the blade of the dagger was a drawing, like an engraving on the steel. Rosalind examined it in the streetlight and saw it was a red and white bull, head thrown back, wicked curved horns tearing at the air. A girl clad only in a wasp-waisted loincloth was leaping over the bull's back, as if she'd just vaulted through the horns. Another girl in the same costume stood in the bull's path, hands raised to make the leap.

"I got the idea from a mural at the palace at Knossos, the bull leapers. I set it inside a dagger as a kind of joke," Taryn said, her head in profile on the mattress.

"As a joke?" Rosalind asked, stroking the picture with her whole palm.

"Yeah. Bulldagger."

Rosalind bent down and kissed the blade of the dagger, kissed the girl vaulting between the horns of death. It didn't seem quite like a joke to her.

Taryn turned over, and Rosalind continued kissing her, trailing up to her mouth. She climbed on top of Taryn, her hunger directing her. Her tongue urged Taryn to life, opening her mouth, calling her out. She felt a moment of doubt that she'd be able to please her lover, inexperienced as she was. Her hand hesitated on the top button of Taryn's jeans, trembling. Taryn took Rosalind's hand away, capturing it, refusing her access. She felt arms close around her and moaned into her open mouth. The distraction worked; she couldn't think enough to protest the distance that Taryn maintained.

Rosalind pressed her hips against the rough denim of Taryn's jeans in mute appeal. Taryn's hands nearly covered her back, stroking down to her hips, grabbing her buttocks. The fingers dug into the muscle, and Rosalind pulled away from Taryn's mouth, gasping. She plunged back down, claiming the girl's lips again, letting her swallow the cries that came from her throat. Rosalind sealed their mouths together, trying to flow into Taryn, to claim a part of her with that connection. She felt Taryn's hand move surely between her thighs. Rosalind moved her hips in anticipation. Taryn thrust two fingers into her, curving them, driving Rosalind upright. She broke the seal of their lips, straddling Taryn, impaling herself on Taryn's long fingers.

Rosalind rode Taryn's hand, feeling the slick fingers plunging in and out in a frenzy, grinding down to meet them. She felt herself cresting, felt the fingers in her center, then the agonizing withdrawal. Sweat stood out on her skin, her muscles tensed, she went blind with the motion. Her climax ripped through her, and she clamped down on the thrusting hand, claiming it.

Rosalind folded back over Taryn's body, lying on top of her with her fingers still inside. She felt them start to leave and grabbed Taryn's wrist. "Leave them inside. Please?" she breathed, desperate not to break contact with Taryn. Having Taryn there, underneath her, inside her, felt like coming home after a long journey. Taryn accepted, kissing her hair, lying still in companionable silence.

Rosalind lay with an ear against Taryn's chest, hearing the ragged heartbeat under her cheek. That, and Taryn's breathing, told her what she wanted to know, that Taryn was as moved as she was. The certainty she felt, after the rawness a moment before, was staggering. She felt Taryn exhale, her breath moving Rosalind's hair.

"You are gorgeous," she rumbled, and Rosalind closed her eyes at the sound. She felt Taryn's free hand stray to her back, lazily stroking her cooling skin.

"I'm glad you think so," Rosalind said, kissing the skin over her heart.

"Anyone would think so. You're magnificent. A walking miracle."

"I've never..." Rosalind said, struggling to find words large enough to fit the moment. Her whole world had just opened up, and the immediate, overwhelming emotion she felt for Taryn scared her. She was ready to fight and die for Taryn, ready to follow her anywhere, to make her a home. It made no sense, but it couldn't be argued with. Her body was coming apart, reshaped by the pressure of her expanding heart.

"You have now."

Taryn reached one long arm down and pulled a blanket up over them. Rosalind surrendered, falling asleep on the length of the girl, feeling perfectly safe. There would be time enough to find words for it in the morning.

❖

The heat of the sun on her closed eyes woke Rosalind. She mumbled against it, rolling over and flinging out her arms. Her hands crossed empty space, and that snapped her to attention. Her eyes flickered open, realization of where she was flooding them. She was naked under a thin red blanket, lying on a mattress on the floor, in Taryn's house. Taryn was nowhere to be found. Sunlight from the unshaded windows filled the room, giving Rosalind her first glimpse of it.

The mattress was set apart from the room in an alcove. The walls of the room were stripped plaster, covered in drawings and small paintings held up with thumbtacks. A peeled wood monstrosity of a dresser faced the alcove, next to a closet with a sliding door.

Rosalind saw her skirt and blouse folded over a chair. The floor was spotted with piled clothing, pieces of paper and books, in no discernible order. She sat up, holding the blanket over her breasts, wondering where Taryn was.

At the foot of the mattress was a pair of black sweatpants and a T-shirt. Rosalind assumed they were for her and picked them up, the oddness of the situation flooding her. She hadn't pictured a morning after quite this way. Rosalind smiled wryly at that thought. This was a morning after she never had the language to imagine, even if she'd had the time between meeting Taryn and ending up on her mattress.

"I've gone and turned into a wanton woman," Rosalind said aloud, testing her voice in the space of the room. The memory of the night came back with a vividness that made her grow warm, Taryn making love to her until she passed out in her arms. No wonder she'd slept through her getting up.

Rosalind stood, feeling stiff from the mattress, her body still shivering from the night's aftereffects. She felt bruised, sore, and wonderfully sated, but she missed seeing Taryn's eyes in the sunlight. She vaguely recalled dreaming of that, while she'd been sprawled on top of her, the way the light would strike the clear blue. Her nakedness felt too vulnerable; she slipped into the clothing left for her. She was grateful for the softness of the sweatpants. Her body felt too changed and new to be buckled back into her jacket and skirt. She held up the T-shirt, reading it. FUCK ON! DON'T DESEXUALIZE THE MOVEMENT! Rosalind felt her face grow warm again, but slipped it over her head.

Feeling like a spy, Rosalind looked around the room at the drawings tacked up on the plaster. They were familiar to her, similar to Taryn's tattoos, done in pen and ink. There were dragons and skulls, pictures of snakes and lions, a tiger shredding through the paper. Many of them she glanced over and kept going, but interspersed between the expected images there were a few surprise moments of Taryn's personality shining through. These she examined in detail: one of Alexander taming Buchephalus, and an early sketch of the bull dagger that gave her an odd but not unpleasant feeling.

The top of the dresser drew her eye. It was set up as an altar, with a bronze statue she recognized as a dancing Shiva inside his wheel of flame, red and yellow dried flowers, apples on a ceramic plate, a few stones of curious shape. There was a brass goblet with incised characters in no language she'd ever seen, a Greek coin with the profile of a man's head, and next to it a knife, its hilt in the shape of a dragon.

In the back corner was another bronze statue, nearly hidden behind the spray of red flowers. It was a woman, many-armed, her hands raised in a variety of gestures, some holding weapons. The bronze had gone green with verdigris at the edges, tinting the belt of skulls she wore, highlighting the edges of the blade of her scimitar. Her face had been painted at some point, black or deep blue; flecks of it still showed on the metal. The statue's whole aspect was ghastly, bloody, and unsettling. Rosalind looked closely, but was unwilling to touch it.

She left the bedroom, feeling a determination to seek Taryn. Barefoot, she padded down the polished wood floor, trying not to wake anyone who might be in the house. The hallway she vaguely remembered from stumbling down it the night before, wrapped around Taryn. There were three closed doors along the hall, other bedrooms, and a staircase leading up. At the end of the hall was a raised marble step and an open door, looking in on a bathroom. The bathroom walls were tiled in a burnt orange, half of them missing. An old-fashioned claw-footed bathtub dominated the room, making access to the freestanding sink and the toilet a dance exercise. Rosalind ran cold water in the sink, splashing her face.

She looked at herself in the mirror over the sink, seeking signs that the world had changed. Her face bore marks from sleeping on the sheets; her hair was wild, bristling up like the ruff of a boar. Rosalind fought down the urge to immediately tame her hair and kept examining her face with the diligence of an archeologist. Her lips were bruised, there was a suspicious color in her cheeks. Her eyes looked the same to her, calm and focused, the surprised curve of eyebrows giving her a perpetually questioning look.

Rosalind sighed, touching her reflection. *I look happy and anxious, which seems appropriate. Wonder if Taryn got a good look at me in the morning light and fled?* She reached for a brush and started wrestling with her hair, bringing civilization back to her appearance.

There was a narrow staircase at that end of the hall, plunging down at a vicious slant. Rosalind leaned over the edge, hearing sounds of pots banging. A grin tugged at her lips. She crept down the stairs, keeping one hand on the wall. At the foot, to the right, was an open doorway. Rosalind stood in it, viewing the kitchen. It was huge, running the entire length of the house. The ceiling had been stripped, leaving exposed wooden beams. The walls were spotted plaster, in the same state of permanent reconstruction as the rest of the house.

Opposite the doorway was a round table, in the corner near the stairs to the backyard. A cast-iron stove stood on the facing wall, diagonal to a sink loaded with dishes. Bundles of dried herbs hung from the rafters, and cast-iron pots on iron hooks. There was a wall of nothing but coffee mugs parading up to the ceiling, each on its own hook. A counter bar stood under the mug wall, protruding halfway into the room, with three barstools tucked under it. At the far end of the room was a closed door, with three food dishes arrayed in front of it. Four large cats surrounded the dishes, pushing over one another as they ate.

A man stood in front of the stove, his back to Rosalind. He was reaching up to grab an iron skillet from a hook. Rosalind thought him to be in his late thirties, not quite six feet tall, and powerfully built. His reaching move revealed a play of muscle under his thin T-shirt, stretching it tight. He was humming something in a low voice. She didn't recognize the tune. When he set the skillet on the stove and turned to reach for a knife, Rosalind got a look at his face. His hair was cut military short, receding over his temples. A tight beard covered his jaw, well trimmed, above a throat rough from shaving.

He glanced up and saw her, his eyes a pleasant chocolate brown that wrinkled at the corners as he smiled at her. "Morning. You want coffee?"

"Uh, sure," Rosalind said, thrown off.

He nodded and took a blue enameled cup off the mug wall, pouring her coffee from a pot on the stove. "Sit. You take anything in it?" He turned toward the fridge.

Rosalind, not knowing what else to do, sat down at the table. The strangeness of the moment carried her along on its current. The man didn't seem surprised to find a stranger in his kitchen. He handed her the blue cup, looking at her expectantly. "Oh, nothing, thanks. Black is good."

"Just like that kid," he said, then shrugged. He took up the knife and started chopping mushrooms, piling them along the cutting board.

"I'm Rosalind," she said, trying to get a feel for the etiquette of the moment. *How do you introduce yourself to the housemates of the girl you just slept with?* The man smiled at her again and set the knife aside. He wiped one large hand on his jeans and held it out to her. His grip was strong but not crushing, an unmistakable impression of strength being restrained.

"I'm Joe," he said pleasantly.

Rosalind liked the sound of his voice. There was a burr to it that reminded her oddly of Taryn's voice. Rosalind remembered Taryn talking about the people she lived with, listing them off. What had she said? "Papa Joe?"

Joe's face twisted up in a grimace. "Taryn insists on calling me that." He picked up the knife, sweeping the mushrooms onto the counter, and reached for a pepper. "Relax, I'll fix you an omelet."

Rosalind sat and sipped her coffee, watching Joe wield the knife and skillet. It was comforting to watch the man cook, to accept his automatic friendliness, to sit in the warm kitchen and drink coffee. Rosalind was relieved not to be explaining anything—what she was doing here, who she was, what she intended. She basked in the anonymity. The coffee cup was warm in her hands. The sweats were soft against her skin. The banging of the cast-iron skillet against the stove took on a rhythm. She relaxed, finding pleasure in everything— the rough plaster walls, the exposed beams, the cats pushing at one another around the food dish. It was wonderful, she discovered, not to be known, but to be accepted anyway.

"Rhea should be up soon," Joe commented, taking a plate out of the cabinet and sliding an omelet onto it in one smooth motion. He set the plate in front of Rosalind, then handed her a fork. "No meat. If you're a carnivore like that punk kid, I hope you'll survive," he said, his smile taking the edge from his words.

"She'll be fine."

The sound of Taryn's voice drew Rosalind's eyes up immediately, and she felt her heart leap in response. It was her first look at Taryn in the daylight, and it made her ache. She was dressed in jeans and a red and black flannel shirt with the sleeves ripped off, exposing her powerful arms. The tattoo of Alexander looked out on unfathomable distances. Rosalind remembered biting down on it during the night, when Taryn covered her, and blushed at the memory. There was a faint redness to the skin. She hoped that there weren't any visible tooth marks.

Taryn held up a paper bag like a hunting trophy. "Bagels. Had to walk up to Solid Grounds. Cybele's was closed." She loped into the room, passing the bag to Joe.

"Cybele's closed on a Saturday morning?" he asked, opening the bag.

"You can't set a clock by them. They run on their own time," Taryn said. Rosalind felt a surge of electricity when she walked near, a jumping of energy from Taryn's skin to hers. She reached out to touch her, but Taryn kept walking to the counter. "I see you met Joe."

"Yes, we met. Good thing, because your skill at introductions is sadly lacking," Joe said, cutting the bagels.

Taryn fished a coffee mug off the wall, a blue glass mug with gold stars painted on it. She poured herself coffee from the pot on the stove, then leaned her back against the counter.

"You're lucky it was Papa Joe in the kitchen. You'll at least get a decent meal out of him. Rhea would make you eat puffed millet with soy milk," she said, her eyes catching the sunlight.

Rosalind felt her skin hurt, felt the need to grab her and press against her. Taryn's distance, and the presence of Joe in the kitchen, prevented her. She couldn't keep herself from staring at Taryn, devouring the sight of her—the firm jaw, the carved lips, the tangle of black hair falling into her eyes. Rosalind let her eyes roam over Taryn's body, knowing more of it than was now revealed—the play of muscle in her shoulders and back, the lean hips, the feel of her hands. Dressed as she was, in loose jeans hanging low on her hips, unlaced combat boots, and the sleeveless flannel shirt, she could easily be taken for a boy. She looked handsome, cocky, and it made Rosalind tremble.

"You cold?" Taryn asked, watching her over the rim of the blue glass mug.

"No. A little, maybe," Rosalind admitted.

Taryn jogged out of kitchen with a clomp of combat boots.

Joe shook his head at Rosalind. "She sounds like a platoon in those things. If I could get her to lace them up, they wouldn't be so bad."

Taryn returned with another flannel shirt. She walked to Rosalind and draped it over her shoulders like a cape. When she set her hands on Rosalind's shoulders, Rosalind reached up and covered one with her own. She couldn't resist touching her. Taryn didn't move away immediately. She gave Rosalind's shoulder a faint squeeze before retreating to the counter.

"How was the show last night?" Joe asked, handing Taryn an omelet. She ate standing up, her back to the counter.

"Good. Rosalind was there, ask her," Taryn said around a mouthful.

Joe glanced at Rosalind. "How'd she do?"

"She was magnificent," Rosalind said, looking at Taryn.

Joe snorted. "I meant during the show," he said, from the stove.

Taryn lashed out with the back of her hand, catching him in the stomach. "Bastard. The show was good. Egyptia was on. I want to work on a few things for next week. Maybe you can help me, after we work out," Taryn said, polishing off the omelet. She grinned at Rosalind. "Joe's my masculine role model."

"Like you need one. You're the poster child for butch." The man laughed, taking the plate from her.

Taryn poured herself more coffee, then refilled Rosalind's mug. "Where's Goblin?" she asked Joe, leaning on his shoulder as he cleaned up.

"With her dad this weekend. Laurel's at her girlfriend's. Rhea's sleeping in. Seems there was quite a racket last night, kept us up." Rosalind choked on her coffee, felt herself blushing furiously. Joe looked at her mildly. "Some idiot left his car alarm on half the night. Didn't you hear it?"

"Must have been off by the time we came in," Taryn said, a sly grin on her face.

Taryn strolled to the fridge and peered at a chart that was written in several bold colors of marker and held up with cat-shaped magnets.

"Rhea has me down for dishes this week?" she asked, disgust in her voice. "I hate dishes," she added, talking to the chart.

"It's character building. It'll help domesticate you someday," Joe said, dropping the skillet in the sink.

"Aren't you eating?" Taryn asked him.

Joe washed his hands, then wiped them off on a towel. "Already did. I'm gonna go wake Rhea. You want to help me with my shot first?"

Taryn looked at Rosalind, silent for moment. "Yeah. I'll be right back," she said, before following Joe up the back staircase.

Rosalind finished her omelet. One of the cats, a massive calico, decided that she was interesting and came meowing across the floor. It circled around her chair, rubbing and crying, until she picked it up. The cat knocked its skull against Rosalind's knuckles, kneaded her lap with its front paws, and purred loudly. "You are such a friendly one," Rosalind said to the cat, as it circled in her lap, too excited to settle.

"She likes your energy."

Rosalind looked up into the face of the woman watching her. She was in her early forties, Rosalind guessed, with thick, curly brown hair threaded with gray. It stood out in a halo around her head, like the rays of the sun. At first Rosalind thought her eyes were a shade of ebony; then at second glance, they looked pure jet, swallowing the pupils. Her face was angular, severe. She was about Rosalind's height, not much over five feet four, and very thin. She wore a blue cotton dress, the hem hanging down to bare ankles.

"You must be Rhea," Rosalind said, her stomach knotting with apprehension. The woman hadn't smiled at her yet.

"I must be. You're Taryn's new friend."

"Uh, yes. I think I am." The cat left Rosalind's lap, running over to rub on Rhea's calves.

"You either are or you aren't," Rhea said, walking to the stove. She was unnerving in her composure, in the biting way she spoke. Her voice had a strain to it, as if words were a clumsy form of communication. The fact that Taryn spoke so highly of her only added to Rosalind's nervousness. She sensed that this woman's opinion mattered to Taryn more than anyone's in the world.

"Then I am her friend," Rosalind said, asserting her right. This earned her a cool appraisal over one thin shoulder, as Rhea put a kettle on the stove.

"Joe's fed you."

It was a statement. Rosalind nodded in confirmation.

"He's good with that. Whoever shows up, he feeds. Would you like tea, or do you drink coffee?"

"I've had coffee, thanks," Rosalind said carefully.

Rhea made a tching noise in her throat. "Another one. Two coffee drinkers in the house is bad enough."

Rosalind stood up, conscious of the large sweatpants hanging off her body, how the T-shirt with its screaming message hung down to midthigh. She no longer felt comfortable and easy in the unstructured clothing. She felt ridiculous, an adult playing at being a teenager. She pushed her hair back behind her ears, then held her hand out to Rhea. Rhea took her hand and held it. The woman's hand was thin and sharp, like the blade of a knife. Rosalind could feel the bones through the skin. It was stronger than Rosalind expected, all sinew over the bone. There was no spare flesh anywhere on Rhea, and unlike Taryn, she wasn't padded with muscle. "I'm Rosalind."

"You're Rosalind. Well, that was inevitable," Rhea said, dropping her hand as if burned.

"Excuse me?" Rosalind asked her, not wanting to follow the turn the conversation was taking. She had the distinct impression that Rhea did not like her, and that scared her.

Rhea looked at her levelly, the way she might look at a rat sneaking across her floor. "I warned Taryn. But I know her. Naturally she ran right out and did the opposite."

"I'm sorry—" Rosalind began, but Rhea cut her off.

"You never were one to take a hint. You are not welcome here."

The sound of boots came clomping down the back stairs. Taryn galloped into the kitchen, surprise on her face. "Hey! Just went in to wake you up," she said, kissing Rhea on the cheek. The woman accepted the kiss, her eyes never leaving Rosalind.

"I should be going. Walk me out?" Rosalind asked. Taryn looked at her sharply, but inclined her head. Rosalind had a clear impression of Rhea's eyes following her out of the kitchen, pushing her.

She took her clothing from Taryn's room and walked down the front staircase.

"Keep the sweats."

"Thanks. Please thank Joe for me, for breakfast," Rosalind said, not looking at Taryn. Her confusion was cutting her in half. She wanted to grab on to Taryn and never let her go. She wanted to run away from this house and the fierce woman in the kitchen, who was even now waiting for Taryn. She had been friendly but distant in the sunshine. It bruised Rosalind's heart. She had put a different meaning on last night.

What had been life changing for her seemed the normal course of events for Taryn. Just another weekend. She remembered Taryn talking about Colleen, how clingy she was. By Taryn's own admission, they'd slept together a few times, and Taryn didn't seem to think they were involved. Grief settled on her, killing off the joy she'd felt since waking up. Rosalind wanted to get away before she started crying. She opened the door.

Taryn took Rosalind and pulled her in, kissing her slowly and thoroughly. Rosalind resisted for a moment, then gave in, melting against her strong body, her hands closing on Taryn's arms. "I'll see you later," Taryn said when they broke apart.

Rosalind nodded, unable to speak. She walked gingerly down the stairs, back into her own life.

CHAPTER FOUR

B ack in her own apartment, Rosalind didn't know where to begin. She'd shed her skin overnight. She was convinced her apartment would be different when she got back. It was, stubbornly, exactly as she left it—neat to the point of museum quality, tastefully furnished with natural wood and neutral colors.

Rosalind couldn't help but compare it to the house she had just left, with its constant state of restoration, the unfinished walls and exposed beams, the kitchen big as a stable, a haven against the world. Rosalind's own kitchen was small, perfect for one person, as the landlord had said. But there was no room to sit down, no room to linger and talk.

She tried putting the bright copper kettle on her electric stove, but the sound was unsatisfying. She poured hot water over instant coffee in one of her mother's teacups, and remembered the feel of the blue enamel mug in her hands. Her state of unrest was getting worse. Rosalind drew in a deep breath and faced her own confusion. She did what the women of her family line had done for generations when under emotional stress. She did laundry.

The sorting was the best part. Everything had a place, had a specific set of instructions on how to maintain it, keep it beautiful. There was no ambiguity, no fear. This was a skill her mother had taught her, insisting on it as a civilized virtue. "Other people may cook for you or buy you gifts, to impress you. But no one will ever care for your appearance as well as you do." You don't wash the cashmere in the machine; you put it with the delicates. You don't put the red blanket in with the socks; the dye will bleed. And so on, until it became a meditation.

At last it was ready. Rosalind stripped out of the T-shirt and sweats, her hand hesitating over them. They didn't fit anywhere, exactly, but her mother's training took over. It would be civilized to wash them, set them aside. Maybe she could give them back at some point.

The phone rang and Rosalind, who had been convincing herself that she was not thinking about anything or anyone in particular, answered it before it rang a second time. "Hello?" Her voice rose sharply at the end of the word, making it more of a question than she'd wanted.

"Well, hello! So, I'm waiting. You're home. It's morning. How was coffee with Elvis?"

"Ellie," Rosalind said, as both identification and reproval.

"You find out anything good? Like, she's really straight, or she votes Republican? Must be good, you're not talking."

"I slept with her." There. She'd said it out loud, to someone in her own life. It existed now. There was no turning back. Shocked silence met her from the other end of the phone.

At last Ellie started breathing again. "When I said coffee is never just coffee, I didn't mean it. Wow, Ros. How was it?"

Rosalind closed her eyes. How was it? How did she answer a question like that? She was a professor. She insisted on context for everything, but there was no context for this. There was just a memory of one incredible night, one awkward morning, in the arms and out of the arms of a splendid young drag king. How could she fit this into her life narrative as anything other than an adventure? So Rosalind decided to give it context, make the story fit the category.

It would be an adventure she had had, while feeling daring. Something to titillate her much more exciting friend with, an anecdote. Taryn would become a colorful character to be brought out at cocktail parties, entertaining people she didn't care for. The night would become manageable, under her control, not something that unsettled everything she'd ever believed about herself.

"It was incredible. She lives in this rundown Victorian in Allentown. We went back there and made love all night long on a mattress on the floor. In the morning some of the characters she lives with made me breakfast. She cavalierly kissed me goodbye and sent me on my way. Very *Casablanca*. You'd have loved it." Rosalind realized that tears were streaming down her face as she spoke, the words twisting a knife in her gut. It wasn't just an adventure, and trying to make it into one was agonizing.

"Oh, sweetie. You're doing laundry, aren't you?"

"How'd you know?" Rosalind asked, giving up on masking the sounds of crying.

"You sound like you're crying. If you're upset enough to cry, you're probably doing laundry. I'll be right over."

Ellie had a key to her apartment and lived nearby. She let herself in, walking right to Rosalind, who sat on the couch surrounded by piles of neatly sorted laundry. Ellie pushed a pile out of the way and sat down. She examined the piles of laundry, a spot of black drawing her eye. She plucked the T-shirt from the top of the pile and fixed her eyes on Rosalind. "DON'T DESEXUALIZE THE MOVEMENT? This is not yours. You okay, honey?"

"I feel like my skin has come off. We had the most incredible night. Taryn was…I thought she was feeling the way I felt. But the next morning, she was so distant. It's like she turned back into a stranger. I don't know what to think," Rosalind said, taking the T-shirt away from Ellie and refolding it.

"Men are dogs," Ellie said sincerely.

"Taryn's not a man." The image of Taryn in her black suit flashed into Rosalind's mind, blurring gender lines.

"Well, no. But that's the standard line the best friend is supposed to say, and she doesn't actually fit in the 'women are dogs' category. It's the best ad-libbing I could do."

Rosalind laughed and wiped tears from her eyes. "Egyptia warned me she was a dog. But I don't listen to warnings any better than Taryn does. I met Rhea the Witch."

"What's she like?" Ellie asked, her face betraying interest.

"Fierce. She didn't like me at all." Rosalind recalled the way Rhea had dropped her hand, and the explicit warning. It wasn't a comforting thought.

"I can't believe that. You are the most universally likable person who ever existed. Disney called. He wants to market you as a character. Rosalind the Cuddly Professor."

Rosalind looked at the piles of laundry that surrounded her. She reached out and knocked one over, watching as it tipped toward the floor. "I don't want to be cuddly anymore, Ellie. I want to be beautiful. Gorgeous. Heart-stopping. I've never wanted that before. It scares the hell out of me. I'm playing a game where I don't know the rules."

"Whoa, rewind. That sounds suspiciously like The Continuing Adventures of Elvis. You going to see her again?" The question was valid, the interest on Ellie's face was genuine, but something in Rosalind hesitated in saying what had immediately jumped into her mind, that unqualified *yes*. She didn't know where that yes was coming from and didn't trust it. She knew well enough that spoken words keep growing, once you let them go.

"That wouldn't make any sense. We hardly have a great deal in common, and she gave me the literal kiss off-on the porch. I'm not a teenager. I can recognize danger a mile away," Rosalind said, ignoring the way her heart started to clench.

"Not to mention the heterosexuality thing. You haven't mentioned that," Ellie said, rubbing her chin.

"Thank you very much, Dr. Freud. Not because it hasn't been running in circles in my head. I had a great time last night. It was so easy, it was almost scary. No, it was scary. But whoever went home with Taryn last night wanted it enough not to care. I'm just not sure who she is yet. Or how to go about finding out."

"Way too heavy for a Saturday afternoon. You need distraction, not more thinking in circles. I suggest the three of us go shopping—you, me, and whoever slept with Elvis. Great sex should always be celebrated with a new leather jacket," Ellie said. When Rosalind hesitated, Ellie took her hand. "Trust me, this too shall pass. Everything seems less dramatic after a few days."

Rosalind spent the rest of Saturday heeding Ellie's advice to pamper herself, take long bubble baths, read trashy novels, and sleep. In the evening she walked, the memory of Taryn's hands far too vivid to allow her to rest. She prepared lectures for the next month, graded papers, saw a foreign film at the North Park with lots of subtitles and weeping women on rocky coasts. She couldn't shake the feeling that Taryn was supposed to be beside her, for everything. When she caught herself walking toward her car, thinking that maybe she would just drive by Mariner Street to see if Taryn was walking around, she got scared. *I've turned back into a teenager.*

When she was a teenager, she'd never acted like this. She'd been very levelheaded, responsible. Her mother never hesitated to loan her the car. Her father trusted her dates to keep her out late. She'd tried to experiment with shoplifting in seventh grade, smoking in eighth, but none of it stuck. Drinking cases of light beer by the river bored her. Marijuana made her hungry, but little else. In rural Poughkeepsie it took an incredible amount of drive to be a problem child. She was, by default, the definition of a good girl. Was it her fault that she actually liked to read, that school wasn't a chore, that she liked succeeding at it? She was the kind of student teachers loved and other students disliked with glee.

There had to be a measure of adolescence that every person is doomed to go through. If you missed it when you were an adolescent, it didn't mean you led a charmed life, were too enlightened for all that hormonal frenzy. It waited for you, lulling you into a false sense of security, until you were convinced you were an adult. Then, BAM! The fist of life got you, right between the eyes. You went from rational to obsessive in the blink of an eye.

Her mind chased its tail all night as she lay in bed. She reviewed every crush she'd ever had, male and female. Hadn't that English teacher in seventh grade been a definitive sign? No, wait. There had been the softball coach. That was definitive. If you didn't count Paul. Of course, there had been that one night with her college roommate. Tracey had broken up with her boyfriend, and they'd gotten sloppy drunk on strawberry wine, commiserating about the lack of good men.

She'd put her arm around Tracey's shoulders, just to be comforting. Tracey had turned into the embrace, and somehow they were kissing. The next morning, though, the only evidence it had ever happened was a throbbing hangover and Tracey's marked discomfort in being alone with her. Rosalind stared at the ceiling and thought about it. That might have been the closest to heartbroken she'd ever been.

Rosalind turned over on her stomach and hugged her pillow. Sleep was not just eluding her; it had left her vocabulary entirely. It took her a moment to admit, even to herself, that what she was feeling was loneliness. It wasn't the loneliness she'd felt in the cemetery. It was fixed on a certain face, a certain arrogant smirk, a certain set of hands. She wondered what it would be like to fall asleep with Taryn's arms around her. Rosalind groaned and covered her head with the pillow. This was not happening. She was not obsessed with a girl she had known for one night. She sat up and threw the pillow across the room. If sleep wouldn't play with her, she would scorn it in turn.

Rosalind walked into the living room and turned the television on. Piles of laundry still dominated the couch, evidence of her disturbed mental state. She took a perverse pleasure in that and sat between them, feeling rebellious. A girl had to start somewhere. She started flipping through the channels, looking for a documentary, a film, anything but an infomercial. She saw opening credits and gave a small cheer. A late-night movie would be a perfect distraction. Marlon Brando, an excellent sign! *Sayonara*. She'd never seen this one. Rosalind settled back with gratitude. An old movie would keep her mind quiet.

Pilot, Southern boy, engaged to a general's daughter, reassigned from Korea to Japan to marry her. Good, simple plot, nothing to break the state of receptivity. His friend is dating a Japanese woman, the army has fits, fine. He goes to see a show with his friend one night; apparently the star performer is spectacular. Oh, didn't anyone mention that she performs with an all-female troop and the tall women play male roles?

Rosalind sat disbelieving, staring at the screen, while Marlon Brando fell in love with Hana Ogi, male costume and all. She sat up as Marlon waited by the bridge day after day, hoping to get Hana Ogi to speak to him. The beautiful Hana Ogi, dressed in her male clothing, would stroll by, surrounded by adoring female fans. The women and girls would mob her, seeking her autograph, while she pointedly ignored her suitor. *I can't get away from it for a single minute*. Drag kings were haunting her. All right, she could admit it; she wanted to see her again.

Rosalind watched with great interest while Marlon Brando courted Hana Ogi, waiting by the bridge every morning and evening in the same spot, under the tree. It wasn't until he tried a new tactic and hid, watching from a different spot, that he saw the performer looking for him. It was like a sign from God, brought to her by way of Brando. She had to go stand by the bridge. There wasn't any bridge near 34 Mariner, not that she recalled, and none near Marcella's. It was getting very late; Rosalind's thoughts were getting hazy. She resolved, as she drifted off, to stand by the porch steps at 34 Mariner every night until Taryn noticed her.

The certainty she'd felt about the message from Brando had vanished in the night, leaving her feeling a little foolish. She'd slept lightly, jumping back and forth across the river of sleep like a child jumping a brook. Her dreams had been similarly capering, her mind refusing her access to the heart of her own mystery. In dreams, she hid from herself in a maze of symbology she couldn't decipher. Moments of the night had bled into images of Shiva dancing; the entanglement of mortal limbs became the swirling of multiple bronze arms. The crow landed again on the blue stone. Joe handed her coffee in Taryn's blue glass mug.

Rosalind awoke exhausted, lonely, her body knotted with unspent desire. She got out of bed just to make a cup of tea and found herself getting dressed. The laundry was still in piles on the couch. She put it ritually away. The black T-shirt and sweatpants were left, not having a space of their own. When her body started walking to the car, she mentally whistled and ignored it. Thinking had gotten her nowhere. In a suspended state, carefully avoiding looking beyond the moment, she drove, letting her destination be a surprise.

The house at 34 Mariner faced east. Rosalind watched the sun start to gild the green shutters, pour across the front windows, and reveal Taryn's room. The sun would be creeping across the mattress in the alcove soon. Rosalind imagined the light touching Taryn's shoulders, the warmth moving down her back, along the bull dagger. She'd have to talk her into buying some shades. She couldn't keep getting up at this hour.

The red convertible wasn't parked out front. Rosalind wondered where Joe had parked it. He always used the spot in front of the house. He'd be up already, in the kitchen cooking, if he were home. Somehow, she didn't picture the household as likely to be at church. The porch was looking like a bridge to her, so she looked away. Rosalind's eye moved over the September garden. It would be gorgeous in the spring, with the roses and azaleas. Beyond the azalea bush, to the left, was a brick path, curving around the side of the house.

Curious, Rosalind left the car, carrying Taryn's clothing. The path ran along the side of the house, around to the back. Stacks of firewood, clay pots, an axe all lined the purple wall. Grass grew up between the bricks. Rosalind walked, feeling absurdly happy to be approaching the house. It took her a moment to realize she was humming "Will You Love Me Tomorrow?" Rosalind grinned. The door at the end of the path was open, looking in on the backyard. The state of energetic disarray of the house extended to the yard, with its overgrown grass littered with gardening tools, what looked like a compost pile the size of a burial mound in the back left corner. The calico cat was sleeping on the back step, its paws folded away in the secret cat hiding spot. "Good morning," Rosalind said, softly. The cat opened its eyes, squinted in pleasure, and closed them again. That was enough of a welcome to make her feel wanted.

"Why are you creeping around my backyard?" Rhea asked from the open kitchen door. Rosalind froze. Her mind took a sabbatical, leaving her without the power of language. She stood at the foot of the steps up into the kitchen, looking at the one person she did not want to see. Rhea put down the teacup, folded her arms, and regarded Rosalind. "Well?"

Rosalind held out the clothing she was carrying. "I wanted to return Taryn's sweatpants."

"I'm surprised she didn't tell you to keep them. She says that to the others. I'm constantly buying her new sweatpants." Rhea picked up her cup of tea.

"Uh, well, she did. I just thought that…" Rosalind cudgeled her brain, screaming at it to come up with something clever. The look in Rhea's eyes paralyzed her, kept her from even approaching the screen door. It was like a confessional booth, and Rosalind had to fight down the urge to admit her impure thoughts. The look of humor on Rhea's face was cold.

"You thought you could see her again and ended up in my backyard at sunrise. Am I going to have to set a warding against you?" Rhea asked. Rosalind wasn't sure what that meant, but it didn't sound good.

"Of course not. I'll just drop these off and be gone. Is Taryn here?" she asked, trying to gather a sense of annoyance at this gatekeeper. It wasn't often that she felt like a complete fool before the sun had been up for half an hour.

"If I tell you she's here, what then? You want to go up to her bedroom and wake her up?"

"Look, I can just…" Rosalind began, feeling lost. Brando had it easy. All he had to face was the disapproval of two nations and the US Army. She had to face Rhea, and the idea of explaining about the bridge made her feel ridiculous.

Rhea sipped from her teacup, her eyes opaque. "What makes you think Taryn is upstairs alone?"

It hadn't occurred to her, not for a moment. Her mind had pictured Taryn waking on the mattress alone. She had relived the lovemaking of the night they'd spent. But Taryn waking with someone else? Her mind balked at the thought, her stomach clenched. She recalled the way Taryn had kissed her goodbye, with the noncommittal "I'll see you later." Later meant never.

How often had her mother told her that? Taryn hadn't called her, had she? Taryn hadn't even asked for her number. Last night had been Saturday; of course the drag king wouldn't come home alone. Some other woman would be waking up under the thin red blanket, wearing a borrowed T-shirt.

Rosalind felt sick with shame. She had been saved from making a complete ass of herself by the disdain of the woman now watching her with the detached interest of a scientist. She set the black clothing down on the steps. "Would you see that Taryn gets these?" Rosalind asked. She didn't wait for a reply before slipping back down the path.

Rosalind spent the morning in her office at the university clearing away the pile of papers, getting caught up on the business of moving in. She shuffled files like tarot cards, trying to see a future in work alone. She dropped her head down on her desk, exhausted by the thought. This was ridiculous, she told herself. She couldn't be missing something that flitted through her life like a hummingbird. Taryn wasn't interested. Her mind was chewing on the disastrous visit to 34 Mariner, dissecting her own motivation. Paul had been solid, steady, a guarantee.

In the end, stability hadn't been enough to hold her interest. She thought she was getting too old to start picking out love objects based on their unavailability, their youth and arrogance. If this was going to be her pattern, why hadn't she started in her teens? It would make it much easier to berate herself now, she thought wryly. She felt a moment of humor break through. She pictured herself listening to Carole King and drinking wine, Patsy Cline and drinking whiskey. "Brando, you let me down," Rosalind said to her empty office.

Sunday night was unbearable. Ellie had gone out with friends from the theater department. She'd invited Rosalind along, but Rosalind had refused. The thought of company was unappealing. Smiling and making conversation sounded like hard work. "Just let me brood a little, write in my journal, listen to sad songs. I'll be fine," she'd said.

The plan had worked, for half an hour, until the sad songs made her double over on the couch, sobbing. It felt good to have that release, but it left a lingering feeling of overindulgence. Her body went to war against her mind, demanding things she couldn't give it. Desperate, she picked a book at random from her bookshelf, Stephen Hawking's *A Brief History of Time*, and settled down to read. Surely this had to be a safe, pure distraction. When Hawking started talking about the universe and the mind of God, she started to see Shiva dancing and threw the book across the room.

By Monday night's class, she was enervated, ready to crawl out of her skin, tired of the spinning of her mind and the demands of her body. She didn't want to think anymore. She wanted Taryn naked and in reach. Her desire was clarified, making it that much harder to admit that it probably would never happen again. Whatever rules had been suspended for that one night were back in force; life turned on its accustomed wheel. Her temper was short. She felt sorry in advance for any student she snapped at during class. The room was filling up; students were brushing by her to take seats. Rosalind glanced down at the stack in her arms, wondering if she'd remembered to correct all the papers she was handing back.

"Dr. Olchawski."

The voice was enough to make Rosalind nearly drop everything she was carrying. She looked up, disbelieving. Two thoughts fought for dominance: *How did she find me?* and *Oh, Lord, she's here*.

There, leaning against the doorway, was Taryn. The girl grinned at her, and all other thought fled out of reach. Rosalind's heart started banging so hard, she thought it might disconnect a few of her ribs. There wasn't a rational thought left in her, only pure reaction that seized her like the force of gravity. She was here, and nothing else seemed important. Taryn strolled forward, hands in the pockets of her jeans, a look of pleasure on her face for surprising Rosalind in her own territory.

"I was wondering if I could have a conference with you," Taryn said casually.

"Sure. I've got a minute before class," Rosalind said, trying to appear as if this was any other conversation. Taryn was young enough to be a student, so standing in the hall chatting with her certainly looked innocent enough, despite the way it felt.

Taryn glanced down the hall at the staircase and smiled. "Take a walk with me?"

"Sure." Rosalind, giddy with adrenaline, smiled back, her bad mood a memory.

The top of the stairs had double doors, usually propped open by impatient students hurrying to class. Rosalind, concentrating on breathing normally, stepped through them. Taryn kicked the stand, and the doors swung closed. In a moment the papers she'd been carrying were dropped on the floor, Rosalind was pressed back against the wall, being kissed like the world was ending. Her arms were around Taryn's neck, her body was reveling in the length of the body covering her, forcing her into the wall.

The urgency of the kiss took her breath away. The need she felt staggered her, but Taryn seemed to feel it as well, claiming her with impatient hands, kissing her savagely. One of Taryn's legs was between hers, pressing up against her, the muscle flexing in the most interesting way. Rosalind ground down against it, wanting to feel more.

Footsteps. Rosalind felt Taryn's mouth pry away from hers and groaned. "Don't—"

There was the sound of running, some student late for class. Taryn hopped a step away. Rosalind tried to fix her skirt. A boy ran past them, up the stairs, smashing through the doors, barely noticing them. Rosalind was conscious of her pulse doing the tango, how flushed she felt. Taryn stepped in again, and Rosalind reached for her.

"I haven't been able to think about anything else since you left," Taryn said, leaning down to kiss her. The doors to the stairs banged; they barely had time to jump apart. They stood with a foot of distance between them, breathing irregularly.

"How did you find me?"

"I have my ways. Miss me last night?" Taryn asked, her smile devilish.

Rosalind closed her eyes. "Yes." She wanted to know who had been in bed with Taryn on Saturday; she wanted to go on kissing her. The latter desire won out, when Taryn moved a few inches closer.

"I have to get to class," Rosalind said, but her hands ignored her and reached for Taryn.

Taryn leaned back in, nipping at her neck. "I'll meet you in your office afterward. There's something special I want to show you."

"What would that be?" Rosalind gasped, arching her neck. She felt Taryn's lips ease up to her ear.

"Why a butch always wears button-fly jeans," she whispered, sending a shudder through Rosalind. She grabbed her purse, fumbled through it, and dropped her office keys into Taryn's outstretched hand.

Rosalind made it through class. It was a unique blending of sublimation and anticipation, but she was inspired. The lesson she had carefully prepared was ignored. Instead, she stood in front of the room, so wet that if she sat down, she was afraid she'd soak the chair. Her students surely found the lecture about writing a personal essay passionate, gripping. When Dr. Olchawski spoke about writing what you know, a smile of beatific glory came across her face. Rosalind was firm with herself. She fought down the urge to cancel class, then the urge to let them go early.

The waiting, knowing that Taryn was in her office, was delicious. She lectured about surrendering to the control of your muse, following the urging of the artistic mistress, and her mind played. She pictured Taryn lounging in her chair, unbuttoning her black shirt. Her mind struggled with the mystery of the button fly, but it eluded her. Her energy was extraordinary. Her students caught it and left class eager to attack their projects.

Dr. Olchawski's office was on the fifth floor of Clemens. She set a new university speed record in getting back to it.

The door was open, and Taryn was there, settling one fear and bringing on a host of new ones. Taryn was reclining in her chair, boots up on her desk, and Rosalind didn't mind a bit. She was holding the picture of the Renaissance Festival, turning it over in her hands. "I like this. You should dress up for me sometime."

The thought that there would be a sometime was very welcome to Rosalind. It indicated more contact with her. She agreed readily. "Whenever you like."

"That's what I love about you, Dr. Olchawski. Your enthusiasm. How was class?" Taryn set the picture on the desk.

"What class?" Rosalind asked, as Taryn stood up.

"Yeah. I've been the same way. I went drinking with Joe and Egyptia on Saturday. They were giving me hell all night for not being able to think straight."

"I've had that problem myself," Rosalind admitted, her mind capering with joy that Taryn hadn't been out with another woman on Saturday. This was getting entirely out of hand. Her body had a will of its own and an elaborate sense of what it wanted.

"Good," Taryn said, and kissed her. The desire that had her wound like a bowstring roared to life. Rosalind grabbed her, impatient, and pulled her closer. Taryn let herself be captured for a moment, before pulling back. "Rosalind, do you trust me?"

She had nothing but emotion to inform her answer, and emotion was a kind of drunkenness, making reason suspect. She didn't have to reach for the word; it was waiting on her lips as she looked up into the sapphire eyes of her tormenter and gave her soul up willingly. "Yes, I do." It was as sweet and honest a response as had ever existed.

Taryn kissed her, lightly, in acknowledgement. "Thank you."

Taryn stepped back from her. "I want you to undo the middle two buttons. Not the top, not the bottom," Taryn said, her voice firm. She took Rosalind's hand and put it on her fly.

It took a great deal of concentration to do only that, without giving in to the temptation to fondle her or rip her clothing off.

Taryn smiled at her when she was done. "If you're not wearing a harness, and most of the time I don't unless it's a special occasion, you can get caught without any way to wear your toys. If you have button-fly jeans on, you can do this." Taryn eased a dildo through her open fly. "That will keep it in place. I've got my cock on. I'm going to fuck you. You can do anything you like, except scream," Taryn said, her voice low and urgent.

Rosalind gasped, the words making her body leap in response. "Yes," she managed to say, not recognizing her own voice.

The toy was a piece of latex, held in place by her jeans. Rosalind reached out with her left hand, touching it shyly, finding it warm from Taryn's skin. Taryn smiled encouragingly at her, letting her explore. She put her right hand on Taryn's hip, stroking the toy with her left. It was the blatant declaration of what was coming, and it surprised Rosalind how much she enjoyed it. It was like claiming the space, announcing her desire. She felt the coursing of power along her veins. She was doing something simply for her own pleasure, not because it made any sense. It made her feel lightheaded.

She thought, when she saw Taryn pull out the toy, of the fumbling nights in the back seat of cars, the sweaty, awkward, needful stumbling of adolescence. Of wanting so much that never happened, waiting for her body to miraculously spark to life, waiting. She remembered the fear of living her entire life without knowing why this physical entanglement was supposed to be sublime. It was numbing, and it seemed like work. Were those who spoke of it in rapturous terms kidding? Her own inability to lose herself, to make her mind shut up, her distance from what seemed by all report to be a good thing frightened her.

It's hard, when you are sixteen, to decide you'll never be normal, that your senses are blunted beyond repair. Rosalind covered it well, but inside she knew the truth. There were things she was never going to know, and she'd best get a sense of humor about it. Marriage hadn't been much better, for now the silence in her flesh was disappointing someone she cared about. In the end, it was easier not to attempt it at all.

The memory of that awkwardness, that numbness in her body was right there, waiting. She looked into the burning eyes of the lover who stood in front of her, wanting something to assure her that she wasn't that teenager anymore. What she saw was herself reflected, magnified, desired. The hunger was naked on Taryn's handsome face, hunger for her, coupled with a look she didn't recognize. It was playful, and passionate, the look in Taryn's eyes, and it gave her the space to be the same. She felt her body remember their first night together with a surge of longing.

Taryn put her hands on Rosalind's waist, guiding her. "Bend over the desk," Taryn said. The professor bent over with her stomach and breasts on the desk; the drag king stood behind her. Rosalind felt Taryn's hands lift up her skirt, caress her thighs. When her hands felt how wet she was through her panties, she thought she heard Taryn sigh. Then the cloth barrier was gone, torn away. Rosalind closed her eyes in anticipation. Her body had been tormenting her for days; even Taryn's impatient pace was taking too long.

With her hands still on Rosalind's waist, Taryn entered her, pushing her hips forward. She was so wet Taryn slid right in, filling her. Rosalind gasped and threw her head back. Taryn started sliding in and out, easing only the tip of her cock into Rosalind. Her breathing took on a rhythm to match her thrusts, the swivel to her hips working wonders. Rosalind let herself fall into the sensation, enjoying the penetration, enjoying the fact that it was Taryn who was fucking her. Her mind started floating. She saw everything start to dance.

Rosalind gripped the sides of the desk, rising up to meet Taryn's thrusts. The ungraded papers on her desk crumpled with their motion. Some of them would be inexplicably moist when Rosalind sat down to grade them. She found herself biting down on a student's paper and spit it back out. "Taryn," she breathed, and that name was a caress and a command. She felt Taryn's thighs meeting hers, heard her growling.

"This is all I can think about, being inside you. All day. What have you done to me?" Taryn said, covering Rosalind's back.

She closed her eyes, thinking everything, nothing, unable to form the words. Rosalind felt Taryn move into her, slowly, then agonizingly back out.

"No, stay inside. Please?" Rosalind asked. She felt Taryn immediately respond, felt the weight of her body, her teeth close on her shoulder. Rosalind threw her head back at the sensation, nearly cracking her skull against Taryn's. One of Taryn's hands reached out and captured Rosalind's, drew it down to her clit.

"Touch yourself. Show me what you like," Taryn said in her ear, lifting her hips off the desk.

"Anything," she said, and it was true. Everything was unbearable and marvelous. It was the feel of Taryn's hand on top of hers as she guided them that finally sent Rosalind over the edge. She moved her hand frantically, rubbing hard, arching off the desk into the protective curve of Taryn's body. Rosalind came, her muscles tensing all at once, her arms sweeping out across the face of the desk, grabbing for purchase. The motion threw the rest of the papers to the floor in a crash. Her mind spun; her girl-boy, her drag king, was covering her, holding her down.

She felt Taryn move, slowly, out of her. It hurt. She'd closed around the cock, but Taryn took her time until she relaxed. Rosalind felt a sense of grief at Taryn's standing back up, uncovering her. She turned over on the desk, eyes wide and questioning. Was Taryn about to turn back into a stranger on her? She didn't know if she could bear that. Taryn's eyes were warm, her smile gentle. She took Rosalind's hands and helped her up. "That can't be comfortable."

Taryn sat down in Rosalind's chair and drew the professor into her lap. Rosalind went willingly, feeling very much like purring and turning in circles. Taryn stroked her hair, her neck, wearing an expression Rosalind had never seen before. It was part wonder, part humor, and something she couldn't place. "What's on your mind?" Rosalind asked, feeling brave.

Taryn tilted her head back against the chair and looked at Rosalind from that angle. "'The gate between her thighs was golden, the road beyond meant only for kings.' Tanith Lee, from a book of hers I read when I was fourteen. That line stayed with me. I just never knew what it meant until now."

There are words that, when spoken, ignite the air around them, falling like ash on the listener's bare skin, leaving a tattoo. That was how Rosalind heard those words.

"Careful. I'll get used to you saying things like that to me," Rosalind said with a nervous laugh. Her heart trip-hammered in her chest. She wanted to melt around Taryn, take all of her inside.

"Would that be so bad?" Taryn asked, and Rosalind glanced at her face. Taryn seemed to mean it. There was no mocking edge to her voice, and the look on her face was open, unguarded.

"No. It wouldn't be bad at all. The road beyond is meant only for kings." Rosalind took Taryn's hand and curled it between her thighs.

Taryn gasped and closed her eyes. When they opened again, she looked into Rosalind's face in awe. "You mean so many things when you talk."

"It's my training. Six years of Renaissance lit, it's lucky I can say anything without meaning. You'll get used to it," Rosalind said, curling up on Taryn's lap. She sat there, feeling wonderful, basking in the arms around her. Something was beginning. She didn't need to fear it anymore.

"Can I stay with you tonight?" Taryn asked, her lips in Rosalind's hair.

"I'd like it if you did." Rosalind managed to hide her smile of triumph at her own restraint. She'd been planning on tying Taryn up and hauling her home. *Funny, I never supported hunting before.*

"Yeah?"

"Yeah. But a few ground rules first," Rosalind said, and felt Taryn stiffen beneath her. "One, we go get something to eat first. Two, no rising before 6:00 a.m. Three, I sleep on the left. You can try to change that, but I'll just end up on top of you." Rosalind felt Taryn's whole body shake with laughter. "Whoa! Careful, you're bouncing me around here."

"Thought you liked me bouncing you around," Taryn said with a leer.

"Oh, I do. But I have to keep you from getting too cocky. You're impossible as it is," Rosalind said, meaning every word.

❖

They ate at Kostas, one of the Greek diners that lurked on every street corner in Buffalo. It was close to Rosalind's apartment over on

Crescent. Taryn ordered coffee and a souvlaki breakfast, to Rosalind's surprised look.

"Breakfast, at this hour?"

Taryn shrugged. "I always feel like breakfast after sex."

"Okay, I'll note that down. Takes coffee black, likes breakfast after sex. Anything else I should know?" Rosalind asked, lightly. This was an experience she'd never had, trying to get to know the person she'd been having sex with. There was something about the way Taryn was slouching comfortably in the chair across the table from her that seemed perfectly natural, like they'd been lovers for years.

Taryn was giving the impression that she was feeling something as well, but refused to be explicit about it. Rosalind thought she could live with that, as long as they had the time to go slowly. She felt a sense of urgency whenever she looked at Taryn. Physical urgency to be sure, but also a sense that if she wasn't careful, Taryn would vanish in front of her eyes. The thought sent a wave of pain through her, so she set it aside. It was too soon to be feeling bereft about a handsome girl she barely knew.

"Yeah, a lot, but you can learn it a bit at a time. I don't know anything about you," Taryn said.

Rosalind smiled and spread orange marmalade on her English muffin.

Taryn made faces at her. "How can you eat that?"

"I like sweet things. What else do you want to know?"

"Family. Got any?"

"Mom and dad, one brother Eric, younger. He's a computer geek, works in Rochester. Lives with this gorgeous Bengali lawyer, Sandhya. They've been together since undergrad. Drove our parents up a wall for a while, but they've started to come around."

Taryn appeared to consider that, while she drained her cup of coffee. Rosalind thought she was about to ask something else, but she shook her head and asked a neutral question about pets.

"Growing up, a dog. A Lab. You look in the dictionary under dog, you see a picture of Roscoe. You?"

"You asking me to be your pet?" Taryn asked in mock surprise.

"No, genius. If you had any pets growing up."

A flicker of anger passed across Taryn's face, quickly masked. "None. Tell me a story about Rosalind as a kid."

Rosalind accepted the change of topic. She could feel the anger still simmering under Taryn's skin, but knew it wasn't directed at her. If telling stories would distract her, get her to smile again, she could tell stories all night.

"All right. We lived outside of Poughkeepsie growing up, Dutchess County. Real rural area. We had this big mulberry tree in the front yard, overhanging the road. Huge, sweeping branches. I used to climb it all the time. I was a bit of a tomboy. I got it into my head that the branches hanging over the road were just too good for coincidence. I convinced my little brother to climb up there with me, and when a car drove under, we'd shake the branches. Big, fat purple mulberries would splat down on the car. It was great fun, until our neighbor Mr. Manning drove his brand-new white Cutlass under the tree. He stopped the car, dragged us down, and marched us right up on the porch. He rang the bell until my mother came out and told her what we'd done."

"And you got the life beat out of you?"

The question surprised Rosalind, but she didn't let that show. "No, but we did get reprimanded. Poor Eric, he was just following my lead."

"You were a rebel, Olchawski," Taryn said with feigned admiration.

"I got away with it because I looked like such a nice girl." Rosalind flipped her hair back over her shoulder and batted her eyes at Taryn. The girl snorted.

❖

Taryn walked into Rosalind's apartment with an easy sense of ownership, claiming the space by moving through it. After spending the weekend fantasizing about having her here, Rosalind couldn't believe it was happening. But there she was, sitting on her couch, her arm thrown over the back. Rosalind kept looking sideways at her, to see if she'd vanish.

"Nice place. Clean," Taryn said, picking up a glass globe with leaves suspended in it. She looked quizzically at it.

"Would you like something to drink? Anything I can get you?" Rosalind asked, feeling like a new hostess. The absurdity of playing Martha Stewart to a girl who had just been fucking her on her desk at school wasn't lost on her.

Taryn grinned, seeming to read her mind. "Relax. Come sit over here and put your arms around me."

Rosalind did and heard Taryn sigh.

"Better?" Taryn asked, and Rosalind nodded.

"Much better."

"This feels good. I didn't know," Taryn said, to the room or to herself.

Rosalind settled in against her shoulder, unable to believe that she was sitting on her couch with Taryn. She seemed perfectly relaxed and not at all distant. The newness of it made Rosalind want to hold her breath, to preserve the moment, but her mind would not let her rest.

"Did you know that I stopped by your house Sunday?" Rosalind asked, biting her lip.

"Nah. When?" Taryn started lazily stroking her back, nearly derailing Rosalind's train of thought. She made a valiant effort to focus and seek out the information that would destroy her or loosen the knots in her stomach.

"Early. I wanted to drop your clothing off. Didn't Rhea mention it?" Rosalind asked, hoping that Taryn wouldn't notice how her voice slanted upward on Rhea's name.

"No. I was in bed all morning with a hangover. She let me sleep," Taryn said. Her hand had included Rosalind's arm in the stroking and was moving closer to her breast.

There was a moment when she could have changed her mind and not asked the question, but Rosalind let that moment pass. She had to know.

"That all you were in bed with?" she asked, trying to make a joke of it.

Taryn turned her head and looked down at her, puzzled. "Of course not."

Rosalind's stomach knotted. She pushed away from Taryn's shoulder and sat up. She couldn't ask the next question. It would brand her as possessive, a mortal sin in Taryn's world. She recalled how Taryn had spoken of Colleen with distaste when she had gotten proprietary. If Rosalind let Taryn know how possessive she already felt, it would be the death knell for whatever they had between them.

Taryn noticed the immediate change in Rosalind and sat up as well. "Didn't Rhea tell you?"

"She intimated that someone was upstairs with you, yes," Rosalind said, through clenching jaw muscles. The immediate, red streak of jealousy that blinded her was a complete surprise. She'd never been a jealous person in her life.

"Egyptia was too drunk to go home, so she crashed with me."

Rosalind managed not to repeat the drag queen's name in amazement. Rhea had left that part out. Somehow Rosalind couldn't see the omission as a simple mistake.

"I didn't want to wake you, so I left the clothes with Rhea," Rosalind said, feeling absurd. She settled back against Taryn's shoulder, hoping that the stroking would begin where it left off. Taryn seemed to be thinking about something. Her hands were still.

"Rosalind? Can I ask you something?"

"Sure, honey." The endearment slipped out before she could stop it, but Rosalind was glad. Every moment she was around Taryn was becoming a struggle not to say what she was feeling. She didn't want to scare Taryn away, but it felt like the missing part of her heart had come home.

"Would you go out with me? Like, on a date?"

Rosalind turned and looked right at her. Taryn's tone was unsure, and she had never sounded like that. For the first time, it occurred to Rosalind that this might be new for Taryn, too. She was serious, and gentle, when she answered. "Of course I would." Rosalind managed not to tack sweetheart to the end of her sentence.

Taryn beamed. "A real date. Dress to the nines, go out to dinner, all that," she said, almost as if she were informing Rosalind of an obscure cultural practice that might be unpleasant or dangerous.

There was no need to hesitate. Rosalind offered her best smile. "Just say when, and I'm yours."

"Tomorrow night. Eight o'clock. Come by and pick me up."

Rosalind leaned in and kissed her, letting that be her answer.

When her bed's structural strength had been tested, when her pale peach sheets needed replacing, Rosalind slipped into her nightshirt and dropped back onto the bed. Taryn was leaning up against the headboards with the smug grin of a boy who has nothing left to prove. She'd stripped down to her boxers and sat with her arms behind her head. Rosalind couldn't shake the feeling that Taryn was still performing, still showing off. Not that she was complaining, exactly. Rosalind drew a lazy hand along her thigh, tracing the winged lion.

"Tell me about doing drag," Rosalind asked, feeling bold.

Taryn's grin lost some of its self-satisfied edge, softened by unexpected pleasure in the question. "What it's like or why I do it?"

"Both. Whatever you want to tell me. I know about women passing as men during the Civil War. I've read about girls disguising themselves as boys to be sailors. I know Hatshepsut declared herself a man by the will of the gods to rule as Pharaoh. I don't know much about modern drag. Just talk. I like the sound of your voice when you talk about what you love."

"There are some who do it for money, deadly serious passing. Some do it for sex. It's righteous. I do it to hear the women howling for me."

"Dog." Rosalind's hand stopped its stroking. Taryn reached down and nudged it into starting again.

"Never claimed different. But it's more than that. For me it's natural. You know Egyptia? She's in drag when she ain't in a dress, you know? Male clothing isn't right on her. It fights against who she is. It's hard to watch."

"I'm not sure what you mean."

"Picture me in a dress."

Rosalind tried. Her mind balked, finally producing an image that looked like a Milton Berle skit—Taryn in combat boots and a pink chiffon prom dress, the straps hanging off her broad shoulders. "Yikes."

"You see what I mean? That's not how nature intended it. All clothing is costume. But we don't live like it is. When I put on a suit it's illusion, sure. But the illusion can be more real than the real thing."

Rosalind saw Egyptia sighing in the chair, surrendering to the beautiful boy who sang to her. "That I willingly believe."

"Illusion and revelation are powerful magic. Rhea taught me that the trickster gods all do drag. They move between the male and female worlds and have secret knowledge."

"Drag as a sacred act. I like that. But I think you were being a little too honest when you told me you do it to hear the women howl for you."

"Hey, the gods have to have a sense of humor. They made me. I feel right in a suit. I feel sexy. I'm just glad that some women agree."

There was a note of vulnerability in her tone that made Rosalind's heart ache. It gave the hint of a well of pain underneath the words that Taryn silenced. Rosalind pulled Taryn's head down and kissed her, softly.

The night had been sweet beyond imagining. Taryn had wrapped Rosalind up in a tangle of long arms and legs and fallen directly asleep. She was like a puppy. Her whole body was engaged in capturing her bedmate. Rosalind, frustrated by the amount of heat Taryn gave off, finally shucked her nightshirt and slept naked. She considered that having someone so warm-blooded might be an evolutionary benefit in Buffalo winters and so let it go. Taryn slept like the dead, leaving a quietly stunned Rosalind bouncing from an aching tenderness to a barely withheld lust.

It was the first time Taryn had been so close to naked with her. It was close, but still far enough that Rosalind could barely see the shore. Rosalind couldn't stop looking at her—the naked length of her legs, the tattoo of a winged lion on her right thigh, the muscle bunching as she shifted in her sleep. Lean hips were seductively draped in the boxers, a veil drawn across the mystery. All the time they had been together, Taryn had gently but firmly moved her hands away whenever Rosalind reached to undress her. That had worked, but Rosalind was determined not to be put off forever.

She loved Taryn's body—the feel of her muscled arms, the width of her shoulders, the span of her hands. She wanted to be able to touch her, bring her the kind of pleasure she so willingly gave. She knew that she'd have to be patient. She'd been around Taryn enough to recognize a stubborn streak a mile wide. She would have to be talked out of her boxers an inch at a time. *Wonder if it's all butch girls, a cultural thing, or just some of them?*

There was something there she didn't understand yet, something she knew she'd come up against. It might be something bruised inside, it might be something else, but she wanted to know. She wanted to make Taryn her lover, in all that implied. Taryn slept on, innocent of the plotting done over her sleeping body. "My sweet bad boy," Rosalind whispered, and kissed her brow.

Taryn woke in the morning to find Rosalind walking in with a soup-bowl-sized coffee mug. She handed it to Taryn with a smile of triumph on her face.

"I went out and bought a French press and some new mugs. Just in case," Rosalind said, unable to reduce the size of her grin. *Lord, I must look like a lunatic.* She debated telling Taryn about the new bathrobe that hung on the back of the door, the toothbrush and set of towels, all purchased just in case.

Taryn sipped at the coffee like a leopard testing a water hole. "This is good. From Spot?" she asked, giving her approval.

Rosalind smiled brilliantly. "Mhm. Thought it was your favorite."

"You pay attention." There was no mistaking the note of approval in Taryn's voice.

Taryn slid over on the bed and slapped her hand down, requesting Rosalind to join her.

She did, crawling up next to Taryn, her hand dropping on Taryn's thigh. She traced the winged lion idly. "I thought you invited me up to see all your tattoos. Now I find one I haven't seen."

"I didn't say when. There's still one I have saved for a special occasion."

"Like when?" Rosalind asked, knowing she was teasing but unable to stop.

"Soon, I think," Taryn said, her eyes chips of sapphire over the white rim of the mug.

❖

Rosalind pulled up at the Metro stop. Taryn had refused a ride home and requested a lift to the subway. She seemed easy, not twitching with restlessness, but Rosalind was afraid that was coming. She glanced repeatedly at Taryn, at her proud profile in the early morning light, at the relaxed way she slumped her long body in the seat. Taryn looked like the picture of ease, but Rosalind thought it might be deceptive ease. Like a panther before it breaks your neck, she thought, then wondered if that made her a gazelle or a wildebeest. She shook her head to clear it, then felt Taryn's hand massaging her neck.

"You're shaking. You okay?"

"I'm fine. Just wondering if I'm a gazelle, or...never mind." Rosalind took a deep breath, preparing herself for the girl's exit. *Lord, one quiet night with her, and you think she's tamed? Ros, get a grip!* her mind howled at her. Taryn wasn't someone who could be domesticated. She probably never has more than coffee with her new friends. An image of Taryn hopping from bed to bed, surviving on coffee and a raw charm, watching the sun rise from a different window every morning paraded through Rosalind's head.

"Hey. You in there? Your eyes keep glazing over," Taryn asked her, tightening her grip on Rosalind's neck.

"Yeah, yeah, I'm fine. I'm good. Peachy," Rosalind stammered, lost in the open regard. *I'm fine, just don't sit so close. You're percolating my hormones…*

"I'll still see you at eight tonight, right? You're not having second thoughts?" Taryn sounded earnest.

"I'll be there with bells on," Rosalind promised. *Bells, on a gazelle? I'm turning into Dr. Seuss.*

"There's a mental picture." Taryn opened the car door, looking at Rosalind with hooded eyes. Thoughts swam across her face and vanished, too fast for Rosalind to follow. *That's what it looks like when she realizes I'm too old, or boring, or—*

Taryn threw herself across the seat, pinning Rosalind back. It was like the strike of a panther, no warning, and Rosalind found herself being kissed with a ferocity, an urgency she never would have read from Taryn's face. Rosalind shifted to catch up with Taryn's mercurial mood, abandoning all nagging thoughts and diving into the kiss. It was unlike any kiss Taryn had given her or she had given in return.

The passion that lurked just below the surface was familiar, the madness threatening to overtake them, but the kiss was a plea, an emotional baring of the soul, an offering. Taryn was giving herself in that kiss, not seeking to rouse her body into a response. Taryn kissed her like her soul would fall out of her mouth if she moved away. Rosalind thought she could start to hear Taryn's thoughts with that kiss, hear the uncertainty lingering beneath them.

Taryn finally pulled back like leaving Rosalind's lips was an agony she had to endure. Her large hands held Rosalind's head captive, staring into her eyes from inches away, the look as naked as the kiss had been. "Thanks for letting me stay last night."

"You can stay anytime you want," Rosalind said, giving her the freedom, knowing that Taryn had to know how welcome she truly was. The sapphire eyes lit and glowed, gems over the heart of the sun.

"Meant only for kings?" Taryn asked, demanded, disbelief and hope fighting in her voice, making it rough.

"Meant only for kings," Rosalind repeated like a prayer, a call and response. It was true, and true things have a life of their own.

The blinding smile that came over Taryn's face was the most beautiful thing Rosalind had ever seen. It spoke of a raw, boundless joy that she had given someone she valued, with her words. That response, that overflowing of happiness, was for her. The pleasure that filled Rosalind from giving that gift made her drunk. Taryn's face transformed with it, bright as the sun, glorious. All from her words, from what she offered with them.

It was the first time in her life that Rosalind got a taste of her power as a woman, as a lover, to dispense joy. She wanted to give Taryn everything, to keep on seeing that smile. Taryn's hand stayed holding Rosalind's face. They both stayed, locked with each other. It was all Rosalind could do to keep from shouting her love. Not yet, a voice cautioned her. Let this moment be what it is. Savor it. Don't rush.

Rosalind knew her own urge was to grab everything with both hands, born of newly discovering her own heart. She found out how good it could be, and wanted it all NOW! She took this part of her aside and had a gentle chat with it, explaining how there had to be a rhythm, a measure to things, that rational adults didn't just go around proclaiming undying love for youthful drag kings, no matter how overwhelming that feeling was. The chat worked, Rosalind managed to bite back the words, but her eyes spoke every one.

"You better drive me home. I can't even get out of the car to leave you," Taryn said helplessly. Rosalind laughed. There was nothing else to do with the overflow of emotion, the joy blazing out of her heart. It was the laugh of a woman first tasting the depths of her own passion and finding it good. She put her head back on the seat and laughed until tears ran from her eyes. Life was a joke, not a sick joke, but a good-natured one, where the punch line makes you groan and cover your eyes, it was so apparent.

Why hadn't anyone told her how this felt? Her laugh filled the car, and it made Taryn's smile get even broader, taking over her whole face. Her muscles ached from it, and she couldn't stop grinning. She was delighting her. Not just bringing her pleasure in bed, she was delighting her. The responsibility of it skimmed by, barely brushing her, the heady sweep of power claiming her first.

"Do you feel as good as I do right now?" Taryn asked, recklessly.

Rosalind coughed and wiped tears from her eyes, her smile rivaling Taryn's. "I think I do. You sure you want me to drive you home?"

Taryn exhaled and rubbed her hands on her thighs. "No. But it will be sweeter tonight if we spend the day apart."

"You're certain of that," Rosalind said, fingertips tracing a dangerous pattern on Taryn's thigh.

Taryn groaned and closed her eyes. "No. But I'd like to try it. Work with me here, Olchawski. You're killing me."

"Can't have that. All that fabulous potential, wasted. I'll be good."

Rosalind placed her hands firmly on the steering wheel. She kept them there, in a death grip, until they were parked in front of 34 Mariner. She took a deep breath, keeping her word to be good, then abandoned it. She reached for Taryn, but she was already there, in reach, too tempting to ignore. Rosalind wrapped her arms around her. Taryn held a finger up to Rosalind's lips, separating them.

"If you kiss me, I won't get out of the car," she said as a warning. It didn't seem to work.

"That would be bad why?" Rosalind asked, kissing the offered finger. She drew it into her mouth, sucking gently on it, her expression one of absolute innocence.

"I don't remember," Taryn said, drawing her finger out of Rosalind's mouth. She traced Rosalind's lips, then pushed it back in, her eyes gone feral.

"Hey! Get a room!"

Taryn snapped around with a vicious speed, only to find Joe leaning against the car, grinning amiably. He had a garbage can in either hand and hefted them, giving reason for his being on the curb. "Morning, Taryn. Good to see you again, Rosalind. I wondered where that kid went last night," he said, pleasant, genial, and very annoying.

"Good morning, Joe," Rosalind said, forgetting to blush. It was hard to keep working up shame around this household. Nothing seemed to faze them. Joe looked like he had just shaved. Dots of blood showed on his neck.

"Care for breakfast? I know you probably do," he said to Taryn.

"Go away." She drew her hand across her throat.

Joe refused the signal and set the cans down. He inhaled deeply, folding his arms over his chest. "Won't have a lot more mornings like this. Just beautiful. Makes you glad to be alive, doesn't it?"

"It's a problem you won't have much longer unless you get your ass off the car and go back inside," Taryn growled.

Rosalind put a gentle hand on Taryn's arm, easing the tension. "It's okay. I was being bad. Why don't we behave, and I'll pick you up at eight?"

Taryn leaned in and kissed her, a bare brushing of her lips. Then she leaped out of the car, tearing off after Joe, who bolted up the steps with an impressive speed. *No wonder she keeps acting like a thug teenager with Joe as a role model*, Rosalind thought.

She sighed, gazing up the steps after them, then started the car. It wouldn't be too long until eight. She could be good for one day.

CHAPTER FIVE

When Rosalind pulled up in front of 34 Mariner at seven forty-five, after circling Allentown for twenty minutes, she found Joe sitting on the steps. He was dressed in jeans and a denim shirt, the sleeves rolled back over his powerful forearms. He was smoking a cigar, exhaling with pleasure into the fall night. He looked like the picture of contentment. He spotted her car and waved the hand holding the cigar. When she stepped out, he dropped it.

"Good God! Who are you, and what have you done with Rosalind?" he cried out, jumping to his feet. Rosalind stood, shyly, pulling at the hem of her dress. He trotted down the stairs, looking her over in awe.

"You think it's all right?" Rosalind asked, feeling like she could trust his response. Joe had befriended her the moment they'd met. It was a welcome that he kept extending. Rosalind knew that must be his nature, but felt that he actually liked her as well. It was instantly calming to see him sitting on the steps of the house. The thought of facing down Rhea had kept her stomach in a knot all day.

"You are the reason the little black dress was invented. You look stunning." He took her hand, kissing it. The praise helped enormously. Rosalind had spent all day getting ready. The dress was an inspiration of Ellie's, something she never would have considered wearing for a minute. It was more the idea of a dress—a sheath of glossy black, strapless, revealing her shoulders and neck, a deep plunge down her back.

She felt like a different person putting it on—daring, a little dangerous, and sexy. She had imagined Taryn's response, wanting her to all but faint when she saw her. The thought of looking gorgeous for Taryn made her weak in the knees. Her appearance had never mattered to her before. Overnight, it mattered more than she could say, because it was a gift she could give.

Her hair was down, flowing over her shoulders in a soft wave, curled just enough to give it life, each strand of red, white, and saffron picking out a different refraction of the streetlight. Joe stood looking at her, eyes wandering over her body so ably presented in the dress. Rosalind could tell that it wasn't idle flattery on his part, and it made her glad.

"You think she'll like it?" she asked, turning around.

"She has a pulse. She'll like it. You would induce cardiac arrest in a priest, let me tell you. Seriously, you look wonderful. You sure you want to date a punk kid? Woman like you could have anyone she wants," Joe said, flirting outrageously.

Rosalind laughed. It made her feel welcomed into the household. She guessed that it was harmless, that Joe was spoken for by Rhea, and his affection for Taryn was evident, so she relaxed into it, enjoying the banter. "I know who I want," she said, running a finger down his cheek, over his rough beard. "And she's upstairs, isn't she?"

Joe sighed heavily, and his shoulders drooped. "That damn gender thing again. All the good women want all the good women. Lord, grant me the strength…"

He stepped back, letting the flirting fade. "Yeah, she's upstairs. She set me out here to keep you busy until she's ready. Between you and me, I've never seen this kid so worked up over a date. She's been getting ready all day. You know how boys are. 'What tie should I wear? I need a haircut! Joe, did you get my suit pressed?' Whatever you're doing to her, keep on doing it. She's got the biggest, goofiest grin I've ever seen in my life plastered on her face, all the time."

He held out his arm to Rosalind and helped her up the steps. His manners were courtly, with a touch of humor, and Rosalind recognized Taryn's odd moments of chivalry in them. She really did use Joe as her masculine role model, Rosalind thought. From what she had seen, Taryn could do far worse. Joe made her feel at ease the minute she showed up. He managed to be funny and charming without being overbearing.

"Just between you and me, I've had a pretty goofy grin on my face all day, too," Rosalind confided, as Joe carefully led her past the staircase, into the living room.

The room had no doors, opening on the front hallway through an arch and on another open room that looked in on the kitchen. The walls were plaster, in the eternal state of reconstruction. An Indian print cloth of brilliant yellow hung over the couch, tacked halfway onto the ceiling.

Tall drums stood in the corner, with a rain stick. There was no furniture other than the couch, against the wall facing the fireplace. Joe sat her down on the couch and leaned against the mantle. The fireplace had been swept clean and had dried flowers in place of logs, burnt orange and deep red, simulating flames. The mantle was covered with pictures in old-fashioned frames—heavy silver, tarnished with age, carved and lacquered wood. Joe glanced at the pictures, a smile breaking over his face.

"Hey! This is great! Taryn told me to keep you busy. I can do all the papa stuff she accuses me of doing anyway. C'mon, I'll show you pictures she wouldn't want you to see and tell you embarrassing stories. It'll be great practice for when Goblin's old enough to date."

He grabbed a handful of the frames and sat down on the couch next to Rosalind. He shuffled through them, handing her a few to hold. Rosalind examined the one on top, the picture of Rhea with much longer hair, her arm around Taryn's shoulders. The girl glared at the camera like it was a mortal enemy. She looked very young; her hair was shaved down to a blue hint on her skull, her face was thin over sharp bones. Taryn's eyes looked wild, savage, out of her face, eyes no person that age should have. She wore a military coat and a dog chain knotted around her neck. Her body was lost in the clothing, indistinguishable as male or female.

"When was this?" Rosalind asked, caught by the wary eyes.

"When Taryn first moved in. Four years ago? No, more like three and a half. Taryn had just turned seventeen. Taryn's Angry Young Man phase. She was a handful, from what Rhea tells me."

He handed her another picture, this one a world of difference. Taryn sat on top of a picnic table in profile, her face turned toward a lake. Wind ruffled her hair, capturing it forever in a moment of disorder. She'd put on some weight; the starved, angry look had subsided. Her skin was pale against the black of her hair and the dark denim of her jacket, but the deep bruises under her eyes had faded. She looked like she was watching something out over the water and didn't know she was being photographed. "That's…a year later. Winter. Rhea took the shot. It was her family's cabin up at Waverly Beach. Taryn must have been eighteen or so."

It was a rare treat to see Taryn looking so peaceful, so absorbed, unaware of being watched. She had a performing nature and loved an audience. Rosalind hadn't seen her that relaxed and unguarded while she was awake. It said something to Rosalind about Taryn's relationship with Rhea that she'd let her guard down enough with Rhea there for the shot to be taken. It sent a wave of jealousy through her, along with envy. She wondered if Taryn would ever be that unguarded around her. She wondered if they had been lovers then.

"Here. This was last spring. I talked the both of them into going horseback riding. Taryn was a natural. It was like she was born for the saddle. But I don't think I'll ever talk Rhea onto a horse again."

Rhea was in the foreground, clinging to the saddle of an enormous blood bay. Her face was drawn down in a series of sharp lines, looking sternly at the camera. Next to her, Taryn grinned devilishly, one leg curled around the pommel of the saddle of her buckskin.

Rosalind took it, liking the look on Taryn's face, the teasing, recognizing it. "How old is she here?"

"Twenty. Just turned, in fact. Her birthday was March seventh, and we went riding on the tenth." Joe took the picture back, smiling down at it.

"Goblin and I moved in right around then. I think I have that shot..." He handed Rosalind a picture of himself carrying a table up the front steps. A girl of around twelve, thin legs poking out of cutoff denim shorts, followed him, hefting a chair. Rosalind could see that she had long brown hair pulled back in a ponytail. "That's Goblin. My daughter. You haven't met her, have you? You may get a chance, if Taryn keeps dawdling. She went to the store with Rhea and Laurel. They're having some friends over tonight."

"I didn't know you had a daughter," Rosalind said, looking closely. "She's lovely. She looks like you."

"Don't tell her that. She wants to look like Kate Winslet. Can I tell you how many times I've seen *Titanic*, now that I have a fourteen-year-old in the house? Leo this, Leo that. I'm glad the jerk drowned. Couldn't act his way out of a paper bag. I didn't just spoil the ending for you, did I?" he asked, looking concerned.

"I wasn't about to see it," Rosalind said, with a laugh.

He handed her another picture absently, rooting through the pile. "There has to be something incriminating here. Did you know that when she thinks nobody else is home, she goes around the house singing?

Swear to God. I once caught her singing…oh, I shouldn't tell you that, she'd kill me."

"Now you have to tell me, or I'll die of curiosity. Please, Joe? I promise I won't use it against her." Rosalind crossed her heart, putting on her best Girl Scout face.

Joe glanced at the stairs, then back at Rosalind. "All right. Remember, my blood is on your hands. I caught her singing 'Achy Breaky Heart.'"

"You did not."

"I did. Billy Ray Cyrus. Our walking attitude problem, dancing around the kitchen in her boxer shorts, singing the Achy Breaky. I just about died on the spot."

Rosalind's mind had a habit of taking whatever it heard and producing a graphic representation, not unlike a short film. The minute Joe finished saying it, her mind raced off with glee, producing a complete fantasy of Taryn in her boxer shorts, singing and dancing around the kitchen. She tried valiantly not to give in to the laughter, to remind herself that this was Taryn, whom she loved, whose dignity and power were unquestioned. It didn't work. She burst out laughing, hysterically.

Joe joined her, and they all but dropped the pictures they were holding. "Shh! She'll kill me, I swear," Joe said, drawing a heaving breath into his lungs.

Rosalind tried to focus on something, anything, to get that image out of her mind. She looked down at the picture Joe had handed her, an old one of a young girl holding on to the hand of a woman. It looked like Goblin at age seven or eight. The woman resembled her. She had the same brown eyes and long brown hair. "Who is this?" she asked, pointing at the photograph.

Joe glanced at it. "I didn't know that was still up. That's Goblin," he said, looking back though the pictures.

"Who's the woman?" Rosalind asked, wondering if she were an aunt of Goblin's. They looked related.

Joe stopped shuffling the pictures and looked at her. She glanced up at him. "That's me. Before I transitioned."

Rosalind absorbed the information, letting her eyes find the clues in Joe's face. He sat patiently, allowing her to do this, allowing himself to be regarded in light of the new information. She had to look hard to see the face of the woman in the picture, in the face of the man sitting next to her. The jaw was broader, the nose larger; the full beard hid the mouth and chin. Only the eyes were the same, looking out quizzically at the world, seeing the joke that few else bothered to listen to. Rosalind put her hand on Joe's powerful forearm, feeling the hair under her fingers. "Goblin has your eyes, you know," she said, and Joe broke into a grin.

There was a clatter of footsteps coming down the stairs. Joe jumped, grabbing the pictures and tossing them back on the mantle. He stood, leaning against it, and started whistling, as if he'd just been leaning there innocently all night. Rosalind stood up and faced the hallway.

Taryn was wearing her black suit, with a silk tie done in a deep shade of green. She'd gotten her hair cut close to the neck in the back, just over her ears on the sides, with a hint of length on the top, gelled back. It showed off the strength of her face, the muscles in the column of her neck. She looked wonderfully handsome. It made Rosalind start to ache in the nicest way.

But it was the look on Taryn's face that was most wonderful. Taryn strolled into the living room and stopped dead. Her eyes flew wide, drinking in all of Rosalind. She'd forgotten about the dress in talking with Joe, but Taryn's reaction brought it back. She saw herself mirrored in the drag king's eyes, and she liked what she saw. Taryn looked on her like she was the most beautiful woman to ever walk the earth. The stunned quiet was a tribute, and Rosalind basked in it.

The girl took a step into the room and took Rosalind's hand. "You are so damned beautiful. You could make God weep with envy." Her voice was hushed.

Rosalind laughed and gave her a kiss on the cheek. "You look remarkably handsome tonight," she said, enjoying it when Taryn ducked her head. Was that a blush she saw, creeping up the back of Taryn's neck? Couldn't be.

"You make me wish I had my camera. It's like sending my boy off to the prom," Joe said, breaking the moment.

Taryn didn't even glance at him. She stood holding Rosalind's hand, her eyes burning over Rosalind's face, her body.

Rosalind felt the heat from that gaze and nearly lost her resolve, nearly said it right then and there, consequences be damned. She was in love with this girl, who was now looking at her like the sun shone from her face, and she couldn't keep it a secret much longer.

"You like Japanese food? I made reservations for us at Kuni's."

"Love it, but I've only had the basics. You can guide me."

"Dangerous thing to offer to that kid. You know she only speaks enough Japanese to get her slapped? I know. I taught her myself."

"You speak Japanese?" Rosalind asked him, to divert Taryn's attention. She could feel Taryn tense up, but when Rosalind squeezed her hand she relaxed.

"I was in the service, stationed in Okinawa for a while. That was a lifetime ago. You kids run along. Rhea will be back in a minute. I have to get the place ready for the Better You than Me." Joe strolled into the kitchen, casting a broad wink over his shoulder to Rosalind. He started humming something that might have been "Achy Breaky Heart."

Taryn took her arm, escorting her down the steps. She walked around to her side of the car, holding the door for her. There was something so earnest about these manners, like they'd been practiced a thousand times in private, but never put to the test in public, that it charmed Rosalind. She pictured Taryn sitting down in the kitchen with Joe, asking for pointers on how to behave on the date, and it warmed her head to toe. *Funny, I've never been a sucker for chivalry, but there's just something about a gallant woman. And she is so damned handsome.* Rosalind watched Taryn get in the car, then asked, smiling, "Where to?"

"Elmwood. Up by the old Village Green. Kuni used to be the sushi chef at Saki's downtown, but he opened his own place. You're in for a treat."

"Say something in Japanese," Rosalind said, with a glance at Taryn's profile.

"Do you speak any?" Taryn asked cautiously.

Rosalind shook her head. "Not a word."

"*Watashi wa anata o aishite imasu,*" Taryn said, her voice dropping down. There was a harshness to her delivery; the words sounded like they were working against the tone.

"You sound like a Kurosawa film. What did you say to me?"

"Maybe I'll tell you later," Taryn said, looking quickly out the window.

Kuni's was a tiny storefront restaurant, with a few tables outside, six inside, and a sushi bar. It was close and packed. A line had formed outside; people were waiting to get to the bar, to jostle for a place. Taryn used her height to part the crowd, making a space for Rosalind to follow. Rosalind felt a twinge of guilt sliding past the waiting people, but once inside, she forgot to feel bad. Kuni's was tiny, but it had great presence. The wall behind the sushi bar was decorated with teacups and sake cups; mechanical fish swam in a fish tank right behind the chef's head.

A dark-haired girl with a disarming smile greeted them as soon as they got inside. She took Taryn's arm, squeezing it. "It's so good to see you! You never come around anymore. How's Rhea and Joe?"

"They're great. Maria, this is Rosalind. Rosalind, this is Maria." Taryn put her hand on the small of Rosalind's back and presented her.

Maria took Rosalind's hand. "Nice to meet you. You're in the back, I couldn't get you the window."

The table was in the back corner, by the step down into the kitchen. Taryn held out Rosalind's chair, then slid in with her back to the wall. "No, she was never my girlfriend. Yes, she knows me. Through Rhea and Joe. No, I don't come here all the time with a new girl."

Rosalind smiled sheepishly. "That obvious?"

"I can read your mind, you know. And your face. You're very open," Taryn growled.

Despite the harsh tone, Rosalind heard the note of respect and what might have been envy. Rosalind sat forward and linked her hands. "What am I thinking now?" she purred.

"I can't do that to you in public," Taryn said with a grin.

"Not that thought. Read the other one."

"You can't mean that," Taryn said, her eyes widening.

Maria came and brought them hot towels and cups of steaming green tea. "Do you trust me?" she said to Rosalind, with an evil smile.

"I do. Go ahead and order."

"We'll have the house miso to start, shrimp tempura, and sushi. Yellowtail, tuna, eel, octopus, salmon. And a bottle of sake."

Rosalind found the sight of Taryn wielding chopsticks fascinating. It added a layer of civilization to Taryn she never would have expected. The sure delicacy of her movements, the ease with which she maneuvered the slender pieces of wood spoke of skills yet unguessed to Rosalind. She watched Taryn pluck a piece from the wooden board and dip it in the soy and wasabi.

"Careful. The green stuff is Japanese horseradish. Hot enough to make a statue bleed. Just a hint is plenty. More will blow the back of your head off." She stared at Rosalind, holding out the chopsticks.

Rosalind leaned forward and opened her mouth. Taryn placed the sushi on her tongue. "That's good. Which is that?"

"Yellowtail. You might like the eel, but I'd be careful of the octopus. Something tells me you aren't an octopus fan."

Taryn took the tiny cup and poured clear liquid into it. "Sake. We should drink it while it's hot. Don't sip at it, just toss it back."

Rosalind picked up the cup. "Can we toast first?"

"Sure. Whatever you like," Taryn said, raising her cup.

"To beginnings," Rosalind said. Taryn tapped her cup against Rosalind's and snapped her head back. Rosalind tried to do the same, but it was like drinking jet fuel. It burned her throat. She started coughing and choking. Taryn jumped up, concerned. Rosalind reached for her tea, waving at Taryn to sit. "M'okay. Just not used it yet. You sure this is pleasurable?"

"Have a few more glasses, then ask me again," Taryn said with a leer.

"Oh, stop. I have a present for you," Rosalind said, reaching for her purse. It had been a very long day, refusing to get to eight o'clock. She had kept looking at the digital clock in her bedroom, expecting it to be time to go on the date, but it never was. She finally gave up and indulged her second favorite passion, going to the bookstore.

"For me?" Taryn said, genuinely puzzled. Women never bought her presents.

"Of course," Rosalind said, handing the present to Taryn with a triumphant smile. "Go on. Open it."

Taryn eyed it oddly, as if she expected it to jump up and bite her. She started tearing the paper away a half inch at a time, driving Rosalind mad. This girl had no concept of Christmas etiquette as she was raised to it, where the recipient of the gift was supposed to rip the paper off in a nanosecond. Taryn acted like she was completely unused to getting presents. Rosalind restrained herself and let Taryn take her time. When the paper came away, and Taryn looked at the cover of the book in her hands, Rosalind held her breath. Taryn sat staring at it, her face unreadable.

"I thought you'd probably have a copy already, but I found the last signed one they had at Talking Leaves and just couldn't resist," Rosalind said, hoping that Taryn's silence forebode good things.

She was as still as a statue, cradling the book in her open palms. She finally looked up, and Rosalind could swear that there were tears in her eyes. "*Stone Butch Blues*. This is like the Bible to me. How did you know?"

Rosalind knew that she'd done something utterly, permanently right, and felt like singing. The look on Taryn's face was priceless. She was taken completely off guard, stunned, pleased, unable to gather herself to respond.

Taryn opened the cover and looked at the handwriting. "In the Spirit of Stonewall—Leslie Feinberg," Taryn read aloud, reverently.

"I'd heard that Buffalo was Leslie's hometown. I went to Talking Leaves and asked about books on drag kings. The guy behind the counter grabbed this down. I confess, I read it."

"You read it, because you were thinking about me?" Taryn's voice was incredulous.

"I saw so much of you in it. It helped a lot," Rosalind admitted. Taryn looked back down at the book, then up at Rosalind. "Do you already have a copy?" Rosalind asked, not sure of how to read Taryn's silence.

Taryn shook her head. "I read Rhea's. A signed copy…and you got it, you read it, because of me…I don't know what to say."

"Tell me you like it," Rosalind prompted.

Taryn looked down at the book and swallowed, before looking back up at Rosalind. "Leslie is a hero of mine. When I met Leslie, around the time this was published, s/he was doing a book talk and signing at a local church. I saw hir. I heard hir speak. I didn't have the cash to get a copy. When s/he got offstage, his wife, Minnie Bruce Pratt, the poet, walked over and just took Leslie's arm. It was…perfect. The look Minnie Bruce gave Leslie, like she loved hir, she understood all of it, the pain, the good stuff, too. S/he walked by me, I was just standing there. Leslie looked me up and down, held out hir hand, and said, 'Nice wingtips.' I just about died on the spot." Taryn looked up, her eyes glinting in the candlelight. "You giving this to me, reading it, it's like Minnie Bruce giving Leslie that look."

It took Rosalind's breath away, hearing it. She wished they weren't in a very crowded public place, with people watching on every side. She wanted to take Taryn in her arms, feel that quiet awe and joy she was projecting, let her know that she did understand.

Taryn turned the book over in her hands. "It's one of the older ones. It still says Leslie grew up a young butch in Buffalo. The later ones, and the next book, *Transgender Warriors*, says Leslie grew up as a drag king in Buffalo. Guess more people know what a drag king is nowadays."

Taryn sat with the book, just holding it gently in her open hands, looking at Rosalind in a way that made her want to cry, to dance. Something remarkable had happened; an understanding had passed between her and her drag king.

Rosalind felt like she had succeeded in letting Taryn know how much she wanted to know all of her. How welcome she was as who she was. She had found a way to get inside. She sat in the glory of that recognition, too scared that it might vanish if she spoke.

Maria came back with hot tea and poured into the silence between them. Taryn sighed, at last, and set the book aside. "Thank you."

"You're welcome," Rosalind said, picking up her teacup.

The meal had been remarkable, but Rosalind couldn't recall much of it afterward. She remembered how Taryn looked in the candlelight—the shadows on the planes of her face, the sharp edge of her cheekbone, the way the new haircut left her neck exposed. The way her eyes got soft and swimming the minute they fixed on her.

"You know, Joe told me tonight about him," Rosalind said, remembering.

"About being trans? He must like you. He usually waits to mention it."

"I think he likes me because I like you. I get that impression from him. He loved playing papa while you were upstairs. I see a lot of him in you."

Taryn leaned back in her chair, a smile easing across her face. "There was this film they showed at Hallwalls, several years ago. Part of the Ways in Being Gay Festival. It's called *Shinjuku Boys*. It's about the drag kings who work at the New Marilyn Club in the Shinjuku district of Tokyo. This club is staffed by male impersonators who are hired to charm the customers, flirt with them, sing karaoke to them, get them to buy drinks. And all the customers are women."

"Gay women?"

"Nah, that's the thing. Straight women flock to this place. They eat the drag kings up. Call them, page them, send them gifts, try to get them into bed. There was this whole romantic culture built up about being with one of the kings, drove these women nuts." Taryn paused, sipping at her tea.

"Oh, I can relate. In a distant way," Rosalind said, fanning herself with her hand.

Taryn grinned. "They profiled these three drag kings. Tatsu was a transman. He was on hormones, his voice was lowered. I don't think he'd had surgery, but he was living as a man. He had this gorgeous nineteen-year-old girlfriend, Tomoe. She wanted to marry him. They seemed very devoted to each other, very happy. Joe's like Tatsu. He always knew he was a man, he just had to make the outside match the inside."

"I can see that. What about the other two?"

"Well, this one, Gaish, looked pretty femme, but dressed like a king. She lived with her partner, another performer at the club, a transwoman. They seemed pretty solid. But the third...she was a real dog. She had all these women calling her, paging her. She was cruel to them, but they were all over her."

"Wonder where I've heard that before?" Rosalind said, thoughtfully tapping her temple.

"Stop it. I'm not that bad. But I am like her. I know I'm a woman. But I'm a masculine woman." Taryn paused to see if Rosalind was following. She took Rosalind's hand from the tabletop, kissing it.

"What's that for?" Rosalind asked, pleased.

"For listening. For caring."

"Finish your story," Rosalind said tenderly, to keep from saying I love you.

"Joe said to me, after we saw that movie, that he thought it might be even harder for me sometimes than for him. Once he transitioned, the whole world saw him the way he saw himself. Few people are ever going to see me like I see me. I don't make sense, like he does. I don't fit what's expected out of a woman," Taryn said, spinning her teacup on the tabletop.

"I see you the way you see yourself," Rosalind said, every word from her heart. "I see a handsome young woman whose courage will change the world. I see a hero. I love...who you are." She realized what she had almost said and buried her face in her teacup.

Taryn looked at her, shaking her head. "You have this remarkable effect on people, worming right under their skin. I knew you for an hour, and I felt like I never wanted to stop talking to you."

"Not all people," Rosalind said, remembering Rhea. The evening was going so well, her first date with Taryn, that she didn't want to bring Rhea up just yet.

"I can't imagine anyone who wouldn't be charmed by you. You're just so...good. Loving. And you're smarter than anybody, but not pretentious about it."

"Why, Taryn, do you have a crush on me?" Rosalind asked in her best professor tone.

Taryn blinked at her, blue eyes innocent and wide. "Yes. But I'm all confused about it. You're so pretty, and everyone tells me it's just me admiring you, wanting to be like you, but all I want to do is take you home and fuck you till you scream."

"Taryn! You are bad," Rosalind said, delighted and scandalized. Her body responded to the suggestion with enthusiasm.

"I'm a dog. Come take a walk in the park with me. I promise I won't try and hold your hand."

"If you promise that, I'm not going anywhere with you," Rosalind warned, and Taryn hung her head.

"Okay. I'll be a gentleman. Not perfect, but a gentleman."

Delaware Park was a haven of green and black trees standing against a sky lit charcoal and orange from the city lights. Taryn led Rosalind down past the Rose Garden, where Shakespeare in the Park was performed during the summer. Taryn pointed to the hill, her arm disappearing against the gunmetal gray sky.

"People come and set out their blankets, bring a picnic and a bottle of wine, and watch the show. You'd be in Heaven. I always have trouble following the language, so I make Rhea translate, or I just drink the wine with Joe and ignore the whole thing. It'd be fun with you, though. You know all that stuff."

"I'd love to see a Shakespeare play with you. A comedy to start, I think, but I'd work you up to the tragedies. I'd have you reciting Hamlet by the end of the summer," Rosalind said, as they strolled down the path.

The hill was dark; the lights were fading between the trees. The park closed at ten, and she should have been afraid. But...she wasn't. It was being on Taryn's arm, the rightness of it, that made her feel immortal. Like nothing could touch her. It helped that Taryn looked male, especially in the darkness. Another couple walked by them, saw Rosalind on Taryn's arm, and nodded a greeting before vanishing into the trees. "They thought I was a nice young man escorting you. You can tell when people don't get it. They don't give you the double take."

"Does that bother you?" Rosalind asked, leaning against Taryn's shoulder.

"Nah. It's a benefit, at night. People don't fuck with you if you're a straight couple, not the way they would if they saw us as two women. It's when the sun is up, and they get a good look at me, that it gets more complicated."

Rosalind looked at Taryn's profile, etched against the darkness of the trees, her hair blending with the night. "You know, there's a Shakespeare play where a young woman named Rosalind dresses as a young man and has a few adventures in a forest. She takes the name Ganymede," Rosalind said, folding her hand over the arm of the handsome girl.

"So you should be the one in the suit?" Taryn asked, amused.

"I don't think I'd look nearly as good as you do. It's funny, Ellie told me I'd meet my Ganymede. And here you are."

Taryn tilted her head. "So you're Zeus? Funny, you don't look like him without the beard."

"You know the story?" Rosalind asked, pleased.

Taryn stopped walking. "One day Zeus, King of the Gods, was looking over the earth. He saw this beautiful boy in a field, the most beautiful boy in the whole world. Zeus went crazy with lust. He did that all the time apparently. This kid, Ganymede, was just hanging out, minding his own business, maybe playing a game, and this big eagle swoops down and grabs him, drags him off to Mount Olympus. He ended up fetching drinks for Zeus, being his boyfriend. I know most of the gay stories. They're the only ones I paid attention to. They don't talk about that one much in school."

They walked down the hill, down to the edge of the lake, where the path curved and became paved. Benches sat along the walkway; the water shone dully in the starlight beyond the lip of the stone wall. Taryn stopped and faced the lake. "Here, stand next to me. This is the most powerful spot in all of Buffalo."

Rosalind stood at Taryn's side, looking up at her profile. "Why?

Besides being next to you, I mean," she whispered, slipping her arm around Taryn's waist.

"Draw an imaginary wheel around us. The Albright-Knox Art Gallery is to our left, across the road. The Historical Society is in front of us, off that way. Forest Lawn Cemetery is to the right. Behind us, that building is the Casino. The city rents the space out. I think there's a wedding reception starting, from the sounds of the music, up on the second level." Taryn said this as if it explained everything.

Rosalind was enjoying leaning on Taryn's shoulder, enjoying the warmth. Her brain was pleasantly floating in the sensations of being in contact with Taryn. It didn't help her comprehension at all. "I'm not sure I get it."

Taryn gestured out into the night, the sweep of her arm taking in the lake, the building, the lights on the water, the wedding reception beginning above them. "Art on our left, death on our right, history before us, and love behind us. What could be more powerful than being in the center of that?"

Rosalind considered this. "Turning around. So history is behind us, and love is in front of us." She gently guided Taryn around, until they faced the Casino.

Music started up on the level above them, the bridal dance. Taryn stepped away from Rosalind, bowing from the waist, holding out her hand. "Dance with me?" It was a question, but the force of Taryn's charm was behind it, making it an invitation guaranteed to be accepted.

Rosalind had stepped forward and taken Taryn's hand without even thinking about it. Truthfully, she'd started moving the minute Taryn held out her hand, whatever invitation was being offered. She put her arm around the drag king's shoulder and felt her hand on her waist.

Taryn led, and they danced in the night, on the shore of the lake, moving in and out of the light that spilled from the wedding reception above. Rosalind could see, as she turned, an old woman sitting on the stone wall to get some air. She watched them until the song ended before turning back to the reception.

The song ended. Taryn spun Rosalind to a slow stop, reluctant to let her go. Rosalind was entertaining the nicest fantasy, with Taryn in her arms, dancing in a public place, people looking on and commenting on how well they looked together. She was still warmed by this thought when Taryn leaned down and breathed in her ear. "You dance great."

"Ballroom dance lessons. My mother insisted on them before my wedding." It slipped out before Rosalind could think about it. Funny, she hadn't thought about Paul much since meeting Taryn.

"You're married?" Taryn said, disbelief in her voice. She dropped Rosalind's hand and stepped back, her eyebrows climbing up into her hairline.

"Divorced. Almost ten months now," Rosalind said, mentally kicking herself.

"You never said anything about it," Taryn said, her voice cooling.

"Hey! Don't you dare do that to me," Rosalind said, grabbing Taryn's hand.

"What?" Taryn asked blandly.

"Disappear. You've been here, really here with me, all night. You don't get to vanish now." Rosalind could see the struggle on Taryn's face, knew enough to read the shock, the hurt, finally covered with a thick layer of attitude, like the formation of ice on the lake in winter.

Taryn took her hand back and walked away, crossing to one of the benches by the Casino. She sat down and looked out over the lake.

Rosalind felt her heart crash into a flaming wreck. Why had she mentioned it at all? Now Taryn was gone, after things had been going so right, so…

Taryn slapped the bench next to her. "Come sit down," she said in a weary voice.

Rosalind did, carefully, inches from her. Tears were threatening to spill over in her eyes, misery clouding them.

"Did you love him?"

"No. Not like…We were good friends, for many years. But it wasn't more than that." It would kill Paul to know that. He'd survived their divorce by thinking that it was just the affair that ruined things in an otherwise sound marriage. How was she ever to tell him that it had never been sound for her?

"How long were you married?" Taryn's voice hardened like steel. The tone made Rosalind flinch, but she answered.

"Three years. We were still in graduate school. He had an affair, admitted to it, and offered to divorce me. I accepted. I was relieved, actually, to get out." Rosalind squeezed each word out like a drop of blood from a wound she never expected to be torn open. Taryn was right next to her, but that might as well be a million miles away, for all

Rosalind could reach her. "Taryn, I'm sorry I never mentioned it. Paul did love me, but—"

Taryn's head snapped up, her eyes savage and undone in her handsome face. "No!" she snarled, cutting Rosalind off. "No. Don't tell me any more about him. I don't want to know. I don't want to hear his name." Taryn stood up, stalked to the edge of the lake, and stood on the stone lip over the black water.

Tears spilled over, running down Rosalind's cheeks. She felt them, but it was nothing compared to the black hole in her chest where her heart had been. She couldn't bear losing Taryn now. The thought propelled her off the bench. She crossed behind her and put her arm on Taryn's shoulder.

She half expected to be shrugged violently off, but Taryn turned at her touch, eyes glassy with agony. "I don't want to know that anyone else ever loved you. I want to be the one, the only one."

Rosalind gasped, the words as sharp as new steel. She threw herself against Taryn's chest, above her heart. "You are. You are." She half spoke, half sobbed the confession, soaking the white shirt. Taryn's arms around her were demanding, fierce, a bear hug of an embrace.

She lifted Rosalind's head and stared hard into her face. "Tell me you love me."

"I love you, Taryn," Rosalind whispered, the words eager to escape into the air, to seek their own life out in the world.

"No one else," Taryn insisted, capturing Rosalind's chin in her hand.

"You are the only one I've ever loved. And I'll die if you turn away from me." The words were spoken; the intensity of them shocked even Rosalind, in the grip of the overwhelming realization of her first love.

Nothing in her experience had prepared her for this, for the way Taryn's words would slay her, make her want to cry out, fight and die, live for her. Everything she'd spent a lifetime fearing she would never feel came roaring through her veins, making her shake. Rosalind Olchawski admitted to loving another person for the first time. The need for Taryn was so strong it nearly made her beg. *How do people ever survive, walking around feeling like this?*

Taryn kissed her. Rosalind drew Taryn's head down, taking it in her hands as if she could mark her, set a brand on her. She willingly gave over her heart in that kiss, knowing she no longer owned it. That honor belonged to Taryn, whatever she chose to do with it. Rosalind was committed.

Taryn brushed the tears from Rosalind's cheeks with her thumbs. "You okay?"

"I think I'm better than I've ever been. I feel like I'm waking up." Rosalind looked at Taryn and, with a mix of wonder and determination, saw her tremble, slightly. Was Taryn scared? Rosalind felt no fear, only certainty coupled with a desire to bring Taryn back to her. Rosalind wiped at the tearstains on Taryn's shirt. "I got you all wet."

"Promises, promises."

It was a relief to hear her make a joke, to watch Taryn get her stance back, to be cocky and young. It also made Rosalind smile, and the sweetness of that was like wine, drowning the fear. Rosalind took Taryn's hand and placed it over her heart, holding it there. The jolt of emotion staggered her. In her confession, in her abandon, Rosalind had found a strength that made her feel wise and gentle.

Rosalind kissed the side of Taryn's neck, above the life vein. She saw the pulse dancing there, so fragile, obliquely shielded by the muscles of neck and shoulders. It was ridiculous how close to the surface that life ran, how easy it would be to threaten it. Rosalind felt very tender, wanting to shelter the girl's vulnerability, shield it from the world so it couldn't hurt her anymore. She kissed the muscle surrounding that vein, as a knight's armor might be blessed.

"So…I guess you'd go out with me again."

Rosalind smothered a chuckle against the skin of Taryn's throat. "Maybe. Are you asking me out?" Rosalind said, pleased with the language. She hadn't been asked out since high school. It had a nice symmetry to it, going through her second adolescence, discovering sex, finding out new things about herself every five minutes, and being asked out in an awkward, charming way. The fact that she was all but sharing the blood in her veins with this girl already made it seem silly. Would she go out with her? Taryn would be lucky to pry her off in order to change clothes.

"Rosalind, would you be my girl? I know, you are a woman, not a girl, but…you know what I mean," Taryn said, biting off the words.

"Going steady? I don't know. It's such a big step. We've only been on one date. I don't even know your last name…" Rosalind said, raising her head from Taryn's shoulder.

"Cullen."

"I need to think about it," Rosalind said primly.

"What, you need references? I can provide them," Taryn said in a dangerous tone. Rosalind gave ground, not wanting to hear about the number of references Taryn might be able to provide.

"All right," she said into the lapel of Taryn's suit coat. Taryn didn't seem to hear her.

"I know I'm younger than you, and I don't have the education you have, and…this is all new for you. But I'll be good to you, Rosalind. Give me a chance." Taryn's voice was defensive, rising into anger.

Rosalind put her fingers over Taryn's lips. "You didn't hear me, baby. I said yes."

"You did?"

"Yes, I did. I love you. Of course I'll be your girl. Go out with you. However you want to say it. I'll make you a part of my life and become a part of yours. Fair enough?"

"Careful. I'll get used to your saying things like that to me."

Rosalind cupped the back of Taryn's neck. She could feel the heat from it singeing her palm, but she didn't flinch away. It was only the heat of Taryn's blood, a heat she knew she could take. "I think you'll have to. I'm not going to be able to stop."

Music started up, spilling over the ledge. Rosalind's head perked up. She tilted it, listening. She tried, Lord knows she did, not to give in, not to let the hilarity win, but the short film had been planted in her brain by Joe. She saw the kitchen, saw Taryn, in her boxers…Rosalind grabbed the lapels of Taryn's coat, burying her face in the drag king's chest. Her shoulders shook from the effort of trying to restrain herself, but it only made it worse.

Taryn stood like a post, letting the hysterical woman cling to her and laugh herself sick. "What's so funny?"

Rosalind mumbled something that might have been Billy Ray Cyrus.

"'Achy Breaky Heart' sends you into hysterics? Just wait until they play the Macarena."

Rosalind collapsed again into her jacket, helpless with laughter. Taryn shrugged.

There was a jangle of chain, a rush of footsteps. A dark form bounded out of the trees and headed right for them. Taryn pushed

Rosalind behind her and balanced on her toes, instinctively. It was a dog, Taryn saw, when it danced through the light coming from the reception. A chocolate Labrador, springing and cavorting around them, wriggling with pure happiness. In its mouth it had a huge stick, and it grinned crazily around it. The dog ran forward, nosed Taryn's outstretched hand, wagging its tail frantically.

"He just wants to show you his stick." A voice came out of the darkness between the trees. Taryn looked and saw a black wool coat, short brown hair, glasses, and a broad, handsome face. The woman looked at Taryn, her eyes staying a few seconds longer than necessary. A small smile appeared, out of nowhere, and she nodded. She whistled, and the dog exploded away from Taryn, back to her side. "Sorry to interrupt." She walked off down the path around the lake, taking the stick from the dog's mouth and throwing it for him. "C'mon, Grizzly."

"Good thing you were there to protect me," Rosalind said, from behind Taryn's shoulder.

Muscles still twitching from the fighting instinct, Taryn flexed her arms. "Hey, if that had been a Dalmatian, I'd have had him." She turned and faced Rosalind, holding out her arm. "Come home with me?"

Rosalind raised her head and smiled, letting that be her answer.

CHAPTER SIX

Rosalind drove very carefully on the way back to 34 Mariner, convinced that Taryn's hand resting lazily on her thigh was not a very good idea. Oh, it was a good idea for her thigh, which enthusiastically endorsed the slow caress of Taryn's fingertips, but her brain had sense enough to recognize when her body wasn't anywhere near engaged in driving. When Taryn's fingers dipped to her inner thigh, Rosalind drew in a sharp breath and swerved hard to the right, nearly clipping a parking meter.

"If you keep that up, I'll owe the City of Buffalo a fortune to replace all the meters I'm going to plow over."

Taryn grinned and kept her hand right were it was. Rosalind filed that away under Taryn Response: Can't refuse a challenge. It was infuriating and very enticing. It kept Rosalind completely distracted as she turned down Mariner. Her mind cavorted about, seeking a way to divert the girl without actually putting her off. If she could manage to park before that motion made her jump into Taryn's lap…

"I got a call from my brother today. He's going to be in town with his girlfriend tomorrow night and wants to have dinner. Would you like to go?" Rosalind asked, trying to keep the catch out of her voice. Taryn's fingers had wandered again. The question stopped the hand, which was not exactly what Rosalind had wanted.

"Go out to dinner with you and your brother?" she asked, as if this were absurd.

"Yes. I'd like him to meet you."

Taryn's eyebrows climbed up together. "You would?"

"Sure, honey. You want me to be your girl, right?" Rosalind asked with a sweet smile.

"You know I do." The hand started moving again.

"Then I get to show you off. The handsomest butch in Buffalo, on my arm."

"I'm…not much good with families," Taryn admitted with a rueful smile.

"Eric's harmless. I want you to meet him and Sandhya. And I want them to get a chance to meet the person I love," Rosalind said, looking at Taryn.

She sat very still, her hand frozen. "You keep saying that so easily. You really mean it, don't you." It was a statement, not a question, and spoken in a voice of wonder.

"You know I do, baby. It's a wonder I didn't say it before." Rosalind pulled the car up in front of 34 Mariner, not really looking at anything but Taryn's face.

Taryn leaned forward and kissed her reverently. "Okay. I'll do dinner with your brother and his girlfriend," she said, her face inches from Rosalind's.

Loud clapping interrupted them. Rosalind raised her eyes to the porch, where a full contingent of people was watching them and applauding. Joe even stuck two fingers in his mouth and whistled.

"What's going on?" she asked Taryn, who had the most annoyed look on her face she'd ever seen.

Taryn groaned and set her head in her hands. "The Better You than Me. I forgot all about it. Guess I was thinking about something else tonight. We've been spotted. We'll have to go in."

"What in the world is a Better You than Me?" Rosalind whispered, but Taryn didn't have a chance to answer. A teenage girl skipped off the stairs and flew at the car. Taryn got out and was nearly knocked down by Goblin, who grabbed her in a swinging hug.

"You're all dressed up! Did you do a show tonight?" Goblin asked, hauling Taryn around in a circle.

"Nah. I had a date," Taryn said, putting her arm over Goblin's shoulders.

Rosalind got out of the car, and Joe whistled again. "The kids are back from the prom!" he called out, grinning. He was leaning against the rail, his arm around Rhea's waist. Rhea had her arms folded, her head tilted to the side, watching Rosalind very closely. There was something in her Rosalind couldn't read, not a warning exactly, but a distance. She looked like she was sizing Rosalind up all over again, but from a different angle this time. Rosalind's dress felt very short suddenly, when she saw Rhea's eyes fix on it. But it wasn't condemnation coming from the fierce woman now, rather a sort of interest, as they approached the porch. Rhea took in Taryn's arm closing around Rosalind's waist, the way the professor moved automatically closer to her. Her face became unreadable, as Goblin hauled them to the steps.

"Everybody, this is Rosalind. Rosalind, this is Goblin. Laurel, you know Egyptia, Joe, and Rhea. That's Irene and Garnet," Taryn said, sweeping her hand toward the crowd. Rosalind looked them over one at a time, to get a sense of them.

Goblin had Taryn's other arm and used it to pull Taryn up the steps. She was tall, and thin, and wore an Ani DiFranco T-shirt with a pair of jeans. Her brown hair was braided, her eyes circled by wire-rimmed glasses. She grinned at Rosalind as she took charge of their progress, acknowledging Taryn's arm around the professor's waist. "You must be special to get Taryn to dress up on a weeknight."

Seated on the step was a young woman in a paisley shirt, her long, white-blond hair falling in her eyes. She looked red faced, as if she'd been crying, but flashed a smile at Taryn, then at Rosalind. The professor added the name to the image. Laurel, the other housemate. She wondered what she had been crying about.

Egyptia sat behind her, combing the white-blond hair though graceful fingers. Rosalind recognized the emerald eyes, the perfectly smooth chocolate skin, but without the platinum wig and makeup, Egyptia looked different. Less mythic, more on a human scale. She smiled in recognition, perfect dimples carving into her cheeks. "Hey, girl."

The other two women were in their late thirties, Rosalind guessed, and stood on the porch next to Rhea and Joe. Irene was the shorter of the two, and heavy, with close-cropped brown hair threaded with gray. She wore a T-shirt with a vest over it, jeans and boots, and stood with her thumbs hooked into the pockets. Garnet was as tall as Joe and wore enameled earrings that showed through her light brown hair. Her blouse was a cream silk, open over a series of Goddess charms and necklaces. She wore a pair of lavender drawstring pants and sandals. They both nodded to her, almost in unison.

Then there was Rhea. The dress she wore was a blue that matched the shade of Taryn's eyes, embroidered with sunflowers. Joe's arm around her waist was the only acknowledgment she made of the people near her, her stance seeming to be that of a woman alone in the space. She held her weight on one hip, her slender body an exclamation point even in repose. It was a complement to the easy, muscular form of the man next to her, but not an extension of it, even with the contact between them.

Joe's immediate smile spoke of genuine pleasure at having them back. It was unsettling to see the openness of his welcome, next to the unreadable but seething emotion coming from Rhea. Rosalind wasn't sure what to make of it and tucked herself under Taryn's arm. The motion caught Rhea's eye, and, for a moment, Rosalind could have sworn she saw approval. It was gone as quickly as it came, so she couldn't be sure.

"We're almost done with the storytelling. You have to pay the ferryman to get by, T," Egyptia said, barring their way up the steps. Taryn sighed dramatically, but nodded.

Joe addressed Rosalind. "We're having a Better You than Me. Old house tradition, whenever life kicks you in the teeth. Laurel's girlfriend dumped her, so we're dedicating tonight to her."

"Everyone has to tell an embarrassing, painful, or funny story, and it has to be true. The goal is to get everyone to say better you than me. Make the person who's suffering feel better. Gallows humor as sympathetic magic," Taryn said to her. "We won't get by if we don't contribute."

"You wouldn't want to break the circle and diffuse the power, Taryn," Rhea said quietly.

"Of course not." Taryn smiled at Laurel. "She wasn't good enough for you anyway. Swim team, what kind of crap is that? You can get a basketball player in two snaps, if you want a jock."

"Thanks, T," Laurel said, tearing up.

"Whoa, none of that. I'll go, to keep the energy moving." She carefully helped Rosalind sit on the step next to Egyptia, then took her stance like the porch was a stage. From the way that everyone responded to her, immediately giving over wholehearted attention, it might well have been, Rosalind thought. As much as she wanted to haul Taryn upstairs, it was a delight to watch her with her family, as Rosalind thought of her housemates. It showed the tender side of her that didn't often come out.

"All right. One I haven't used yet, a powerful one, to dispel

Laurel's misery. Ah! I was in the mall. I stopped in the bathroom. It was pouring down rain outside. I'd taken the bus, so I was soaked to the skin from crossing Walden Avenue. Right where that girl got killed, you know? I had on my army jacket and a pair of boots, normal stuff, and was slicked down, leaving puddles when I walked. Must have looked like a drowned cat. I walked past this housewife. Orchard Park written all over her. Suburbs! Flower plastic raincoat.

"She gasped when I went in the doors, but I didn't think anything of it. When I was coming out, a security guard grabbed me in a half nelson and wrestled me to the floor. I didn't know what the hell was going on, so I fought. The jerk got his knee in my back, slammed my head against the marble floor until I stopped struggling. He hauls me to my feet. I'm bleeding all over, and he slaps cuffs on me and muscles me to the mall office. Seems the housewife reported a guy going into the women's room. I didn't have any ID on me. When they told me what was up, I told them they were stupid bastards, and I was a girl.

"Jerkoff told me to prove it. I told him to go fuck himself. Told him I was going to sue his ass, sue the mall. He grabbed my crotch and got this look on his face, like he couldn't decide if he should apologize or spit. I helped him decide by kicking him in the groin. Mall management let me go. I was already bleeding and had a hell of a temper on. Rhea called a lawyer, but I didn't have any witnesses, and I had fought back. He told us to drop it, so we did," Taryn finished, looking at her audience.

The group responded as a chorus, "Better you than me!"

Rosalind saw Taryn's eyes seek her out first. She said I love you, without moving her lips.

Laurel shook her head. "That sucks. Thanks, T."

"Anytime," Taryn said with a grin.

"Okay. Your turn, Rosalind," Goblin said, looking at the professor.

"All right," Rosalind said, thinking back. The household seemed to take the storytelling ritual with a sense of humor, but seriously as well. It wasn't just a party, or a gripe session; they were working magic. Rosalind cast an eye at Rhea, who had gone still as a stone, watching her from the side of her dark eyes. *Is she looking to see if I'll disrespect the ritual, make a fool of myself, or shame Taryn?* Rosalind had no intention of disrupting the emotion even she could feel gathered on the porch.

I may not be a witch, but I understand the magic of language, how stories change the world. She looked back at Rhea. Taryn had managed to tell a horrible tale with a shrug and a grin. The pain was there, acknowledged, but not submitted to. Rosalind took her cue from that and silently gave thanks to six years of Shakespeare in the Park. Taryn's eyes hadn't left her. She wanted to show that she understood the dispelling of pain by sharing it, making it communal, that she could fit into Taryn's world.

"I grew up outside of Poughkeepsie, down the street from the Methodist church. Mom was a Catholic when she married Dad, Dad was an atheist. So we compromised and went to the church the closest walking distance to the house. I was in the third grade. They had this huge Christmas tree in the church, right up by the pulpit. It was decorated with gold bells, white snow wreaths, gold-painted Styrofoam cubes with Greek letters on them. But the best thing was the snakes. They were made of rope, spray painted gold, with gold sequins glued on for scales. They had red plastic gems for eyes that would catch the light and look like they were alive. They were the most beautiful thing I'd ever seen.

"So I took one. While everyone else was in the parsonage for coffee fellowship, I snuck back into the church, unwound a snake from the branch, and stuffed it down the arm of my winter coat. I took it to the woods behind my house and wrapped it around the highest branch of the dogwood tree that I could reach. I would go visit it after school every day and made my brother Eric stay away. I knew he would tell my mother. I figured that since it came from a tree in church, it was a holy object. And it was sacred, I could tell, because it was beautiful. So I prayed to it. My mother started wondering where I went every afternoon, so she followed me into the woods. She came on me praying to the snake in the dogwood. She just stood there looking at me, like she couldn't believe what she was seeing.

"Whatever she had thought I was doing, playing with matches, playing with myself, would have been better. She didn't say a word. She just took the snake off the branch and walked back to the house. I followed her. She sat down at the kitchen table, resting her head on one hand. 'Whatever you were doing, I don't want to hear about it. You will never do it again. And you will never tell anyone you did it,' and I got grounded for a month. It made me scared that I'd done something so horrible, my mother couldn't even put words to it. I lost my sense of God. And I never saw the snake again."

Silence greeted the story, then Joe shook his head.

The group joined in with him in their chorus, "Better you than me!" It was like winning the Academy Award, like the Nobel Prize. Rosalind knew she'd been accepted into the circle, added to the magic.

Taryn looked at her with pride, fairly radiating it. "Okay. We paid the ferryman. We're heading up," she said, holding out her hand to Rosalind.

"Night, kids," Joe said with a smirk.

Rosalind found that she didn't mind walking past the group, hand in hand with Taryn, when everyone knew they were going upstairs to make love. The openness of it precluded shame. It made her feel bold. "Night, Papa. Don't wait up," Rosalind said, grinning.

Joe laughed out loud, and Egyptia sent a "You go, girl!" up the stairs after them.

In Taryn's room, Rosalind felt high as a kite. Though the house was full of people, though the ceremony and party might well last through the night, she didn't want to go back to her empty apartment. This house, she was starting to understand, had a feel to it, a life, a running of joy along the veins. Energy, Rhea would say, like it had been built on a powerful spot or become one through ritual and inhabitance. She knew it was starting to get to her. She could feel the difference when crossing the threshold. It was Taryn's home. She couldn't think of a better place to be welcomed into her body, as she had been into her life. Rosalind was determined. Taryn would be her lover tonight.

Taryn eased up to her, wrapping arms around her from behind and resting her head against Rosalind's. "You feel good," she murmured into Rosalind's ear.

"So do you, baby. I like it when you hold me like this. I feel safe," Rosalind admitted, stroking Taryn's hand.

"Have I ever held you like this?"

"No…I suppose not. It feels so familiar, somehow." Rosalind cudgeled her brain, wondering where that thought had come from. All she could find was the sense of familiarity and ease, or perfect connection, when Taryn took her in her arms. It made no sense, but it was too sweet to be argued with. *This is how love must feel. I've just never been here before.*

"You know, no one's ever attached the word 'safe' to me before," Taryn said, her teeth closing playfully on Rosalind's ear.

The professor shivered and arched her neck. "You should think about changing your reputation. You're really a big teddy bear, not the Defiler of Maidens that you pass yourself off to be."

"Defiler of Maidens? Oh, I like that," Taryn said in a low voice.

Rosalind turned and put her arms around Taryn's neck, rubbing the back of her head. Taryn was arrogant, and impossible, and infuriating, and just so damned handsome it hurt.

"What's that look for?" Taryn asked her, cocking an eyebrow.

"You. I was wondering how I made it this long without meeting you. I know we were supposed to meet sooner." It was the energy of the house, partaking in the ritual of storytelling that was making her think like this, Rosalind knew. She didn't talk like this. But standing there, looking into the face of the girl who held her, she thought about the story she'd told about the snake. It was beautiful in a way that she knew was sacred. It was the last moment she remembered feeling sure about God, or gods, in her life.

Rosalind looked into the burning eyes of Taryn and felt that certainty return, knew the same truth she'd learned and forgotten in third grade. What was sacred was beautiful, and being in Taryn's arms was beautiful. She might never convince her Catholic mother or atheist father, but she was looking into the face of the divine and caught it looking back at her.

"Rhea says I was born late, a decade or so. She told me, when we stopped being lovers, that she was meant to be my mother this time around, but I refused to come back, to get born. She had to settle for other ways to be close to me. She still gives me hell for being late for everything, says it's just me being stubborn from my last life. If you and I had met any sooner, I'd be jailbait and you'd be arrested." Taryn's lips quirked up in a smile.

"You're in time enough for me. But I'm glad you didn't wait another few years. I might not have survived it without you. It was getting cold out there." The words were out before Rosalind examined them.

"I waited for you. I had to know you'd be here," Taryn said in response, her voice as naked as Rosalind's had been. The implication was too much for both of them, so they shied away from it, falling into the physical connection they shared, joining their bodies. It was sweet, and easier to handle, the way their bodies spoke to one another. That language would be enough for them, for this night.

Rosalind loosened Taryn's tie, slipped the jacket off her broad shoulders. The streetlight showed her the glow of the drag king's dress shirt, the knot of her green silk tie half undone, her hair too short to be mussed the way it was the night they met, but that didn't keep Rosalind from trying. Her hands were roaming over Taryn, hungry for her but not ready to rip her clothes off yet. She was enjoying undressing her, prying her out of her suit one button at a time. It was playful, it was arousing, the way Taryn accepted the game and waited as Rosalind explored her, unbuttoning her shirt, drawing off her tie. This was Rosalind's night.

The tie found its way to the floor, following the suit coat. Rosalind smoothed her hands across the front of the shirt, feeling the binding Taryn used. She pulled the shirt out of Taryn's pants, opening her belt to do it easily. Taryn obligingly raised her arms and held them out as Rosalind drew the shirt down off her shoulders. Impulse made her leave it halfway down her arms, trapping them. She didn't want Taryn getting away.

She saw the ace bandages Taryn used to bind her breasts, wound tightly from her rib cage to her armpits. She touched the clawed metal clasps, wanting to undo them, but not sure how Taryn might react. She risked a glance at Taryn's face and found only encouragement there.

"It's okay," Taryn said, reading her look and her intent.

The permission was all she needed. Rosalind took the clasps off, setting them aside. She could picture herself stepping on one in the heat of passion and nearly giggled. It was like unwrapping a mummy, taking the bandages off Taryn, but the flesh underneath was warm and alive. She'd seen her naked to the waist before, but there was something wicked about unwrapping her like a Christmas present that appealed to Rosalind. The surprise of finding a girl's body under the suit, sheathed with muscle under smooth skin, but still a girl, sent a jolt from the base of her spine up to her heart. It was that tension between seeming opposites that was so arousing, the beauty of Taryn unique in its form. *My Ganymede*. She took Taryn's breasts in her hands and bent her head to them.

Taryn groaned and arched her back, bracing her legs wide to keep on standing. Rosalind was gentle and insistent in her exploration, the level of comfort she felt amazing for her first foray. She had done this before, she had to have. It was too familiar, the taste of the flesh, the way she tried not to make any noise but did anyway, small sounds in her throat. Rosalind reached down and grabbed Taryn's ass, digging her fingers into the muscle. Taryn pressed her hips against Rosalind, the metal of her belt buckle getting snagged on Rosalind's dress. Rosalind responded by grabbing the belt and pulling it out of the loops, tossing it to the floor without ceremony.

She took Taryn's pants and eased them down over her hips, but left her boxer shorts in place. It took a moment of gentle insistence on Rosalind's part, but Taryn finally kicked the pants off and lay down on the bed, reclining like the statue of a young god. It didn't make any sense to be in her clothes when she wanted to feel Taryn's skin against her, so Rosalind knelt and gave her back to Taryn. Taryn obligingly unzipped her dress, then lay back down, head propped on her arm. She watched as Rosalind took the dress off, inhaling sharply when the professor raised it over her head.

Rosalind stopped when Taryn made the sound and looked at her, concerned. Was something wrong? The look on her face was like music and wine, like the first signs of spring after the months of snowed-in death sleep. It melted her. She had to sit down on the mattress; her knees refused to hold her up. Here she was trying to seduce this girl, and she was slain by one small noise of appreciation. Taryn sat up and kissed her, drawing Rosalind back down on top of her. Her brain wasn't firing on all synapses, drowning in the sensations this girl drew forth without effort. Rosalind remembered her determination and pulled away.

She ran her hands over Taryn's face, down her neck, across the tattoo of Alexander on her right bicep. She wanted to make this girl feel the way she felt and didn't know if that was even possible. She'd never been sexually confident, but had never had occasion to mourn the lack. Men were easy. It was a shame to admit it, but they bored her silly; her husband had, in any event. Not that he didn't try, but it always felt like that, trying. She'd never swooned in his arms, never felt carried away. Taryn just looked at her, and breathing was difficult.

Rosalind stroked the face of Alexander, the winged lion on her right thigh, and wondered how much of this was love, how much of it was sexual frenzy. She wanted Taryn so much it hurt. She wanted to bring her shuddering into her arms, to have her desperate and undone, the way she felt. She'd never really cared that much how Paul felt about it. With Taryn, it was vitally important that she know it was her, Rosalind, doing this to her, making her feel this way. She scratched her nails across the back of Taryn's neck and she moaned.

"Yes, baby. Let me hear you," Rosalind said, loving the sound of Taryn's voice in pleasure.

"You're killing me."

She pressed back down on top of Taryn, bringing her whole body back into contact. It wasn't enough to stop and think about what she was doing. Her body was surging with response; every time Taryn moved, or sighed, it went right into her blood. She couldn't separate herself enough to launch a campaign of careful seduction. She pressed her hips against the girl's closed thighs, kissed her mouth like the only air left in the world might come from Taryn. She cried out against her open mouth when she felt Taryn's arms close around her. She had wanted to be careful, and delicate, but she was eating her alive. "Take these off, honey," Rosalind said, hooking her hand into the boxers.

Taryn froze. Her face, her body, all movement ceased. Rosalind raised lust-filled eyes to Taryn's face and found panic there. "I don't…I mean, it's not…"

Rosalind took her hand away and Taryn started breathing again. The look of panic didn't fade, it just receded. It was too much for Rosalind, seeing the pain being pushed down. She took Taryn's arms and drew her in, pressing Taryn's head to her breast. "It's okay, baby. It's all right. I'd never hurt you."

Rosalind followed her instincts and held her close, crooning to her. She felt Taryn's body relax in stages, the masked trembling reduce to a stillness. She could almost feel her gather herself, pushing the air out of her lungs. The tension remained in her back and arms, muscles bunched up like startled cats, thrumming with adrenaline. Rosalind felt Taryn shift, felt her raise herself up on her arms and was sure Taryn was going to push away. When she sighed and cuddled closer, Rosalind's heart nearly burst out of her ribs. She had never experienced anything like the fierce tenderness she felt, the desire to protect and cherish this girl lying in her arms. She felt ten feet tall, with the way Taryn surrendered her pain and accepted the comforting. She had no idea how rare that moment was.

Rosalind started singing. That halted all attempts at flight; the very uniqueness of being sung to kept Taryn there, in Rosalind's embrace, long enough for her guard to drop.

It was a song Rosalind's mother used to sing to her, when she couldn't sleep. Rosalind kissed her neck as she sang, and Taryn laughed.

"The bushel and the peck sound familiar. But I thought it was a hug around the neck," she said, her lips against Rosalind's breast.

"Not according to my mother." Rosalind was so glad to hear Taryn speak and sound even again, that she was ready to sprout wings and fly.

"Mrs. Olchawski can't be wrong."

"Oh, she was wrong about a lot of things. Don't get me started. Are you okay, sweetheart?"

Taryn closed her eyes and nuzzled against Rosalind's breast. "Yeah. Funny, I think I am. I've never done that before."

"Gone away?"

"No, I've gone away plenty. I've never gone away and come back. It just seemed like it was more fun to be out here with you than trapped in my head," Taryn said, grinning up at Rosalind.

"You can tell me, you know."

Taryn's eyes narrowed. "It's not such a big deal."

"So share it with me. Then it will be even less of a big deal," Rosalind said, reasonably. It worked, it was the right tone to take with Taryn.

Taryn sat up and wrapped an arm around her knees, looking across the room at the altar on top of the dresser. The headlights of a car going too fast up Mariner cut across the room, lit on the statue of the dancing Shiva, sending sparks from the bronze. For a moment the statue flickered, as if it were moving; the hands changed gestures subtly. From the darkness at the back of the altar the face of the bloody woman glared out, until it was still again, the trick of the light past. Taryn sighed. In that sigh Rosalind heard the span of years since Taryn had told this story. Who had ever heard it? Rhea, certainly. Rosalind couldn't imagine anyone else.

"My family lived in Lackawanna. Probably still do, but I wouldn't know. I was thrown out when I was sixteen." Taryn's voice was flat, unemotional. She spoke from a cool distance, as if describing a movie she had seen long ago.

Rosalind waited, biting her tongue, letting the welling silence encourage Taryn to continue. It was a silence with as much texture as language. Rosalind filled it with her presence, but kept her words out of it. The way Taryn spoke had the feel of events reduced to shorthand, a symbol removed from the actual blood and fire to become manageable. She let it unfold, knowing she couldn't change what had already happened.

"Ever been there? Don't bother. If a place can be depressed, Lackawanna is depressed. Not just economics, the feel of the place. Like hope died there a long time ago. Rhea says there's no love in Lackawanna. Anyway, my cousin came to live with us because his parents couldn't deal with him. Funny, my parents couldn't deal with me. They should've traded."

Taryn got up and padded to her suit coat, fishing out her lighter and cigarettes. She opened the window, perching on the sill. Her face was backlit by the streetlight, smooth and white; the smoke hung yellow in the blue light. "I was trouble. I never liked school. I got in a lot of fights. My parents wanted to send me to a counselor for my behavior problems. I kept dating girls and refused to look like one. I went once, for three sessions, but we didn't have the cash, and I was, quote, unrepentant.

"Anyway, Dean moved in. We…didn't get along. He would steal my stuff and hock it for crank. I found out and flushed his stash. We fought. One afternoon he raped me. Floor of the family room, by the pool table. I think he wasn't setting out to. He was just going to beat the shit out of me, but I fought back. He got a pool cue and broke it across my head. It knocked me down. I went to my mother, told her to kick the son of a bitch out, you know? Know what she told me? I asked for it. She believed me, she just thought it was my fault. I was a truck driver, she said. A challenge to boys like Dean. They had to prove something on me. She told me to put on a dress, he'd be nicer to me. Nicer. I was sixteen."

Taryn tapped another cigarette out of the pack and lit it thoughtfully.

Rosalind sat up, watching her through the haze of smoke. "What about your dad?"

A smile twisted on Taryn's lips, bitter and full of bile. "This was his brother's son, who had been sent to him to keep out of trouble, and here I was making trouble. He actually told me to pack my shit and get out. So I did.

"I knew some friends of friends in Buffalo. I stayed with them for a while. I moved around a little. I ended up working in this restaurant as a dishwasher. A gay boy, real sweet, by the name of Steve, was a waiter there. He let me stay with him. That was cool, until his boyfriend broke up with him and we both had to move out. I was bussing tables, thinking, oh shit, now where do I go, when I heard something.

"I looked up, and there was this woman with wild hair, like snakes, just looking at me. I had a bus pan full of coffee mugs. She was staring at me. So I said 'What?' She just smiled a little, came over and touched my cheek. She didn't say anything. When my shift was over she was there, standing outside. I went home with her. We were lovers for a year, then we were friends. Friends was better. She still gave me a home, but she started doing things like making me eat, making me read books she picked out. She had me take the GED when I was eighteen. I fought her, but Rhea isn't soft. She didn't put up with any of my shit. She told me she was my family, and I could make all the noise I wanted to about it, but it wouldn't change. I've been here since." Taryn shook her head. "I don't know how I got off on all that."

She stubbed out the cigarette and came back to the mattress. "Changed your mind about me?" she asked, half cocky, half defensive.

Rosalind reached out and took her hand, knowing Taryn wouldn't crawl right back into her arms just yet. "Damn them all for hurting you," Rosalind said, the words burning her throat. The anger was instinctive, hot, hard to contain. That wasn't like her at all.

"I'm okay," Taryn said stubbornly.

"I know you're okay, sweetheart. I still want to kill them all. It doesn't mean I don't see how strong you are."

"You think I'm strong?" Taryn asked, tilting her head.

"You survived and you kept going. I don't know if I would have in the same place. And you kept a sense of humor. Of course I see how strong you are." Rosalind held her arms open in invitation, and Taryn accepted.

She lay down with her head in Rosalind's lap. "I get jumpy about…letting go. But I'd like to. With you." Taryn gave Rosalind an open, pleading look. "You want me?" she asked, sitting up.

Rosalind gasped. Keeping up with this girl's moods would give her whiplash, she thought, but she wasn't complaining. She answered truthfully, letting the hunger show on her face. "More than you know."

Rosalind leaned forward and kissed Taryn, softly, then pulled back. Her eyes darted from Taryn's eyes to her lips. They were thin, sculpted, splendidly shaped. Taryn kept them parted invitingly. Rosalind leaned back in, magnetized, tasting them. She offered herself to Taryn's strength, coaxing it out, letting only their lips touch. Their bodies, so close, called out for more, but Rosalind kept back. In that kiss was the promise of surrender, the hunger of a woman. It worked its magic.

That kiss spoke to the things she loved best in Taryn—her confidence, her passion, the way she accepted the mantle of control. It gave life to Taryn and offered her more. Taryn accepted. She leaned forward and took Rosalind into her arms, pulling the woman to her chest, kissing her with intent now.

Rosalind gave her every gift a woman could offer in the expression of her desire—her trust, the welcome of her body, her faith in Taryn as a lover. She gave these gifts consciously, deliberately, from love of Taryn. She gave them in the light of her love for how Taryn had kept her heart intact, despite the pain.

Rosalind gave wetness as a gift to her. Rosalind showed her in a hundred small ways—the movement of her hips, the tension in her thighs, the way her head arched on the pillow—that she was welcome. Expected even. When Taryn came into her body, it was like a woman going to her mystery. When Rosalind's skin was flushed and mottled, and her hands tensed on Taryn's shoulders, Taryn increased the speed of her plunging hand. When Rosalind called out her name, she thought that Taryn cried. Taryn looked up at her like the magic that made the world was closing around her hand. When Rosalind stilled and folded back from the arch of her climax, her hand pulled weakly at Taryn's shoulders.

"Come here," she said, her voice passion drunk. Taryn covered the body of her lover, keeping her warm. "It just gets better with you," Rosalind said, her eyes still half shut, dreamy.

"I love you, Rosalind."

"I love you too, sweetheart," Rosalind said, opening her eyes.

"That's what I said in the car. When you asked me to say something in Japanese," Taryn said, nuzzling at her neck.

Rosalind's hands combed Taryn's hair. "Say it again."

"*Watashi wa anata o aishite imasu.*"

"That suits you. It sounds harsh and restrained, but it means something so beautiful."

"You won't leave me, right?" Taryn asked, out of nowhere.

Rosalind smiled, a lazy, satisfied smile that spoke of grace. She took Taryn's large hand in both of hers and placed it over her heart. "Meant only for kings," she mumbled, grinning.

Rosalind pulled Taryn's hand up to her lips, kissing Taryn's fingers one by one. She drew Taryn's index finger into her mouth, her tongue caressing it, tasting herself. The caress went from lazy to interested; she started to kiss her wrist, nipping at the soft skin under her hand.

From there it only made sense to sit up, so she could keep on exploring Taryn's arm—the bulge of the bicep in its bed of shadow, the face of Alexander watching her with wide, knowing eyes. Rosalind moved around behind Taryn, spreading her hands across the width of her back. She pressed her lips to the black eagle, ran her nails down the dagger with the bull of Knossos, left impressions of her own over the lines.

The draw of her hands was as persistent as the needle; the thousand sparks her fingers cast were a pleasure as constant as the pain, raising Taryn into another realm. Taryn closed her eyes and leaned back, as if giving over her control to Rosalind. It had been a night of firsts, many of them building to this one, and Rosalind knew that Taryn had an excellent sense of ritual. She must feel the perfection of the symmetry. When Taryn leaned into her hands, Rosalind hoped that she knew she'd be looked after.

Rosalind touched Taryn's body with proprietary interest, claiming the territory as she went—from the curve of her shoulders, across the blades, down the spine shielded by the columns of muscle in her lower back. She kept her pace slow, far slower than she wanted, after starting. She restrained the urge to claw down Taryn's back, rip her way through muscle and bone to her heart. There must be an invitation before she went inside.

She let her hands wander down to the base of her spine, to the place it vanished into secrecy and night, the curve into the top of her boxers. Rosalind let her hand draw slowly down to that point, waking all the flesh up in its path, then moved away. She curved her hands around Taryn's ribs, embracing her from behind, feeling her breasts press into Taryn's muscular back. Her lips found the hollow of her neck and lingered there, seeking to make the pulse dance under Taryn's smooth skin. It did.

When she heard the catch in Taryn's breathing, when she felt Taryn melt, all her tension go out of her, leaning heavily into her embrace, she knew it had begun. She moved with hesitancy, just enough to make Taryn confirm every new motion with her breathing, the ragged slamming of her pulse in the life vein. She risked sliding around in front of Taryn, where she could see her face, see her reaction. Rosalind risked looking into her eyes, the eyes of a girl who knew the territory she was only now discovering, the body of a lover, the body of a woman. She found only encouragement there, coupled with a pleading that nearly broke her heart. If anyone, ever again, hurt this girl, she would rip them apart with her nails and teeth. Pacifism be damned, this was love.

Rosalind could read every emotion. Taryn was a windswept plain, as empty and as complete. She hesitated, not wanting to trip over any broken bones of memory, not wanting to trigger anything that would make the girl hold back a portion of herself or fight to keep control. She knew what she wanted to give Taryn—a confirmation of her strength, even while asking her to surrender it. *I know who you are, baby. Let me love every part of you. Let me draw you out, let me take you where you've taken me so many times. It is a gift, baby. No grief. You're still my boy, my king.*

Rosalind saw the moment the decision had been made, the way Taryn's eyes swam half closed, the way she leaned forward, presenting herself. She kept her heavy-lidded eyes on her lover's face and reached for her boxers. Such a simple thing, to be the beginning. But in the hooking of her powerful hands around the waistband, in the impatient shucking of the cloth, a new world came into being. Taryn handed the boxers to Rosalind like a flag of victory, but her lover tossed them aside, not interested in a trophy. The real prize was yet to be reached.

Rosalind's eyes ran down Taryn's body, wanting to go slow, wanting to grant her a respectful time, but she'd waited so long. She saw the triangle of dark hair and felt a shiver run up her spine, then loop around the pulse in her throat and gallop back down to her groin. In the shadow of the curve of Taryn's hip, just below the bone, was her last tattoo. In a three-part black border, simple as the ribbon on a funeral car, was a yin/yang, the eternal turning of the balance of opposites. A common enough symbol, given personality and life only by its location.

It was the first thing Rosalind touched, as a promise, an understanding. She expected to feel the heat of Taryn's body on her open palm, but she wasn't prepared for the jolt of energy that slammed up her arm. She looked down at her arm, expecting to see a nimbus of fire running along it. Taryn seemed to feel it as well. She swayed, lips parting, and wrapped her hand around Rosalind's wrist.

"Is this okay?" Rosalind asked, her voice a stranger to her in its intensity and pitch.

"If you don't touch me soon, I'm not going to survive," Taryn growled, fierce even in surrender. Her voice worked wonders on Rosalind, who felt herself get wet again. This gave her a clue as to how to proceed. She wanted to know if Taryn was wet, if her arousal had traveled from her voice to the gate between her thighs. It was a lovely way to think of it, Rosalind realized with a shock, as her language expanded to match her experience.

Taryn was the union of opposites—pale white skin like alabaster, the darkness of her hair curling around Rosalind's fingers. The skin on her inner thigh was so soft it stopped Rosalind, stroking it with curious fingers, enjoying that, until Taryn squirmed. Her hips pressed forward, seeking Rosalind's hand. She obliged, pressing her palm down, letting herself feel for the first time the heat and the wetness. Lord, Taryn was as excited as she was. She wondered if this was how Taryn felt, the mix of pride and triumph, every time she became aroused in response to her caress. She hoped so.

"Sweetheart, there's something I'd like to do," Rosalind said, looking up into Taryn's face. She expected a clenching, a momentary shift into uncertainty, but Taryn's face was calm, easy, even with the tension gathering in her body. It was a compliment that Rosalind felt to the core. She knew Taryn's answer before she spoke.

"Whatever you like."

"Okay. Um, you'll have to lie down."

Taryn lowered herself to the mattress indolently, first easing down on her elbows, then lying flat, a smile of invitation on her face. Rosalind's hands parted her thighs, lingering on the muscles shifting under her skin. Rosalind climbed between Taryn's legs, not familiar with the maneuvering yet, landing on her calf. She let the smile sneak across her face, the warmth she felt having everything to do with affection. Her lover returned the smile. Taryn could tell she was nervous; Rosalind knew it from that smile. Rosalind knew she could supplant that smile when her hands closed on Taryn's thighs, parting them farther. The warmth Taryn was about to feel had to do with much more than affection.

She waited and hung there in midair, until she knew Taryn could feel her hot breath, then the touch of her lips. Rosalind kissed her. It was just that at first, the embrace of her lips, the offering of love first, before all else. She felt her wetness all over her cheeks and moved side to side in it, wanting to be covered in the evidence of desire.

Taryn was so wet, it was astounding. *All this, just from making love to me?* Rosalind thought. Well, sure, some from her touching Taryn, she could admit that. But to have this immediate and overwhelming effect on another person was staggering. The power of it, and the fact that she'd longed for just that power, wasn't lost on Rosalind. She had wished to have Taryn in her arms, shuddering and undone, just like Taryn made her. Now, here she was, her hands, her lips, on her, and it sure looked like exactly that.

This was the moment of truth. Could she be the lover of a girl dedicated to passion, who delighted in loving women often and well? The voice in the back of Rosalind's head asked her what made her think that her clumsy attempts at lovemaking would ever be enough to hold the interest of this splendid youth. For all the clarity her love gave her, she still feared the difference in their experience. Rosalind had mocked her for it, but Taryn was an experienced lover. How could she be happy with a novice?

In the chorus of doubts, the wetness on her face gave her something to believe in. There was no shame in her desire. Taryn wanted her. So Rosalind bade the voices in her head be damned and made love to her girl. The first stroke of her tongue made Taryn sigh in relief, the second took that relief away. Taryn's hips pressed down toward her; Rosalind had to grab her thighs and hold them apart to keep from being crushed. There were mechanics she learned, quickly, like not getting her nose in the way of Taryn's snapping pelvic bone, how not to nick sensitive flesh with unshielded teeth, how to bring pleasure to the point of pain by denying it, repeatedly. There were other flourishes inspired by a playful mind, a careful watching of her response, a delight in exploring her body, claiming it.

There are moments when you know why you are alive, when the reason behind all things becomes clear and the veil fades away like smoke. In those moments you see why you chose to come back into the flesh, and the only emotion big enough is gratitude. All things make sense. The profound becomes simple and reachable. It was a moment of such clarity for Rosalind. Everything made sense, and everything was perfect.

Rosalind knew why she was alive at long last. She was almost sorry when Taryn started coming. She didn't want to stop. Taryn came, one hand clenched in the sheets, the other on the back of Rosalind's head, calling out her name. There are times when words aren't enough to convey the whole of an emotion, when the lightness of freedom can only be expressed in the shy smile of a lover.

Taryn opened her arms, Rosalind climbed up her long body, watching the muscles still dance and twitch. The drag king wrapped the professor in a possessive embrace, tucked her head into her shoulder, and wept, softly. Just a few tears, blending into the sweat-damped hair of her lover. They both fell asleep, holding on to one another.

CHAPTER SEVEN

Rosalind woke first. A glance at the window showed the glow of dawn. They hadn't slept all that long. She could have sworn a single chime of a bronze bell had woken her. The sound echoed in the room, but wasn't repeated. Taryn was sound asleep, curled on her side, pressed up against Rosalind's arm. Rosalind reached out and stroked her cheek, drawing the back of her hand over the sharp cheekbone, down to the soft flesh in the hollow of her throat. Taryn stirred, smiled, and slept on, pleased by whatever she was dreaming. Rosalind couldn't bear the thought of waking her, but found she was fired with energy, unable to rest in the warmth of the blankets. She slid out carefully and pulled the covers over Taryn's naked shoulder.

It was cold in the room; the wood floor chilled her feet after being trapped under a blanket with a heat source like Taryn. Rosalind selected a pair of sweatpants from the dresser and a heavy maroon sweatshirt with a Harvard logo on it. She raised an eyebrow at it in a perfect impression of Taryn, wondering who had left it here and how long ago. She sniffed at it, but it only carried the scent of her, a scent as familiar to her now as her own. It was cold, the sweatshirt looked warm, so she shrugged into it, promising herself she'd ask Taryn about it when she woke. *Have to get this mess cleaned up. I can't be hopping around town in all the clothing of her former girlfriends*, Rosalind thought, then stopped. A huge grin worked itself across her face, met by the first rays of the sun coming in the window, striking her face.

Former girlfriends. Past tense. That part of Taryn's life was over. She was Taryn's girl now. She laughed, then covered her mouth at the thought. *I'm a grown woman, a professional. I've been married and divorced, for Christ's sake. There's no call for me to be weeding the wardrobe of my lover because I'm jealous of her former girlfriends*, Rosalind told herself reasonably, but it didn't help.

The language was silly, applied to her. Girl indeed. But there was fun in it. Play. She certainly wanted to lay some public claim to Taryn. *Wonder if I can make her wear my college ring on a chain around her neck?*

Rosalind glanced at the mattress, at the sleeping bulk of Taryn under the blankets, the shock of black hair against the pillow. She had the oddest urge to find a teddy bear and tuck it in with her. Taryn didn't seem like the teddy bear type, though. Nothing in her room was stuffed; a statue of a dancing Hindu god wasn't quite the same. She looked back at the sleeping Taryn and pictured a dog, a Lab, curled around her, head on the pillow, snoring away. It made her smile. She would have to get them a dog someday. Taryn had never had one.

She looked around the room for a stuffed anything, convinced she wouldn't find it. Something caught her eye on the floor of the closet, in the back. It looked like it had fallen off the shelf and laid there, forgotten, for a long time. What was it? A snake? An alligator? Rosalind fished it out and held it up by the wings. It wasn't plush, didn't have any fur, but it was made of cloth, and, when she squeezed it, Rosalind could feel the stuffing. It was a pterodactyl, something from a science museum gift shop, she thought. It wasn't cute or cartoonish, it looked rather naked in its ivory cloth skin and bat wings, but it was a toy. She returned to the mattress and tucked it in, setting its pointy head on the pillow next to Taryn. It would have to do, for now. Not a dog, but a start.

She pictured Taryn waking to coffee and found she liked the idea. She eased out of the bedroom and padded down the hall, past closed doors. The floor was familiar enough to her that she could manage it without creaking, a feat of no small skill. She snuck down the back staircase to the kitchen, listening for sounds of inhabitance. She heard nothing. Joe must not be up. Funny, she had expected him to be. Like a kitchen elf or a household god, he was always there, preparing something.

The party must have gone on late into the night, following the ritual. The kitchen was dark. Rosalind crossed to the wall of coffee mugs and turned on one of the overhead lights. It lit the center of the room, leaving both ends in elliptical shadows.

She spied the blue coffee pot on the shelf above the stove and reached for it, stretching up on her toes. There was a water purifier attached to the sink. She ran the water into the pot, enjoying the mechanics, and lit the flame on the cast-iron stove. She felt like Joe for a moment, savoring the joy of being the only one awake in a house full of people, knowing that she was preparing to surprise them when they woke.

"Coffee is in the fridge. Back of the top shelf." A voice from the darkness at the end of the room spoke, frightening Rosalind.

She whipped around, eyes wide. She wasn't alone. There, her eyes adjusting to the gloom, she saw a shape at the table at the end of the room. It was Rhea, sitting half in shadow. She leaned forward and rested her elbows on the table, a teacup clenched in her hands. She must have been there, in the dark, since Rosalind came into the kitchen. The thought unnerved her. "Been there long?" she asked, trying to keep her voice steady.

Rhea's face was in shadow, just catching splinters of light from above. "Long before you arrived," she said, and Rosalind knew she wasn't just talking about the kitchen.

Rhea reached behind her and turned on the light. The single bulb over the table revealed a weary looking woman in a brown robe, her hair in disarray. In the light of the kitchen, Rhea didn't look fierce; she looked haggard, worn.

She extended a hand to the chair opposite her. "Have a seat." Her voice was the only part of her that held her normal spark and emotion, layered in between the words. Rosalind found her feet moving. She sat at the table facing Rhea. Rhea sipped thoughtfully at her tea, watching Rosalind over the rim. "Making her coffee. That's good. She'll like that." Rhea squinted, crinkles appeared at the corners of her eyes. She looked long at Rosalind, then shook her head. "It's happened already," she said, to herself or to her teacup.

Rosalind knew she wasn't even in the conversation Rhea was having, but she wanted to be. She'd recovered from the shock of finding her sitting in the dark and calmed down, observing this woman. She saw the fragility of Rhea for the first time, like the brittleness of steel. *It's still bright, and hard, and sharp enough to lay you open to the bone if you grab it with naked hands, but a tap at the right angle will shatter it.* "What's happened?" Rosalind asked, proud to find her voice steady.

Rhea sipped her tea. "Her energy is all over your aura. Threaded through, actually. You couldn't tear them apart without causing damage."

"How do you know it's hers?" Rosalind asked, knowing she was leading up to the hard question. This cryptic conversation, in the semidarkness of early morning with the witch former lover of Taryn's, was taking on a life of its own.

Rhea smiled, deepening the wrinkles around her eyes. "There's none like her. You can't mistake that signature. And…it fits yours perfectly." Rhea's voice dipped down into sadness at this last admission.

Rosalind found the strength to ask what she wanted to know. "Why do you dislike me, Rhea?"

Rhea raised an eyebrow at her, then sighed and put the teacup down. "Your coffee is ready."

"I'd like it if you answered my question," Rosalind said, surprised at herself.

"No, you won't. But go get yourself a cup of coffee and come sit down. I'll tell you."

Rosalind did. She didn't hurry in pouring the coffee from the enameled pot into the blue glass mug with the gold stars. She didn't remember that it was Taryn's mug until she sat down, but Rhea did.

Her smile was secret and layered with bitterness. "If I had the luxury, I would hate you, Rosalind. But you are a part of someone I love, unto my own death. I know you, and so I fear you. I know who you are, and I know who you were. And I know what it means for Taryn that you've finally come back."

"I don't understand what you are saying," Rosalind said, and Rhea snorted.

"Don't be dense. You're thinking from your academic training. Stop. You're smarter than that. You always were too hung up on the formal organization of knowledge. If it wasn't written in the temple scrolls, it didn't exist under the sun. When you met Taryn, in the first moment, you knew her, yes?"

"I…yes. There was a recognition there," Rosalind admitted.

"So. Of course there was a recognition. She felt it too, she just likes to forget. It's harder for her. I saw it in her the next morning, when you first spent the night. You two have old, unfinished business. It's tangling you up."

"You mean reincarnation? Old souls, past lives, all of that?" Rosalind asked, afraid and terribly excited. She wasn't sure if she believed in any of it, but something in it spoke to her, called to that same part of her that was able to see the godhead in a snake in a dogwood tree. To her surprise, Rhea laughed.

"Taryn, an old soul? She's an eternal adolescent! No, you two only go back a few lives together. You are both fairly recent. We are going to play a game. I will begin a story; you will finish it, with whatever comes into your mind. Don't think about it, just speak." Rhea waited to see if she argued.

Rosalind sat back and curled her hands around Taryn's blue glass mug as if it were a talisman. There was a red candle burning on the table. When had Rhea lit that? The flames distracted her, making the room unreal as Rhea began to speak. Rosalind started to see the images Rhea invoked, between the dancing spatters of light.

"In a city of enameled tiles on mud brick walls, a city of heat and luxury in a barren waste, there was a certain gate. This gate was not one of the gates that arched above the main avenues that the army might march down, or the processions of the Goddess, or the retinue of the Great King. This was a side gate, a place that might be easily overlooked for its plainness in a city of beauty. The gate was unadorned, had no name. It faced west, in a city that looked to the east, out toward old trading routes no longer in fashion, out toward the hinterlands, out toward the yellow hills of the desert province. A woman came to that lonely gate, every morning before sunrise, and looked out to the west. Tell me about the woman," Rhea said, sitting back.

Rosalind hesitated, trying to pick up the thread of Rhea's story. Her mind wasn't focusing very well. The room had gone a shade of blue-black, like a night sky far away from city lights. Was that haze from the candle, or was it from the knot of bitter herbs smoldering in the copper dish?

Rhea waved at her impatiently. "Don't think! Tell the story that is in you."

Rosalind gave up trying to think and started speaking, letting the words surprise her as they came out of her mouth. There was a difference to the sound of her voice, a little like her mother's, or more like her grandmother's. "The woman went to the gate every morning because it was the last place she saw the person she loved. The gate was the place they said good-bye, before her lover left. Not death. Her lover was exiled, out into the desert. Someplace out in the yellow hills, her lover is waiting for her. They can't be together because of their status.

The woman is a priestess, her life is devoted to the Goddess. She's been trained for years and years in the temple and knows literature, philosophy, politics, theater. Priestesses pledge seven years of their life to serving the Goddess, and during that time, they belong to the people and cannot have lives outside the temple. But in a city of luxury, where love is all around her, she'd never known love. When love came to her, it was a complete surprise, something that threatened to tear down the structure of her whole life." Rosalind looked at Rhea and saw her grimace, as if in pain.

Rhea's voice had the same hazy quality to it as the air in the room, threaded with smoke. The story she told sounded so familiar to her, as if Rosalind had heard it as a young girl and was only now being reminded of the details. She could see the gate in the wall, could start to see the priestess who stood there every morning.

Rhea took up the story, weaving in strands of scarlet and vermilion. Rosalind could see the colors hanging in the air. "I will tell you of the priestess's lover. The Great King of the city had a dream that his newborn child must be raised and educated as a prince, or surely he and his city would fall. So the Great King took his daughter and gave her to her uncle, a retired general from the Goddess's army. The uncle, following his instinct, put the child into the hands of the first woman he met, out in the wasteland.

"This woman was a fortune-teller, a woman of old, wild magic, unregulated by the temple. The rural people came to her for charms and potions, for the reading of dreams and the laying of ghosts. When the uncle held out the child, wrapped in a simple soldier's cloak, the fortune-teller looked on her and knew this was her fate. She could feel the Wheel turn as she accepted the child and vowed to raise it in disguise, hiding even from the eyes of the gods.

"The fortune-teller knew two things about the fate of the child. The first, that it was royal, and so must receive the training and education that would befit a prince of the royal house. The second, the child must grow as the trickster gods grow, in disguise to deflect all ill luck. So the child from birth was raised as a boy. This disguise, it turned out, was no disguise at all. It rather followed the nature of the child's heart and revealed more than it concealed.

"Out in the desert, in the yellow hills, the handsome girl grew into a beautiful boy, her heart burning at her exile from the city she had never seen. She had been cared for by the fortune-teller from the beginning of her life, grown up in the same house with wild magic and spirits. Yet she had a restless nature and yearned for adventure, for danger and destruction. Her heart ached for something she could not name. The fortune-teller watched as the prince grew restless and felt fear. There was no standing in the way of the urging of the heart. Something larger than life called the prince back to the city.

"The fortune-teller knew that it was her fate to go, but she had come to love the prince beyond all sense, and so she grieved. With the madness of youth, the prince abandoned her exile and stole into the city. And what happened there?" Rhea said, stirring the dish of smoldering herbs with her teaspoon, in a slow, circular motion.

It drew Rosalind's eye, mesmerizing her for a moment. She set her hands flat out on the table, to make sure it wasn't spinning too. It was her turn to speak. She wasn't sure if she had started already.

"The priestess had a vision during the night of a black eagle rising to embrace the sun. The eagle had fallen in love with the Goddess in her solar aspect and went mad. The eagle flew into the heart of the sun, knowing that the single embrace would mean immolation. But for one moment, one perfect moment, the eagle knew divine love. When the priestess woke from this vision, she walked to the gate like a woman drunk on uncut wine. There, as the first rays of the sun struck the gate, a beautiful boy slipped into the city. The priestess took one look at the boy, at the handsome girl, and her heart fell at the prince's feet," Rosalind said, not recognizing her voice at all.

Rhea stood up and walked to the cast-iron stove. She reached up into the rafters, drawing down a knot of herbs hanging to dry. She crushed them, sniffed them, then sprinkled them over the copper dish. Rosalind watched the gray-green specks fall like rain into the embers as Rhea spoke.

"In this city, when a person fell in love, their friends would offer condolences and a hope for a speedy recovery. Love was rightly seen as a form of madness, a hunger that builds on what it seeks to devour. The hungriest heart is one that has never known its own appetite. The fortune-teller advised the prince against this affair. There are certain kinds of love that are sendings directly from the Goddess, a perfect balance between souls. The danger with these kinds of love is that they flare too hot for mortal flesh to contain, and they spill over, pulling with them destiny. The fortune-teller knew that this love might well alter the course of the Wheel of Fate. So she warned. Naturally the prince ignored her advice and ran with open arms toward the priestess."

Rosalind sat up. "The prince really loved the priestess. It wasn't just stubbornness on the prince's part. They were happy together."

"Of course they were happy together. That was the Goddess's gift to them. But the Goddess can be jealous as well as magnanimous, and the priestess belonged to Her. The gift had a price. The news of their affair got out, through various means. A satrap who yearned to overthrow the Great King of the city got the news and prepared to use it to destroy the prince, the priestess, and the king. He was very powerful, this satrap. He did not follow the Goddess of the city, and so he did not have the citizens' reverence for Her ways. He learned that the girl-prince was sneaking into the city to see the priestess, through that gate. He captured them and ordered them put to death, knowing it would break her father the Great King's heart. There was no hope." Rhea set her teacup down and leaned her arms on the table, staring into Rosalind's eyes, challenging her.

Something stubborn rose up in Rosalind, something that refused the story Rhea told. "But the prince's friend, the fortune-teller, loved her too much to let her die. She managed to smuggle word of the execution out of the satrap's palace, to the temple of the Goddess. The women of the temple told the army, and they marched on the satrap's palace in time to stop the execution."

Rhea shook her head. "Not in time to stop the execution. The archers had already fired their first arrows when the army came through the door. The fortune-teller knew that this love carried a price. Death had already visited that room, Death who is sister to the Goddess of the city. She cannot be denied. Who died?"

"The arrows were aimed at the prince. But the archer looked at the beautiful boy, and his hand shook. He was unable to get a clean shot. The arrow went wide," Rosalind said, desperately clutching Taryn's blue glass mug. She saw, again, the crow shift its clawed feet on the blue gravestone.

"You know better. You know that the archer's hand did not shake. You have the other memories. Tell the truth about this," Rhea said, acidly.

Rosalind felt a great weight pressing her down. She wanted to put her head down on the kitchen table. "No," she said, exhausted.

"Tell the truth about the arrow, Rosalind."

"It went right at the prince's throat. But..." Rosalind stopped, unable to speak.

"The fortune-teller could not see her die. While the priestess stood frozen, the friend saw Death reaching out for the prince. She did what must be done and stepped between the arrow and her throat. She did what the lover could not do. So Death had her portion, and the Wheel of Fate turned as it must," Rhea finished, sounding as weary as Rosalind. The smoke from the copper dish had dispersed, leaving only the single candle burning down into a puddle of red wax, congealing like blood on the table.

"But, I never—" Rosalind blurted out.

Rhea held up her hand. "You, no. The first of your line, yes. The woman who waited by the gate passed her blood down the ages. As did the prince, and her friend, who gave up her life. It's a cycle as old as the city of enameled tiles, now dust so long men do not remember her name. Great love leaves echoes. The women of your line have always loved the women of Taryn's. You carry the memories of your ancestors, and frankly I'm surprised at how clear they come through to you. Souls return again and again with the turning of the Wheel. When a single moment changes the direction of the Wheel, it spins off ripples that do not fade until they all meet the shore."

"You mean that the friend who saved the prince's life changed things. That it shouldn't have happened that way. We're still living out what happened then," Rosalind said. The story had the quality of fable; it was sufficiently outside of time that she didn't take it seriously. Her focus was starting to return, and with it came the warning of a headache. *Probably from those damn herbs Rhea burned.*

"Is that so odd? Children live out the mistakes of their parents, over and over, and pass them down to their own children. Families pass down quirks, habits, secrets. Souls pass on the same things to their kin. The Death was meant for the prince, the fortune-teller took it on, and so her family must now live it, again and again. The world is full of signs. I'm sure they've been trying to speak to you. You were born with two gifts. You come into the world knowing that love is waiting for you, and you recognize it when it arrives. She has what you need, and you have what she needs. You two have been lovers before, three times. You are both very young," Rhea said, wearily.

"How old are you, Rhea?" Rosalind asked, suddenly, feeling a chill pass through the kitchen, like a wind off a lake of ice.

Rhea opened her eyes, perhaps not expecting this question. "A woman of my line was in Babylon when Alexander rode in. She threw flowers before his golden chariot. I remember. A woman of my line saw Rome fall under the sandals of the Northern tribes. I remember. I saw Europe lit by fire and blood, one war or another. I am old enough. Women remember."

"Was the fortune-teller, your ancestor, the lover of the prince?" Rosalind asked without knowing why. It was important to know, even if it was before her time.

"For a moment, no longer. It was never meant to be. The priestess was meant to come and bring love like a gift to the prince. So the pattern was set in motion. The women of my line have always been irresistibly drawn to the women of her line, but we can never hold them. We are their teachers and healers when they are young, when their anger is the most alive part of them. But then we die. We have to, to make room for the women of your line to come. And you always come.

"There is more. Taryn told you I was supposed to be her mother this time around, yes? I was. I thought I could love her, teach her, and spare her pain that way. But she is Taryn. She is as stubborn a creature as any of her line since the first. She refused to come back, refused to get born into the flesh again, because of what you did to her."

Rosalind was shocked. "What I did to her? Not the first of my line?"

"You, Rosalind. Your soul, your new soul. Oh, it's a pattern as old as the first pair, true. But you betrayed her last time around. It was a hard time in history then, to be lovers and women. Not so long ago, really. I had already come and gone. She waited to meet you and she did, as magnets draw steel. You were lovers, for a short time. As I said, this was a hard time in history. You felt the weight of the world's hatred. You gave up and pulled back. The women of your line have always flinched at the last moment, and Rosalind is no different.

"You left her alone, after the bonding had happened. She's never been as strong as you are, you know. Her line is never as strong as yours. When you left her, told her never again, and married a man, she couldn't survive it. She killed herself. Go ahead, look horrified. She can't live without you, once she's met you. She never could. The original couldn't, either. You, the women of your line, give them life in a way no one else can. You can also take life away. She was so distraught, Taryn was, that she refused to come back. She missed the chance to be my daughter. She had to know that you were already here, in the world.

"She waited a decade and more just to be sure. You know, I thought I could protect her this time, change the direction of the Wheel of Fate. I thought you wouldn't show up, after…that. But you did, just like you always do, like the women of your line always have. Taryn's tied to you. She will never be free," Rhea finished, clenching her hands in her lap, looking away around the room.

Rosalind couldn't swallow, could barely breathe. After all her anger at the people who had hurt Taryn, her lover, now she found she was one of them. The one, from the sound of it. How much of this could she believe? Stories, fables. Hadn't love been a fable to her, until a few days ago?

"I…don't remember ever doing that to her. But if I did, I learned from it. I love her now, Rhea, with all my heart. I will never hurt her again." Rosalind found herself speaking with conviction, but didn't know where the conviction came from.

"Of course you love her. You have always loved her. Even women not soul-bonded to her fall in love with her easily, but the balance between you two is perfect. The pattern will keep repeating until the last echo of the first Death has settled, until the Wheel is free to turn again. The memory will be hazy for you for a bit, but it's woken up now. You'll start to see more and more of it.

"You know, we never did get along. How could we? The women of your line come and take from us all that we have ever valued. I let myself grow lazy this time, when so many things seemed different—Taryn's age, our ability to live as a family, Joe and Goblin. I've never had the chance to have a family of my own. I stopped watching to see if you were coming across the horizon, Death on your heels. But the Wheel turns.

"Old arguments, prayers, and invocations set against the ritual and direct action of street magic. Argue with me when you know what I say is true. I am not optimistic, Rosalind Olchawski. Prove me wrong." Rhea rose from the table and walked to the stove.

Rosalind sat, stunned, feeling the weight of history collapse on her. Something from the mass of information jumped out at her. "Rhea? You said that you...the women of your line die when, well—"

"When you show up. Before, usually. We can't stand the sight of you," Rhea said easily.

"Maybe that pattern is being broken, then...I mean..." Rosalind began, only to face Rhea's suddenly turned back.

"No."

"But, I'm here, and you..." Rosalind started, desperate to find a loophole.

"Are dying," Rhea said, putting the kettle on the flame. "She doesn't know. I would appreciate it if you didn't tell her yet." She turned to Rosalind, her face half in shadow. "Don't take her away. I know she's yours now. I have eyes. But Joe and Goblin will need her. Let her stay with the family." It was a request. Rhea had actually asked her for something, almost pleaded.

"Of course I won't take her away," Rosalind vowed.

Rhea smiled, just a little.

"Why don't you tell all this to Taryn?"

Rhea looked at her steadily, until Rosalind dropped her eyes. "Go ahead. Go ahead and tell her everything, not just the ancient bond. Remind her of what you, Rosalind, did to her last time around. I guarantee that you will lose her in the next breath. I don't think you're willing to risk that. You have a set amount of time with her, Rosalind, as do I. I will allow you your time. Allow me mine. Accept what Fate has given you. Silence is the price of love. I will be kind. I have prepared it so that you won't remember this talk with me." Rhea blew out the red candle.

Footsteps came creaking down the back stairs. Joe ambled into the room, his masculine presence altering the space that had grown up between the women. He waved at Rosalind, then crossed behind Rhea, lifting her hair and kissing her neck. "You were up early," he said in his burring voice.

"Couldn't sleep," Rhea said, accepting his caress.

"The season's changing. It always affects you," Joe said, smiling at Rosalind. He took over the space in front of the stove, moving into his accustomed place as if it were his kingdom. The skillet began to heat, the knife danced in his fist, the edge blurring with the speed. Rhea sat down at the table again, watching Joe.

Rosalind saw her face soften, saw the hard lines ease away when she looked at the man cooking breakfast. It was a look of love, of relaxation, that she was starting to recognize. Joe gave Rhea a place in the world to rest; she could see it. Rosalind shook her head, not sure where her headache was coming from. She and Rhea had been talking about something. It had gotten her upset, but she was having trouble remembering exactly what it had been. It was about Taryn, it had to be. There was a picture in her mind of a handsome black-haired girl leaning in a doorway, smiling with an arrogant charm.

The thought of Taryn asleep upstairs made her ache. She wanted Taryn next to her; she needed to feel Taryn's living warmth after everything Rhea had said. The feeling became intense, as if she wouldn't survive if she didn't have Taryn's skin on hers. Rosalind pushed back from the table, fighting down the rising panic. Taryn was fine. She was just upstairs asleep. What Rhea had told her might be true, or it might not. But Rosalind refused to believe it until she saw for herself. A door might open at any moment, sweeping the girl away from her, into the darkness. She had to get to Taryn before she woke without her and thought she was gone. She headed for the stairs, starting to run. Rosalind rounded the corner to the back stairs and came crashing into Taryn, who had just descended them.

Taryn rocked back on her heels from the impact. "Whoa! What's the hurry, chief?" she asked, holding the wall to steady herself.

Rosalind saw her, heard her voice, but it wasn't enough. She threw her arms around Taryn's long body, burying herself against her chest. Her head burrowed into her neck, seeking the warmth of her skin over the collar of her flannel shirt, lips parted, seeking the life vein. She felt the hot tears against her eyelids, moved beyond reason at the thought of Taryn being alive, here, now.

Rosalind collapsed against Taryn and just clung to her, not speaking. She felt Taryn close her arms around her, exerting her strength. She felt safe here, in the circle of Taryn's arms. Rosalind didn't know why it mattered so much, but when Taryn flexed her arms, drawing Rosalind in, she gave a small, choked sound that might have been a sob.

"Don't cry, angel. Whatever it is, I'll fix it," Taryn said, brushing her cheek against her lover's hair.

It was too much—the confirmation of Taryn's warmth, the pulse of the blood in her veins, the sound of her voice, pitched low and close.

It undid Rosalind. "I just love you too much," she said into the front of Taryn's shirt.

She could hear the smile in Taryn's voice when she responded. "Never too much. Not from you."

"How can you know that?" Rosalind asked, raising her head. She saw Taryn's face suffused with emotion, like the light of the sun showing through clear marble. It trembled on her lips, the whole story that Rhea had passed on to her, the history of love and death, betrayal and sacrifice. She couldn't bear the thought of the love in Taryn's eyes turning into something else. The words died on her lips. Silence is the price of love, Rhea's voice said to her. A haze-like smoke filled her head. She couldn't think. What had Rhea been saying to her? "Sorry. Guess I'm just feeling a little emotional this morning," Rosalind said, wiping tears away with the back of her hand.

"Guess I'm a little emotional too," Taryn said, kissing her. They leaned against the wall, blocking the narrow staircase, until Joe poked his head around the corner.

"Breakfast!" he called over them, up the stairs.

"Don't you ever knock?" Taryn complained, tearing her lips away from Rosalind's.

"On a staircase? Please. You have public sex, you invite public participation." He managed to duck back around the corner before Taryn's lashing hand caught him.

Footsteps answered his shout, and Goblin came down the stairs. She saw the obstacle in her way, saw that neither woman looked like she was going to move, so she stepped over them, squeezing between Rosalind and the wall. "Gangway."

"Can somebody use the front stairs, please?" Taryn yelled, her head back against the peeling plaster wall.

Laurel, from the top of the stairs, stopped in her tracks. She turned around with a reproving look and headed down the hall.

"We should move, baby," Rosalind said, leaning back against Taryn. She didn't want to move. She wanted to stay suspended with Taryn in the hallway.

"I'll move when I damned well feel like it." Taryn tucked her lover into her arms and closed her eyes, ignoring the noise and chaos of the house. Moments like this needed to be stolen from the day at all cost. They wouldn't last forever.

They ate in the kitchen, at last. Taryn stood in her accustomed spot with her back to the counter. Rosalind sat on a stool next to her, one hand hooked in Taryn's belt loop. She felt more normal now, convinced of Taryn's presence. The mundane world was pushing the conversation with Rhea away. The witch gave her a single look when she came back into the kitchen, seeming to read something in her face, perhaps seeing the complicit silence. Neither woman looked at the other again.

The mystery was hard to hold on to, in the warm kitchen full of people talking and eating. Joe continued to provide a mix of food and entertainment, handing off plates as he got them filled. Taryn made a move toward the stove for coffee, but Rosalind's hand on her belt loop restrained her. Taryn looked at her, quizzically.

"I have your mug," she admitted, holding up the blue glass.

"We can share," Taryn said. She raised an eyebrow at Joe, who immediately strolled over with the coffee pot.

He refilled the mug without comment, but Goblin, seeing this, stopped eating. "You're sharing your coffee mug?" she asked, fork frozen in midair.

"Yeah," Taryn said, letting Rosalind sip from it.

"Great Goddess! Taryn's in love!" Goblin crowed.

"Knock it off, Goblin," Laurel said, elbowing her.

"Come on. Has Taryn ever, in the forever she's lived here, let anyone ever touch that mug? You know I'm right. It must be love. It's a sign, like the Virgin Mary appearing in a doughnut," Goblin said to Laurel and Rhea.

"It is. She's my girl," Taryn said quietly. All other sound in the room abruptly stilled. She took the mug from Rosalind's hands, sipping her coffee in the silence of the kitchen.

Goblin got up from the table and went over to Rosalind. She threw her arms around the surprised woman, hugging her. "Welcome to the family!"

Joe patted her on the back. "Honey, go sit down. We don't want to overwhelm Rosalind," he said, looking at the woman. He knew it was sudden; he didn't want to scare her off, push her too far with their welcome.

To his relief, Rosalind smiled at him from over his daughter's narrow back. "It's fine. Thank you, Goblin. That means a lot to me," she said, returning the hug.

Goblin smiled at her before sitting back down.

"Wow, T," Laurel said, looking to her housemate.

"You people act like I've never said that before," Taryn said, hiding behind the mug. She raised her arm and wrapped it around Rosalind's shoulders, a gesture not lost on anyone watching.

"You haven't," Rhea said, in a tone that brooked no argument.

Rosalind could read the look on her face and tried to understand the mix of grief, affection, and weariness. It was a hard combination to face, but Rosalind didn't look away.

"Oh, no," Goblin said.

"What's wrong?" Joe asked her, his attention pulled away from the look passing between Rhea and Rosalind.

"T, have you forgotten about the auction?"

"Shit," Taryn groaned, and closed her eyes.

It was a welcome distraction from the depths of Rhea's eyes, from the pain that was starting to knife into her head whenever she tried to think. "What auction?" Rosalind asked.

"It's a fundraiser for Community AIDS Services. Egyptia and some of the queens came up with the idea. They're having this Bachelor Auction. You know, bid on a date with some volunteers, the money goes to CAS, the highest bidder gets a date with their choice. It's mostly guys, but with the way people have been responding to me at Marcella's, she wanted to try a drag king," Taryn said, trying to sound offhand.

"They're auctioning you off for charity?" Rosalind asked, in the most interested tone of voice.

"A night with me. Not like that! Just a date. Dinner," Taryn finished weakly.

"I know how dinner with you can go, Defiler," Rosalind said, her tone dipping into dangerous territory.

"I agreed to this before I met you! It's for charity," Taryn mumbled, looking away.

"I'm playing with you, baby. You can do anything you want."

"You're okay with me going on a date with someone else?" Taryn asked, anger creeping into her voice.

"Did I say that? No, I'm far too reactionary to be okay with you dating anyone else. I'm okay with you volunteering to help Egyptia with the fundraiser. I'm going to be front row center, with the biggest pile of cash in the known world," Rosalind said, taking the coffee mug from Taryn's hands. She smiled at Taryn from over the rim. They became aware of the rapt attention from everyone else in the kitchen, watching them like a tennis match.

"You can go back to eating now," Taryn growled.

"This is much more interesting," Joe said, ignoring Taryn's evil look.

❖

It was like tearing off her own skin, when Rosalind finally made the move toward the door. Taryn didn't want to help, so she didn't. She kept distracting Rosalind with everything she could think of, and succeeded, for another hour and a half. Finally Rosalind begged for mercy, and Taryn relented, walking her to the front steps. She hung her head, refusing to let go of Rosalind's waist. "You sure you want to leave?" she asked again.

Rosalind's eyes snapped open. She grabbed Taryn and hugged her hard enough to crush the breath from her lungs. "I never want to leave. But I have to. I have to get ready for class. My brother's coming into town tonight. I'll see you at seven."

"It's too long," Taryn said stubbornly.

"You have to work out with Joe, I heard you promise him. And you should have some time to yourself. We were able to manage as quite independent people, oh, three or four days ago. We can do this," Rosalind said with a smile in her voice.

"I don't want to manage. I want to drown in you. I want to keep you under me until I don't know if it's my blood or yours running in my veins," Taryn said, her eyes pinning Rosalind. "I love you. It's like saying the world is round. The words aren't big enough anymore."

Rosalind ran her fingers through the spiky black hair still disordered from their passion. She touched the back of her hand to Taryn's cheek. "I never thought I'd be standing with my lover, looking into her devastating eyes, after a night like the one we just spent. I love you too, Taryn. The words aren't big enough."

❖

Back at her apartment, Rosalind opened the door to a swirl of dust and a handful of leaves, like opening the door to an abandoned house. She must have left a window open, she thought. Dust didn't have time to gather in her apartment before she eradicated it. The air was cool, hanging without movement, undisturbed by life. It was too much like the air in a tomb, and it brought back a snippet of conversation she'd had with Rhea. It was like trying to catch the shadow of a hummingbird in her bare hand, recalling what had been said. Rosalind concentrated, but it only made her head ache.

The blinking light on her answering machine told her that someone in the world loved her, outside of the house at 34 Mariner. It was a strange thing to be reminded of. Was it only Wednesday now? How could her whole life have changed so quickly? She'd gone to Marcella's on Friday night, the blind date with Greg. Rosalind smothered a giggle at that memory. The poor man, having his date stolen away from him. She felt a moment of sympathy for him, Taryn's love making her feel expansive. It would be a crime if people lived and died without feeling the way she felt now.

Rosalind hit the button and walked into the kitchen, throwing her keys on the counter.

The long beeeeep sounded, then Ellie's voice poured into the living room. "It's me. It's Tuesday. You didn't call me on Monday, so I guess you went ahead with the plan to entrap Elvis. Let me know how the Wild Kingdom is going, Marlon Perkins. I'll be right behind you with the tranquilizer gun. Say hi to Eric for me. Wednesday, right? I have class, but thanks for the invite. He's a doll. To bad he's taken. Sigh. Love you."

Beeeeep. "Rosalind, this is Dr. Grey. Please call me."

Beeeeep. "So, I was asking my students, what is the definition of absence? We decided it was when someone you love doesn't call you for three days in a row when you leave them countless messages. I've got it! You haven't called because aliens have kidnapped you and are performing unspeakable acts on your body. One alien, at least, and I'll bet it's unspeakable." Ellie's voice chided her from the machine.

Beeeeep. "Hey, Sis. Sandhya and I will see you at seven. Anchor Bar good? Bye." It was her brother's voice, surprisingly like hers, even with the depth of it. She smiled to hear it.

Eric had been her best friend growing up, so much so that when Rosalind went away to college, he'd taken it as a personal abandonment. She'd missed his high school years, seeing him only in snapshots of visits home. When she'd left Poughkeepsie, he'd been an awkward, gangly boy in the full horror of adolescence. In a matter of visits he'd grown tall, filled out, his body transformed into a hulking young man. The boy she remembered, who couldn't wait to tell her everything about his friends, his projects, the books he read, was now unable to more than grunt when he shambled through the room.

It had been as personal a betrayal to her, his journey into his teenage years. It was a foreign place. Suddenly her wisdom no longer had any bearing on his experiences. Her advice was less than useless. A teenage boy has no use for an older sister, particularly one who was too bookish to offer sound dating advice.

It wasn't until she was at Cornell, buried in her PhD, that she'd gotten to know him again. He'd gone off to college a few months before. Rosalind remembered seeing him off with the awkward one-armed hug that her family employed for public leave-taking. She'd returned to Ithaca, the sadness old enough now that she didn't feel it as a fresh loss. Her baby brother was leaving to find himself, outside of Poughkeepsie. If he'd asked, she might have been able to identify the depth of the stabbing pain that took her breath, just for a moment. He didn't ask, and she had stopped offering.

The phone call at midnight was unusual. For a moment she thought it was Paul. He was off visiting his family, making plans for their wedding in the spring. The male voice was ripping with excitement, a voice strange enough to her that she couldn't place it until he said her name. "Ros? It's Eric." The first thought was, *Disaster.*

"Are you okay?" Rosalind had blurted out, unable to think of another reason he'd be calling her. He laughed. It was the first time she'd ever heard that laugh from him, a man's laughter.

"Yeah, I'm okay. Better than okay. Ros, I'm in love."

The story had poured out of him in a rush, while Rosalind sat listening with a stunned tenderness. Who was this gregarious young man, his conversational skills unleashed by falling in love? He'd met Sandhya Bharadwaj in a computer science class. They ended up in the same study group. They'd started e-mailing one another. Joy made hash of the story. Eric threw details in at random, conveying his delight with everything about this girl.

"She's gorgeous. She's brilliant. She's gorgeous. She can seem so nice and sweet, then cut you to ribbons and you won't even see it coming," Eric had said, reeling on the line like a drunken Boy Scout.

"She sounds wonderful. When do I get to meet her? Are you going to bring her home for Thanksgiving?"

"No. That's kinda why I called," Eric had said.

Rosalind, who had been delighted with the sound of Eric's voice, listened to it go flat in a heartbeat. "Tell me what's up," she'd said to the man who was still her baby brother.

There was a moment of silence, then Eric began. "I was gonna bring her home for Thanksgiving. I mean try, anyway. I called home. I told Mom about Sandhya. Well, you know Mom. She didn't take it well that Sandhya's Indian. Gave me the minispeech about dating suitability, all that shit. So I said I'm not coming home without her. Can we stay with you?"

There had been things she could have said—her place was very small, she was working all the time, she and Paul were planning their wedding. Rosalind said yes without hesitation.

It had been the start of years of campaigning. Rosalind had gotten to know Sandhya and had been charmed to the core. Eric was a different person around this fiercely intelligent young woman. Sandhya argued with him, challenged him, and looked at him with a tenderness Rosalind could not believe. She'd taken up the banner for them before the first afternoon was over.

It had been Rosalind's idea to approach their mother, to spend countless hours gently talking her into meeting Sandhya. Olchawskis were known for their stubbornness. In the end, when Eric and Sandhya showed no signs of breaking up after years together, their mother had come around.

Wonder if Eric would go to bat for me now? Their mother had been heartbroken by her divorce from Paul. She hadn't asked Rosalind if she were dating anyone since the divorce became final. There hadn't been anyone worth mentioning.

Now, she felt like Eric in that midnight phone call—overwhelmed with emotion, unable to believe the miracle that had struck. She was in love. It was stunning enough that she wanted to tell someone, everyone, to alert the world to what had happened. She wanted to share the happiness that threatened to rip her apart. It was that fierce and immediate. She finally understood Eric's need to talk about it. Her heart was outside her body.

The phone rang. Rosalind, chilled by the emptiness of her

apartment, dove for it. Funny how she had just spent all morning saying good-bye to a certain someone, but was still hoping she was calling. "Hello?" she asked in a tone that added darling, and it's about time.

"No, it's not loverboy. Lovergirl. Just your poor neglected best friend in all the world. You gonna be home for a bit?"

"Sure," Rosalind said, glad to hear Ellie's voice. Her own life was surrounding her again, making her feel more at home. She was loved, out in the world. It was good to remember. Meeting Taryn had thrown the moments of genuine affection in her life into high relief. She could see the rarity and treasure in each of them now.

"I'll be right over. I have a present for you," Ellie said, a smirk in her voice that came right across the phone line.

Ellie walked into the apartment five minutes later, carrying boxes. "Go sit," she ordered, and breezed into the kitchen.

Rosalind did, sitting on the couch. "What are you doing?" she called, but Ellie ignored her.

"Close your eyes."

Rosalind did, resisting the urge to peek. She heard Ellie come closer, then something landed on the coffee table.

"Open 'em," Ellie commanded.

Rosalind did, and saw a cake. It was chocolate, with tiny red roses sculpted of candy trimming it. Candles were lit around the edges. Rosalind's brow wrinkled. It wasn't her birthday, not even close. She peered at the cake, seeing the lettering for the first time. **Good For You! You're Gay!** it read in a cheerful scrawl.

"Ellie!" she said, half shocked, half delighted.

Ellie dropped down on the couch next to her. "Hey, I watched Ellen. I know what this calls for. Blow out the candles. You disappear for three days, not a word, then you come back quiet as a cat, with a smile on your face that makes me die of envy. You need a new leather jacket, don't you? Thought so. I'm hardly ever off the mark with this." She shook her blond head and handed Rosalind the knife. "Cut the cake."

"You are too much," Rosalind said, making the first cut.

"So did you spend the last few days rolling around with lovergirl or not?" Ellie asked, accepting a slab of cake.

"Yes, as I'm sure you know," Rosalind admitted around a mouthful of cake.

"I only ask because my own life is so sad and drab, I envy you your new distraction."

"She asked me to be her girl," Rosalind said, grinning like a fool.

"How very 1950's. She's been watching too many Elvis films. You said, 'No, I couldn't. I'm in mourning for my failed marriage. I have too much work to do. I couldn't possibly have a life too.'"

"I said yes. I said I loved her."

Ellie held up her hand. "That sounds serious. No serious until after cake and presents. Then we can do serious." She plucked the box from the table and handed it to Rosalind.

"Purple tissue paper? That's not like you."

"Lavender. It sets the mood. It's a theme present."

Rosalind undid the ribbon with the cake knife, getting frosting on the paper that she ripped away in one healthy swipe, then opened the box.

"It's a Lesbian Starter Kit. I talked to a dyke in the theater department, and she gave me a list of things no beginning lesbian should be without," Ellie narrated, as Rosalind held up each item. "One Melissa Etheridge CD, any one at all. One scented lavender Goddess candle. One brochure to the Michigan Womyn's Music Festival, note spelling of Womyn's. A copy of *Rubyfruit Jungle*, a videotape of *Desert Hearts*, one of *Claire of the Moon*, but you can only watch that one stoned. A reading list: Judy Grahn, Paula Gunn Allen, Dorothy Allison, Minnie Bruce Pratt, Joan Nestle. The phone number of the Lesbian Herstory Archives. And a gift certificate for Taryn. For a toaster."

It was the toaster that did it. Picturing the household congratulating Taryn on another successful conversion, then picturing Taryn walking casually to a closet, where she kept her hundreds of toasters stacked like Legos, just broke Rosalind up. She laughed until tears ran from her eyes, until her ribs ached and she couldn't see. She collapsed against Ellie's shoulder, both of them too hysterical to talk for minutes.

When she could draw in a breath, her sides felt sore. "You're the best. You know that? A good-for-you cake, for Christ's sake. Where's all the oppression and hatred I'm supposed to get?"

"It'll come, don't go looking for it. But what they don't tell you is one, how much darn fun it can be, and two, how some people get over it quickly. If they let everyone know that, lots more people might come pouring out of the closet, and then where would the world be?" Ellie exhaled and patted Rosalind's leg. "She's a lucky butch to land you. Does she know that?"

"I think so," Rosalind said shyly.

"The cake is done, the presents opened. We can do serious now. She asked you to be her girl. Not to throw a bucket of cold water on your new flame, but what does lovergirl mean by that? She wants a steady fuck for a few weeks, she wants to wear your ring, something in between? How serious does this girl get?"

"She didn't seem like the type to get serious at all when we met. But…she's so intense. It's like we can't bear to be apart, even for a few hours. She's in love with me," Rosalind said, pride in her voice.

"Snaps for taste, at least. You think you two might last?"

Rosalind looked down into her lap, at her folded hands, then back up into her friend's face. She nodded, unable to speak.

"Then I get best-friend rights. I get to grill her extensively on her intentions—how she plans on treating you, who she thinks she is to waltz right offstage and grab the best woman in Buffalo." Ellie's tone was indignant, comic, but there was something else to it.

"Do you believe in love at first sight?" Rosalind asked. She halfway expected a flippant answer, but she didn't get one.

"I'd like to. I'd like to think the world is a good enough place for things like that to happen. If I did believe in it, I'd say you guys had a case." Ellie ran a hand through her hair. "Confession time. I don't think I've ever been in love, not the way you seem to be. Three days and BAM, you're certain she's the one. I've had some wonderful affairs, a good relationship or two. But I've never felt that he's 'the one.' I don't know if there *is* a one for me. Maybe not everyone has that out there waiting for them. So, on behalf of the disillusioned romantics of the world, don't squander this. It might be rarer than you think."

"Oh, Ellie."

"Don't you 'Oh, Ellie' me. I'm being honest with you, rare for an actress. I'm envious. I'd give my right arm to have someone drive me crazy. But you know what? If it could have been a woman for me, it'd have been you."

Ellie said this, then looked down at the cake, at the ruins of the lavender tissue paper. Rosalind looked at her friend, then leaned in and kissed her on the cheek. She sat with her head on Ellie's shoulder, in silence, as they both adjusted to what had been said.

"Do you believe in reincarnation?" Rosalind asked, at last. Something from her conversation with Rhea was itching at her mind, a thought that kept spinning just out of reach.

"I think souls travel in groups, like field hockey teams. You usually end up knowing the same people over and over. I've known you before. Minute I met you, I felt it. Like, this woman is cool. You can tell her anything, and it'll seem like you already have. Conversational déjà vu," Ellie said, with a trace of her humor returning.

"Why does that sound familiar?"

Ellie's head perked up. "Déjà vu sounding familiar? Very funny."

"No, it's not a joke. Damn this headache. It makes it so hard to focus." Rosalind rubbed her temple with her right hand.

"Too much sex. Gives you a headache every time," Ellie said in her best talk-show-host voice.

"I have not had too much sex. I think Rhea put a spell on me," Rosalind complained, leaning back down on Ellie's shoulder.

"Rhea the witch guardian angel. Oooh, this'll be good. She jealous? Elvis hard to let go of?"

"I don't know. I'm sure Taryn would be hard to let go of. I don't plan on finding out. Rhea and I had some sort of heart-to-heart in the kitchen this morning, and I can't seem to remember much of it." Heart-to-heart. Rosalind pictured, for one wild moment, a beating heart sitting in a copper dish, torn from the body that housed it. She saw another heart, blue and throbbing, placed next to it. She shuddered down to her marrow, disturbed by the uninvited image.

"You know, blue agave has that effect on me. I just never thought of blaming it on a hex before."

"Not a hex. A warding. First time I showed up in the backyard, she asked if she'd have to set a warding on me. What's a warding?"

"Something the Academy does."

"I'm serious. You know more about this than I do."

Ellie considered this and didn't seem to think it was a strange turn for the conversation to take. Perhaps they discussed this sort of thing in the theater department all the time. "It's a protection against something, a warning. Usually put on a house to keep unwanted things out."

Rosalind shook her head. "Charming. Rhea wants to keep me out of the house. She's put up psychic no-pest strips."

Ellie smiled in approval. "That was really funny. The headache is good for your sense of humor, at least. Try some caffeine, and a few minutes lying down in a dark room. Good for spell recovery and migraines. I've got to go, sweetie. Acting 108. I'm teaching them how to be chairs today." Ellie stood up from the couch and stretched her arms over her head.

"How do you be a chair?"

Ellie looked at her with a grave, still expression. "First, you meditate on the essence of a chair. Then you bring that primal 'chairness' into form. You become the chair. Plays are just real life on stage," Ellie intoned.

"Do they ever ask you why you make them do these things? My freshmen always fight me about writing exercises." Rosalind's headache was subsiding to a dull throb.

"Nah. I have them play freeze-tag on the first day of class. After that, they accept anything I tell them to do. Tell Eric I said hey. And call me, for anything," Ellie said over her shoulder as she left.

It was six thirty when Eric rang the bell, as Rosalind knew it would be. She and her brother shared a family passion for being early to everything. Friends grew used to it, automatically deducting half an hour from the time the Olchawskis promised to arrive and adding an hour to invitation times. It almost evened the trait out. She went to her window and tossed her keys down to him. He caught them one-handed, displaying an athletic grace that belied his day job.

Rosalind heard him opening the door seconds later and knew he'd jogged up the stairs. He entered the apartment, his face dappled red from the exertion, a smile creasing his cheeks. That smile, and his eyes, were the only indication that he and Rosalind shared blood. He towered over her, standing six two; his hair was a soft, dusty brown like the pelt of a deer. His stint in the army reserves had left him with a solid frame and a penchant for crew cuts. He looked like a hearty farm boy, handsome in an unfinished way, ready to extend his hand to anyone. At twenty-eight, he still had the energy of a teenager.

Eric hugged Rosalind, engulfing her. "You look great. What have you been up to?" he asked her, holding her by the shoulders and looking her over.

Behind him, Sandhya entered the apartment at a dignified walk, having foregone running up the stairs. Sandhya was Eric's physical opposite. Only Rosalind's height, graceful as a dancer, where he was rough, explosive. She wore her black hair loose to her shoulders, a fall of jet silk with highlights like water.

Where Eric was ruddy and fair, she was brown and gold, and her smile had the prescience of a gift carefully bestowed on worthy subjects. She was gorgeous enough to instill hatred in women and envy in men, but managed to treat her beauty as a minor fact of her being, behind the force of her intellect and personality. It was a devastating combination.

"Hi," Sandhya said, taking Rosalind away from Eric and hugging her. "You know that all he's talked about all day is having wings with you. It's not like we don't have wings in Rochester."

"Yeah, but they aren't Buffalo wings. And how often do we get to see Ros?"

"I'm glad you guys are early. There's something I wanted to talk to you both about."

Eric frowned, and his whole face became a comic mask. "You in trouble? You need money?" he asked immediately. Sandhya put a hand on his arm, and he quieted down.

"No, no trouble. Maybe you'd better sit down." Rosalind led them to the living room. Eric sat on the edge of the couch, his elbows on his knees, his brow wrinkled in concern. Sandhya was calm, one hand resting on his back, granting Rosalind space for whatever she needed to say. "We're having company for dinner," Rosalind began, then wished she'd picked another way to say it.

"What, that's all? Ellie, right? She's always invited. Jeez, you had me worried it was—" Eric said, but Sandhya gracefully halted him.

"I don't think that's it, sweetie."

"Oh. Guess who's coming to dinner?"

"There's something I want to tell you guys, but it's not coming out well. I've met…there's this person. I'm madly…Remember back when you broke it to Mom and Dad that you were dating Sandhya, and it was serious?"

Comprehension showed on Sandhya's face, but Eric broke into a broad grin.

"You're dating a Bengali woman and can't break it to us?" he said with a laugh.

"Half right," Rosalind said softly.

"You're dating a Bengali guy?" Eric said, confused.

"I think she means the other half is right," Sandhya said, her eyes gentle on Rosalind.

"You're dating a woman? Whoa," Eric said, rocking back on the couch.

"Yes, I am." Dating seemed an odd word to apply to her relationship with Taryn. Do you date a tornado, or do you get swept away? Dating sounded so civilized, so removed from the truth. She wanted to say, I met Desire in the form of a handsome girl and surrendered to it. I left my heart like an offering before the divine fire, and like the phoenix, I was immolated and reborn. The words were bubbling up in the brain, old words she might have heard once. The headache slashed at them, shredding the thought.

"Are you happy?" Sandhya asked, and Rosalind looked at her gratefully.

"Happier than I think I've ever been. I'm in love with her." The headache receded when she spoke of the present, when she kept her thoughts narrowed down to the last few days.

"So we get to meet her?" Sandhya asked.

"I invited her to come to dinner with us. I should warn you, she's a little younger than I am. A lot younger, actually. And she'll be very nervous to meet you, so I wanted to get you ready. You aren't saying much. Are you...okay?" Rosalind asked Eric.

He sat, his forehead wrinkled up, his eyes wide. "How come you haven't mentioned it before?"

"It's pretty new. I wanted to talk to you in person, and it worked out that you were coming into town for dinner."

"Am I okay? I just found out my sister is a dyke. Yeah, I guess I'm okay, but jeez, why didn't you ever talk to me about it? Didn't you think you could trust me? After everything I went through with the folks over Sandhya, I guess I thought you'd open up to me."

"That's what's bugging you?" Rosalind asked, carefully.

"Ros, you really think I care who you sleep with? I'm glad you found someone who makes you happy. I wish you'd trusted me enough to tell me."

"Would it help if I said I'd only been seeing her since Friday?"

Eric's head snapped up. "Yeah, it would help," he said, his smile returning. "Waaait a minute. You've only been seeing her since Friday, and you're in love? You're not easy, are you, Ros?"

She smacked him on the arm, so relieved that she nearly cried. "I'm easy, but I'm not cheap. Unlike some people I could mention."

"Too bad you didn't figure this out earlier. I could have gotten mileage off this with the guys in drill. My sister, the hot lesbian." His smile was evil.

"Eric, that's enough," Sandhya said.

"So what's her name? Let me guess, Monique? Genevive? Buffy?"

"You're thinking in 1-900 numbers again," Sandhya said, pushing him.

"Her name is Taryn. And I think you're in for a bit of a surprise."

CHAPTER EIGHT

Eric, I want you to be nice to her. I mean it," Rosalind said, turning around to face her brother. She'd convinced Eric and Sandhya to go in her car to pick up Taryn and was now regretting it. From the way Eric was sprawled too casually across the back seat, arm around Sandhya's shoulders but eyes fixed on the window, Rosalind was afraid of his interest. What in the world would he make of Taryn?

"I'll be nice to her. She's just a kid, right? I won't scare your girlfriend off."

"That's not what I'm worried about," Rosalind muttered to herself.

Rosalind parked in front of 34 Mariner, behind Joe's red behemoth of a car. She hoped she'd get a chance to go inside and see Taryn privately, even for a moment, but there she was sitting on the porch, talking to Joe. Her head was turned. Rosalind caught a glimpse of her sharp profile, the curve of her neck, the tattoo of the eagle embracing the sun above her shirt collar. She was wearing one of Joe's blue shirts, open at the neck, tucked into a pair of black pants that disguised her hips.

She was saying something to Joe that looked serious; her brows were drawn down. Rosalind got just that glimpse of her and felt her heart expand. Merely looking at Taryn did the most interesting things to her. What would it be like sitting next to her all night, in a restaurant, in front of her brother? Ellie's warning to savor it came back to her. It had only been a day, not even a full day, but the sight of Taryn was like water—clear, brilliant, and shining, a relief her body craved. She took the moment to taste her presence, loving her; then Taryn's head turned, and the blue eyes found her.

There was no one else on the porch, on the street, in the city. Only her lover, whose expression made it plain that the sun shone only in Rosalind's direction.

Rosalind started walking to the steps, pulled on by that look. It took her a moment to recognize the sound of a car door slamming; Eric was right behind her. Taryn stood, brushing dust from her pants. She met them at the foot of the steps, pausing like a leopard on a hillside.

She didn't reach out to Rosalind the way she usually did, though her hands began the motion. She checked, awkward, and held herself away. "Hi," she said to Rosalind, lifting her hand in an unfinished gesture that might have ended in a handshake or a caress.

It broke Rosalind's heart, the thought behind it, the fear. Taryn was holding back in front of her brother, for her benefit. Rosalind got the feeling that it was something Taryn had never done and had no interest in learning to do, but was trying to do for her. Taryn was protecting her from any displays of emotion in front of Eric.

It would be easier for Eric to have a chance to get to know Taryn, to get used to seeing them together, before they displayed any public affection. Rosalind knew that this was the sensible and humane thing to do. After all, he hadn't asked to know that his sister was dating a girl. It was the calm, rational, adult, and understanding way to break the reality of her emotional life to her family, even her beloved brother. No sense in shoving it down his throat by greeting Taryn like she normally would, was there?

Taryn's awkward approach signaled her willingness to play along. Rosalind could relax. Taryn wouldn't cross any boundaries in front of her family. There would be time to talk about it later, undo the damage of hiding.

Rosalind moved with a speed that would make a striking snake proud. She slid an arm around Taryn's neck and kissed her surprised lover with a passion that Joe hadn't even seen. Taryn's hands were held out away from Rosalind's body as if afraid to come in contact, but she kissed the woman back.

Joe caught Eric's eye and smiled. "I'm Joe. Taryn's housemate." He held out his hand and firmly shook Eric's.

"Eric. Ros's brother." He managed to take his eyes off the spectacle in front of him and look at the man he was talking to. Eric felt a sense of relief immediately. From his build to his stance, Joe was military. An understanding passed between them when Joe took in Eric's haircut, his size. Eric widened his own stance automatically and held his shoulders back.

"Rosalind is great. We're very fond of her here," Joe said amiably.

"I can see that," Eric said. His sister was sucking the tonsils out of Taryn, who looked to him like a boy.

"So, where are you guys thinking of going for dinner? Care for one?" Joe asked, pulling a cigar out of his shirt pocket.

"No, thanks. Anchor Bar. I like hitting it whenever we're in town."

"Great wings. Though I've heard it argued that Duff's are better. Can't beat La Nova for barbecue, though." Joe lit the cigar evenly, rolling it in the flame of his lighter.

"You got that right. I lived on them during college." Eric noticed that his sister had stopped kissing Taryn, but still had her arms around her. They stood like that for a minute, like they were the only two people on earth.

"Taryn, this is my baby brother Eric. Eric, this is Taryn," Rosalind said, opening herself away from the girl to present her.

Taryn looked at him with a mix of pride and confusion, a little flushed from the kiss. She held her hand out, as Joe had. "Hey, Eric." Her voice was low, but not unpleasant, and her handshake was firm.

"Hi," Eric said, abrupt and manly.

Rosalind could read his thoughts, in order, as her brother stared at Taryn. He was wondering what in the world his gorgeous sister saw in this boy/girl teenager. When she'd revealed to him that she was dating a woman, he'd pictured a woman like one in a magazine, who looked like she did, maybe a little taller, with long red hair, or auburn, nice build, makeup, femme. The only kind of lesbian that mattered to a straight man, the high-class lipstick girly ones. It was, in its way, a compliment. Clearly he thought she could have any woman she wanted, if she wanted a woman. He would naturally assume that she'd get the best; she was his sister.

She watched him puzzling it out, taking in Taryn's build, her clothing, her stance, her hair. Slight curl to the lip there, he didn't approve of her appearance. Easy to read. He didn't understand why she wanted a boy. He was in the army, he could spot a dyke a mile away. Or so he'd said, a hundred times. Taryn was the kind of kid they'd recruit into the service. Tough, fearless, annoyingly competent, but hardly feminine. Then everyone would not ask or tell, as long as she did her job.

They staked out a table in the back room of the Anchor Bar. Jazz played on Wednesday nights, but not until ten, so there was space available. Eric held the chair for Sandhya, Taryn held the chair for Rosalind. She slid into the chair next to her lover, where she could touch her knee to Rosalind's under the table. Eric sat to her right, Sandhya across from her.

"Everyone good with wings?" Eric asked, disdaining the menu.

"Sure, but I'm not in the mood for the suicidal," Sandhya said. "Why don't we get a double medium? Ros and I can share them. You can gnaw on your nuclear waste by yourself."

"What about you? You don't look like the type to get scared off by a little hot sauce," Eric said, directly to Taryn.

She raised an eyebrow at him. "Very little scares me," she said. She felt Rosalind's hand close on her thigh and smiled. "Suicidal sounds great."

The waitress took their order, speaking only to Eric, who seemed to expect that. He ordered a pitcher of Molson along with the wings. The conversation stalled after ordering.

"How's the work with the project going, Sandhya?" Rosalind asked.

Sandhya didn't let on that she'd already given the update on her work to Rosalind in the car on the way over. She smiled as if delighted Rosalind had asked. "Brilliantly. We secured the funding from the city for another year, despite the political morass. I'm working on a grant to get matching federal funds. I've had less time in court, but after the grant is finished, that should change."

"Except for the new paper you're writing," Eric said.

"What paper?" Rosalind asked.

"I was asked to compile a paper on domestic violence statistics in the States for the Southeast Asian Women's Conference. I only have a few months until the conference, so it will be a bit of a crunch."

"So I'll be abandoned. Guess I'll have to put in a lot of overtime and microwaving dinner," Eric said.

"Don't let him fool you. He's gotten to be a great cook," Sandhya said to Rosalind.

"That's a change," Rosalind said.

"Well, once you train them on how to keep a woman satisfied— cook for them every night—it's a breeze," Sandhya said lightly.

Taryn sat silent while they laughed. She picked up her beer glass and looked around the room.

"I never thought of Buffalo as your kind of city. It's not Ithaca. You liking teaching here?" Eric asked Rosalind.

"It was a little bit of an adjustment at first, but I love it. My students are great. The city really surprises you. There's a magic to it. It sneaks into your blood."

"Like zebra mussels in Lake Erie," Eric said and laughed.

"It's a border town. You're always on the frontier. It's the perfect place for people in between," Taryn said.

"So, Taryn what do you do?" Eric asked, pouring more beer. Sandhya declined, Rosalind accepted a glass. Eric tilted his head at Taryn and she nodded.

"Do?" she asked, taking a drink.

"Yeah, for a living. You in school?" He persisted.

"No," Taryn said flatly.

"You work?" Eric asked.

"I do some design work. And I perform."

Rosalind froze. Either direction the conversation went might be disastrous.

"An artist, huh? Funny, I never figured Ros would go for an artist. What do you design?"

"I design tattoos," Taryn said, evenly. The gauntlet was thrown down.

Eric's face lit up, much to Taryn's surprise. "No shit?"

"No shit," she said, enjoying his reaction. He showed interest, for the first time. Maybe they'd gotten lucky, hit on a topic they could discuss.

"When I was in the service, this guy wanted to have me get a tattoo. He was using me for practice, you know? But he wanted to do something stupid, like a Tweety bird on my butt or something queer like that."

"Eric…" Rosalind began, and he turned to her.

"What? Oh, sorry," he said directly to Taryn. "I don't always think before I speak. It's a little new, you know?"

"Yeah. I know. A Tweety bird is dead wrong for you. You need…a Bettie Page, on your arm, and across your back…a leopard, on the left shoulder, reclining. Holding a Masai spear, with the sun setting on the grassland, across the back."

Eric's eyes widened. "That's perfect! I've always wanted to go to Africa on a safari. How'd you know?"

"Taryn has a gift for knowing what Olchawskis need, even if we can't name it yet," Rosalind said, and was rewarded by a look that made the air burn.

The wings arrived, Taryn and Eric took to out-machoing each other with the suicidal, Sandhya and Rosalind ate the medium and talked about their work. Halfway through the pitcher, Eric ordered another one and refilled Taryn's glass first. Sandhya was telling her about her work with the women's shelter and the new work going into prisons to confront rapists. She became engrossed in the conversation. It took her a while to notice that Eric and Taryn had their heads bent together and were talking military strategy.

"Julius Caesar, I'm telling you," Eric said. "Greatest general who ever lived."

Taryn snorted. "He was a politician who got into the army as a middle-aged man. He could manipulate the Senate, not fight. Alexander conquered the known world by the time he was in his thirties. And he had charisma, his mystery. His men loved him. He would lead in battle. They'd do anything for him. He was recognized as a god during his lifetime."

"He was a fag, right? Sorry. Gay man."

"Yeah. His lover, Hephaistion, was one of his generals," Taryn said, taking no offense.

"Don't ask, don't tell, my ass. The service would fold up if we drummed all the gay people out. I think it shouldn't matter who you sleep with, you know? If you can do your job." Eric poured more beer for Taryn and himself.

"Does though, doesn't it?" Taryn said, accepting the glass. They noticed that Rosalind and Sandhya had stopped talking and were paying them extravagant attention.

"Don't stop on our account," Sandhya said.

"I get the hint," said Eric. "We'll be debating tactics at Gaugamela next."

Dinner relaxed into a companionable silence, broken by the click of bones in the bowl in the center of the table. Rosalind asked Eric about his job. He complained for a few minutes about the ignorance of managers on all things technical. She watched Taryn out of the corner of her eye, glad to see that she looked less likely to bolt as the evening went on. She was silent during their discussion on family news and updates, but her attention didn't wander.

They seemed to have worked out a shorthand between them. He seemed more comfortable with Taryn, despite all the obstacles, than he had with Paul. Though he'd never said a word against her husband, Rosalind had always gotten the feeling that Paul had bored her brother to death. Taryn was many things, but boring was not one of them. She'd gotten absorbed in watching them interact and was surprised to catch a snippet of their conversation.

"Let me ask you something. You ever get hassled? In public. You know what I mean." Eric gestured with his beer glass, confident that Taryn would follow his meaning.

Taryn watched him for a moment as if reviewing his qualities. "Of course," she said at last.

"Because of how you look. You ever get jumped? Like, there was this guy in our unit. He went out one night, and he got the crap kicked out of him by some other guys who didn't know he was one of ours."

"Yeah. I've been jumped," Taryn said, as if it were quite common.

Rosalind looked at her. She hadn't heard this tale, or tales. She wondered how many times it had happened. The way Taryn said it, it wasn't a singular event.

"See, I know about the guys," Eric said. "I didn't know if it happened to the girls too."

"It happens. I bet you and Sandhya have trouble," Taryn said, glancing at Eric's girlfriend.

Sandhya nodded to her. "Depends on where we are. If we're holding hands we get the most looks and comments. In the Indian community, people aren't comfortable with me dating a white, non-Hindu man. It's too modern. But Eric's family had the hardest time with him dating an Indian, non-Christian woman. We didn't tell them for a long time."

"Everybody's got a closet," Taryn said.

"Rosalind was great," said Sandhya. "She did all the smoothing over of the parents, until they came around."

"How long did that take?" Taryn asked.

"How long have you guys been together, six years?" asked Rosalind. "Took them a good four. Mom still worries what religion the grandkids will be."

She felt Taryn's leg shift under her hand and looked into her lover's face. "What's wrong, baby?" she asked, forgetting that Eric and Sandhya were still with them.

The look in Taryn's eyes was bleak. "Four years, to accept Sandhya. And she's a lawyer, she's...sorry. I got lost there for a minute." Taryn realized what she was saying, and stopped.

Rosalind took her hand on the tabletop, in front of her brother. "They've been warmed up. They'll accept you in no time."

"I love you," Taryn said, her voice vibrating on the word.

"I love you too," Rosalind said, her hand tightening on Taryn's. She knew that she had just declared herself in front of her brother. It felt good, better than good, to have him know just how serious this was getting. And it was worth it all to see the look in Taryn's eyes, the pride, when she was claimed, acknowledged. Rosalind had to fight down the urge to ask Taryn to marry her; the emotion was that strong.

They stopped and got a bottle of red wine to take back to Rosalind's apartment. Eric and Taryn strolled in together, talking.

Rosalind and Sandhya followed them, shaking their heads. "I was afraid Eric and Taryn wouldn't get along. Now I can't pry them apart," Rosalind said wryly.

"He hasn't had someone to male bond with in a while. The minute Taryn mentioned tattoos, then knew military history, it was all over," Sandhya said, smiling. "You might not get her back."

"One Olchawski is as good as another. You think they'd notice if we just kept walking on without them?"

"Not for a while. Taryn might notice first. She keeps her eye on you. I noticed that during dinner, whenever you were speaking, she'd keep looking over at you. Just checking to see if you were there, I suppose, but it was charming."

Rosalind looked at her back; the drape of the blue shirt gave just a hint of the curve of muscle beneath. "Charming. Yes. She sure is something," she said, with a wistfulness she couldn't check. Taryn paused, rolling up her shirtsleeve to show Eric the Alexander tattoo.

"We don't always find who everyone else expects, but we always find the right one," Sandhya said, taking Rosalind's arm.

Rosalind poured the wine, Taryn sat on the floor, Eric and Sandhya on the couch. Eric leaned forward, his arms on his knees, debating the finer points of kung fu films with Taryn. From the kitchen, Rosalind could hear the ongoing discussion and shook her head. Taryn was as bloodthirsty as her brother was.

"Jackie Chan. With Bruce dead, of course."

"No way. Jackie's a great stuntman, good charisma on film. But he's a comic," said Taryn. "Jet Li."

"Samo Hung," Eric offered, but both shook their heads after a moment.

"Okay. Best film?" Taryn asked.

"*The Flying Guillotine*. Can't beat that birdcage with knives thing. Thanks, Sis," Eric said, taking a glass from Rosalind.

"*The East is Red*," Taryn said. When Eric looked blankly at her, she snorted. "Come on, man. You haven't seen it? Asia the Invincible? You have to. Go rent it tomorrow, then try to talk to me about heroes." She drank the red wine, reaching out her free hand to take Rosalind's.

Rosalind sat on the edge of the coffee table, where she could stroke Taryn's back without effort.

"You do any fighting?" Eric asked.

"Only when I have to. Joe does. He shows me some stuff. Says I have a gift for it."

Eric leaned back on the couch and put his arm around Sandhya's shoulders. He sighed, a grin appearing on his face. "This was great. I never get to talk about half this stuff. You must bore Ros to death with it."

"She hasn't bored me yet. I'll let you know in a year or so," Rosalind said, lightly, but Taryn's head turned very quickly.

"So how did you two meet?" Sandhya asked Rosalind.

"I went out on a blind date, with someone else. Taryn was performing, I saw her on stage, and that was it," Rosalind said, her fingers tracing a pattern on Taryn's back. It didn't feel like it had only been a few days since she first saw the sex god in the black suit, on stage with Egyptia.

"One of her friends sent me a drink. I went over to the table to say thanks. I sat down opposite this woman, looked kind of quiet and all. But then she looked up, and I saw her eyes. It was like staring into the sun. I went blind. I haven't been able to see anything else since," Taryn said with a glance at the woman next to her.

At the end of the bottle of wine, at the end of the evening, Rosalind walked Eric and Sandhya down to their car. She knew that the evening had been a success. She could feel it. It was something so different from anything she'd ever felt, this desire to have her brother like her lover. Paul…er…well, yes. That was a mistake. He had been so…acceptable. Eric had been polite to him, but never seemed to enjoy his company the way he enjoyed Taryn's.

"When I saw her, I wondered what a woman like you could see in somebody like her," Eric admitted, hesitating at the door. Rosalind glanced up to the window, where Taryn's silhouette waited for her.

"I know," Rosalind said. It was a reaction she'd have to get used to. Outside of the tight-knit community Taryn moved in, they wouldn't make any sense as a couple.

"I may not get it, but I like her," said Eric. "She's weird, but it's kind of cool."

"She makes me happy," Rosalind said, and hugged him.

"Then you should keep her around for a while."

Later that night, Rosalind dreamed. She saw a gate, a black eagle that launched itself into the sun, a flight of arrows. There was something she desperately needed to remember, something she needed to take back across the veil, but it turned to smoke in her fingers when she tried to carry it. Her spirit fell heavily back into her body; her arm flailed out, seeking her lover.

When her hand closed on empty air, she woke without transition, eyes jolting open. She could feel her heart hammering in her chest, feel the sweat cooling on her bare skin. Her eyes darted around the room, but Taryn was really gone. It wasn't just the dream; Taryn had wandered off sometime during the night. Rosalind threw back the covers and went into the house, trying to remain calm. It was only a dream, whatever it had been.

Taryn was in the kitchen, sitting on the windowsill, staring out. She wore her black pants and the blue shirt, open. In the morning sun the edges of her face were gilded, her hair was coal. In that moment of stillness, she looked older than her years. Rosalind's age at least.

The dark head turned and saw Rosalind, naked, standing on the kitchen tiles. "There's a sight for sore eyes." Taryn held out her hand.

Rosalind took it, sitting down on her knee. "You're up early." Rosalind felt the large hand roam over her back, the touch very warm and welcome after the clinging effects of the dream.

"I'm crazy about you. You know that?" Taryn said, as Rosalind slid her hands inside the open shirt, warming them.

"I know," Rosalind said, her voice honeyed, her certainty out of nowhere, but no less sure for that.

"I've known you for a week. Less. But you're becoming the whole world to me. That's weird enough. Know what's worse? I see the same thing happening to you. Like I'm becoming the whole world to you."

"You are." Rosalind curled her hands around Taryn's rib cage.

"I feel funny when you say things like that to me. It's like there's this ache in me, it's been there so long I don't remember being without it. And it only stops hurting when you speak to it." Taryn looked up into her lover's face, questioning.

"Maybe it's time for it to stop hurting."

"I'd rather believe it's all you." The grin came like a flash of sunlight on metal—quick, blinding, then gone.

"You can, if you like. I credit you with everything good that's happened to me, and there has been a lot," Rosalind said, spreading out her fingers across her smooth skin. If she tried, maybe she could claim all of her with her hands.

"You teach tonight, right?" Taryn's tone changed, withdrew a bit.

"Yes."

"So you'll get out late. You haven't had a lot of time to yourself. You said something like that yesterday. I know I can be…intense, and I don't give anybody space. I've given this a lot of thought." Taryn broke off and took her hand away from Rosalind's back, fishing into the pocket of her pants.

Rosalind felt the warmth leave and protested immediately. What had possessed her to say a thing like that? Here she was, feeling like she'd jumped a hurdle in having Eric and Taryn meet, and she was pulling back. "I didn't mean—"

Taryn held out her hand.

Rosalind pulled one hand away from the safety of the blue shirt and took what Taryn was offering her. The bit of metal dropped into her palm, warm from Taryn's pocket.

"I won't expect it. But if you happen to crawl into bed with me, I won't kick you out."

The relief was enough that she nearly cried. She felt tears, gathered and ready, and blinked them back. "You won't, huh?" Rosalind held up the key. "Isn't this a little sudden?"

"Joe liked it. He wants you to move in already. If you were single, and he were, he'd fight me for you. It would be sudden if I told you to pack your gear and head for 34 Mariner. A key seemed like a good start."

"So you wouldn't kick me out of bed. If I showed up," Rosalind asked, her heartbeat doing an odd dance.

"I wouldn't kick you out of bed for eating crackers. I wouldn't kick you out of bed for eating peach flambé," Taryn vowed, hand over her heart. "But I won't expect anything."

"Be careful of what you don't expect," Rosalind said, and she kissed her.

CHAPTER NINE

The night had been magic. There was no other way for Rosalind to think about it—from Eric and Sandhya's acceptance of Taryn, to the new intimacy they seemed to reach every moment they were together. It was almost too easy, the way the walls were coming down, the way Taryn exposed her heart. It was like they had done all this before, old lovers renewing their acquaintance. That thought kept nagging at Rosalind during the morning, from her late breakfast at a café near the campus, to a session of book shopping. The feeling of unease surprised her. Things were going beautifully. Better than she had any right to expect. Why should she be feeling so off balance?

The used bookstore offered a quiet place to hide. Rosalind browsed through the fiction shelves looking for books by Mary Renault. She found one of her Greek historical reconstructions but none of the Alexander books.

"Do you have any more Mary Renault?" she asked the clerk who was sitting behind the counter.

He raised his eyes and squinted at the shelf. "Just what's out. I can always order for you. Did you have anything in mind?"

"Some books on Alexander the Great."

"History texts are on aisle nine."

Rosalind thanked him and headed where he pointed. There was a surprising number; Alexander seemed popular for a man dead more than twenty-three centuries. A red leather-bound copy of Arrian's *The Campaigns of Alexander* found her hand on its own. The leather was worn smooth from generations of readers. It fit into her palm like the grip of an old friend. She turned it over, scanning the back for mention of the battles Eric and Taryn had been discussing. "I have a lot of catch-up reading to do," Rosalind said, amused. Greek history had never been her love.

A picture flashed into her head, a scene so detailed Rosalind gasped. She saw in an instant a room, a library or a study. The walls were lined with bookshelves; piles of books were stacked around the armchair. A fire was burning, and snow dusted the panes of the window. She'd never seen that room before, but she knew it. As surely as she knew that the book of Alexander's campaigns was open on the chair and the person reading it was about to step back into the room.

Rosalind dropped the book. She put her hands to her head, not sure if she were ill or crazy. Certain types of brain tumors could cause headaches like the one tearing her skull apart. They might be able to cause hallucinations as well. The walls of the bookstore closed in on her, choking her. She needed air; she needed to run like her heels were on fire. She could not leave without the book. The clerk quoted a price; she threw a pile of money on the counter and fled.

The street was lit with the clear blue light of a late September morning, harmless and without portent. Rosalind forced herself to walk very calmly down the street. It had been an intense night; things were getting serious with her new lover. That alone was enough to make a sane woman act mad. She'd been book shopping because she wanted to know more about what Taryn loved. She was, she told herself very calmly, in a highly irrational state, emotional and prone to suggestion. It was probably a scene from the dreams she'd had all night. She might be imagining things.

The thought was comforting until midmorning, when Rosalind was in her office. She managed not to think about what she and Taryn had used the desk for; she managed not to think about Alexander, or the book, or Marlon Brando, or Shiva. It was a perfectly ordinary moment.

The book sat on the corner of her desk, where she practiced not looking at it. Nothing to it. Rosalind graduated to practicing not touching it, but failed miserably. Her hand inched across the desk until the red leather slid underneath her fingers. No explosions, no sudden shift into madness. She breathed a sigh of relief and let her hand rest on top of the book.

"What in the world are you doing?" Ellie asked, causing Rosalind to jump like a cricket.

"Nothing." Rosalind tore her hand away from the book.

"Nothing?" Ellie nodded. "Looked like you were stretching out across your desk in a new form of yoga. Keeping up our flexibility for lovergirl?"

"Something like that."

Ellie sat down on the edge of the desk, pushing the book aside. "How was dinner with Eric and Elvis?"

"Wonderful. They ended up talking martial arts movies. Sandhya and I drank red wine and watched them."

"Fabulous! Can I pick them for you or what? I'll be generous and not even mention that a few days ago you weren't going to see her again. Have you bought her a new leather jacket yet?"

"No," Rosalind said, rubbing her temples.

"You okay, sweetie? You look pale." Ellie leaned over the desk.

The office was hazy, the air gray and thick as the inside of a shell. Rosalind felt like she was sitting in the center of a merry-go-round watching the world spin out of focus. "Yeah, I'm okay. I have this killer headache I can't shake. I had these weird dreams last night, but I can't remember what they were about. It's got me in a funny mood. I'll be all right after I get this class over with."

She managed to make it through class despite the headache, despite the lingering feeling of anxiety. Everything was going extremely well, she reminded herself. So why did she feel like the world was about to crumble away beneath her feet? Taryn was home waiting for her. There was no reason to feel the blind panic that rose up at the thought of Taryn.

She drove to 34 Mariner very calmly, parked the Saturn very calmly, and managed not to bolt up the stairs. For once, Joe wasn't sitting on the porch. He must be a morning person, Rosalind thought, with a corner of her mind. She used the key, letting herself in a door she expected to groan on its hinges like a horror movie, but it was well oiled.

"Rosalind! Hi." It was Goblin, stretched out on the couch, her long legs draped over the arm. She held a book at arm's length from her face and squinted at it, her glasses on the floor.

"Can you see that way?" Rosalind asked, unaware that she had just sounded exactly like her mother, in tone and delivery.

"Sorta," Goblin said, bringing the book closer. "I wanted to see if I could see without my glasses. You looking for T, right?"

Rosalind spoke as casually as she could, for all the leaping her heart was doing. "Yes."

"She's up on the third floor with Joe, sweating with the oldie."

"At this hour?" Rosalind asked, glancing up the stairs.

"T had rehearsal all night." Goblin said, as if that explained everything. "Joe took her to the mall today. They bought a new suit. I shouldn't tell you, but Taryn looked gorgeous. She wanted to surprise you." Goblin swung her legs off the arm of the couch and sat up. She patted the cushion and Rosalind obliged, sitting down next to her. "Potato chip? I have to finish them and hide the bag before Rhea finds it. She thinks I eat too much junk." Goblin held up a bag.

"No, thanks."

Goblin drew out a handful of chips, then rolled the bag, hiding it behind a cushion. "T told me about the key. You took it, right?" Goblin asked, glancing at Rosalind's face.

"I sure did," Rosalind said with a big smile.

"Good. She's a lot happier since she met you. It's kinda funny to watch. Like you're housebreaking her. She bought another surprise today, but I promised I wouldn't tell that." Goblin reached down and fished her glasses from the floor.

"I guess I'll just have to find out for myself. What are you reading?"

"Tolkien. Joe says he used to read it to me in my crib. It was the only thing that would calm me down when I cried. You ever read it?" Goblin held up the book, *The Hobbit*.

Rosalind shook her head, sheepishly. "I have to admit, I haven't. I never read a lot of fantasy."

The look Goblin gave her over the rim of her glasses mixed pity and disbelief. "We'll fix that. Who wants the world the way it is?"

Footsteps came from the kitchen, the sound of bare feet on a well-polished wooden floor. Goblin pushed the bag of chips down further in the couch.

Rosalind felt a touch on her back and turned around. Rhea was standing at the end of the room, one hand on the archway between the living room and the hall. She looked tired. Her hair was bound up in a braid. It made her look smaller with the wild strands restrained. Her eyes were opaque as jet, brooding. "Rosalind. I was expecting you. Would you…join me for a cup of tea?"

Rosalind patted Goblin on the knee. "I'll take a rain check on the book." She followed Rhea down the hall.

"Goblin, no more chips," Rhea said, not looking at her

Rhea poured hot water into Taryn's blue glass mug and set it in front of Rosalind. The gesture wasn't lost on Rosalind, who pulled the mug closer. Rhea sat down opposite, curling her hands around her own teacup. The silence was as awkward as a wake. Rosalind thought that Rhea must know about the key and had called this conference to register a protest.

Rhea looked up, the corners of her eyes crinkling without mirth. "Do you know what Joe and Taryn are upstairs doing?"

"Working out, or so Goblin told me."

Rhea shook her head. "They are working, but not lifting weights. They are putting together the frame for Taryn's new bed." Rhea watched Rosalind as the realization slipped into focus. "Yes. She went out and bought a bed today. She said, quote, Rosalind is too good to keep sleeping on the floor. It was too big for the alcove she sleeps in. So she moved up to the third floor. Because you took the key."

"She said she wouldn't expect anything," Rosalind said, and Rhea snorted.

"You know better. She thinks with her heart. And her heart is yours."

"I don't—"

"How is your head?" Rhea asked, changing directions.

"It's fine," Rosalind said, despite the solid tempo of the pain.

Rhea nodded, looking out at the kitchen with what Rosalind might have called wistfulness in any other person. On Rhea that look read as grief, or barely stilled rage.

Rhea hadn't invited her in for a cup of tea and a little chat. "Look, Rhea, I know you disapprove of Taryn and me. You can't be happy about the key."

"You have invaded my home. You have taken from me what I am not ready to give up. And you think a key would make me unhappy?" Rhea said quietly.

Rosalind sat, stunned.

One thin hand raked through Rhea's wild hair. "Forgive me. You can't know, I've seen to—Never mind. We are adults, Rosalind. We both love Taryn. I expect we can be civil. Go on, she's waiting for you," Rhea said. Rosalind knew that she'd been dismissed.

The pain in her head was a spike. The cryptic conversation with Rhea had intensified it. Her mood was dangerously unbalanced. She felt herself yearn for Taryn, as if being near her might bring her back to herself. With that half-conscious hope, Rosalind climbed the back stairs from the kitchen, listening to the sounds of furniture being moved above. She heard Joe grunt, then a thud. Taryn's voice ripped out an oath and a warning. Rosalind nearly laughed and spoiled her entrance. She hesitated in the doorway, getting a good look at the space.

The third floor was one large room, running the length of the house. She'd known that the third floor was the weight room and Joe's office, but she hadn't been up to see it. From what she could tell, Taryn and Joe had been busy. The weight bench was gone; Joe's desk and file cabinets were gone. She recognized Taryn's dresser and piles of clothing, but not the rug set down over the hardwood floor, not the bed that dominated the domestic space being constructed.

Taryn and Joe had been maneuvering the dresser. Taryn was leaning on it, arms folded, while Joe bent down, looking at the legs.

"Break anything?" Rosalind asked, and was gratified to see what an effect the sound of her voice had on them. Joe jumped. Taryn looked like someone had lit her on fire. The smile that came over her was almost painful to look at, the emotion so raw and unshielded. She glowed with it, her whole body echoing it, extending a welcome automatic and complete. Rosalind felt very lucky to be on the receiving end of that look.

"Hey. Thought you'd be later," Taryn said, taking a step toward Rosalind.

"Not that you were expecting anything." Rosalind reached out and took her hand as she spoke.

"Nah, me? I wanted to surprise you, but you busted in here and caught us. Come look." She pulled Rosalind over to the bed.

"It's huge," Rosalind said, getting a look at it.

"I'm kinda tall. I wanted to get something more like normal people sleep in, you know? I've been sleeping on a mattress for years."

"A mattress is easier to pack up and move. Not to mention easier hauling up three flights of stairs and putting together," Joe said, wiping his hands on his jeans.

"You're Mr. Toolbelt, you love this shit. Don't let him fool you. He was all, like, let me get my wrenches and we can put it together."

"You've done a great job, both of you. I'm duly impressed. It's a great space up here, but what about the weights, and your office?"

Joe smiled and picked up his tools. "We put the bench in Taryn's old room. I put my desk in there as well. It'll be nice to have the sun in the afternoon, when I'm working. It's good for the house to have changes, keeps all the energy flowing. It's late, kids, and I'm too old for all this exertion. I'll see you in the morning."

"Thanks, Joe," Taryn said, as he headed down the stairs.

She slid her arms around Rosalind's waist and pulled her close. "So, you like it?"

"Mhm. Whatever possessed you to move up here and go buy a bed?"

"There's this girl I'm seeing. She might be spending some time here, you know, sleeping over. I wanted a nicer place for her." Taryn's face was a mask of indifference, her voice bland.

"I'm sure you've seen other girls who slept over. What's different about this one?" Rosalind asked, drawing her hand along Taryn's collarbone.

"She's a hot lay. I wanted a real bed, so I can hear the springs squeal," Taryn said, leering.

"You are a dog. You're a pretty hot lay yourself, Cullen. I should be buying you leather jackets every other day." Rosalind's hand moved up to Taryn's neck, scratching at the short black hair.

"Leather jackets? I don't get it."

"Something Ellie said. Great sex should always be celebrated with a new leather jacket."

There was a definite reaction in Taryn when Rosalind said it, a surge of energy. Pride suffused her features. "I like that. A new leather jacket every time…yeah. I could do a whole leather wardrobe, wear nothing else," Taryn said, and smirked.

It was the smirk that hooked Rosalind, reminded her of the drag king's reputation. That reputation was not a comfort to her, more so now that she was starting to feel proprietary about her. Her bad mood reared its ugly head.

"How many leather jackets did you collect before you met me?" Rosalind asked, wishing she could just bite her tongue off and get it over with.

There was no safe answer to the question, and the trapped look on

Taryn's face was evidence that she knew it. "Why'd you want to know that?" Taryn asked in a strained voice.

"You afraid to tell me?" In her own estimation, when she woke up that morning, Rosalind had been a rational adult. She was in love, true, and that made madwomen out of the sanest adults, but she was still functioning on her expected level. This sudden dip into adolescence took her by complete surprise, but once the idea had presented itself, there was nothing to do with it but ask. It became very important to get Taryn to tell her how many leather jackets there had been, crowding up her closet. She heard, in a distracted kind of shock, the words leave her mouth, hating herself for asking, but determined to get an answer.

"Rosalind."

"Don't try the rational tone with me. Answer the question." Rosalind took her hands off Taryn and stepped back. "What is it? Can't count that high? Afraid I won't be able to handle the truth?"

The pained, surprised look in Taryn's eyes was enough to make her relent, but the words had been spoken, and she had heard them. Taryn walked to the bed and sat down on the edge, resting her hands on her knees. "I never pretended to be a virgin before I met you," she said, her voice strange to Rosalind's ear.

Sanity poked through the fog of pain in her head, making her hear how she sounded. "Taryn, I'm sorry, I don't know what—"

"No, you asked. That's fair. Double digits. I don't know exactly. I didn't keep notches on my bedpost, no matter what people say about me. I fucked my way through Buffalo. And I'm sure that's still what is said about me. Satisfied?" Taryn said, not looking at Rosalind.

Satisfied? Rosalind thought, in a kind of numb shock. *I managed to insult Taryn, when I came to wrap myself around her.* Taryn's dark head was bent down, inspecting the floor. Rosalind could feel herself bleeding into the air, feel the wound in her side where Taryn should be. She had performed surgery on herself with her words and was now paying for it. She stared at Taryn in anguish, wanting to take back her words, her eyes full of her apology. But her head was bent, so Taryn did not see it.

Rosalind knew that silence wasn't good, that Taryn would swiftly fill that silence with meaning and react like a wounded animal.

"Maybe you'd better go. I want to be alone tonight."

The words went through Rosalind like a stiletto easing between her ribs to reach for her heart. Taryn had given her the key, gone out and purchased a new bed, moved up to the third floor just in case she came over. And she did come over and promptly kick the girl she loved in the teeth. "Taryn—" she began, agonized, but Taryn's head came up, and her eyes were cold and remote.

"Maybe you didn't hear me. I told you to get out."

It was the sound of Taryn's voice that reminded Rosalind she was an adult; she was just behaving like an adolescent. Taryn had fought against the words, speaking each one in a clipped efficiency that spoke of pain. It was a first for Rosalind, facing the aftermath of an unconsidered remark to someone she loved. She'd never had a fight like this with Paul. He'd never interested her enough to get heated about. She'd hurt her lover, she'd have to work to get back in. Rosalind thought about what she was doing, but did it anyway. She crossed to the bed, standing in front of the seething Taryn, who turned her head, looking anywhere but at her lover.

"I deserve that. It was a stupid, childish thing I said to you, and I regret ever opening my mouth," Rosalind said steadily.

Taryn's shoulders twitched, but she didn't look at Rosalind. She shrugged off the hand Rosalind tried to place on her arm, and rose from the bed. "Don't."

"I never want to hurt you, Taryn." Taryn's body was close enough to feel the heat of her skin.

"Then why the fuck say something like that to me? You decided that it isn't cool anymore, sleeping with somebody with experience? You seemed pretty damn happy about it until now." Taryn turned her head, looking at Rosalind from the corner of her eye. "I'm not just some stupid butch you can pick up and ride. That's not what I thought we were doing here." She backed up as she spoke, as if being physically close to Rosalind was unmanageable.

"That's not what we are doing," Rosalind said softly. It was getting worse, not better, with every word spoken.

Taryn walked away, the length of the room. She stood in front of the windows, her back to Rosalind, arms folded protectively. The distance between them might not be bridgeable, if she left it to harden overnight.

Rosalind took strength from the certainty she'd felt when Taryn had given her the key. She walked slowly toward her, watching her back stiffen as she approached. She started speaking ten feet from her, letting her voice cover the remainder of the space open between them. "I was twenty-eight when I got married. I wasn't a virgin, but I might as well have been. I didn't know that what I felt mattered. I didn't know anything much at all about my body."

Rosalind paused, watching the set of Taryn's shoulders change, just a fraction, a motion only visible to the eye of a lover, who translated such things. She waited for three heartbeats, until she could hear Taryn's breath easing in and out, hear a sound that might have been just a figment of her imagination. She started speaking again, as everything faded down to a vivid silence, punctuated with Taryn's breathing.

"It's funny to admit, as a feminist, but I never gave my own body a lot of thought. It never caused me pain; it was pleasant, but it was very manageable. Eric used to get mad if he didn't eat every few hours. He was like a bear or a lion. He'd get all grumpy and evil. It was fun to watch sometimes, seeing him so in thrall. I never felt enslaved by my needs. I didn't have many."

Rosalind paused again, feeling the weight of the silence. The change in Taryn's breathing was definite, the air coming more quickly into her lungs. If she tried, she could hear Taryn's heart clench with each beat. "In high school I never thought I was pretty. People said it to me, but no one ever said it in a way I believed. When you don't believe that about yourself, but people say it, it does something to you. To your trust. It was like a red flag, indicating when to tune someone out. They were complimenting me, so they'd just started lying. There were things I could be complimented about, and believe. My mind. My work. My warm personality. Warm. I heard that so often, I started to think of myself as a sweater or a pair of mittens, warm and fuzzy. When was someone ever going to go mad for me, call me gorgeous, heart-stopping, to die for? The thing is, I wouldn't have believed it, even if someone had said it to me. I had a pretty good setup, airtight." Rosalind chuckled, softly.

"I had a good handle on things. I had friends, a good job, got along with my family. The divorce was a relief in the end—no more of looking into Paul's eyes and seeing a need I couldn't meet, couldn't share."

Rosalind saw Taryn's shoulders tighten at the mention of Paul's name and knew how much she hated to be reminded of her husband. But it was important for her to feel that surge of instinctual anger right now.

"Then, one night, I went to a club with my best friend. She'd tried to fix me up on a blind date, again, with some sensitive guy she thought might do. He bored me silly the moment we met. I looked up at the stage and saw this girl. Just like that, my whole life changed."

Rosalind took a step toward Taryn's back. "My body reacted to her without knowing her. All those needs I thought I had handled rose up and grabbed me by the throat. It didn't make any sense, but if I didn't get close to her, I'd die. It helped that she was the sexiest, most handsome swaggering thing I'd ever seen. But there was something more to her. A presence. A soul. Like I knew her. I just had to remind her of that.

"The first night she took me in her arms, I knew who I was. And the first night she let me hold her in my arms, I knew why I was here. I'm not who I thought I was, I don't have anything handled. Lately I think I have more needs than anyone who ever lived. My skin hurts when I'm away from her. I'm lucky if I can string two sentences together without wanting to say her name. Nobody has ever loved her the way I do. It's arrogant, but I'll die defending it. So when I picture her in bed with someone else, it doesn't matter if it was two years ago or two minutes ago. I want them dead. And it makes me into a jealous asshole, who's spending her time apologizing when I should be holding her now, on the bed she bought for us."

Taryn turned so fast she was a blur, spinning on her heel. Rosalind froze at the suddenness of the motion, not knowing how to interpret it. She wanted to see Taryn's face, her eyes, read the emotion there, but Taryn didn't give her a chance. One minute Rosalind was standing, inches from her back; the next, she found out just how strong Taryn was. Her feet left the floor—one muscled arm catching her behind the knees, the other around her back. In one smooth motion she was midair, being carried across the room. Her arm went around Taryn's broad shoulders for balance. Taryn's face was set. She carried Rosalind as lightly as a child over to the bed and deposited her with a rough grace.

Taryn crawled onto the bed, over Rosalind's body, covering her. Rosalind could feel the tremor in her back, as if she were chilled to the bone. She coiled Taryn into her arms, not easy to do with her height. Taryn's face was buried in her hair, turned away, so Rosalind couldn't see her. She felt Taryn's weight pressing her down into the bed and welcomed it, opening her legs for Taryn's thigh to slip in between. "I'm so sorry, baby," Rosalind whispered into her ear.

"Shut up," Taryn said, her voice clogged with emotion. "No more words. They hurt." She turned her face until her lips were pressed into the fragile skin of Rosalind's throat. They parted and rested there, her breath hot on the woman's skin, as if she readied to drink her blood.

"Words suck," Rosalind said, solemnly. She felt Taryn's shoulders hitch.

"Don't make me laugh, I'm mad at you," Taryn growled, but the anger was gone from her voice. She shifted her weight and pressed her hips into Rosalind's.

"You should be. I'm a jerk."

Taryn moved her head against her lover's neck, a motion of negation. "No. You make me crazy. I want to be all mad at you, but then you come near me and all I want to do is crawl into your lap. You think you had it all handled? I'd bury you. I never got tied down by anyone, not even Rhea, and I loved her. Now look where I am."

"Right where you belong." Rosalind tightened her arms. "I just want to squeeze you until the stuffing comes out your ears."

"I'm not a teddy bear," Taryn said, in an aggrieved tone.

"Sure you are. You've got big round eyes, a fuzzy head, and you are very huggable. Textbook case," Rosalind said, and grinned as Taryn pushed up on her elbows, staring down at her in disbelief.

"I do not have a fuzzy head."

Rosalind's hand brushed the black hair down toward Taryn's face, making it stick out at all angles. "Fuzzy. Just like a baby duck. I rest my case," Rosalind said triumphantly.

Taryn pulled her head away and started smoothing her hair back down. "You're lucky I love you."

"Still?" Rosalind asked, serious now.

"Still." One word, spoken in the mostly empty room, carried to the far walls. It was enough. And when Taryn leaned down to kiss her, it was more than enough.

Rosalind felt a barrier give way, a wall she'd built so long ago she didn't remember gathering the stones. Taryn's skin moved under her hands—the head of Alexander, the bull dagger. The abandon came on her and she welcomed it, hearing her own voice whispering like the notes of a muted chime. *Know love and remember.* Her soul woke to beauty, called out by the handsome girl, and began to climb, recognizing its own at last.

Rosalind luxuriated on the bed like a cat, her headache blissfully gone. "If I knew that was the cure I'd have tried it years ago," she muttered.

"Tried what?" Taryn asked, rolling out of bed.

"Nothing, baby. What in the world are you doing?"

Taryn had gone to the dresser and picked up what looked like a knot of dried grass and her lighter. "Blessing the room," Taryn said, as she lit the knot.

"I feel like we just did bless the room," Rosalind said, with a saucy grin.

"Right, I don't want to lose that energy we created. It's good magic."

Rosalind watched as Taryn walked to the far corner, stretching her arm above her head. On her back the bull dagger elongated; the Cretan girls leapt between the razor horns. On her left shoulder, the snake in the tree watched Rosalind with eyes of old humor. She thought of the golden snake in the dogwood tree and felt a shiver travel up her spine, more of anticipation than fear. Clothed in line work and shadow Taryn stalked the edges of the room, marking her new territory. She was saying something in a low voice, too low for Rosalind to catch.

Taryn went to each corner and held the knot up, letting the smoke drift up, around the windowsills and the door. She crossed the block of shadow back toward the bed, emerging head and shoulders first, as if the darkness gave birth to her.

"The room's blessed now?" Rosalind asked, opening the covers for her.

"Getting there. Rhea came up with the broom and sage earlier while Joe and I were setting the bed up. Once I get it all the way we want it, I'll finish the blessing." She set the knot in a bowl on the floor, next to the bed, and crouched there, watching Rosalind.

The idea that Rhea had helped bless the room left Rosalind stunned. By all accounts, the woman couldn't stand her. "What was that you were saying?"

"Let all who come in peace be welcome here. It's Rhea's welcome. It's her house, so I used it. I'm a little more like, if you want to fight, come on! But she says that's too belligerent for a blessing."

"You practice witchcraft with Rhea, I take it." It was a statement. Rosalind had seen the statue of Shiva dancing, seen Kali Ma with her belt of skulls, seen the altar she kept on the dresser top. They hadn't spoken of it yet.

Taryn sat down cross-legged on the bed, facing Rosalind. "I circle with her. The whole house does. I'm not a witch, though. I don't follow enough of the Craft. Laurel is, and Rhea."

"What about Joe?" Rosalind had a hard time picturing Joe as a witch, for some reason, although she didn't know exactly what that entailed.

"Joe's a sorcerer."

"Do you believe in it? Goddess worship, right? I don't have a lot of experience with it."

"Believe? That's a strong word. I believe that Rhea has power. Whatever is out there, she can reach. I like some gods. I guess I like the idea of them more than anything. Power we can talk to. The thought of One God scares me. Are you a Christian?" Taryn said, tilting her head.

"No. I can't say that I am. But I believe in goodness. Whatever that makes me."

"Makes you a good person to know."

"So why the blessing, if you don't follow the Craft?"

"It's respectful. This is a witch's house. And it's ritual. I like ritual. Rhea says it's like cooking. You put the ingredients together in the right order, something happens. Can't hurt," Taryn said, and the words snagged at the edges of Rosalind's mind.

There was something there for her to get, but it hadn't made itself clear yet. She tried to focus on it, but felt the warning stab of her headache returning. It was easy to set it aside and think of other things. "You auction your body off for charity tomorrow," she said, running her hand down Taryn's arm.

"You sure you want to come?" Taryn asked, her eyebrows knitting.

"This body is mine now. I'm not letting it out of my sight. Some shaven-headed femme girl with a rich daddy will snatch you up." Rosalind's hand closed on Taryn's arm.

"Most of Buffalo doesn't know I'm not available anymore. It might get—"

"The only reason I'd stay away is if you didn't want people to know

I'm seeing you. I'll be front row center with my checkbook, elbowing like it's Christmas Eve," Rosalind said, cutting her off. "Do you not want people to know?" she asked, the idea presenting itself to her for the first time. Funny, she'd expected herself to have a problem with going public. She'd never expected Taryn to. But she had a reputation for not settling down. What would it be like to change that so quickly? Her housemates were one thing; this was a public declaration.

"You're my girl," Taryn said firmly.

"And that means?"

"That you can go where I go. Let everyone know. I love you. It makes me proud you picked me."

"If they knew how sweet you were, they'd never forgive me. I'll be there, with bells on," Rosalind said, dragging her lover's head down for a kiss.

CHAPTER TEN

She was supposed to pick Taryn up at five. Rosalind kept looking at her watch, hoping the meeting wouldn't run over. Who had scheduled a departmental meeting on a Friday afternoon? *Don't these people have lives?* She rolled the agenda into a tube. It occurred to her that she'd never objected to a departmental meeting before, but then she'd never had a compelling reason to rush home. It was getting downright silly how much time she'd started to shave from her day just to spend it with Taryn.

I'm a cliché, Rosalind thought without regret. She'd fallen in love, and it had short-circuited her brain, making anything other than rolling around in bed with the handsomest boy in Buffalo completely irrelevant. It was unfortunate timing that her awakening to desire came her first month into her first real teaching job.

The worst part about being a new professor was the endless committees you got suckered into. Nothing like departmental politics to get in the way of a night out. Dr. Pearson was babbling again about 1947; she could never understand why he fixated on that year. *That's tenure in action.* She smiled. Means she could turn into a wild old woman and not worry. *I'll make them all listen to Joni Mitchell once I'm tenured. And I'll make them listen to Billy Ray Cyrus.* That led her mind off on a Taryn fantasy, starting with Taryn singing in her boxers, which led to thoughts involving getting Taryn out of her boxers. A pleasant, stoned smile crossed her face, and suddenly Dr. Pearson's rambling was bearable.

Dr. Grey was saying something. She'd missed it in her daydreaming. Was the meeting finally over? Rosalind looked up, right into the steady gaze of the chair of the English department.

"Is that acceptable, Rosalind?" He asked, his voice burring.

"Sure," she answered, not having a clue as to what he meant.

"Good. Why don't we go into my office?"

Dr. Grey stood, the signal for the end of the meeting. Everyone else grabbed their papers and coats and fled for the hills, making her wonder what she'd gotten herself into now. *More delay, that's what I've gotten myself into. I still have to stop by the bank before I go to 34 Mariner. Maybe I should call and see if she needs anything—*

"Rosalind?" Dr. Grey asked, his eyebrows rising.

Lord, he's been talking to me and I'm off on Mars.

"Great. Let's go into your office," she said, hating the chipper sound her voice took on when she was kissing ass.

Dr. Grey was in formal mode, she saw, from the way he motioned her to a chair, then shut the door. *Why shut the door, with everyone leaving?* Dr. Grey had two chairs, arm to arm, facing his desk. Rosalind always felt like it was a psychological test, choosing a chair in front of him. She sat in the chair on the right and wondered what that indicated about her. Dr. Grey sat down at his desk and folded his hands, a bad parody of a schoolmaster from an English film Rosalind had seen once, years ago.

"Is something wrong?" Rosalind asked, not wanting to add his title for some reason.

Dr. Grey removed his glasses and set them in front of him. "I tried to call you about this matter, several times, but received no word back. There's no easy way to broach this. You know that we are very impressed with you here, Rosalind. The feedback from your students has been very positive."

Rosalind felt her stomach clench. His tone was too soothing. "Thank you. I've enjoyed them a great deal." *Now get to the 'but,' you bastard. You're ruining my evening*, her mind hissed. She told it to be quiet.

"We've had a complaint about you. Nothing formal yet, so I felt I could have a private chat with you. Maybe straighten this thing out."

A cold hand reached in and squeezed Rosalind's heart. "May I ask the nature of the complaint? A student was unhappy with a grade?"

Dr. Grey moved his glasses around on the desk, and Rosalind thought of a boy playing with a toy car. "No, not exactly. You understand that this is never an easy topic to broach, but we do have to manage it before this becomes a formal complaint filed with the university. A person has accused you of sleeping with a student."

"Excuse me?" Rosalind asked, unable to help herself.

"That's the accusation. You see how it could get complicated. We have policies against this sort of thing. It can be considered harassment, if the complainant decides to take it to the university. It's my job to investigate the complaint before it becomes formal," Dr. Grey said, driving his glasses around the desk.

"That's ridiculous. I would never sleep with a student. Who got a crazy idea like that?"

"You know I can't tell you that. I am pleased with your reaction, however. Am I to understand that this complaint is without merit?"

"It's completely without merit. I haven't done anything that could be misconstrued on that level. It's a vicious, unfounded attack," Rosalind said firmly. Her mind raced. Who could have said something like that about her?

"Good. That makes things much easier. In cases like this, it's usually a misunderstanding. You know how young people can be. Just to be on the safe side, it's best to do a little good PR. Be seen with an appropriate escort at an event, a concert or a play. Just to keep things straight. You understand what a close community a university can be. Are you...er...romantically involved with anyone?" Dr. Grey said, putting his glasses back on.

A host of reactions danced through Rosalind's mind, but the first one was incredulity. "What?"

"Seeing anyone. I understand that you are divorced. It would be easier to present a positive image, put these rumors to rest, as it were, if you had a steady escort. Just a friendly question, you understand."

Just an illegal question, you bastard. The answer came to her lips, unbidden. "Yes, I am seeing someone."

"Splendid. Go out to some public event this weekend, friendly advice. That should handle this nicely. I'm glad we don't have to take this any further. I know these charges are painful. It's terrible, the amount of power they exert over our lives. Just be circumspect for a few weeks. Don't give any fodder to the rumor mill, eh?"

"Right. Be circumspect," Rosalind repeated. She left Dr. Grey's office like she was moving underwater.

Her life had taken a left turn sharply away from circumspect a week ago. There was cause for concern. Any complaint in her first semester would be scrutinized. That was perfectly rational, especially for someone as eager to please as she knew herself to be. It was almost a disease, her desire to be liked, to be a good girl. It came out whenever she was faced with an authority figure, a response so automatic she rarely questioned it. It came to her now that what she was doing was reacting like she'd been caught stealing from the collection plate. She hadn't done what she'd been accused of doing. That didn't stop her from feeling as guilty as if she'd actually committed the offense.

This was not the time to go Freudian on herself, but she couldn't help it. She walked through the hall toward the parking lot, feeling naked. A man held the door for her. She jumped aside. Was he mocking her? What did he see in her face as she walked? What did her body give away? *Get a grip, Ros. They can't tell who you're fucking by looking at you.*

Her mind contradicted that immediately, presenting her with a picture of Taryn in all her glory. Taryn never had to say a word; her body, her stance, her clothing all spoke for her. Even her devil's eyes gave her away, the way they looked right into you and promised profane knowledge. Women did not look at women the way Taryn did, not with that explicit hunger and appreciation.

❖

There was a pay phone in the parking lot. For years her mother had been after her to join the modern era and get a cell phone. Rosalind always agreed that she would, then put it off. Cell phones were too intrusive, much more likely to cut into the time she set aside for thinking. The world was drowning in methods for communicating; what it needed was more time for reflection.

There was a humming like bees in her head. She had trouble focusing around it. She saw herself drop the quarters in, heard the phone ring, but it was far away.

"City morgue, you stab 'em, we slab 'em." It was Joe's voice that finally broke Rosalind's trance. She looked down at the phone in her hand, amazed. "Joe?"

"Rosalind? That you? You sound funny. You know that boy of yours is using all of my aftershave. You have to buy her some of her own. I tell her Christmas is coming, but does she listen? You on the way?"

"Could you do me a favor?" Rosalind asked, not recognizing her own voice.

"Sure," came the immediate response, not waiting to see what the favor might entail.

"I'm stuck in a meeting here at school, and it's running late. Could you give Taryn a ride to the auction?"

"Well, okay. T loves the convertible. It'll mess her hair out of all that gel. Too bad about that meeting. Don't those people have lives? You want to talk to her? I think I hear her singing up in the bathroom."

Joe's voice pulled away from the phone, and Rosalind could see him, in the kitchen, about to shout up the back stairs. "No! Don't disturb her if she's getting ready. It's a big night."

"Gotcha. See you there."

"See you there," she echoed, and hung up.

She drove around North Buffalo, up Parkside, past the zoo, around to Delaware Park. She left the Saturn and started walking, along the path from the Rose Garden, down by the lake. The wind blew leaves around her feet; the lake was green and brown in the early evening light. It was the last week of September. All the leaves would be coming down soon, the fall was in full gear. Winter was coming.

Rosalind looked off toward Forest Lawn, across the road. Hills covered in mausoleums showed through the trees, white and gray stone mixing with spots of red and amber. She stared at them, thinking of nothing.

A flash of light on metal drew her eye to the left. She looked up at the statue of David on his hillside. She saw the set of his broad shoulders, his noble head turned toward the giant he was about to fight. He paused, forever on the brink of action, eyes calm and quiet in the planes of his face.

There was a pay phone outside of the Casino, at the foot of the stairs. Rosalind walked toward it, not hurrying, but still moving. "Ellie? I need to talk."

It seemed like an eternity between Ros's saying the words into her best friend's answering machine and the phone picking up. Ellie fumbled with the receiver, dropped it, swore concisely, then picked up.

"Hey, sweetie. Great news. I'm coming to your auction! I talked my friend from the department into meeting me there. I told her it'd be right up her alley. Actually, Taryn would be right up her alley, but that's a moot point now. Can you stand it? I was thinking of bringing her to see the show at Marcella's, before I brought you. Right place, wrong woman. I give myself one point for instinct, at least." Ellie paused at the expanse of silence on the other end of the line. "But that's not what you wanted to talk about, is it? What's up?"

"Can you meet me?" Rosalind asked, closing her eyes.

"Sure, honey. Where are you?"

"Delaware Park, by the Casino." Rosalind leaned her forehead against the smooth metal casing of the phone.

"You don't sound good. What's going on? Did you fight with lovergirl?" Ellie's voice was deliberately light.

"No." A tremor went through Rosalind's body, shoulders to heels. She hadn't fought with Taryn. But the thought of her, on her way now to the auction, made her weak, in more ways than she liked.

"Never mind. Sit down on the steps. Pretend you smoke, smoke about three cigarettes. I'll be there before the last one is out."

Rosalind had never gotten the habit of smoking. She'd tried, a few times, to be social, to see what the fuss was about, but it left her perplexed as to the attraction. She thought about what Ellie said, and her mind played. She remembered the night Taryn had sat on the windowsill, backlit by the streetlight, a cigarette hanging from her long fingers, speaking dispassionately about the past. She couldn't get away from her for the length of three imaginary cigarettes.

If her mind wasn't conjuring Taryn's image, her body was listening for a familiar footstep, the sound of a long easy stride, a pair of combat boots striking the pavement. Rosalind shook her head, unable to fight it. Taryn was a part of her. It wasn't just poetry, and sex, and madness that she could dive into and walk away from. Taryn was in her bones.

Ellie came walking up the path, hands in the pockets of her leather jacket. She spotted Rosalind sitting on the steps and strolled over, kicking leaves as she walked. Ellie dropped down on the step next to her friend and looked out over the lake.

"You don't look like you're bleeding, so I'll assume it isn't medical. I'm supposed to be the dramatist. What's going on?"

"Grey called me into his office. Someone has issued a complaint that I've been sleeping with a student," Rosalind said, her voice surprisingly even.

"Jesus! You? What kind of bullshit is that? You denied it, of course."

"I denied it. He said it wasn't formal yet, so it didn't have to go any further. But he advised me to be seen in public with an appropriate escort. He kept using the phrase 'straighten things out.'"

Ellie absorbed this for a moment. "I see. Somebody knows about you and Taryn and either wants to destroy your reputation or thinks lovergirl is actually a student. Grey was covering his ass. He couldn't come out and tell you to act straight to shut things up, but he did, in his own special way."

"Yeah," Rosalind said, resting her head in her hands. "Remember when I asked you where all the hatred and bigotry were? I take it back. I can't even handle a taste of it."

"Honey…do you know who is doing this?" Ellie asked, rubbing her back.

Rosalind raised her head, her eyes red. "I thought about it, but it doesn't really matter, you know? It could be anyone. And it doesn't have to be true. It doesn't have to be a student. It's enough that my lover is a girl thirteen years my junior. All I need is an informal complaint, and my reputation is shot. And if it escalates, my chance at tenure goes up in smoke. Don't look at me like that. I know how university politics work. You don't get a job by being a rebel. You get enough unwanted attention for the department, and they start thinking about how expendable you really are."

"Too bad you're not in theater. It's a scandal if someone starts a rumor that you're straight."

"I don't know what to do. I can't fight it. It's just an informal complaint. If I call for a hearing, I do myself more damage than they could. I can't take Grey's friendly advice, be seen in public with an appropriate escort. Taryn's a lot of things, but she's not—" Rosalind broke off, horrified.

"Finish the sentence. She's not appropriate. She couldn't pass if you threw a wig and makeup on her, put her in a dress and heels," Ellie said sharply.

"I wouldn't want her to. I love the way she is. I just hate that it makes such a difference." Rosalind looked at Ellie's face. "All my life, I wondered if there would ever be anything that made me crazy, made me forget everything and everyone else. A grand passion. Now I have one, and the minute it gets challenged, I get scared. I feel like the whole world is looking at me, like people I don't even know get to judge what

I'm doing. So I'm sitting here talking to you, instead of driving to the auction. I'm an asshole, right?"

"I think you had a week of bliss, and now the real world is biting you on the tail. It gets complicated from here. You'll have to make choices about who knows, how they get to know, what you're ready to risk and ready to lose. Love is like that, or so I hear. This is your Waterloo, Ros. Do you let the people watching tell you how you live, or do you tell them?" Ellie's voice was firm and offered no comfort. It was strangely comforting for that reason. Rosalind knew her friend was telling her the truth and challenging her.

"Lord, Ellie. I've never had to make a choice like that. I don't know how," she said, shaking her head.

"Start from the basics, what we know to be true. Taryn's a sexy beast. She's also inappropriate, and thirteen years younger than you, and hardly a charm school graduate. You are, despite your week of vacationing, a woman who's been straight her whole life, now divorced. You're an adult, a professor, you love your job, people think of you when they think respectable. You'd be the designated driver in any group; you'd be the one to take the minutes at the meeting, send thank you cards, remember birthdays. Doesn't make any sense in the world that you'd risk anything for a weeklong fling with a girl who is, to put it bluntly, butch.

"Face it, girlfriend. You walk down the street with her, you out yourself. Everybody knows what you are doing together. Clerks in the Galleria will know your business. If you feel like people are looking at you now, you ain't seen nothing yet." Ellie watched the color drain from Rosalind's face.

"You're right. It will only get harder."

Ellie brushed her hands together. "So, break up with her. Don't show up at the auction. She'll get the picture. She'll have a broken heart for a while, but there's plenty of women out there who will want to help her ease her pain. And you can forget it ever happened."

Rosalind let herself experience the thought fully. She saw Taryn's face when she didn't show up at the auction. She pictured leaving an unmarked envelope on the steps at 34 Mariner, a single key inside. She saw Taryn, broken, sitting on the bed in the space she'd created for them. Rosalind's heart lurched; the blood started pumping back toward her skin. Her mind, cruel to the last, added a new player in, a woman walking up behind Taryn, embracing her, stroking her hair. It could be anyone, anyone but her. Then she saw herself going back to her own apartment, alone.

Rosalind felt the air of the tomb crawl across her skin. Even if she took up the knife Ellie offered and cut off Taryn, she couldn't staunch the bleeding. And she saw herself placing Taryn's hand over her heart, repeating the vows she'd already made. Meant only for kings. She knew then. She wouldn't be able to forget. She might break Taryn's heart. Taryn might even recover someday. But she wouldn't forget. She would walk back into her own life, sundered, knowing what she was missing.

"No." It was spoken quietly, an internal conversation that slipped out into the air.

Ellie tilted her head, listening. "What was that?"

"No." It was stronger now, life returning to the voice under it. "I couldn't forget. Even if I broke up with her. I love her, Ellie. That makes everything else different." Rosalind turned and looked at her.

"So we go from there. Do you go to the auction or not?"

The fear bit at her, but she had a place to start from now. "Yes. I don't know if I'll be front row center, but I have to be there. I'm her girl," Rosalind said, raising her head.

"Never thought I'd hear you say that with pride. Good for you." Ellie patted Rosalind's knee. "Come on. Time's a wasting. Some other wench might have snapped her up already."

Rosalind took her friend's hand and stood up. "You were pretty harsh there. Thanks."

"My job. When you aren't being as fabulous as I know you are, I have to kick you around." Ellie smiled, taking the sting from the words.

"You were a little too convincing with how hard it's going to be. I almost thought you wanted me to break up with her."

"I like Taryn. But I love you. I wanted you to choose. I got your back, no matter what." Ellie put her arm across Rosalind's shoulders.

CHAPTER ELEVEN

The auction was being held at an old brick building on Franklin Street that Community AIDS Services often rented for events. A cash bar came along with the small auditorium and proscenium stage. Egyptia knew enough about hosting a spectacle that she could transform the room from a high school cafeteria into a palace. A runway had been rented and set up perpendicular to the stage. Some of the lights from Marcella's had been pressed into service. Lance, the Saturday night DJ, brought in his own sound system. Red and blue lights hit the facets of the disco ball; crepe paper streamers were self-consciously draped across the ceiling, just tacky enough to be camp.

The auction was underway by the time Ellie and Rosalind walked in. Rosalind had insisted on stopping home and getting dressed up first. Whatever else happened tonight, this was her first public event with Taryn, and she was determined to dress accordingly. Her dress was the color of fresh blood, an eye-hurting scarlet that vibrated into the room. Ellie had questioned the choice, until Rosalind put it on.

"I get it. Leave no doubts, take no prisoners. Subtlety isn't in your vocabulary tonight," she'd said, watching Rosalind unfurl her hair.

Rosalind hadn't expected this much of a crowd for a fundraiser. From the front porch, the building was packed shoulder to shoulder. She could hear music and shouting coming from the back room and moved toward it, slipping sideways into the crowd.

"I can't even see the runway from here!" Ellie shouted in her ear.

Most of the crowd was men; the smell of aftershave was thick. Drag queens dominated the crowd, demanding passage from the press of bodies. Rosalind saw one queen use a football player-sized escort to divide the room like the Red Sea, passing unharmed through it.

Rosalind broke to the right, seeing an opening in the crowd. There was a familiar head and shoulders near the back wall, facing the stage. She headed for it, pulling Ellie along by the wrist.

Joe was leaning against the wall, a beer bottle hanging from his hand. He wore jeans and a dark green button-down shirt, looking out of place in the gorgeous costuming of the crowd. His eyes were wandering over the crowd with bemusement. He spotted Rosalind and smiled, lifting the bottle in a salute. Rosalind felt a sense of relief, seeing him, and headed for the back wall.

"I was hoping you'd get here! That boy has been driving me right up a wall. I've had to call your house five times, mine three, and promise to send out a dogsled team to look for you, if it got to be eight. If they didn't have to keep her backstage, she'd be on the porch, I swear. You look like a beacon in the fog, Rosalind. Would you please stop getting more gorgeous every time I see you?" Joe extended his hand to Ellie as he spoke, his eyes shifting from Rosalind to her friend. "I'm Joe."

"Ellie. You're not Papa Joe, are you?"

Joe swore and lifted the bottle to his lips. "Gonna kill that kid," he mumbled.

"Joe, was she really worried?" Rosalind asked, putting her hand on the man's wrist.

He paused with the beer bottle halfway to his lips, his eyes wide and unguarded. "She loves you, you know?" he said quietly. He put the beer bottle down on the floor. When he straightened up, he rolled his shoulders, looking uncomfortable. He looked into Rosalind's eyes and rubbed his chin. "I'm not good at this stuff. She would die before she admitted it, but yeah, she was worried. T got this…feeling this afternoon, and it nearly kept her from coming tonight. She thought you wouldn't be here. That if she came tonight, she'd lose you." Rosalind looked at Joe and saw the concern, as well as the relief, that Rosalind was here.

"You knew I'd be here?" she asked, aware that Ellie was watching their exchange with fascination.

"There's lots of ways to know things," Joe said, lifting his chin. "I knew you'd wear a dress so red it made the air hiss. I knew you loved her."

"Ellie gave me a swift kick where I needed it. Is there any way I can see her?" Rosalind asked. The need to connect with Taryn, to reassure her, was so strong it burned her. Whatever else was going to come from tonight, she knew she was in the right place. Her body proclaimed it, crying out for her lover.

Joe shook his head. "She's about to come on. When this intermission is over, Egyptia will start auctioning again. She's next on the program."

Ellie took Rosalind's arm. "She's a performer. Trust me on this. You don't want to see a performer right before they go on. You'll shatter her focus."

"I want her to know I'm here," Rosalind said stubbornly.

"If we get in front of the stage, she'll know you're here. That dress announces you," Ellie said.

Joe took Rosalind's other arm. "Shall we go let your boy know you're here for her?" he asked with a nod to Ellie.

"Lay on, Macduff. And damn'd be him that first cries, 'Hold, enough!'" Rosalind proclaimed.

"The Scottish play. That's upbeat," Ellie said as they pushed through the crowd. They made it to the end of the runway and claimed the space, thanks to Joe's judicious use of his shoulders and Ellie's natural ability to part a crowd. Rosalind felt like a queen with her attendants, a nice sensation. The festive mood of the audience was seeping in, the level of excitement in the room humming like high-tension wires. She looked to the right and left, getting a feel for her fellow bidders.

More women were coming in, or perhaps coming to the fore; the men gave back, granting them space. Rosalind saw Irene and Garnet, the couple she'd met on the porch during the Better You than Me. Garnet waved, and Irene nodded to her solemnly.

"Looks like you're a celebrity already. I thought you didn't know anyone," Ellie said.

"I don't. I bet I don't know another person here."

"Hey, Ros! Joe!" A voice called out in excitement, from behind them. They turned and saw Laurel coming through the crowd, trailing a very tall, handsome black girl behind her. Laurel stood next to Joe and Rosalind. "Glad I found you! Has she been out yet?" she asked both of them, her face flushed.

"Not yet. She's about to. We just got our space for the bidding wars," Joe answered.

"Great dress, Rosalind. I saw it clear across the room. Guys, this is Robbie. She goes to Buff State. This is Joe, my housemate, and Ros,

Taryn's g—oh, is that common knowledge yet?" Laurel asked, casting a worried look at Rosalind.

"If it isn't, it's about to be," Rosalind said with a laugh. "This is my friend Ellie. Nice to meet you, Robbie, is it?"

"Robbie is fine." The handsome girl unleashed a killer smile.

The lights all came up. Lance stopped the music. Egyptia strolled down the runway, casting sparks like a firefall from her platinum wig and dove gray evening gown, threaded through with silver, like lines of rain. She wore embroidered gloves and had an evening bag in the crook of her left arm. She struck a pose and waited, examining the back of her gloved hand, until a boy ran from the sound booth with a microphone for her. She bent gracefully down and took it from him, a feat of Olympic gymnastic ability, considering the tightness of her dress. She waited until the cheering and catcalls stopped before she spoke.

"That's better. Now you know we do this fundraiser every year and bring you and your wallets out for a good cause. You've been very good tonight. We've raised nearly three thousand dollars for CAS. Give yourselves a hand." Egyptia paused until the clapping subsided. "We decided to do something different this year. Ladies, get your purses out. You know her from Marcella's as the boy who gives trouble its capital T. Taryn."

Egyptia stepped back, to the right of the stage. The lights went to black. A single follow spot came up, hitting the curtain. The music started. Rosalind felt the anticipation grab her by the throat, felt her heart start pounding madly.

A hand parted the curtain, a glimpse of somber black from the shirtsleeve, a spark of gold from a cufflink. The gesture was indolent, the very slowness of it brazen as the curtain was eased open and the figure stepped out into the light. A gasp went around the room, a collective indrawn breath.

Taryn stood, hands in her pockets, head bowed, while the light revealed her. Her shirt drank the light, a black so thorough no details could be made out, buttoned to the neck, no tie. The jacket fit smoothly, draping from her broad shoulders, unbuttoned. Her suit was the complement to Egyptia's gown, a gray that spoke of rainy afternoons under gunmetal skies, the dull glow of old pewter. It was the specter of the twilight time between the burning glory of autumn and the deep death sleep of winter.

It was a color that made Rosalind want to grab Taryn and cuddle with her in front of a roaring fire, to bring warmth back to her, to banish the melancholy that exuded from her. Taryn raised her head slowly, eyes brooding and sad under black brows, and Rosalind felt a shiver caress her spine. Taryn had a goatee, as black as her hair, carving out the shape of her firm jaw. Standing there, for all the world, was a young man, sullen and beautiful.

He looked out over the crowd, the young man with the brooding eyes, resting on nothing. He took his hands out of his pockets and started to walk. Rosalind learned all over again what it was like, staring at Taryn with a room full of people, all focusing on her as an object of desire. Heal me, his walk said. Only you can touch my pain. She wanted to compare it with the stalking of a great cat, but it wasn't that unconscious.

It was the walk of a performer who knows he is being watched, desired, devoured, who can feel the hunger in the room and string it out. The very indifference was calculated to pull more response. It was a challenge, a dare. Could you be the one to break that shell?

It took a moment before her eyes allowed any other sense's input, before she recognized the music. It was a splendid conceit. Probably Egyptia's idea: "I Touch Myself." Taryn walked to the right, to the edge of the runway, her eyes skimming the crowd. The mask of her face didn't change, but her eyes stopped, meeting those of a woman pressed up to the edge of the stage. Taryn leaned forward, just an incline of her upper body, but the impression was one of coming out into the audience. The woman reached out for her, grabbing at the edge of her suit coat. Taryn shook her head and stepped back. She pivoted on her heel, looking down into the crowd to the left.

A woman howled like a wolf; it drew a momentary flash of a grin from Taryn. Jealousy rose up and tapped Rosalind on the shoulder. One of the leather jackets, perhaps? There was no way for her to know how many of the women cheering and catcalling in the crowd had had the pleasure of the drag king. Bile dripped into her stomach. Something of it must have showed on her face.

She felt Joe's hand rest, lightly, on her shoulder. "They don't know her. They look at her, that's all. She looks back at you."

Rosalind reached up and squeezed his hand.

Taryn started walking again, down the runway. Her step had

gathered some bounce; the energy of the crowd was lifting her. Now there was a deliberate effort to make eye contact, to give each woman a second of infinite time when they and they alone had Taryn's attention. Just that moment of total attention, a tilt to the dark head, a smile that hinted at fulfillment. Just a whisper of a promise. I know what you need.

Rosalind could hear the checkbooks being dragged out as Taryn passed. Given a glimpse of her intensity, what would a night be like? The thought was loud enough to be shouted in the tightly packed crowd around the runway.

"This is obscene. They're salivating!" Rosalind said to Ellie. She turned to her friend to find a suspicious blush on her cheeks. "Oh, Ellie. Not you too."

Ellie grinned. "I'd say it was professional interest, but damn, if I could find a man who looked like that! I sure hope Linda made it. She'll kick herself for missing this."

Rosalind had studied Shakespeare for over six years and thought she knew a thing or two about theater. She knew, intellectually, that the stage was only an elevation of a few feet, that the lights were a simple hang, that this person before her was the same girl who had lain naked in her arms. But the stage worked its magic, making Taryn in the suit the color of old pewter seem like a stranger. Her charisma was staggering, amplified by the desire showing on the women's faces.

Rosalind felt the urge to make her presence known, to let everyone in the room know that Taryn was hers. She felt possessive, proud, and confused, her desire to be anonymous warring with her need to have Taryn acknowledge her. Taryn certainly wasn't appropriate, she thought, watching the drag king walk. She was magnificent. Taryn was headed for the end of the runway. She looked out over the crowd, eyes sweeping the room, catching sight of Joe, Laurel, then—

She stopped dead, letting the mood of the crowd carry itself along without her. Her eyes found Rosalind, and her face transformed. The character fell away, and Rosalind saw the joy break across her face, saw the blinding smile of welcome. It was a look as intimate as a touch, heedless of the audience; it reached right out to Rosalind and embraced her. It was a naked look, offering Rosalind whatever she wanted for showing up, for coming through. Rosalind put two fingers over her heart, in a gesture she hoped Taryn would read.

The music stopped. Egyptia took up the microphone. "I'll start the bidding at fifty dollars. Any takers?"

"Fifty!" The woman called from the left of the runway, her hand shooting up. Rosalind looked over at her. It was the woman Taryn had bent down and flirted with. She was blond, in her thirties, and her face had the flushed look of a woman seeing something she wants. She kept her eyes on Taryn as she bid.

Rosalind recognized that look. It'd been hers, the first night at Marcella's. She felt a moment of empathy for the woman, then remembered what she was bidding on was a night with her lover. Before Rosalind had a chance to adjust, to respond, the figure had climbed up to one twenty-five and kept going.

"Are you waiting to let it top out before bidding?" Joe asked, concerned.

"No! I can't get an edge. They keep skipping over each other."

Egyptia was working the crowd, mike in hand, stirring the women up. She avoided the front of the runway and Rosalind, refusing to walk over or make eye contact.

"What is she doing? Egyptia ignored me!" Rosalind asked Joe, grabbing his arm.

"It's a fundraiser. I'm sure she's just driving the price up," Laurel said.

"She doesn't have to. It's at three fifty already. None of the men went for that," Joe said.

"We have three fifty, can I get three seventy-five?" Egyptia cooed into the mike.

Colleen pushed to the edge of the stage, holding up a fistful of cash. "I've got that!" she called, getting Egyptia's attention.

Two things happened inside Rosalind's head so quickly that they might have been simultaneous. The first was a light going on, a recognition of who might have had a motive to issue a complaint against her. The second thing was simpler, a primal reaction, like a wolf baring its fangs. In essence it said, *Oh no, you don't.*

The rational part of her brain, the part that had carried her with great success through her life as an academic, recognized this as the moment to practice Dr. Grey's recommended circumspection. Buffalo had many of the elements of a small town, particularly the community she now moved in.

The traditional distance between teacher and student broke down rapidly if you hung out in the same bars, went to the same events, and, in this case, slept with the same people. It was her responsibility to recognize that potential problem and adjust for it. Making a public statement right now about who she was seeing could easily backfire. All she had to do was express interest in Taryn, and she was outed.

"Five hundred," she called out, in a voice trained to reach into the head of the most bored freshman in the back of a lecture hall. She threw one arm up and felt like a neon sign, in her red dress. Egyptia couldn't ignore her now.

No one could ignore her, as it turned out. The crowd turned and looked. Egyptia was forced to acknowledge the bid.

"We have five hundred from the fierce sister at the end of the runway. Can I get five twenty-five?"

Rosalind looked directly at Colleen, her stare as steady as a cobra's. *That's right. I'm throwing five hundred dollars down in public for Taryn. If you're going to have something against me, then it's going to be worth it.*

Colleen looked away, shuffling her bills. Rosalind nearly breathed a sigh of relief, her eyes daring Colleen to keep bidding. Maybe this was over; she could go collect her winnings.

"Five twenty-five!" It was the blond woman off to the left.

Egyptia lit up. She stalked the diameter of the stage, from Rosalind to the blond woman.

"I have five twenty-five! Come on gals, this is for charity. You know a night with the bad boy is worth a few lousy bills. Picture it…" Egyptia slid next to Taryn and draped herself on Taryn's arm. "You get to go out on the town; you got the handsomest boy in Buffalo escorting you. You gonna tell me that ain't worth a little more?"

"Do you have more money?" Ellie asked.

"I cleared out my savings account. I can keep going." Rosalind said, then motioned to Egyptia. "Five fifty."

"Oooh, we got us a bidding war! Honey, I know you want this; I can see it in your eyes. You got five seventy-five for me, don't you?" Egyptia asked, holding the mike out to the blond woman.

She nodded. "Five seventy-five."

"Six hundred," Rosalind said, looking at Egyptia.

The drag queen smiled so hard, her face looked like it might stretch that way permanently. "Good going, sister! What about you? Don't you tell me you're done? You got friends, don't you?"

The blond woman grabbed the woman standing next to her and conducted a swift negotiation. "Six fifty," she said, looking back up.

"Six seventy-five!" Ellie yelled, and Rosalind looked at her. "For you, of course."

"Seven hundred." The voice came from the right side of the stage, a cool, measured voice that carried without effort. Egyptia, Rosalind, and the blond woman all looked simultaneously.

The speaker was a woman in a yellow silk shirt and black pants. She wore her hair in a knot at the back of her neck. It accentuated the proud carriage of her head. She looked, Rosalind thought, the way dancers and choreographers look, in complete control of every muscle in their body. She was gorgeous, and Rosalind felt her stomach drop.

Egyptia shook her head. "We have seven hundred from the sister on the right. Can I get seven twenty-five?"

"Say something! You have to bid," Ellie hissed in Rosalind's ear. Rosalind looked at the new bidder with a sense of wonderment and a sense of recognition. Where had she met this woman before? She had a definite reaction to this woman. It could be because she was bidding on Taryn. Yes, probably that. The recognition threw her for a moment, making the silence following Egyptia's question seem much longer.

"Ros?" Ellie asked.

Rosalind tore her eyes away from the new bidder and looked toward the stage. Taryn was staring at her, eyes wide. It brought her back to earth. There was a business transaction to be handled.

"Seven fifty," Rosalind called out, to a relieved Egyptia. It was obvious that the drag queen could feel Taryn's nervousness and knew she'd get killed for letting someone else purchase her for the night. Taryn was practically vibrating; the energy coming off her was making Egyptia back away. This had gone far enough in the name of charity; now it was starting to turn. Egyptia held up the mike.

"We got seven fifty. Going once, going twice—"

"Eight hundred."

Egyptia stopped, midsentence. "Excuse me?"

The woman simply folded her arms and waited, knowing that the drag queen had heard her. She had the distinct air of a woman who need not repeat herself.

"You girls sure love your charity! We got eight. Can I get eight twenty-five?" Egyptia asked, almost pleading with Rosalind.

"Eight fifty," Rosalind said firmly.

Egyptia sighed in relief. "Eight fifty. Going once, going—"

"Nine hundred" came the bid, from the right of the stage. Egyptia glanced at Rosalind, to see if she was able to keep going.

"Nine fifty," Rosalind said, looking at Taryn. She had the money. It would be a stretch, but she could do it. What mattered was the look on Taryn's face when she upped her bid without hesitating. That look, from those eyes, was worth going broke for.

"Nine seventy-five." The woman wasn't giving up. The crowd watched the exchange in silence, heads darting back and forth like a tennis match.

Rosalind prepared to throw everything she had into the ring, to ask Joe and Ellie and Laurel for all their cash. Her mother, once, had told her that some things are worth begging, borrowing, or stealing to have. She had never said what those things were, but in that moment, Rosalind knew.

"One thousand." Rosalind's voice was steady, her shoulders back, her head up. She was letting everyone in the room know, she was throwing it all on the line for Taryn.

The woman to the right of the stage drew in breath to counter bid. Rosalind could see that Egyptia knew she was about to be in so very much trouble and didn't know how to prevent it.

Taryn moved. She threw her suit coat back, as a gunfighter throws back her duster. With her right hand she reached back and drew forth her wallet. She held up that square of black leather so no one in the room could mistake her gesture. Then she threw it to Rosalind.

It didn't take as long as it seemed for the wallet to pass through the air, for Rosalind to reach out and snag it. But the weight of every eye in the crowd slowed its descent. When Rosalind's hand closed on Taryn's wallet, silence fell. The new bidder recognized the gesture and let her indrawn breath out without sound. Territory was recognized. Ground was given. The bid stood at one thousand.

Egyptia knew better than to let it rest. "Going once, twice, sold! To the fierce sister in the red dress. You can come backstage and meet your date."

Taryn ignored Egyptia and stalked to the end of the runway in three swift strides. The crowd gave back, knowing they were witnessing something remarkable. It was magnificent, the way she paused on the lip of the stage and extended her hand to the woman in the bloodred dress.

Rosalind put her hand in Taryn's and was lifted up onto the runway, Taryn catching her around the waist with one strong arm. Taryn set Rosalind on her feet, but left the arm around her waist. Her eyes locked with Rosalind's, blocking out the room, the lights, the crowd. She looked ready to drown in her lover's gaze, reckless and mad, poised on the edge of a cliff, listening for a single spoken word to lure her back.

Rosalind felt the crowd, the lights, the weight of the eyes on her and on her lover. The public declarations had been made now, in both their worlds. She knew this and knew that there would be fallout from it.

But the blue eyes worshipping her gave her the world in a single, careless gesture, open and vibrating with need. So Rosalind did the only thing there was left to do. There, on stage, before the eyes of friends and enemies, new allies and former lovers, she kissed her drag king. She felt Taryn's arms close around her, and the feeling of unease she'd carried since meeting with Dr. Grey evaporated. The heat of the body in her arms banished the tendrils of fear.

Egyptia stood behind them, hands on her hips. "This is your date, Taryn. Taryn, this is Rosalind," she said dryly.

It was very different kissing Taryn while she wore a mustache and beard. The hair was rough against her skin. Rosalind pulled back, her arms wound around the drag king's neck.

"Lovely to meet you. Karen, was it?"

Taryn grinned, a flash of white teeth through the black goatee. "Yeah, Roseanne."

"Enough. Take it backstage. I'll be accused of fixing the auction." Egyptia pushed Taryn toward the curtain.

A howl came from the audience, followed by more, until the room rang with the sound of a wolf pack. Taryn threw them a smile over her shoulder, generous with all the world, now that her arm was firmly around Rosalind.

The curtain fell closed behind them, leaving them alone in a twilight space pierced by spears of pale yellow light. Taryn pulled Rosalind against her immediately, bending her head down.

"I was hoping you'd make it in time," she whispered, inches from Rosalind's skin, her breath caressing her lover's face.

"And miss bidding on the most devastatingly handsome boy in Buffalo? I'd have to be crazy. You had a roomful of women just panting to buy you for the night." Rosalind's hands moved to Taryn's shoulders, down her arms, feeling their shape through the cloth.

"There was only one that mattered to me," Taryn said, her voice rippling with restrained emotion.

"You managed to let everyone know that, without saying a word. That was clever, but I think I heard a few hearts breaking."

"Are you sorry?"

"No. I almost couldn't believe it when you tossed me your wallet. It was like seeing you at Marcella's, larger than life. It was hard to remember that you were…my lover. I don't think I've said that to you before," Rosalind said, looking up at her face. What she saw there gave her pause.

There was a look of fear on Taryn's face, badly masked. The pain was so raw, it hurt Rosalind to see it, and to see it in Taryn.

"Baby, what is it?" she asked, her heart pushing against her ribs.

"I…you didn't. Say that to me before."

Rosalind smoothed down the lapels of Taryn's coat, her expression softening. "I had a hard day today, baby. I came up against something I wasn't ready to face."

The sudden tightening of Taryn's face was evidence of her fear. Rosalind lay the palm of her hand against her jaw until she felt it relax. "Hear me out, okay?"

Taryn nodded stiffly.

"I didn't know if I was going to make it tonight. The head of my department called me in. Someone issued a complaint against me and accused me of sleeping with a student."

Taryn's eyes flew wide. "What?"

"I think it was…someone who doesn't like my spending time with you and thought they could use your age against me. I got that impression from Dr. Grey. He not so subtly told me to straighten up and fly right, and to do it publicly."

"Bastard," Taryn said, and bared her teeth. "Can he do that?"

"Yes and no. It's not legal, but it wasn't a formal complaint, so he can claim it was a friendly conversation. The advice was to lay low, not give any grounds for rumors to start," Rosalind said, and shook her head.

Taryn's face changed, cooling like wax. "So the auction—"

"Wasn't what Dr. Grey had in mind when he 'advised' me."

Taryn hadn't moved, but Rosalind felt her retreat, felt a distance open between them. She couldn't leave Taryn out there alone in her thoughts. She might not decide to come back.

"I drove over to Delaware Park, to the spot you showed me on our first date. I'm not sure what I was looking for. I called Ellie, and she reminded me of what was important."

Taryn swallowed. "And what would that be?"

"What you love. What makes you wake up at night crying. What you can't live without." Rosalind's smile was tender, offering herself to Taryn. "You."

Tears came to Taryn's eyes. She fought them, blinking them back. "You have a good memory for words."

"There's a lot of things I could have done. I went home and put on the reddest dress I owned, cleaned out my savings account, and came here, to win my boy for the night. I've never wanted much out of life, Taryn. But tonight, I wanted more than anything to be a woman who wouldn't let her lover down."

"You didn't let me down," Taryn almost growled, around the stone in her throat. "I know I'm not an easy person to be with. I carry some baggage, you know? People won't always be as cool as Eric was. Now your job might be on the line. I guess all I'm saying is, if you need to bail, I understand." Taryn's head went up, like a dog expecting a blow.

"Oh, honey." Tears that she didn't know were there spilled from Rosalind's eyes. "I could spend the rest of my life trying to forget you, and that's all I'd be doing, trying. You're in my blood."

"You're not bailing?" Taryn asked, eyes narrow.

"I'm not bailing," Rosalind affirmed, and was crushed in an immediate hug. Taryn's lips were close to her ear.

"Good. I wasn't really cool about letting you go." Taryn relaxed her fierce hold just enough to kiss Rosalind. Rosalind laughed against her open mouth. "What?"

"Sorry, sweetheart. Your mustache tickles."

"Oh," Taryn said, sheepish. "I could take it off."

"What's it made of? It looks real." Rosalind touched it.

"Spirit gum and my hair. I save it when I go to the barber, for full drag."

"I love kissing you. I never pictured kissing you when you had a dark mustache. It seems a little distant. You go take it off and meet me out front."

"You want me to take this off?" Taryn asked, indicating her suit.

"No, you look gorgeous. Just the beard. Go on. I have some explaining to do, I'm sure."

Taryn started to walk away, and Rosalind watched, enjoying the lope of her long legs. She gave in to her impulse and reached out, slapping her on the ass. Taryn gave her a surprised look over her shoulder.

"Just checking the merchandise," Rosalind said, and smirked.

Taryn looked like she was about to object, then smiled. She sauntered off, starting to sing.

Rosalind was humming when she walked back into the crowd. There was a spring in her step, a sense of triumph all out of proportion to winning Taryn for a night. She felt like she'd climbed Everest without gear, clawing her way up with naked hands. But Everest hadn't been all that hard, in the end, and the view from the top was more sublime than anyone had ever told her.

Egyptia had started the bidding again, and the men in the crowd were surrounding the runway. Rosalind glanced off to the doorway and saw Joe, standing with his back to the dark wood frame, guarding the passageway. It was a condition of the light, a reflection from the stage, the positioning between one room and the next, but he looked different to her. For the first time, Joe looked weary. The light made his green shirt look like a patch of a storm-ridden sky; his arms hung down loosely from his shoulders. His head was resting back against the wood, arching his neck, making him look like a sacrifice waiting for the knife. Rosalind stopped in the press of the crowd.

Something whispered in his ear, he turned his head right toward her, a restrained smile offered as a greeting. He took up a glass of red wine from the floor and handed it to her, the gesture carrying some of the easy grace that marked him.

"She seemed happy to see you," he said, reaching for his beer. "Your friend said to meet her by the bar. Listen, Rhea called, she's feeling tired tonight, but she insisted that I invite you to the house tomorrow night. We're having a full moon circle, and it's important that you be there."

"Joe, are you all right?"

"You'll be there tomorrow?" he asked, ignoring the question.

"Of course. What's going on?"

A look of annoyance crossed his face, something Rosalind had never seen. His brows drew down, his eyes narrowed into dangerous slits. "I'm going, damn it! Stop crowding," he said, his head to the side. He turned back to Rosalind. "Sorry. There's quite a mob clamoring to get in tonight, and they all want to talk to you."

Rosalind looked into his eyes and saw the effort at control, like a man blocking constant pain. "You see things, the way Rhea does," she said, letting that realization come over her.

"Different. Rhea has a narrow focus. She can see specific things for specific people. She cultivates it. I get flashes, when I don't look for them. Never did me any good, so I stopped listening. But tonight, it's like somebody put a lightning rod into my head," he said ruefully, rubbing at the back of his neck. "Ros, I'm not much good at this. But we have to talk. It's important."

"You want to go somewhere quiet?"

"No. This is the sort of conversation made for doorways. Just hear me out, then I'll try to explain it. You did the right thing, coming tonight. It may seem like a small thing, but it set in motion a chain of events. Everything is linked, forward and back. A small thing can break a pattern."

"You know Rhea doesn't like me," Rosalind said, despite Joe's request.

"Rhea is afraid of you, Ros."

"But why would she be afraid of me? I won't—" She broke off, unable to finish the sentence. The pain in her head blossomed.

"Rhea is a woman to hold fast to what always has been. Her strength is the keeping firm, the rock. Not time, nor pain, nor death can alter her. She is fixed and set, eternal and unchangeable. I'm her opposite. My strength is water, giving way and moving around. Eternal change unfixed in any form. I am Love that can fill any shape," Joe said, the pain retreating from his eyes.

"I can't accept that, the way things have always been. There has to be another way. We'd still be chopping each other down with swords if there wasn't."

"That's your strength. The belief in goodness, no matter what. The blade of grass that splits the stone. You confront from love. You'll be the one to split the pattern. When a voice comes, listen to it. Don't expect it to make sense. I expect you're pretty good at that already." Joe smiled at her, warmth coming back into his face.

"I've had some practice this week in learning to accept what I would have thought to death before."

"Has it been only a week? Mighty Aphrodite, it seems like we've known you forever, Ros." Joe lifted his hand to his forehead, wincing.

"Pain?"

Joe smiled, with effort. "Pain isn't the worst thing that happens."

"What's the worst thing?" Rosalind asked impulsively. There was a moment of stillness about Joe that was profound. He might have been a statue, but for the life in his liquid eyes.

"Having love leave. I'll see you tomorrow?"

"Count on it." Rosalind clasped his arm.

Rosalind left the doorway and pushed on into the bar. She saw Ellie first, her blond head thrown back in a laugh, the force of her joy like an arc of lightning coming from her. Affection flooded Rosalind. Lovers change the world, but best friends get you through it. She knew she'd never have had the courage to come tonight if Ellie hadn't held up the mirror and offered her a glimpse. What had Joe said? Everything is connected.

Ellie was absorbed in an animated conversation with a woman who wore her hair in dreadlocks. She wore jeans and a black leather jacket, in the way that Ellie wore them. Dramatically. Something the woman said was cracking Ellie up; she was doubling over with laughter. Rosalind walked up behind the woman, catching a fragment of what she was saying.

"Girlfriend, I'd have been like, 'Get your damn hands off my property!' Good thing you warned me she was taken, or I'd have made a fool of myself throwing money down. Yo, Egyptia, got me a trust fund over here!" She laughed on the end of the sentence, a rich, full sound that Ellie echoed.

"Ros! Hey, I ran into Linda, she made it after all. Linda Alejandros, Rosalind Olchawski," Ellie said, presenting them.

The woman turned. She had a striking face, broad cheekbones under red-brown skin, a curve of eyebrow that belonged in movies from the forties. She held out a hand full of silver rings.

"Good meeting you. Congratulations on your winnings. Ellie was just torturing me by telling me she meant to take me to Marcella's last Friday. I see I'm a week too late."

"Or I was just in time, depending on your viewpoint. You wouldn't be the friend from the department that was behind the starter kit, would you?"

Linda held up her hand. "Guilty. When Ellie came to me, it gave me a charge thinking I could make a difference. Sure wish one of those had been ready for me when I came out, with some Audre Lord and Barbara Smith. Although, seeing the cause, I'm surprised you needed a starter kit."

"Call it a cultural introduction. Ros is stuck back in the Elizabethan era," Ellie said, smirking. "When's lovergirl coming out to join us?"

"Momentarily. I was lucky she has a good sense of audience dynamics. I'd never have won her without that wallet toss. I bet that wench across the runway would have—"

"Kept bidding until she got what she desired." The cool voice came from over Rosalind's shoulder.

Rosalind saw Ellie's eyes go wide, saw Linda glance down at her drink, and knew she was in trouble. She turned and saw the woman who had bid against her.

"Rosalind Olchawski, Marilyn Huang. Marilyn is—" Linda said.

"The wench who bid against you," the woman said with a hint of amusement. "I had no idea Taryn was spoken for, until she tossed her wallet. I did restrain myself once the terms had been clearly outlined."

"Marilyn's the artist in residence at ArtSpace for October. I'll be working with her, developing a performance piece, and I thought she might like to get a feel for the community," Linda explained, as Marilyn and Rosalind sized one another up.

Rosalind decided immediately that she had met the coolest, hippest woman in all the world. This Marilyn was gorgeous, and she wore that knowledge openly. Where Sandhya, who had been Rosalind's standard for staggeringly beautiful, made little of how she looked, this woman lived in it. Marilyn Huang looked like the kind of woman who never got ruffled, not in physical exertion, not in hatred, not in the act of love.

Every word, every gesture, every incline of her head was measured, calculated, controlled, and deliberate. Coupled with the detachment was a sense of personal amusement. Her lips quirked at the corners, as if all life was a private joke.

"Where are you from, Marilyn?" Ellie asked, diverting the woman's eyes from her friend.

"New York. I'm here on a NYFA fellowship. I knew about ArtSpace, of course, but I never expected to find a thriving drag culture in Buffalo. I'm pleasantly surprised," Marilyn said, her eyes slipping back to Rosalind.

"You never know what you're going to find when you stop expecting." Rosalind's eye was drawn across the floor.

Taryn was in the doorway, framed against the dark wood, searching. She'd removed the goatee, but still looked like a beautiful young man, unconscious of the way people stared longingly at her when she paused. Her eyes were restless, scanning the room, pale under dark brows, until they found Rosalind. Then the warmth in them would have melted steel, reworked stone.

Rosalind absorbed that welcome, hearing it like music from the doorway. It was as explicit a declaration as the kiss on the runway had been. Women, staring at Taryn, followed her line of sight and looked away.

"Forget what I said earlier. I don't want a man who looks like that. I want a man who looks at me like that," Ellie said to Rosalind.

Rosalind smiled, knowing she was in love, knowing that it was as visible in the room as light. That smile pulled Taryn across the threshold to her side.

"Hello, Taryn. Apparently I'm the cruise director this evening. May I present Linda Alejandros, UB Theater. Marilyn Huang, artist in residence, ArtSpace. Taryn, local performer and drag king," Ellie said grandly, as Taryn slipped in next to Rosalind, fitting herself against the woman's hip.

"Hey," Taryn said, inclining her head to the trio. Her eyes passed from Linda to Marilyn, and she stopped, a puzzled look on her face. "Do I know you?"

"I imagine not. I think we'd both remember that. You have a wonderful presence on stage. Some real potential," Marilyn said, her eyes examining Taryn's face.

"We were going to the Lavender Door for a drink. Why don't you two join us?" Linda said to Rosalind.

It drew Rosalind's attention away from feeling suddenly invisible. She weighed her answer, wanting to get Taryn alone, but not wanting to repeat her fit of jealousy from the other night. Linda she liked and would enjoy talking with. But. There was something about Marilyn that rubbed her the wrong way, and not the least of which was her bidding on Taryn. Or the way her eyes now devoured Taryn as if she were an appetizer. Taryn's arm was around her waist. She felt her fingers against her back, the heat soaking through the thin fabric of her dress.

"Sure," Rosalind said, noting the smile on Taryn's face.

"Wonderful. I think we have a lot to discuss," Marilyn said, looking at Taryn.

CHAPTER TWELVE

Down along the Niagara River, where the lights of Canada can be seen across the black water, deceptively close, there runs a road. Past the bait shops and taverns, past the Great American porn shop, where Niagara Street elbows into Tonawanda, is a wasteland. The warehouses close up at night, leaving the street empty and barren. It's not a place anyone lives. But there is a house, behind a thicket of hedge, just past the curve in the road. You'd never see it unless you knew it was there.

A dirt and gravel driveway climbs the small rise to the right; a billboard dominates the space to the left. At the top of the rise, the train tracks cut across the grass. Makes it hard to tell if there is a right side to the tracks.

There's no sign, no markings to indicate a place of business. The windows in the front are so small they might be postcards. There is a white enameled screen door and a single concrete step up into the weathered purple-gray house.

The Lavender Door was the deep cover of the lesbian community. Some of the men's bars had a high tourist ratio, like Marcella's, or even Heat, depending on the night. Those were the places to go to dance, to hear loud music, to pose and strut in front of disinterested but good-looking young people.

Lavender Door had few tourists. You had to know someone to get in. It was a blue-collar neighborhood bar with no dance floor, no DJ, one pool table, and one bar. There was a jukebox with Melissa Etheridge and Patsy Cline. Up two steps was the back room, a few tables and chairs, a dartboard. Sliding glass doors opened onto the patio, triangular with the train tracks, surrounded by a high wooden fence. Candles in squat red and blue glass holders sat on picnic tables, unseasonable lights strung overhead. There was a redwood bench and a hibachi for the nicer weather.

It was a dyke bar. A place that sponsored softball teams and book clubs, had dinners the third Sunday of every month, Michigan reunion parties, remembered birthdays and anniversaries. It was where you went to get a drink after funerals and family gatherings, to find a piece of yourself again, where nobody would argue with you.

Rosalind let Ellie direct her from the backseat of the Saturn. "It doesn't look like anything is down here," Rosalind said, looking at the stretch of broken windows in the silent concrete buildings.

"There is, you just have to look for it. Linda took me down here once. Have you been here?" Ellie asked Taryn, who was sitting very quietly in the front seat.

"Yeah," Taryn said, looking out the window.

Rosalind put her hand on Taryn's thigh, feeling the muscle through the gray suit. "You okay, baby?"

Her head fell back against the seat, her neck arched, as Joe's had been, an invitation to Fate's knife. The image disturbed Rosalind; she was glad when Taryn sat up.

"Something's changing," she said, her eyes looking like rain-slicked pavement in the streetlight. Rosalind felt a hand close on her heart. She squeezed Taryn's leg, unable to answer.

"What is?" Ellie asked.

"Everything. The season's changing. It's more than that," Taryn said, shaking her head. "Doesn't make sense."

"Tonight was a big night. You showed everyone that you were taken. That might be affecting you," Rosalind said. There had to be more to it than that. Joe had been feeling odd things; even she had a sense that something was off kilter. The warning note of pain sounded in her head, distracting her.

"Finally, a perfect opportunity to assert best-friend rights. So, Taryn, how taken are you?" Ellie asked with diverting cheerfulness, leaning over the front seat.

"What?" Taryn turned her head toward Ellie, her profile sharp against the black outside the windshield.

"Simply put, I'm grilling you. You step off stage and sweep up the best woman in Buffalo." Ellie cleared her throat and lowered her voice. "What are your intentions toward our Rosalind?"

It was a game she could end with a word, Rosalind knew. Ellie was sensing a somber moment and decided not to let that happen. All Rosalind would have to do would be say her name and it would be over. She didn't. She waited, in the growing silence, for her answer. There was a loud sound inside the car that took her a moment to recognize as her own heart beating. She pulled the car into the dirt and gravel driveway and parked along a railroad tie.

Taryn raised her head, speaking to Rosalind, but looking at Ellie. "To love her for as long as she'll let me. To be the one who holds her when she wakes up in the middle of the night. And if the world won't give her everything she deserves, to change the world."

Ellie sighed and leaned back, spreading her arms across the seat.

"Would it be all right if I just said ditto?" Rosalind asked, taking Taryn's hand.

"After that? Sure. I'll forget you're a lit prof. You're going to have to cut it out, Taryn, or I'm gonna forget I bat for the other team," Ellie said, fanning herself.

"Do I get your approval, best friend?" Taryn asked, leaning her chin on the seat and looking at Ellie, her eyes clear and sharp in the planes of her face.

"We'll see. Treat her well through the winter, and we'll talk about it."

"Fair enough," Taryn said. She got out of the car, holding the door open for Ellie, then for Rosalind. Rosalind took her arm, letting Taryn escort her across the uneven ground. Ellie walked ahead of them, then turned on the concrete step, her eyes artlessly open, drinking them in.

We're worth watching, Rosalind thought. It was amazing, to Rosalind, the difference that came over Taryn when she offered her arm. She went from a lanky teenager to a gentleman, a knight whose mail was a suit. And I feel graceful when I'm with her. There's a perfection to us, too seamless to be crafted.

"You two look like something out of a movie, all dolled up. You should be out drinking cocktails at a black tie affair and dancing to a symphony, not getting a beer at a backwater bar in a warehouse district."

Taryn smiled at her. "This backwater is where our people are. 'We go where we love and where we are loved, out into the snow. We go to things we love with no thought of duty or pity.'"

"Paraphrased H.D. Very good. Whoever saw to your education did well," Ellie said, opening the screen door.

"I'll let Rhea know you approve," Taryn said, taking the door from her.

Rosalind could see that Ellie hesitated, nearly protesting, but there was no condescension in the gesture, only a set of manners honed for small occasions, apart from the normal conversations of power. It was a gesture that would go unused in a more public space, for fear of ridicule or violence. Rosalind watched the recognition come over Ellie. In that moment, on the step of the Lavender Door with her best friend's lover holding the portal open, Ellie saw the rift that lay between them. She had never had to think about the consequences of such gestures, as versed in lesbian culture as she was. It was a small moment, but Rosalind saw how Ellie looked at Taryn differently and accepted the courtesy.

A pool game was going on, doubles, the jealous row of stacked quarters testimony to the waiting challengers. Behind the bar a plump, handsome woman in her forties, fair hair cut halfway between neck and shoulders, waved as Taryn came in. "T! Haven't seen you down here in while."

The pool game stopped, the bar stools swiveled, the air in the room grew hushed as a church, drinking in the sight of Taryn casually crossing the floor with Rosalind on her arm. She set her foot up on the rail and leaned on the bar, offering a seat to her lover. It was the gesture of an actor in a play, opening a big scene, courteous and seemingly indifferent to the watching eyes.

"Hello, Sharon. May I present Rosalind, my lover? And her dear friend Ellie," Taryn said, loudly enough to carry to the back of the bar.

Sharon managed to put down, without dropping, the glass she'd been holding and extended her hand. "Good to meet you. You did a show, right? You sound like it," she added, directly to Taryn.

The noise started back up, the jukebox clicked onto a Melissa Etheridge song, play resumed on the pool table. "The auction," Taryn said, knowing that Sharon had heard about it already. No information in the city of Buffalo escaped a good bartender, and Sharon was the best. She had an excellent sense of when not to know certain information and employed it now.

"Oh, really? How'd it go?" she asked, picking a St. Pauli Girl out of the cooler and handing it to Taryn automatically.

"Rosalind won a date with me." Taryn smirked, accepting the beer.

"A good deal more than that, I hope," Rosalind said.

"Ya never know, lightning could strike. You girls want anything?"

"Two St. Pauli Girls," Rosalind said, smiling.

"Comin' at cha," Sharon said, swinging the bottles in her hand and opening them with an economy of motion local to bartenders everywhere.

They walked up the steps into the back room and saw that it was empty. Through the glass doors Rosalind could see two women at the table on the patio. Linda and Marilyn. She quelled an instant feeling of dislike when she spotted Marilyn, not wanting to believe jealousy had such a firm hold on her. True, the woman was a little too collected, and gorgeous, and subtly but explicitly interested in Taryn. So were a few others. She could stand a little competition, she told herself.

There was a candle lit in the center of the table, the flame dancing in the red glass, casting elf shadows on the faces of the women. "Ready to swim with the sharks?" Ellie asked, her hand on the door.

Rosalind looked through the glass and saw Marilyn watching Taryn. Her face gave away nothing; her interest was cautiously divided between whatever Linda was saying to her and the figure through the door. It was a minute shift of her eyes, but to Rosalind, it was as brazen as neon.

The motion of Ellie's hand drawing the door back broke Marilyn's concentration. She shifted her gaze to a neutral spot and smiled graciously. Linda followed her look and smiled at them in welcome. "Thought you'd be right behind us. Pull up a couple of chairs. We were just talking about the auction."

"About Taryn, in particular," Marilyn said, and smiled at Rosalind.

Rosalind managed to choke down the urge to smack her and smiled sweetly in return, as Taryn held out a chair for her.

"I'm glad you're here, Ellie. You can back me up. I was just saying that the auction was great theater," Linda said as they sat.

"It was a spectacle, entertaining, but not controlled enough to be theater," Marilyn said coolly.

"What is theater if not a spectacle or entertainment?" Linda asked her.

"It was great performance. It gave a promise, drew you in, fulfilled it, then gave you what you weren't expecting," Ellie said, leaning forward on the table. "I send my students out to see drag shows in my basic acting class. They can learn more about presentation, gesture, about being responsive to their audience, in one night than a week of exercises can teach them."

"Willing suspension of disbelief. Drag has its own culture built in. The audience is in on the joke, knows what to expect, and feels included. The perfection of the illusion is admired, but not needed. If it were truly about the art of it, the perfection, it would be different. A perfect illusion is more real than the real article," Marilyn said, her gentle tone making the words seem inoffensive. Rosalind wondered why they sent her back up, immediately.

Linda snorted and put her beer down on the table. "Listen, I grew up in Buffalo. It's a blue-collar town to the bone. You can talk about levels of sophistication in an audience, suspension of disbelief. What I saw when Taryn came out on that stage, when she pulled Rosalind up there with her for a kiss, was theater. Buffalo is no arts capital, but it is full of communities that do theater, that give time and effort to put their own representations onstage. Lemme give you an example. There ain't that many Puerto Rican/Haitian dyke professors walking around for me to bond with, you know? But when I go to Ujima and see some Ntozake Shange, I'm at home. Part of me is up there, giving back."

"Validation. When you see a reflection of yourself, larger than life, it creates as much hunger as it feeds. It's like being…praised, for having the courage of your desire," Rosalind said.

Linda looked at her, amazed, then gestured with her beer bottle. "Yes! That's it. Having the courage of your desire. I looked at those women's faces when Taryn threw you the wallet and pulled you up there. I thought I'd see a lot of disappointment, but it wasn't that. These women were eating it up, the sight of the two of you. There was something genuine and powerful. Like it wasn't something they got to see before. Not that way."

"People know when something's real, when they get to see the heart, not something made up to satisfy them. When it's done for love, look out," said Ellie. "An image like that has the power to move the world."

Linda nodded, lifting the bottle to her lips.

Marilyn's silvery laugh cut the silence that had settled on the table. "You are visionaries, more than I expected to find in such a city. It's refreshing to listen to you speak."

"Come on now, Marilyn. Tell me that it didn't knock your socks off when Taryn kissed Rosalind. We can be all sophisticated and all that, and still have a primal need to see our own desire reflected," Linda said.

"It was engaging, of course. Desire reflected is powerful," Marilyn said, her eyes on the candle.

"It was more than that. I think there's something there, waiting. Egyptia had a good idea, but it was only half an idea," Linda said thoughtfully. She looked like a woman in the grip of a vision, at the beginning of something that will change many things. She paused, letting the words form in her mind before she spoke again.

"I sense a project," Ellie said, glancing at Rosalind.

"Yeah. A project. That audience was hungry, and they got an appetizer. What if we gave them a whole meal?" Linda drawled, leaning back in her chair.

"You mean—" Ellie started, but Marilyn cut her off.

"A whole show. All women."

"You're with me now. A little attitude, a little feast for the eyes, some performance. The whole spectrum. High femme, passing drag. Drag kings. Plural." Linda's excitement made the words run together.

Taryn, who had been silent for the entire exchange, leaned forward. "A women's drag show?" she said slowly, as if learning the words.

"Exactly. You saw those women tonight. They were eating it up! Imagine giving them a whole show. The house wouldn't be left standing. Listen, it's something unique we can give back to the community. How'd Rosalind put it? Having the courage of your desire," Linda said.

"That'd be some work to take on," Ellie commented.

"I'm a director, you teach acting, Marilyn has a classical dance background. Nobody can teach movement like she can. And, she has to do a project for her residency at ArtSpace. Why not this?" Linda asked, looking across the table at Marilyn.

"I bow to the enthusiasm of the visionary. It would be quick. We'd have to have auditions right away, workshops, begin training. Taryn would train the kings, naturally."

Rosalind watched as something in Taryn caught fire and burned. The light shone from her face, poorly masked with instinctive attitude. Despite the curl to her lip, the surprised curve of eyebrow, she shone like steel in the sun.

"I don't train anybody," she said.

"Come on, you're the original! The King of kings. Who else would give that enthusiasm and experience?" Linda said.

Marilyn looked across the table, directly into Taryn's eyes. "You have the gift. You are raw and untrained, yet you understand gesture and movement, stance. You have the presence. I can give you the craft, voice and character. A whole performance."

Taryn quickened. Her posture didn't change; the lazy slouch of indolent youth didn't alter so much as an inch, but her attention was riveted. "So I get trained while I'm training?" she asked Marilyn.

"As is always the case," she said with the ghost of a smile.

"I know some students that would love to get in on this," Ellie said to Linda.

"We can hold a workshop, get a feel for the talent pool. A drag king workshop. Think you could lead one?" Linda asked, her voice teasing.

Taryn shrugged. "Yeah. I could show the new boys a thing or two."

The conversation took on a momentum of its own, pulled along by the idea, the lure of the project. Rosalind saw it happening, saw the words being strung together, until the show was real, the date had been set, the workshop organized.

This was how things got born into the world, she thought. One person spoke, and the idea burned in the air like a grail. So a conversation, in the back room of a bar on an autumn night, might herald something remarkable.

It gnawed on her, inside of her ribs, a monster that lacked only a fragment of attention to become a Leviathan, the way Marilyn looked at Taryn. Rosalind clenched her jaw against the pain and refused the beast. If Taryn was being seduced by anything, it was the idea held out to her—performing, training others to perform.

Rosalind looked at her lover and saw Taryn fall in love with the idea, bit by bit. *It's my job as your lover to make sure you get to look that happy.* She softened.

In the middle of a sentence Taryn turned and looked at her, her uncanny eyes reaching right into Rosalind. *Anything,* Rosalind vowed in that aching silence. *I will give you anything you desire.*

"This has been awesome, ladies. But I'm calling it a night. There's the matter of a winning bid at the auction to be seen to." Taryn stood and gave them a bow. She held out her hand to Rosalind.

"So, you down with Thursday?" Linda asked.

"Yeah, Thursday's good. I'll be there."

CHAPTER THIRTEEN

Back at 34 Mariner, Rosalind sat on the bed, hugging her knees, and watched Taryn pace. She'd taken off her suit coat and shirt and now prowled the attic in her gray pants, the belt hanging undone. It was an invitation too splendid to ignore, but Rosalind controlled herself, careful of Taryn's mood. There was a manic energy to her, an excitement that wouldn't let her rest.

"Imagine. Me training a bunch of boys." She walked the length of the room and stood in front of the window, hands in her pockets.

"You'd be perfect. You do it for love, that's the strongest reason there is. They'd learn a lot from you," Rosalind said honestly.

Taryn's head turned, looking off into the shadows of the room.

Her stance reminded Rosalind of the statue of David—the width of her shoulders, the way her arms seemed weighted down by her hands. Her eye followed the tattoo of the bull dagger down Taryn's back, across the column of muscle that disappeared into the black leather belt. "You're like a cat in an electric storm," she said, half to herself.

"Hmm?" Taryn turned.

"You're so excited, you're giving off sparks." Rosalind folded the sheets back and patted the bed invitingly.

Taryn raised an eyebrow at her. She prowled across the floor, hands extended like claws. "A big cat. A sleek, deadly beast, a killing machine, a noble black panther," she purred as she approached, her feet as silent on the hardwood floor as the mythic panther.

Rosalind enjoyed the approach and found the comparison to be apt, with the easy play of muscle under her skin, the deceptive smoothness of her movements. But she'd be damned if she'd feed Taryn's ego any more; she was already impossible. "Morris. Self-satisfied and sarcastic," Rosalind said archly.

She never saw her move, never saw the gathering of her legs under her, only felt the rush of air, the impact of something striking the bed. She blinked, finding herself flat on her back, Taryn sitting triumphantly astride her hips. Taryn was grinning from ear to ear, well pleased with herself.

Taryn leaned down, slowly, her eyes narrowed down to slits of balefire. She opened her mouth, achingly near to Rosalind's lips, then turned, her teeth closing on the skin of her lover's neck. She bit, and Rosalind arched her neck.

"Still Morris?" Taryn purred, her tongue snaking out to taste the salt on Rosalind's skin. "You've graduated to Fritz," Rosalind said, closing her eyes.

Taryn stopped and sat up. "Fritz?"

"Before your time. I forget how young you are, sometimes." Rosalind reached up, soothing the lines around Taryn's eyes, caressing the familiarity of her face, the strangeness of it.

"I'm old enough to know better but too young to care," Taryn said, kissing her.

❖

Sleep was reluctant in visiting them, as if a warding had been set against it. Rosalind held Taryn and stared up at the ceiling arch, lost in thick crow-winged shadows. She knew that she should be drifting off into blissful, exhausted slumber as her lover was. She should be reaching for the vault of heaven, not sitting the death watch. Cold water ran along her veins at that thought.

Hadn't she read somewhere that death could not take you if you saw it first? That had to be an old superstition. Ancient. The Egyptians believed in seven souls; maybe death could pluck them off one at a time like flower petals. Where had that thought come from? She'd never done much reading on old Egypt. Now she was feeling that they were neighbors of hers. Seven souls was typically Egyptian and extravagant. Any educated person knew that there was only one soul, winged to ascend toward the Goddess.

Rosalind's hand found the tattoo of the black eagle and felt a jolt of pain move up her arm. The drifting quality to her thoughts fled. What the hell was going on? Grief came and settled on her like the folding of great, dusky wings. Tears moved down her face, she had no idea why.

The pain in her head was a song. She couldn't focus around it. There was no need to feel bereft. Taryn was just sleeping.

Rosalind took a moment to calm herself as she would a frightened child. There was nothing wrong. See? Your lover is right here. She could feel Taryn's breath on her arm, feel the warmth in her skin. Her mind refused to accept these proofs, insisting that disaster had struck. There was no turning aside of fate.

Taryn turned over and buried her head in the pillow. The tattoo of Alexander regarded Rosalind with his deep-set eyes. Remember my choice, he seemed to say. A short life filled with glory and everlasting fame, rather than a long life of obscurity.

"Your lover was already dead when it was your turn to go. I bet he'd disagree with you if he'd lived," Rosalind said, aware that she was talking only to herself.

At last she closed her eyes and willed herself to sleep.

The dreams were immediate. She saw the study, the fireplace, the chair with the book of Alexander's conquests. This time she was in the room, standing by the window. She caught a glimpse of herself in the snowy pane and thought, *I never wear my hair back like that.* The room was all warmth and invitation, but she stood rigid against the cold stone of the window. She was steeling herself against the familiarity of this room, knowing that it was the last time she would ever visit here. The weight of grief descended on her. She had to turn and wipe away tears.

The door opened and a woman walked in. She was tall and rangy, with a body like knit steel from a lifetime of labor. Her black hair was clipped short, unheard of in this day and age. In trousers and a loose work shirt, she was often taken for a man. Rosalind knew this, from the times they had walked down the street together, arm in arm. She didn't want to look at the woman. She was afraid of the welcome she'd see in her eyes.

Sound was muffled in the room, from the snap and hiss that should have come from the fire to the sound of human words. Rosalind knew that she was speaking, but couldn't hear what was being said. From the woman's face she could read them. The look on her face went from welcoming to disbelief. For a moment there was a look of such open need it made Rosalind falter, but her dream self had been expecting that. She watched as her loved began smashing everything within reach in the eerie silence of the dream. Glass shattered and arched as the lamp was hurled from the table.

Only when that sinewy hand picked up the red leather book did her dream self move, seizing her wrist. At the touch the tall woman crumpled to her knees. She saw the woman's head rise, saw her lips move. It was like fire being lashed along her nerve endings. Rosalind watched, helpless, as her dream self backed toward the door. The black-haired woman stayed kneeling in the wreckage of the room.

Rosalind woke, shivering from more than mortal cold. She inched away from Taryn, unable to bear what she had seen. She sat on the floor by the bed, her head folded down on her arms. The door in her head opened; the pain was no longer enough to keep the memories back. She sat rocking as they flooded back. She couldn't bear to be in the room.

Not knowing where else to go, Rosalind fled down to the kitchen. Rhea sat at the table holding a cup of tea. The sight of the witch was oddly comforting, despite her anger at being manipulated. Slowly, deliberately, Rosalind walked to the teapot and poured herself a cup in Taryn's blue mug. She sat down opposite Rhea, staring like a gunfighter at her opponent. Rhea hadn't reacted to her entrance. Rosalind thought that she was expecting it.

"When did you start remembering?" Rhea asked softly, looking down into her tea.

"The morning I picked up a book in a used book shop. I think we used to own it. It opened a door in my head."

Rhea nodded. "I didn't expect that this soon, not with the fog I cast around your memory. You're stronger than I remember. So you recall the conversation we had."

"All of it. Pieces of the last time, too. I keep seeing a study."

"Have you seen *her*?"

Rosalind nodded stiffly.

"How old was she?"

"In her thirties, I'd say."

"Ah. That memory. You're moving quickly. You saw the fight?"

"In pieces. I know I went there to break up with her. Tell her I was getting married."

Rhea sighed, a sound that a woman in terminal pain might make. "You never see the rest. You never see her kill herself. Stubborn, willful child, no matter her age. I, naturally, have to watch, helpless, having already passed."

"Why did you cloud my memory?"

"You know why. To give her a moment of peace. But now you remember, now the cycle begins, the Wheel of Fate turns. The dying starts."

"That's why so much seems familiar. It's the echoes, the things we've been through before. It's happening all over again."

Rhea looked away, then down at her hands. Her eyes were rimmed with red when she looked back up. "I've known Taryn since she was sixteen years old, when she was all anger. I saw her grow up, saw some of that change, saw her get a handle on her temper. I saw her learn to laugh again. But I have never seen her as happy as I have with you. If I could wish you gone, Rosalind, you would be gone. But I made my vows so long ago, and I will never be able to deny her what she loves."

"Are you sure?" It was the first thing that came from Rosalind's lips, followed by shocked silence.

"When you are as old as I am, you learn a few things. No sense in wasting time resisting. Things change. I could never forestall your coming. You belong here. I saw something, watching her and Joe wrestle that bed up to the third floor. I did exactly what I was supposed to do in warning her against you. And she did exactly what she was supposed to do in running toward you with her arms open. And you are doing exactly what you are supposed to do. The cycle is turning. My anger didn't serve any purpose. Fear, I suppose, the same old mortal fear of death and change. We don't rage against the coming of winter," Rhea said, her voice easy, amused.

"Rhea, are you sick?"

"I have cancer. That's the expression it took, this time around. We don't die of arrow wounds as often these days. I don't know how long, and I'm not sure I'd like to. Yes, Joe knows. No, Goblin and Laurel don't." Rhea pushed away from the table and walked to the stove. Her back was very straight, the dress draped on her like a cloth on a statue, a dull red the color of garnets.

"Taryn should."

"No." It was flat and brooked no argument.

Rosalind argued anyway. "Rhea, she worships you. You can't keep this from her."

"It is still my life, Rosalind. I won't have her knowing. It wouldn't change anything." Rhea turned around and leaned against the stove, folding her arms. "Some knowledge changes you, and you can never go back. She doesn't have to live with Death yet. It's my final gift to her."

"She doesn't need a final gift from you. She needs you. There are so many things she—we could do, so you aren't alone. I'm not at all convinced this is a death sentence. Do you have a doctor?"

"So Western, even now. But your line always was. Hidden off in the temple with your scrolls and tablets, the collected learning of the known world. No wonder you still yearn for that environment. I should have known you'd be a professor this time. You always loved to lecture. I do have a doctor. I also have a homeopath, and other sources. That is my gift to my body. You won't understand this yet, but you will remember it for when you need it. This isn't about the body, isn't about this incarnation. Old webs are dragging me down. It is what must be," Rhea said, and crossed her arms over her thin waist.

"I don't believe that. We can set our own destiny."

"Perhaps you do. Perhaps you always did. We disagree on that, but we've never had much of a chance to get together and discuss it, have we? You are the fall, Rosalind. You herald the coming of winter."

"Are you sure? Things are different already, this time. That could change, too. Tell Taryn what's going on, and let us help you," Rosalind argued. She was surprised by the sudden flaring of anger.

"I want your word that you won't tell her. I may not have any choice about my body, but I have a choice about how I deal with it. It isn't your decision to make," Rhea said harshly.

"I think it's wrong."

"You imagine I care what you think? Leave me be." Rhea walked back to the table and sat down.

"We haven't finished this conversation."

"I have."

Rosalind knew she had been dismissed. Rhea sat with her teacup in her hands, as if Rosalind had already left the room. The stubborn strength emanating from the small woman was staggering, a strength of will gained from lifetimes of facing down death. "There has to be a way to end this differently. We can't be pawns, repeating the same mistakes over and over. I won't let that be it," she said desperately, facing the woman at the table. She wasn't prepared for Rhea's reaction.

The witch stood, her face gone dark with rage. *"You* won't? You are taking away everything I value, including my life. You are robbing Joe and Goblin. I will not speak of what you are doing to Taryn. You have always done this. I have some small time left, and I won't let you steal that as well. Get the hell out of my kitchen and leave me be before I forget myself and curse you."

❖

Taryn rolled over as she crept into the room. "Where'd you go?" Taryn mumbled, eyes shut.

"To get a cup of tea."

Taryn smiled. "You're turning into Rhea."

Rosalind froze. She was full of broken glass. She didn't know if she could sit on the bed without turning to dust and blowing away. The need to feel Taryn's skin overwhelmed her. Rosalind lay down next to her and took Taryn's face in her hands.

"You act like you're memorizing my face," Taryn said, leaning into the caress.

"I am," Rosalind confessed, drawing her fingers along the firm jaw, the hidden softness of the skin underneath. This might be the last moment she had with her lover. "You feel like home. But I'm still partly in shock, only knowing you a week. My body is still getting used to having you near. I keep jumping, expecting to find out it's all been a dream."

"Yeah. Me too. People don't get to be this happy. I don't." Taryn rolled off into the blankets and lay on her side. "Like, who did I bribe in heaven to get that? You looking at me like that, across the pillow."

"How do I look at you?" Rosalind asked, folding her hands under her head.

"Like you'll never stop loving me," Taryn said, her tone like a cat's paw.

"For as long as I'm still breathing. And for everything that comes after."

Taryn went still as death, all at once. Her eyes opened, the glitter in them dangerous, feverish. The blood drained away from her face, leaving it white as a funeral mask. "Don't."

"Baby, what is it?" Rosalind reached out to Taryn automatically, but saw her move her body out of the way. "Honey, please. Talk to me."

"Those words. They're like an echo of something I heard a long time ago. But they make my blood cold. Like I can't believe them."

It was terror that Rosalind saw on Taryn's face, naked terror. In that moment, she saw Taryn, knowingly or not, relive their last parting. She saw Taryn's heart break, saw her give up and decide not to go on. The willful retreat from life was there, under the surface of her skin. Maybe not her, this time out. But the memory of it made her go pale as alabaster.

"Taryn, sweetheart. Come back. Stay here with me, baby." Rosalind reached for Taryn as she spoke and found her flesh chill. She rubbed her hands against her back, calling the blood to the surface. Rosalind saw her eyes swim, unfocused, saw her face go slack. It wasn't like watching Joe as he listened to the voices. It was far more frightening. Taryn was gone, her body a gorgeous toy, empty and limp on the bed. Rosalind pulled Taryn into her embrace frantically.

"I don't give a damn who you think you are right now, you come back!" Rosalind growled, the ferocity in her voice making it almost unrecognizable. "Who the hell do you think you are, giving up on me? You did this to me before. I left you, but you left me, too. You walked out on the ice, and you never said goodbye. It took the rest of my life to forgive you for that."

The words were coming from somewhere. Rosalind didn't have time to analyze them. She focused on Taryn's face, the blue tinge to her lips, as if she had gone under the ice. Rosalind sat up, cradling the body in her arms. It felt wildly unfamiliar, but it was something a part of her had longed for all her life, the chance to hold this form, bled of life as white marble, black hair like a spill of ink. She had come back into the flesh to kill her own anger and shame, to move them, as a stone in the road might be moved, to open the way.

Taryn had done this to her before. She wasn't a girl then. She'd been older, but as willful and as stubborn as this arrogant youth. In her hurt, in her pride, she'd given the final reprove to the lover who'd abandoned her. Rosalind didn't separate these thoughts from the ones that screamed for Taryn to wake up, to stop acting like a sullen teenager and open her eyes. Taryn wasn't responding to endearments or touch. Rosalind, panic eating into her stomach, bent over her, her hands digging into the slack muscle of her arms.

"You get one shot at life, moron. We found each other again, don't you dare squander it. Stop acting like a child and face me!"

There was a hint of blue about Taryn's lips, the human frost of life retreating. Rosalind's reason gave in. She shook her violently, calling out to her in words she would never remember later. Her mouth closed over Taryn's, sealing them together, forcing air into her lungs. Her mind had narrowed down to one impulse. She would not be cheated by life. Not this time. The stars could veer from their paths and fall, the earth could tilt off her axis, but her mouth would not leave Taryn's, she would not leave her. In an act of will stronger than the stubborn pride of Taryn, Rosalind forced breath into her lungs.

Taryn coughed. A simple thing, in the scope of the world, but it reduced Rosalind to tears. She coiled herself around her body, sobbing. The heat of her body transferred to her lover; the chill of memory receded with each indrawn breath. Taryn struggled to sit up; Rosalind refused her, keeping Taryn in her arms. "You're not moving," she said, her voice choked with weeping.

"Rosalind?" It was strange, like hearing Taryn's voice from a great distance, but it was her voice.

"Yes, God damn it, it's Rosalind. I'm not letting you do that to me. If you ever try to leave me like that, I swear on Christ's blood I'll kill you."

Taryn gave a choking laugh. "You'll kill me, if I kill myself?"

"Yes, asshole."

"The endearments are smothering me." Taryn pushed, and this time Rosalind did let her sit up. She pressed her hands against her eyes. "I used to wonder why Rhea was glad I couldn't see the way she did. I think I know." She opened her eyes and drew her hands away, slowly. "I didn't try and kill myself. I had a memory of when I did. Not me, but—before."

"I got that part. I'll still kill you." Rosalind let out a shaky breath. "You scared the hell out of me, you know that?"

Taryn looked at her for a long moment, her face an open wound. "You left me," she said at last. "I saw it. You left me, and I didn't make it. I went out onto the ice."

"I didn't leave you. I mean, that was before…I don't remember any of that."

"You know what I'm talking about," Taryn said. It wasn't a question.

Rosalind exhaled heavily. She'd known it would come to this. "Yes. Rhea told me that she thought we'd been lovers before. And that I left you, and you...did what you did. It's why she warned you against me."

Taryn's eyes went wide. "When did she say that to you?"

"A few minutes ago, in the kitchen. I had a dream. I remembered telling you I was leaving."

"Fuck!" Taryn sprang back off the bed as if she'd been branded. She stood, shaking, in the center of the floor. "You knew that, and you didn't say anything to me?"

She started pacing, a tiger in a cage, leaving no room for Rosalind to reply. "I should have known. Rhea's never wrong, and I ran against what she said. That's why I've been feeling so weird. The memory. You're going to do that to me again. It's happening. All that bullshit about loving me forever. I'd heard that before, just didn't know where. I let you in. Now you're going to rip me open." Taryn's voice rose as she paced, as she worked herself into a frenzy, ignoring the woman on the bed. Her emotion rose with her voice, like a dog slipped off the chain.

Rosalind pushed off the bed, landing directly in Taryn's path. She got right in front of her lover and stopped still. "Taryn!" she yelled in her best professor tone.

It worked. Taryn looked slightly stunned, reminded that there was another person in the room.

Rosalind pointed to the bed. "Sit yourself down. Now."

Taryn sat on the edge of the bed, looking warily up at Rosalind. Rosalind was acting like she'd never seen her, angry, in control, commanding. It captured her attention.

"I didn't tell you because I didn't know it yet. I've just recovered the memory of it. I don't *see* things the way Rhea does, or Joe, or you. What was I supposed to say, sorry I betrayed you in another life? You didn't seem to have any connection to it, and Rhea said it was too hard for you to remember. And it broke my heart, the thought of causing you pain. I couldn't face it."

Rosalind's voice softened. She stood in front of Taryn, not letting her look away. "I do believe it now. There's too much between us that speaks to it."

"So what does that mean for us now? Are you going to leave me again?" Taryn asked, her voice nearly a whisper in the dark room.

Rosalind reached out and caressed her face. "Oh my sweet boy. What Rhea saw, that memory of yours, that's the outcome of choices made in another life. It can't be undone. Maybe it was us, or part of us, but that doesn't have to mean we live the same thing over and over. I won't let it. All I have to go on is what I know. I know that I love you, and not even Death will change that. I think we get to do it different this time, if we choose to. I made my choice tonight, when I bid on you at the auction. If my mistake was leaving you, I won't make the same one this time. I choose you, baby."

Taryn's face was as smooth as marble, unreadable. In the silence that followed and pooled around her, Rosalind waited. She let the fear gnaw at her, let the terror come. She had declared herself, and she told what she knew to be true. It was up to Taryn to choose, now. Trusting her, trusting in the promise she held out, meant going beyond her own fear. The memory that had possessed her was an old one, and Rosalind didn't know what it had been like, experiencing it. Pain like that, even dulled with the passage of time, might be too much to risk again. But that was always the choice. Love or fear. You couldn't have both.

Rosalind took a step back from the bed, then another. She stood, unknowingly, in a shaft of light from the street lamp, sparks of pale gold and scarlet showing in her hair like a nimbus of fire. Taryn looked up at her lover and saw the look of certainty, of grace, that allowed her her own response. She was struck through with this woman, the light that shone from her. Her greatest fear, the one that all but crippled her, was losing this woman. Her lover.

In that moment of recognition, Taryn decided. She took a step, staggered, then fell to her knees, embracing Rosalind. Like a knight, she knelt before her liege and bowed her head. Rosalind's hands were in her hair, combing around the shape of her skull. Taryn, gone nearly blind with longing, raised her eyes to Rosalind. Her fingers closed on Rosalind's waist. Taryn looked up into the face of her lover and laid her heart like an offering on the altar. "Don't go. I choose you."

Rosalind's hands were gentle on her shoulders, light as the touch of a sculptor learning the stone, firm as gravity. With the impartation of her will through her fingertips, she told her to stand.

"Taryn." She said that name, and nothing else had form in the universe. By saying it, spirit was made flesh, delight made visible. She felt a burden lift from her soul, one she'd been carrying before memory was fact. Its weight was so much a part of her that the lifting of it left her giddy, vertigo-struck. Rosalind's soul remembered it had wings and stretched them, yearning upward, set free by the welcome in her eyes. *For me*, she thought recklessly, *after all, for me*. The time had come to set the next burden down. The Wheel was turning.

Taryn kissed her, in the silence that widened like the silence in the moment before creation. Taryn pulled back and put her arms around Rosalind, lifting her in one smooth motion.

Rosalind put her arms around Taryn's neck as she held her, midair. "Baby, we need to talk."

"No," Taryn said, walking toward the bed.

She could let that be answer enough. She could drown in her kiss, forget her resolve, and let the words wait for the morning. It would be easy, and Lord, it tempted her, the chance to forget and join her flesh with Taryn's. But Rhea had been right. There were some kinds of knowledge that changed you. In this moment of Taryn's choosing her, she had taken on a responsibility.

Rosalind let Taryn set her down on the bed, marveling at her strength. She sat, curling her legs under her. Taryn stalked forward, ready to push her down.

Rosalind held out her hand. "Trust me, love. There's something you need to know."

The tone held a warning edge and a glimmer of sadness. Taryn reacted to it, instantly. She sat down on the bed, cross-legged, and squared with Rosalind, eyes narrow. She expected the blow; the tightness around her mouth gave her away.

"This is going to hurt," Taryn said. "You don't have to answer, I can tell from your face."

Rosalind told her the story of her meeting with Rhea, the warning, the past lives, and Rhea's part.

Taryn listened stoically, not twitching a muscle.

"She said she dies when I show up. That's the pattern. The original died from an arrow wound, setting the whole chain in motion," Rosalind said, into the mask of Taryn's face.

"You're here, and Rhea's here," Taryn said, seeing the same glimpse of hope Rosalind had first seen.

She was breaking her word to Rhea. But looking at Taryn, she couldn't deceive her. She was her lover, she had chosen her. This was something that would have to be confronted. Taryn would have to know. It was no longer her place to keep it from her. It was her place to tell her and pick up the pieces.

Taryn didn't give her a chance to finish. She moved with the blurring speed Rosalind had seen her use on rare occasion. One moment she was still and thoughtful, mulling over what Rosalind had said. The next she was off the bed, across the floor and down the stairs, moving as if all the devils in Hell were on her heels.

"Taryn, wait!" Rosalind called, grabbing the nearest piece of clothing, Taryn's black shirt. She struggled into the shirt as she flew down the stairs, glad for the height difference between them. The shirt was almost as long as a dress on her.

Taryn went through the bedroom door like a whirlwind, slamming it aside. It rebounded from the wall, half closing again. Rosalind had to catch it to avoid being struck.

Joe sat up in bed, the sheet falling away from his naked torso. Rosalind could see the scars on his chest, outlined with the tattoo of a dance of snakes. He ran a hand across his face, squinting. "T? What the hell is going on?"

Taryn stood in the center of the room, facing the bed, quivering like a horse run too hard. Joe blinked and focused, recognizing the state she was in, taking in the sight of her, wearing only her suit pants, trembling. He spotted Rosalind in the doorway, wearing only Taryn's shirt. Taryn said nothing, just burned in her silence, staring at Rhea.

Rhea sat up and arranged the sheet over her breasts. Her hair was disordered from the pillow, reminding Rosalind of Medusa. She had a flashback to Taryn's story of their first meeting, when Taryn was sixteen, how this woman with the wild hair had simply walked up to her and touched her cheek. They faced one another now, the burning youth and the contained elder, straining the silence beyond its limits.

"So you know," Rhea said, leaning back against the headboard. "Your lover told you."

"Why." Taryn made the word a statement and punctuated it by walking closer to the bed, her feet silent on the polished wood floor of Rhea's bedroom. Rhea raised an eyebrow, the expression so similar to Taryn's that it hurt Rosalind to watch.

"Why? Because the pattern is older than any of us. Because seasons change."

"No. Why didn't you tell me? Joe knew, right?" Taryn glanced at Joe and read the answer on the man's face. "So what makes it okay for him to know and not me?"

Rhea kept looking at Taryn. "Joe, would you put on a pot of tea? This has the look of a long night."

The man nodded and climbed out of bed. He cast an apologetic look at Rosalind and crossed the floor in his boxer shorts. Rosalind pulled down at the edges of the black shirt.

Taryn exploded. "What the fuck, Rhea! I asked you a question, and you tell Joe to go make tea?"

"Joe is an adult and he understands balance," Rhea said, in answer to one, or both, of Taryn's questions.

She threw back the sheet, displaying her body with a carelessness that shocked Rosalind. Taryn didn't bat an eye or look away. It reminded Rosalind that this bedroom had probably once been Taryn and Rhea's, that she had slept where Joe now did. It hadn't been all that long since she was Rhea's lover, not long enough for there to be any shame or awkwardness between them at nakedness.

Rhea crossed the floor, as fierce as Taryn, her presence blunting Taryn's rage. She stood in front of Taryn, her dark eyes locking with the volatile blue. "Joe knew because he is my lover. You did not, because you would react the way you are reacting. I asked your lover not to tell you. Evidently she felt more loyalty to you after a week, than to me. I should, I suppose, applaud that. It means she'll be there for you in the hard times."

"Rhea…" Taryn dropped her eyes to the floor.

The woman moved away, crossing to the bed and picking up a blue robe. "Laurel and Goblin are sleeping. If we are going to have this conversation, we are going to have it in the kitchen, over a cup of tea, not standing naked in the middle of the bedroom. Put on a shirt and meet me in the kitchen."

CHAPTER FOURTEEN

The kitchen was lit from one end to the other—from the table by the wall, to the counter under the coffee mug wall, to the cat dishes near the sink—by the time Rosalind and Taryn dressed and went down.

Rhea was in her blue robe, seated at the table, a queen waiting to hold court. Her hands were folded in front of her, the fingers laced, waiting for the water to boil.

Joe had snagged a pair of jeans and a T-shirt from the laundry basket near the foot of the stairs. He stood, not in his accustomed place near the stove, but by the counter, absently petting the calico who nested on a pile of magazines. The caress of his large hand drew Rosalind's eye, the way he would begin the motion again whenever the cat bumped against him. It was the reflex of a man used to caring for the needs of everyone and everything around him, she thought.

Taryn had been deadly silent when they went back up to the third floor. She hadn't shrugged off Rosalind's hand on her back, but she hadn't responded to it, either. She had pulled on a sweatshirt and headed for the stairs, moving like a sleepwalker.

Rosalind thought about taking off the black shirt, but her hands refused to unbutton it. She lifted the collar and sniffed. It smelled of Taryn, of the cologne she wore. A shiver went through Rosalind, unbidden. She'd never liked it when her erstwhile husband had worn aftershave, but…She left the shirt on and grabbed a pair of jeans.

The four people looked at one another, waiting for a signal to position themselves in the room. Taryn stood awkwardly in the doorway, hands in her pockets. It took Rosalind's hand on her arm to move her into the room. She took a stance against the counter, facing the table, and folded her arms.

Joe abandoned the calico, who lashed her tail and jumped to the floor. He went to the stove and deftly plucked the kettle off the flame, pouring the hot water into a teapot of deep blue, with a gold embossed dragon entwined about the rim. Ritually, he set a cup out for each of the people in the room and poured the tea. He handed Taryn's to her first, then walked to Rhea, setting it before her on the table. Last, he took his cup and stood next to Rosalind, near the doorway into the hall.

Rosalind accepted the teacup from him, grateful for something to occupy her hands. There was a comfort to the ritual of it, the order that the precise action brought to the room. It was as if Joe had prepared the space for the conversation to begin.

Taryn held the cup in her left hand, ignoring it. She gazed steadily at Rhea, her look bruised and sullen. Rhea concentrated on her teacup and avoided looking at the brooding girl leaning against the counter. The silence lasted for two full minutes, while Rosalind and Joe pretended to be very interested in the designs on their cups.

Finally, Joe cleared his throat. He looked at Rhea, who gazed down at the pattern the steam made rising from her teacup. He glanced at Taryn, who raised her eyebrows, and shrugged. Joe nodded in understanding and took a long sip of his tea. He then hurled the cup at the back door. The cup traveled between Rhea and Taryn in its flight, dragging their eyes with it. It met the door with a crash, shattering.

"I've had enough of both of you," Joe said, his voice surprisingly calm. "Before Goblin and I moved in, this house belonged to you two. Don't argue with me, I have sense enough to know it. I love you, Rhea, and you are like my own child, T. But there is an ocean of unsaid words between you, and it's drowning everyone else near you. And you are both too stupid and arrogant to start speaking. So Rosalind and I are going to take a walk. If you have the conversation that you need to have while we're gone, fine. But I'm done making it okay for you not to speak." He took Rosalind's arm, ignoring wide-eyed stares from both Rhea and Taryn. "Shall we?"

Rosalind looked at Joe, then glanced at her lover. The shock was plain on Taryn's face, but she didn't look panicked. "Yes. I think we shall."

Joe turned on his heel and walked down the hall, his stride measured and deliberate. Rosalind looked back over her shoulder at Taryn, but Taryn's eyes had moved to Rhea. It was like looking in on a moment from the past. It was something she wanted to be a part of, but she wasn't. Rosalind took a deep breath and matched her stride to Joe's. They would have to do this themselves, if they chose to.

At the foot of the steps Joe paused and exhaled, his chest and shoulders moving like a man setting down a great weight. The sadness that had clung to him since the auction hadn't abated. She saw his face, for a moment, give in to it, saw the gentleness of his demeanor crack. The grief came through, water from a broken pitcher. He raised his head and looked at her, unguarded. "I want to go right back in there and make it okay for both of them. Part of me thinks they'll kill each other without a referee."

"Me too. Nobody ever stages emotional upheavals for a convenient hour. So, where would you like to walk?" Rosalind said, doing her best to sound sunny and cheerful.

Joe laughed. It was just a small laugh, at first, but then the laugh caught in his throat, doubled itself, and continued. It reached out and picked Rosalind up, who then had no choice but to be borne along. "There's probably a support group for us," Joe said, drawing air back into his lungs.

"Yeah. Overly sensitive partners of emotionally repressed women."

Joe cocked his head and raised his eyebrows. "Are you attracted to the brooding artist type? Does the thought of spending long hours talking to yourself while your lover barely grunts sound familiar? You know better, but does one look from a pair of moody eyes, one look at a pair of pouting, sullen lips send you quivering into ecstasy? Join OSPERW!" He started walking down Mariner, toward Allen Street.

"We'd need a better acronym. How about Overly Sensitive Partners, Repressed Emotional Youth?"

"OSPREY? It'd work for you, your boy is brooding on the edge of adulthood. I don't have the same recourse. Rhea is a consummate adult. So much so that she forgets she ever was a child."

They turned the corner on Allen Street. Even in the dead hours of a Saturday night, when the time of being drunk gave way to the time of hangovers, when dawn was more than a distant threat, Allen was alive. "You want to get a beer? We could go to Nieztsche's," Joe said, looking off to the left.

Rosalind shook her head. "No, the thought of entering another bar tonight is too much. I don't think I've had five minutes sleep. Coffee, maybe?"

"The Towne it is," Joe said amiably.

They grabbed a table by the window, looking out on the corner of Allen and Elmwood.

"I don't know what it is with Buffalo and Greek diners. I'm starting to feel like I grew up in Greece," Rosalind said, looking at the menu.

Joe pointed at the framed posters hanging on the wall. "Then you remember the Acropolis."

"Oh, sure. Used to go there every afternoon. You get used to these things."

Her eyes wandered to the poster hanging to the left of the Acropolis. It was the head of a statue of a young man, superimposed on a landscape. It wasn't the same statue as the tattoo, but there was no mistaking the deep-set eyes, the lion's mane of hair. She looked on Alexander and saw Taryn.

Whatever was happening in the kitchen of 34 Mariner would change Taryn. The knowledge Rhea had been sparing her was out in the open now. Rosalind's mind pictured a quick succession of images— Taryn crying, shouting; Rhea on her feet, fighting just as hard. She wondered what it had been like between them when Taryn had been younger, and angrier. The Taryn she knew now had a sense of humor, a sense of irony, coupled with her intensity.

What had she been like when she was all raw emotion? Rosalind remembered the photograph of Taryn at seventeen, the rage that simmered just under the surface, as visible as the shape of her bones under her skin. She wondered how much Taryn hadn't told her about those years, and if she could have spared her any of that buried pain.

The waitress came by, and Joe ordered coffee while Rosalind stared at the wall. She was silent until the waitress came back and plunked white mugs down in front of them both.

Joe shot a glance at the poster, then back to Rosalind, who dropped her eyes. "They'll be all right," Joe said, his voice rising on the end of the statement, mutating it into a question.

"That obvious?"

"Staring at Alex? A bit." Joe wrapped his hand around the coffee cup, covering it. "I'm as bad. Old habit, from when Goblin was young. I couldn't stop worrying about her. Not her physical well-being. She was fearless and bulletproof. But how she felt, how she saw the world. Was I doing a good job as a mother? Would she have the tools she needed in the world?"

The distraction, for Rosalind recognized it as such, was very welcome. Joe was as adept as Ellie at pulling the conversation off into interesting sidelines, to keep the emotional morass distant.

"Joe, can I ask you something?"

"Sure, Ros."

"How did Goblin react when you transitioned?"

Joe leaned back in his chair and smiled wryly. "She was young. Her dad and I divorced pretty early on, and he moved in with his male lover, so she was used to a more unconventional family life. I think she was eight, no, nine. She was nine when I started on hormones. I sat her down and had a talk with her about everything, and asked her if she wanted to live with her dad. I told her I was going to change how I looked on the outside, to match how I felt on the inside, but I was still the same person, and I loved her. Know what she came up with?"

Rosalind shook her head.

"If I was going to be a man now, why couldn't I date Daddy again? Ah, the vision of youth," Joe said, and smiled.

They sipped their coffee slowly and tried to distract one another with amusing stories. Rosalind found herself telling Joe about her college days in Ithaca, about her marriage, things about her past that had, until now, seemed outside of her interaction with the household at 34 Mariner. It was as if she'd been born the moment she'd come home with Taryn, and it was strange to remember the entirely different life she'd had before meeting Taryn.

"So T was your first. I admit, I wasn't expecting that."

"I look…experienced?" Rosalind asked, surprised.

"No. But you don't seem like a tourist either. You seem very comfortable, not only with the punk kid but also with how she lives. Her family. We can be a pretty odd bunch."

"I don't think there's another family I'd like to belong to as much. I don't think I could live with going back to my old life." Rosalind looked down at her coffee mug, overcome with what she was saying.

It was Joe she revealed this to, a man as easy to talk to as any she had ever met, but still someone who had only known her a short time. She felt a touch, like the ghostly resting of a hand on her shoulder, and looked up. Joe was across the table and hadn't moved, but the look in his eyes was strange, unfocused.

"You won't have to," he said. A brief shudder went through his frame, as if a chill draft had caught him. He reached for his coffee cup clumsily, his hand knocking into it before recognizing it.

"What's it like?" Rosalind asked gently.

His eyes blinked, then fixed on her. He was at home in his skin again, his attention returned to her. "Like someone shouting in both ears while banging iron skillets together. Kind of insistent." He rubbed a hand across his chin. "I spent years ignoring it. It was like ignoring a migraine. Or a door-to-door salesman."

"The whole household seems to be...gifted," Rosalind said carefully.

"Something in the water?" Joe said and grinned.

It eased Rosalind's fear. She smiled at him in return. "Come on, it does seem a little unusual."

"Not really. We attract each other. Everyone has some ability. Some people are closer to the surface with it. And there is the queer thing." Joe signaled to the waitress, who was passing by with a coffee pot.

Rosalind waited until she'd left again before leaning on the table and almost whispering. "What queer thing?"

Joe sighed. "You know any Native American history?"

"Only what I learned in school, the basics."

"Okay. You've heard of the berdache? Rotten term that the French used, but it stuck."

"Yes. Men who dressed and lived as women."

"I like the term two-spirited. Transwomen, we'd say now. There were women who dressed and lived as men, as well, in many tribes. Most, I think. Anyway, the nations usually respected their two-spirited people. They were often shamans, healers. Some handled the wealth of the tribe, were considered especially lucky. They had a hard road to walk, so they had powers in compensation. Usually a vision at adolescence signaled the beginning of a path such as that. You with me?" Joe paused and looked at her.

"I think so."

"Some of these people were what we'd call gay. Some weren't. But they all had some measure of power from the unique path they followed."

"So there's a propensity toward being…gifted," Rosalind said slowly.

"Yeah. It seems to show up more readily. And people with gifts are always drawn to Rhea's house. It's like a big magnet." Joe set his cup down with a spin.

"So it's perfectly normal if I start hearing things," Rosalind said. She'd meant it to come out light, funny, but it sounded serious to her ears.

"I'd expect you to start seeing things."

Rosalind raised her eyebrow.

Joe reached across the table and took her hand. "Don't sweat it. It usually shows up pretty early in life. Harder then to tell if you have a reputable source or the 7-11 clerks of the Great Beyond. But if you do start hearing things, you can always tell them to go to hell. Ouch, poor word choice. Go to Cleveland. They'll leave you alone. Just be as stubborn as they are."

"Stubborn." Rosalind's voice layered a wealth of meaning into the word.

Joe appeared to catch the layers. He sighed and leaned back in the chair. "Been about an hour. Think it's safe to go back?"

"If the immovable object and the irresistible force haven't slaughtered each other by now, they probably won't."

Joe threw a handful of bills on the table. "So, which is yours?"

"Irresistible force," Rosalind said, with a smile that would scandalize a nun.

"Shouldn't have asked. I'm getting too old to keep hearing about kids' sex lives."

"I'm hardly a kid."

"You're younger now than the day I met you, Ros. And your handsome boy is older. You're good for each other."

They walked in companionable silence back down Mariner. Joe paused on the steps, and Rosalind saw that his hand trembled on the knob. She reached out, set her hand over his, and squeezed. He smiled his gratitude, and they opened the door together.

It was silent in the house. Rosalind had expected some noise, conversation, shouting perhaps. But the hallway was as still as a painting, the light from the kitchen indicating that it was still inhabited.

Wordlessly, Joe and Rosalind peered around the corner and looked into the room.

Taryn knelt on the floor, holding out her right hand. Rhea sat in front of Taryn, her head bent over the hand, her back to the doorway. Rosalind had the oddest impression that Rhea was reading her palm. It took her a moment to recognize what Rhea was doing. There was blood down Taryn's wrist, a brown stain that extended to her elbow. Rhea had a pair of tweezers in hand and was plucking bits of glass from the gory mass of flesh that had been Taryn's hand.

Taryn gave no indication that she felt any pain as Rhea worked free a sliver of glass two inches long. Rhea worked with an intensity, her hair covering Taryn's arm when she looked into the wound. Taryn had a look on her face that Rosalind would have sworn was pride. Her eyes never strayed from Rhea while the fragment was pulled out of her hand, sending forth a fresh jet of blood. Rhea dropped it into a bowl, next to her knee.

It was too much for Rosalind to watch in silence. "Taryn," she said, stepping into the room.

Taryn raised a smile to her of reflected pleasure from Rhea's ministrations. "Hey. Didn't hear you guys come in."

"Honey, you're bleeding. What happened?" Rosalind asked, kneeling down at Taryn's side.

Rhea snorted, and went back to searching the wound.

"I'm okay," Taryn said easily.

"But what happened?" Rosalind asked, watching Rhea pull forth more shrapnel with practiced ease. A shiver went through Rosalind at the sight. Something about her, and blood, and the binding of wounds. It spoke to something ancient in her. She should be sewing up the rents in that flesh. It was her responsibility.

"I punched a window," Taryn said sheepishly.

Rosalind took a shard of glass from the floor. It was shaped like an arrowhead, the edges trimmed with unwitting precision by the force of Taryn's blow. There was a spot of her blood left on it, a jewel on the transparent cutting surface. Rosalind imagined that it still felt warm from the contact with Taryn's flesh.

Whatever had passed between Rhea and Taryn, whatever storm had flared and died, there was a kind of peace in the kitchen now. Rosalind could feel it, even though the sight of Rhea easing glass darts out of Taryn's mangled hand was anything but comforting. The sight of Taryn accepting the ministration of Rhea spoke volumes. Her head was tilted to the side, an odd smile tugged at her lips. There was familiarity in being cared for, after a blooding, by Rhea. The anger that had lived in the air around Taryn was quieted, perhaps by the familiarity of Rhea's attention.

The sight caught on Rosalind's attention like the ghost of a memory, something she hadn't seen herself, but had heard so often as to relive it with each telling. She knew, for example, that Rhea would come across a splinter deeply buried in the flesh between Taryn's thumb and forefinger. That the effort to remove it would only drive it deeper, that fresh damage would be done to that ravaged flesh before the glass worked free. Rosalind knew this before it happened.

She knew how Taryn's face would give away nothing of the pain, how Rhea's eyes, fixed on extracting the glass, would miss the subtle tightening of her lips. Only when a new jet of blood came forth with the wound would Rhea look up and see a glimmer of Taryn's pain.

Joe came over with strips of cloth. He turned Taryn's hand over, examining it for debris. "I think it's safe to wrap it up. I don't want to hurt you."

"Let me," Rosalind said automatically.

Joe handed her the cloth without a word and moved out of the way.

Rhea remained kneeling next to Taryn, her eyes critical on Rosalind as she bound the wound. Finally, as Rosalind wiped away the rivers of blood left on Taryn's forearm, Rhea nodded in approval. "You've done this before."

Rosalind glanced at her. Had she? She couldn't recall. But her hands knew. They moved with an efficiency that her mind couldn't trace.

"I think we've all had enough for one night. I'll clean the rest of this up in the morning." Joe stood and held out a hand to Rhea. She took it, using his strength to pull herself up.

"Yes. Good job, Rosalind. You have good hands," Rhea said to her.

Rosalind felt a surge of pride, out of proportion to the event. It mattered that this woman had acknowledged her caretaking of Taryn. The mantle was being passed.

Taryn stood, examining her hand. "I look like a mummy."

"There are worse things. I will see you in the morning." Rhea set her hand on Taryn's shoulder. For a moment she hesitated, letting that contact be all there was between them. Rosalind thought she could see the moment the decision was made, as Rhea leaned in and kissed her on the cheek. "Sleep well." Rhea looked hard at Rosalind. "Pleasant dreams."

Taryn was silent as they climbed the stairs to the third floor. She sat on the bed, cradling her bound hand, eyes half lidded, as Rosalind climbed into bed. Rosalind propped herself up on her elbow, watching the bent shape of Taryn's back. Taryn's shoulders were bowed, unlike the unconscious arrogance that normally marked her. She made no move to undress or approach her lover.

It was a distance that was new—not one born of a heated moment, not one born of pride, or anger, or a misspoken word between them. This was a distance born of something inside her that she'd never seen, a grief that stretched from her bones to her skin, but didn't pass her lips. Rosalind wondered if she ever would speak of it, without prompting. It wasn't the night for such speculation.

Grief has a life of its own and changes shape with every person that it visits. Rosalind knew that well enough. She couldn't simply reach out and expect Taryn to be able to reach back. Taryn was lost in a landscape that had no maps, no guideposts. Rosalind was left looking into the past, at a girl whose pain she wasn't able to share.

An inspiration hit her. It made no sense, and less than none, but it felt right. Rosalind went with it. She started speaking, in a low, easy voice, not commanding Taryn's attention, but coaxing it. She had no idea where she was going. She let the story take on its own life, as it began.

"Once, long ago, when the first people had left the forests for the grasslands and begun to keep herds and flocks, to till the soil and grow grapes and grain, a fire came at night in the sky. Like the arrow of a god, it flashed across the darkness, dividing it. It crashed down into the land, plowing under a vineyard and a hut, scattering the flocks. The people were justly afraid, for they had never seen such a thing. They huddled in their stone houses and spoke to one another in frightened voices. 'It is a sign!' they said. 'Surely, the wrath of a god is visited upon us. We have been wicked, and we must repent.'"

The slightest twitch of muscle along Taryn's shoulder gave evidence that she was listening to the sound of Rosalind's voice.

Rosalind took her strength from that, and kept going. "The idea caught hold, and the people decided to mollify the anger of whatever god they had offended by offering a sacrifice. They chose, in a hasty council, the strongest and fairest maiden of their village. 'Go and give yourself to the god, that we may live,' they said to her." Taryn shifted her weight, then turned, leaning down on the bed. Sleepy eyed, she leaned on her bandaged hand, not looking at Rosalind exactly, but not exactly looking away. Rosalind trusted her instinct and continued.

"So she did. She went forth from her people, huddled in their stone huts. She crossed the fields, the shattered vineyard, the rent earth, until she came to the place where the arrow of the god had touched down. The edges of the furrow were torn and smoking, the very dirt looked scorched. She trembled before it. She leaned forward, over the edge of the furrow, and…" Rosalind let the story trail off.

The silence lengthened. Taryn opened her eyes. "And?"

"That's all we know. We didn't go down into the earth with her. We don't know what she saw there or how it changed her. We can only hope that her strength will be enough to keep her going, until she can come back and speak of what she has seen."

Taryn crawled the length of the bed and laid her head in Rosalind's lap. She rested there, hot eyed and silent, her body coiled and tense. Her arms were closed around her stomach. Rosalind didn't ask, didn't demand. It had been a night of too many happenings, too much to be dealt with, too many words. Taryn was drowning in the knowledge she'd come up against. With a lover's wisdom, she simply gave what simple comfort Taryn seemed ready to take and let the questions wait.

Rosalind stroked her hair, aware that Taryn might not be able to bear a touch on her back or arms. She did not cry, but every half-restrained shudder that passed through her body was a howl of grief. Rosalind combed the night black hair with her fingers and scratched Taryn's head with her nails. She started singing, softly, a lullaby her mother had sung to her as a girl.

Taryn turned onto her back, looking up into her lover's face. Her eyes were burning with tears that couldn't come, luminescent as rain. She curled her head into the caress, even as she held her body away, rigid as steel.

Though she'd been kicked out of chorus in grade school for crimes against music, Rosalind continued to sing every song she could remember, until the tension in Taryn's body started to ease, the trembling quieted.

Taryn arched her neck against Rosalind's leg and turned her face, kissing her thigh. "This isn't how I pictured spending the night with you. Some auction this turned out to be."

"Hush, sweetheart. Try and sleep."

"Regret your winning bid?" Taryn asked, stroking Rosalind's knee. Rosalind took a chance and put her arms around her. There was a moment of resistance, Taryn's body clenched like a fist. Then, with a sigh, she relaxed into the embrace.

"I'm your lover, baby. This is a part of it."

"Never was before," Taryn said, looking out at the room.

"It was never me before. Try and fall asleep." Rosalind resumed stroking Taryn's hair.

"Yeah. That'll put me out. Am I smashing your lap?"

"You're fine," Rosalind reassured her, and pulled more of her onto her leg. "I'm stronger than I look."

Another shudder passed through Taryn's body, like a cold wind whipping across the bed. "Tell you a secret?" she whispered to Rosalind. "I'm not. Stronger than I look." Taryn's voice was small in the darkness of the room.

"You are to me. Rest, my sweet warrior."

"I need a hero, but all the heroes are dead," Taryn muttered and shut her eyes.

❖

Rosalind sat for an hour, until she was sure that Taryn was actually sleeping. She eased Taryn from her lap and put the blanket over her. She protested and flailed her arm out. When Rosalind took her hand she relaxed, falling back into sleep. Rosalind sat next to her, unable to shut her eyes. It had to be five, maybe even later. Dawn would be coming soon. She kept the night watch over her lover's sleeping form, knowing that Taryn needed protection. In sleep, Taryn looked far too young and far too vulnerable. "I won't let anything hurt you," Rosalind whispered, kissing her hand.

It wasn't the sudden pain that she feared, but its aftermath. For now, Taryn was in shock. But soon, tomorrow even, the changes might begin. The despair would set in, the slow spreading like a mist, the deadening of nerve endings. It would be subtle, at first, the life bleeding out of her. Bit by bit, the things that brought her pleasure or diversion would become stale and dull; the clouds would roll in and not lift. And Rosalind would watch it, unable to reach her.

She looked around the room, at the splinter of light from the window, the altar on the top of the dresser. Her eye stopped on the statue of the dancing Shiva. In the sinuous bend of the god's arms, she saw an echo of the snake in the dogwood tree. An odd feeling came over her, perhaps the lateness of the hour and the emotional night, perhaps the sparking of a childhood memory. Rosalind prayed.

It was a feeling, at first, a longing to protect and cherish. She let that longing grow until it all but choked her, then gave words to it, whispered over the body of her lover to the darkness and anything that listened. "She needs a hero. They can't all be dead. Please, let me be what she needs." It was the voicing of the one pure hope she carried into the potential of the witch's house.

There was no response. The statue was as silent as the snake had been, long ago. Rosalind let a small, bitter chuckle surface. What had she expected? The heroes were dead, and the gods were sleeping.

Her eyes started to get heavy at last, lulled by resignation. She wasn't sure that she wanted to sleep. Sleep was an escape, and she wanted to be present as she had never been before. Taryn needed her to be. She shook her head, but the weight of her eyelids dragged them down. She felt her body sway, her eyes harder to keep open than a freshman's in an 8:00 a.m. class. In the middle of blinking and fighting to stay awake, she saw light come from the end of the room. Had the dawn come so soon?

She must have fallen asleep. She was seeing the walls of the room fade like smoke, a smoke that billowed and thinned into a haze of yellow dust. She saw a gateway of mud brick set into a wall of enameled tiles. She was looking out at the desert, across the yellow dust toward the dun hills in the West. It was the Egyptians who described death as going into the West; she'd learned that in her training. She was here at this side gate in disguise, waiting for her lover.

Through the light pouring down like molten gold she came, the beautiful boy who was a handsome girl, dressed to fool the gods. The black-eyed girl who was a prince and her beloved. The gods were not fooled, though the prince looked so very like the Lord of Sheaves, the adored consort of the Great Goddess. In her youth and strength, she was as gorgeous as a leopard, as splendid as a black eagle. The prince was also reckless and felt free to deny the prophecy.

Rosalind knew that she was the woman who waited by the gate, day after day. She was a priestess, and so this affair was profane. She had been consecrated to the Goddess and could not love where she chose. The prince lived in exile to avoid the death that had been foretold at the hour of her birth. Coming into the city was asking death to find her.

The dreamscape shifted. There was a street, a broad paved avenue wide enough for three chariots to travel abreast. Rosalind walked on the street in her gauzy priestess's robes, her mind full of the prince. She felt her arm being seized. A woman with wild hair like a halo of snakes accosted her. She knew this woman. It was the fortune-teller who had raised the prince in secret.

The fortune-teller had powers of her own, untrained and unregulated by the temple. She practiced her magic in the wild places beyond the walls of the city, called up the spirits of the dead and the small gods under the hills. The fortune-teller knew of the affair and knew it meant death for the prince. So she came to the city to warn and bargain, to ask the priestess to let the prince go.

It was no use. As soon as the fortune-teller set eyes on the priestess, she knew. The Wheel of Fate had already turned, binding them all together. Death was coming for the prince, and death cannot be stopped.

Death took the form of a rebel satrap who seized the prince one night when she snuck into the city to visit her lover. In the lowest reaches of his palace the prince was kept, awaiting execution. Rosalind saw this, saw the room of flat gray stone. As the priestess she was there, captive, helpless. There was the creak of bows being pulled taut, the groan of cane arrows pleading to fly. The prince waited, calm as a priest at a sacrifice, looking out on unfathomable distances. Rosalind didn't move, didn't know why she wasn't moving.

There was a flash of acrid smoke, folk magic used to cover a hasty entrance. The fortune-teller was there, wild-eyed. She saw the prince. She saw death in the room, waiting. She saw the arrows and did the only thing that her love allowed. She stood in the path and took the death meant for the prince.

The world capered and spun before Rosalind's eyes. Every particle of the air, every mote of dust began to dance. In that dance she saw that all things are one. The world existed inside of a drop of water; the sum was the part, and the part was infinite. The flight of the arrow became a spear of light arcing toward the center.

The dreamscape shifted and Rosalind saw a wheel trimmed in celestial fire. In the Wheel, Lord Shiva danced to the music of the spheres, all time bowed before him. Yet it was a woman who danced, the woman with the belt of skulls. In each hand she held a blessing or a weapon. Each arm began to move so sinuously that Rosalind could not tell the flower from the blade. The face of the goddess melted and ran, became the face of the fortune-teller in her moment of sacrifice hurling herself into the path of death in an act of love.

The face shifted, became the priestess who held out a blessing and a warning so interlaced it was the same gesture. The features ran like wax. It was a beautiful boy who danced in the Devourer's place with a smile like a dark star, a handsome girl who mingled deception and revelation seamlessly. In that moment it came down like the sparks from the divine fire, and the goddess who gives birth became the goddess who devours.

Everything was connected front and back. The Wheel became the circle of the sun; the beautiful boy became a black eagle rising in passionate abandon to immolation and reunion with all things. The sun became a snake sheathed in golden scales winding around a branch of flowering dogwood. All motion abruptly ceased. The Wheel lurched to a halt, sending off showers of fire. Blocked by a single arrow caught in the spokes.

Rosalind's eyes snapped open to a room bathed in gold. The spears of sun had come across the floor and were edging toward the bed. She was still sitting holding Taryn's hand. The vastness of the dream mercifully faded; love eased into the spaces it left. It was too much to hold at once, the things she had seen; her mortal senses balked at it. Rosalind concentrated on breathing in and out, taking refuge in the physical reality.

Taryn seemed to be sleeping peacefully. Rosalind raised Taryn's hand to her cheek and held it there for a moment, absorbing the living warmth. She looked at her lover's face—the line of jaw, the high cheekbones. It was the face of a beautiful boy, not quite the face of the prince in the dream. The prince's eyes had been black as obsidian. Only the soul looking out had been the same.

For a moment Rosalind's mind froze, unable to approach the visions. She reached out to touch the crown of Taryn's head and let her hand rest there. "I can't imagine a world without you. Waking up and not knowing Taryn likes this, doesn't care for that. Believes in these things, fights for them. I can't imagine not knowing what you love. None of this makes any sense without you to come home to. What good is revelation without joy?" Rosalind said softly, coming down from the madness of the dreams.

"Plato would have loved you, baby. His idealized, perfect youth. That makes me the dirty old man, I suppose," she said, absently tracing the edges of Taryn's lips.

"I dreamed you were a prince. Not you, exactly, my dear king. Someone you came from." She couldn't have slept for long, her head was still foggy. "You might not be descended from Alexander, my love. This was long before his time. She might have been a warrior, but she had the air of a priest. In the face of death, she was calm, even graceful."

The image came back with the force of a sledgehammer, and the fog lifted from Rosalind's brain. Exactly who everyone had been became clear. The prince, the priestess, the fortune-teller. It couldn't be. But Joe had cautioned her to listen to the message when it came. It appeared, whole and perfect in her mind. She saw it, every motion, like a dance.

It could finally work. After thousands of years, the symbols were too perfect to be ignored. Taryn, scion of the prince's line, was royalty. A drag king. She lived in disguise, had the magic of the trickster, the cross-dresser, the magic that was both illusion and revelation, the revealing of the soul in the assumption of identity. She was a warrior, a soldier on the front lines of the gender wars. She'd been raised by the witch, of the line of the fortune-teller, and so was beloved of the goddess. She was beloved of the professor, of the line of the priestess, the heir to arcane formal knowledge.

The cycle that kept happening wasn't all Fate. There had only been one death foretold so long ago. Rhea's line had spent so many years fighting it, or taking it on herself, that she'd forgotten: death was simply change from one state to another. The goddess that gave birth was also the goddess that devoured.

For the Wheel of Fate to turn again, death had to be surrendered to. Not in the way of a soldier losing a fight, but of a priest going to the mystery, the wholehearted abandon of a lover, the madness and celestial ecstasy of the immolation embrace. The death only persisted because the passionate resistance would not let it go. It was possible to end it. It turned her marrow to water, but she knew what had to be done. Taryn had to accept her own death.

"Taryn?" She shook her, gently. Her lover's body was like lead. She didn't respond. Rosalind tried again, gripping her shoulders. "Taryn? Baby, wake up." Her breathing changed, but her eyes remained glued shut.

Rosalind sighed. Taryn was going to be difficult. She climbed the length of her body, easing her leg over Taryn's hip. That drew more of a response from her; Taryn shifted in her sleep. Rosalind fitted herself to her broad back, sliding an arm around her waist. Taryn's hand closed on her arm. Good. Rosalind leaned over Taryn's neck, stopping to nip at the flesh between her shoulder and the hollow of her throat. She trailed her tongue up to her ear, circled it, and moaned. "Oh, Annie—"

Taryn's eyes flew open. "Who the hell is Annie?" she demanded, her voice thick with sleep.

Rosalind sat up and smiled beatifically at her groggy lover. "Annie Lennox. I always did have a crush on her. Sorry, must have been fantasizing."

"Rosalind, what are you talking about?"

"Sorry, baby. I had to wake you up, and you weren't responding to anything else."

Taryn sat up, her eyes murderous slits of blue. "I'm up now. What was so goddamned important?"

"I've got it! I think I do, anyway. We have to wake everyone up," Rosalind said, springing off the bed.

Taryn's eyes had gone wide when she saw Rosalind throw on clothing. She sat very still, not comprehending. "Now? It can't be past seven o'clock."

"Right now. Get Rhea and Joe and everyone and have them come down to the kitchen." She held out her hand, and Taryn took it. "I had a dream. I think it might be…I think it *is* the key to ending the cycle between you and Rhea. Among all of us. I know it's crazy, but what else has sounded sane here? Go wake them up."

CHAPTER FIFTEEN

Rosalind took the center of the kitchen floor like the front of a lecture hall. Every time she'd addressed a group of people, she'd been prepared. She'd had the time to rehearse, take notes, rehearse again, to know exactly what she was going to say. Some people can speak with no warning on any topic. Ellie was one. Ellie had explained to Rosalind, once, that all you have to do is look like you know what you're talking about. Most people listen with their eyes.

This was different. Rosalind found herself standing in the middle of the kitchen floor, facing an audience whose lives she wanted to change, and she had no idea of what to say. There was no mastery to be had of this topic. It was the realm of dreams, of poets and lovers and madwomen, of stubborn insistence on moving the Wheel of Fate.

Rosalind closed her eyes and thought of a golden snake, coiled about a branch of a dogwood tree. She took a deep breath, then another, and opened her eyes to see the people before her. Joe was the perfect audience, leaning forward on his chair, eyebrows curved in question. Goblin sat with her back against the wall, tipping her chair up on two legs and swinging her ankles. Laurel and Taryn sat at the counter. Taryn was four feet from her right hand, close enough for Rosalind to imagine that she could feel the heat radiating from Taryn. And then there was Rhea.

Rhea sat opposite Joe, and if Taryn hadn't been born with presence, she could have learned it at this woman's feet. Her eyes were hints of lightning in a night sky, old eyes that had seen the cycle of blood come and go. She wore her body like a useful garment, a heavy jacket on a winter night that was about to be put away. Rhea might have been afraid, but she didn't fear her own fear, and so it didn't rule her. She looked at Rosalind with attention, but without interest.

Rosalind spoke. She let the words come in whatever order they chose and didn't try to understand them before she let them go.

"We come into the world knowing ourselves, knowing some that we love, longing to meet others. In growing up and taking on our current life, we choose to forget so that we may be able to bear being alive. So life is a surprise, love is a surprise, and the outcome of things is never certain. When we dream, sometimes we remember—who we've been, who we've chosen to be, and who we've come back to see. When we wake, we forget again.

"Maybe it's a mercy that we do. How else could we stand watching the people we love die? Even if we know we will see them again, we feel the loss every time. No two moments in the river of Time will ever be the same, no moments are wasted, and love is never a mistake. But you forget that you know this and run through life blind and deaf, shivering from the cold.

"Then, one night, you meet someone. It might be in a bar, it might be in the company of friends, it might be that a stranger has the courage to approach you and offer condolences on your loss. But you look up, and you know them. When the voice in your heart gives you that recognition, follow it. Follow it, no matter where it leads you, no matter what form it takes. Sure, it will get complicated.

"Your lives will get tangled up beyond all untying. You will have to be somebody greater than you ever imagined yourself to be, to keep up with a love like that. But follow it anyway, whether it leads to friendship, to family, or to a lover. Believe in it, hold it sacred, honor it, and fight with every ounce of your being to cherish and protect it. What are we here for, if not to love one another and find out who we are?

"We get stuck, sometimes. We give in to anger, or grief, or hate— the fast, hot emotions. Anger can twist your life into a pattern that's hard to break, and hate can bind you. The Greeks called it *kyklos geneseon*. The Wheel of Becomings. Long, long before then it was called the Wheel of Fate. When the wheel gets stuck, maybe by a moment of great anger, of grief, you stop growing. Say, a young woman who's been betrayed, attacked, and is full of anger. A friend approaches her, gives her comfort, speaks to the one unbruised part of her that's still willing to love, but that friend dies, or gets taken away.

"Then there is only the rage, and she gives in to it. Rage has a sweetness to it, a promise that the pain can be stopped if you get angry enough. But it's a false promise. All anger gives in the end is anger. The only way to stop the pain is to end the cycle.

"Love breaks patterns, tears down form, creates new ways when the old ones no longer serve. Oh, it takes becoming something more than you thought you could be to trust in a kind of madness like love. Love promises only itself, but sometimes that is enough. Perhaps there is only a small thing holding back the wheel. A slender wooden shaft piercing the spokes. An arrow. If the arrow is removed, the wheel can turn again. All that person has to do is believe that she has the skill. Love can be that forgetting and remembering."

Rosalind spoke and forgot she was Rosalind, forgot that her lover was Taryn, that the woman facing her was Rhea. Perhaps it was from her heart or from another place, below her memory.

"The arrow is a death. You cannot remove a death," Rhea said, her voice full of dust.

"No," Rosalind said, knowing that this was the true battle. "You can't. Death is change. In this case the death was taken from its intended target. Deflected, if you will. The Wheel will never turn until that cycle is complete. It will stay in that moment, over and over, life after life."

"Complete the cycle. Will you stand in and take the death for her? Is that your way now?" Rhea asked bitterly.

"No. That will only continue the cycle. Don't you see? You took on the responsibility of the death, but it isn't yours. You have to give it up."

"No," Rhea said instantly.

"Rhea. Hear me out. The prince, the priestess, and the fortune-teller all died a long, long time ago. I'm not advocating offering her up as a sacrifice. I'd take her place first. You must know that by now," Rosalind said, laying her heart open.

Rhea's eyes closed as if she were too weary for the world. "You have no right to ask this of me," Rhea said finally.

"Then let me ask it," Taryn said, stepping forward.

Rosalind held her breath. They had discussed this before they called everyone down to the kitchen, but saying it to Rhea was another matter. Surely the prince had never looked so regal as Taryn did at that moment, opening her hands to the witch. "You've given me everything. You took care of me when nobody cared if I lived or died, including me. We need such strength just to get out of bed every day in a world that would be happy to see us gone. You never give in, never let anything beat you down. You take your own space and love who you want and let the world be damned. No way would I be here without you. Rhea, you're my family and my heart. It's time for me to take this on. Let me take what was meant for me, so you don't have to anymore."

Taryn stood with her hands held out. Rhea reached for them. It took Rosalind a moment to realize that Rhea was crying.

"To finish the cycle she needs to accept the death," Rosalind said. The silence in the kitchen was perfect. Rosalind took a deep breath, sent a quick prayer out to whoever was listening, and jumped.

"Death is an ending. It's also a beginning, the razing of the ground for a new building. I think that's what I saw in my dream. The prince was perfectly calm in the face of the arrow. She understood the mystery. Only when you stop raging against change can it have a chance to bring new things. We need something symbolic for Taryn to accept the death. Sympathetic magic, like the Better You than Me. If Taryn accepts the death, the cycle is complete. You don't have to die. She doesn't have to die. And maybe, for the first time in all our memories, we can be together."

Rhea pushed her chair away from the table with the stride of a woman too dignified to run. She walked to the center of the floor, to Rosalind, and held out both her hands. Rosalind took them. "Yes. Simple and complete. And to think I feared your coming. Thank you," Rhea said, and Rosalind felt her heart expand.

"That…that doesn't make any sense," Goblin said.

"No." Rhea stood up and slipped her arm around Taryn's waist. For a splinter of time she looked up at the handsome girl with adoration. In that moment Rosalind could see how they had been lovers. "It doesn't make sense. It's insane. Crazy. But madness is just the gods' way of saying, 'Beware, this person has power. She has a bit of the trickster in her.'"

"Can you do this?" Taryn asked Rhea.

"You know enough about magic, and me, to answer that. The symbol can become the thing itself. Rosalind is right about the perfection of the symbols in this incarnation. It makes sense that once we stop resisting, the Wheel will turn on its own. It's like light through a window I'd painted over and forgotten. It took your lover to scrape that surface away. It's crazy, but it's perfect. I never would have seen it."

"I never would have, either. I'd just go on letting you die for me," Taryn said savagely.

Rhea's hand lay against Taryn's cheek, just for a moment. "I've loved you since the moment we met. Before then, if you ever remember. This might mean that I will never again be your protector, your servant, in the anger of your youth. That cycle between us will end."

"But...what about you? Will it make you be okay?"

"I don't know," Rhea said, and smiled. "When the cycle is completed, it will leave room for other things to happen. Healing might be one possibility. Whatever happens next will be a surprise. That itself is a gift. I haven't been surprised in six hundred years."

"Will I still get to know you? Next time, I mean. Will I know you again?" The sadness in Taryn's voice broke Rosalind's heart.

"You've always been a splendid youth. I'd like to see what a remarkable woman you become," Rhea said. Rhea turned to Rosalind. "The day is yours. Lead us where you will."

Rosalind asked for the day to prepare the ceremony. The circle was set for nine. After outlining everyone's part, Rosalind had asked for a moment alone with Taryn, before the ritual began. She took Taryn up to the third floor and sat on the bed, patting the mattress next to her.

Taryn sat, her arms coiled around one raised knee, her eyes clouded with a look Rosalind couldn't decipher.

"You okay?" Rosalind asked gently.

Taryn nodded.

"Are you up for this?" Rosalind put her hand on the small of Taryn's back.

Taryn nodded again.

"You're awfully quiet. Is the ritual...I mean, does it all make sense? I know it's crazy. I just wanted to...honey, please. Tell me what's going on, why you're looking at me like that."

Taryn cocked her head. "You're giving me the chance to save my friend. Lovers or not, I'll owe you for the rest of my life for what you did tonight. I asked for a hero and you showed up."

The word went through Rosalind like a knife or an arrow. Hero. It was the echo of an old conversation, a conversation that had shaped lives. She had always wanted to be a hero, but there was something missing from it. "I just followed my dream, baby. If there's a hero, it's you. You have to end it."

Taryn snorted. "I'm no hero. If I do anything that resembles heroics, it's because of you. You give me the knowledge and the strength."

"Fine, we do it together. All right?"

A smile of pure joy spread across Taryn's face. "Yeah. That feels right."

"I have to go get a few things for tonight. Baby, I'd take you with me, but I think you're needed here today. After last night, you and Rhea might have a few things left to say. And you should talk to Joe." Rosalind pulled Taryn into her arms. She lay back immediately.

"I didn't tell you what went on between me and Rhea," Taryn said, glancing at her.

"You will, when you can. It didn't feel right to push."

"Do you understand all this stuff because you're older, or because you're just good with people? I can't manage a conversation without smashing things."

Rosalind turned Taryn's bandaged hand over in both of hers. "I'm not convinced I understand anything. But we'll work on the smashing part. Okay?"

"Yeah." Taryn leaned in and kissed Rosalind good-bye.

It was going to be a long day.

CHAPTER SIXTEEN

W hat's next on the list?" Ellie asked, picking up the candles and putting them in the paper bag that sat open between her knees.

"Arrows. An arrow, actually. I think I only need one," Rosalind said, looking up from the pile of debris surrounding her on her living room floor.

"You think. You have a dream about magic and death, and instead of attributing it to bad food or tequila, you go arrow shopping. You don't sound like yourself, sweetie."

"No, I sound like an actress who is so superstitious about going onstage, she won't open a show without a piece of jade in her socks." Rosalind raised an eyebrow at Ellie.

"Low blow. Love the eyebrow thing. Get that from our teenager, did we?"

"She's twenty. I wish everyone would stop calling her a teenager." Rosalind sighed.

"No, you don't, because it makes you feel young and vital to be sleeping with a girl who can't drink yet. What about this one?" Ellie held up an aluminum shaft with red fletching.

"There's no point on it. It has to have a point," Rosalind said, examining it.

"Everything you do has to have a point. You can choose the head—see the little screw marks?" Ellie held up the example.

Rosalind picked up a package of arrowheads and examined them. "These."

The humor left Ellie's face. "Those are for bear hunting. You could punch a hole in a Toyota with that thing. Are you sure?"

Rosalind opened the package and felt the weight of the razor-edged steel in her palm. The original arrows had been cane, fletched with desert eagle, with heads of graceful bronzework. If she closed her eyes, she could still see their flight. The bear-killing head was far more brutal in appearance. It would be perfect as a symbol of death. "Yes."

Ellie shrugged. "Okay, arrow, check. Deadly looking bear-hunting arrowhead, check. We have the candles. We have the costumes. We have enough incense to make a hippie blush. Anything else you need?"

"I don't think so. The important thing is the arrow. I've never designed a ritual before. I'm not sure how to go about it."

"Theater started out as ritual, so you came to the right place. Tell me the basic plot, we'll design something gorgeous. A little spectacle, some emotion, a big climax. It's just like theater. Dress well, pick good lighting, a flashy moment or two to bring the audience in, and have something pretty to say to tie it all up," Ellie said, folding the bag closed.

"You make it sound easy." Rosalind stood up, abandoning her nest of paper, books, candles, and incense.

"Ritual should be easy, I think. Gorgeous, emotional, but understandable. Why else did you ask me to help you on your supernatural treasure hunt? I take it seriously, but not too seriously."

Ellie settled back against the couch, her arm stretched out in invitation.

Rosalind accepted and sat down next to her friend. "I haven't really prayed since third grade. I don't even know who I'm praying to. I asked you to help me because I trust you, with my life and hers." Rosalind's eyes found Ellie's and held them.

"Careful, that sounded serious. Tell me the story again. I'll give you some believable action."

Rosalind took a deep breath, then let it out slowly. "The prince was captured. The fortune-teller threw herself in front of the arrow. She couldn't let the prince die."

"That sounds familiar," Ellie said dryly.

"That act of sacrifice set the whole pattern in motion. Ever since, the women of Rhea's bloodline have loved and protected the women of Taryn's, up till now—"

"But then you come in to end the cosmic codependence," Ellie said, putting her arm around Rosalind's shoulders.

"But then I come in. I can only hope my ancestor was right about this. The dream was hers, just waiting until a woman of my line could understand it," Rosalind said, leaning forward and resting her arms on her knees.

"Forgive me for being blunt, but if you accept all this, how in the world do you think you can change it? Aren't there mystic laws and such playing out?"

"That's the part I have to take on faith. I can't believe that we have no control over our own destiny, that God, or whoever, could be cruel enough to give us the capacity to love then snatch it away. I have no way of knowing. But in the face of not knowing, I choose to live like I have the power to change things. It's all I have."

"I think you're a few bats shy of a belfry. But what the hell. We've got nothing to lose."

"Thanks. I think."

"Okay. Believable action. Stuff the audience can read. I've got it. Start with the scene from the dream. We need to set up Rhea as Taryn's caretaker. Taryn just punched a window, right? Have Rhea change the bandages."

Rosalind remembered the sight of Taryn sitting quietly on the kitchen floor, blood down to her elbow, while Rhea picked glass shards out of the wound. She'd known then that they had done that before. There was too deep a feeling of recognition at the sight. "All right. We'll need to bring the priestess in. The archway between the living room and the middle room would serve for the gate. I could wait there for the prince."

"Perfect. Taryn will have to do drag, won't that be a shame. But you will need to be captured by soldiers to set up the execution. Joe could play one, I could play another. We'll need more, I think. Laurel and Goblin. The important thing is the arrow. Do you want to?" Ellie asked, holding up the shaft.

Light played along the razor edge of the head, designed to pierce a thick wall of fur, flesh, and muscle. It was too savage a thing to belong to the world she knew, but she'd purchased it at Kmart. *Maybe humans haven't changed all that much since we hacked each other apart with swords.*

"No. It's not my symbol. It needs to be one of the soldiers. Would you?"

"Shoot a bear-killing arrow at your girlfriend? Sure. What are friends for?" Ellie said with a straight face.

"Have you ever been to one of these ceremonies before?"

"A Wiccan circle? Sure. They have one every month at the Unitarian Church on Elmwood."

Rosalind whistled between her teeth. "Wow. Unitarians are more liberal than I thought."

"They ain't Methodists from Poughkeepsie, sister." Ellie stood up and stretched, then held her hand out to Rosalind.

"Sister. I like that. We should have been sisters."

Ellie was very quiet for a moment, her face uncharacteristically still. Then she laughed and tossed her hair back on her shoulders. "Maybe we were, in another life. I hear there's a lot of that going around."

"Oh, stop. Tell me what happens." Rosalind started gathering up the wreckage of her living room, unable to suppress the need for cleanliness her mother had drummed into her. Supernatural treasure hunts and mystic patterns notwithstanding, a clean house was a must.

"Well, usually they cast the circle, sort of draw an imaginary line around everyone to create a sacred space. They call the directions and the center. Hail to the Guardians of the Watchtowers of the South kind of stuff. It's an invitation for the spirits, or gods, or powers to come in and play. After the ritual is done, the circle is declared open again."

"Invitation. That has a good feel to it. I think we're ready. What should I wear?" Rosalind started walking toward her bedroom.

"Black is always good. But then, black is always good for anything." Ellie looked at the narrow black pants and black silk shirt she was wearing and smiled.

Rosalind came back out of the bedroom in a black turtleneck and pants. Her hair was loose on her shoulders, arrayed with disheveled perfection.

Ellie looked at her for a long moment, absorbing the changes in her friend. Rosalind looked stunning, even in the simple clothing. There was a lightness to her, almost an aura. In the week since she'd met Taryn, Rosalind's nervous mannerisms had vanished. Rosalind carried herself like a woman who had found who she was and was happy in that knowledge. "You look great," Ellie said, awed.

"You're just saying that because I'm starting to dress like you." Rosalind smiled at her.

"No. You've changed, Ros. Love agrees with you."

The shy smile that answered Ellie was like a splinter of light caught in a gem's facet, a hint of radiance that was painful to look at directly. Rosalind had found her mystery.

Ellie endured the brimming silence as long as she could, before giving in to her impulse to speak, to change the subject, to dance about with words. "Do you know what you'll say for the big wrap-up?"

"I have something in mind," Rosalind said, but didn't elaborate.

❖

It was evening, and the street was crowded with cars. Rosalind parked down near Virginia. They walked up the street, kicking leaves into the air. Rosalind carried the paper bag in front of her chest.

"You look like a schoolgirl with her books. Will you relax?" Ellie whispered to her.

"Probably not. You know that. I'm still nervous."

"Let's see. A house full of witches, meeting for a full-moon circle. One hears voices, one predicts the future and identifies past lives, one flouts gender convention for fun. And you're worried about what they'll think of you?" Ellie rolled her eyes.

Rosalind laughed. "Yeah, it does seem kind of silly."

"She can't wait to see you. I know, because you can't wait to see her. It'll be fine." Ellie put her hand on the small of Rosalind's back and pushed her along.

Joe was sitting on the top of the steps, smoking a cigar down to the band. He was all in green, from the dusty green of his pants, to the deep forest green of his shirt. Next to him, leaning against the column, was Taryn.

The sight of her stopped Rosalind in her tracks. Taryn's posture was meant to be casual, but Rosalind could read the tension in her body, even from a distance. She wore a tank top and a pair of jeans that hung low on her hips. Her dark head was resting against the column. Her bandaged hand hung at her side, a reminder that she was mortal and could be hurt.

"My, she certainly is a healthy specimen," Ellie drawled, looking at the broad set of Taryn's shoulders and the definition of her arms.

Rosalind just looked up at her. Taryn's head turned, slowly, until her eyes found Rosalind's. She could feel it like a touch, the force of her gaze.

"Evening, Ros. Good to see you again, Ellie. Will you be joining us tonight?" Joe said, smiling.

"I believe I will, if that's all right. Ros had something she wanted help with." Ellie left Rosalind on the sidewalk and marched up the steps.

Joe rose and tossed away the end of his cigar. "Perfectly all right. Splendid, even. Why don't you come in? I have some hot cider on the stove, just the thing for a crisp fall night." He opened the screen door and held it for her.

"Sounds great."

They vanished into the house, ignoring the silence between the two left on the porch. Rosalind walked slowly up the steps, the paper bag clutched to her chest. The sheer audacity of what she proposed hit her, hard. She had no idea of what to say to Taryn, and it made her awkward.

Taryn seemed to feel it. She stayed where she was, leaning back against the pale purple column. "You get what you needed today?"

"Yes. I hope so," Rosalind said, then decided that she was being ridiculous. She set the bag down and opened her arms.

Taryn came into them immediately, the ferocity of her embrace assuring Rosalind that she'd done the right thing.

"You okay, baby?" she asked, kissing her cheek.

"I am now. You were right," Taryn said, her voice a low rumble in her chest.

"About what?"

"Staying home today. Rhea and I had a talk, without smashing anything. I made up with Joe. I even apologized for being a jerk. You'd have been proud of me."

"I am proud of you." Rosalind put her hand over Taryn's heart, feeling the irregular drumming under the skin. It beat harder when she left her hand there.

"I don't get it. I'm happy about it, but I don't get it. It's like I've got you fooled. One day you're going to wake up and look at me and be, like, she's an uneducated little punk. What am I doing with her?"

Rosalind laughed. She saw Taryn's face harden into furious lines instantly. Rosalind took Taryn's head in her hands. "No, sweetheart. I'm not laughing at you. I'm laughing because that's what I thought when you first spent the night at my place. You'd wake up and think

I was too old, or boring, or vanilla, and wonder what you were doing with me."

It took a moment for a smile to work through the remains of anger on Taryn's face. She fought it, but it came, a smile that spread from ear to ear. "We're made for each other."

"We are."

"Rosalind, I don't care where it came from, if we knew each other before or what. I want you. I want it to work with us," Taryn said, her voice low and urgent.

"I want that, too. I think that, after tonight, we can have that conversation. There will be room for it." Rosalind leaned up and kissed Taryn.

"So, you gonna tell me what's in the bag?"

"Let's go get everyone, and I'll tell you all at once."

Egyptia and Laurel were serving cider in the kitchen when Taryn and Rosalind came in. Goblin and Joe were sitting at the table with Ellie. Rosalind looked around for Rhea.

"She's upstairs meditating. She wanted some time alone before we begin. This evening has raised her hopes, and Rhea doesn't do well with hope. She'll be down," Joe said to her. Egyptia handed Rosalind a mug of cider.

"I hope you don't mind me being here. Joe said this was for family."

"Egyptia, I hope to be as much a part of this family as you are. I'm glad you're here," Rosalind said warmly.

"It is perfect that she is here," Rhea said, making everyone jump. She'd come into the room quiet as a cat. "Royalty is fraught with its own power, both inherent and cultural. Drag royalty has the trickster power, the crossing of realms. Anyone who walks a hard road to be true to themselves has magic."

Taryn went to the stove and poured Rhea a cup of cider. When she handed it to Rhea, Rosalind saw that it was in her blue glass mug. Rhea took the cup and kissed Taryn's hand, a startling display of affection. Taryn stood behind her chair and massaged her shoulders as she spoke.

"I've been meditating on the symbols for tonight's ritual. I looked everywhere for flaws, but found none. You are right. All the elements align at this time, in this place and incarnation. The season is right.

Autumn at the high end of late summer, with the hint of winter on the wind. The time to secure the house and make ready for the winter sleep, to put away stores against the lean times. A time for changing state in a glorious display.

"The place is right. Buffalo is a city perpetually on the frontier and perpetually falling behind, a perfect place to cross borders. This house has been Taryn's home. She hasn't lived with me before. I've always been outside her immediate family. I planned otherwise this time, but her stubbornness kept her from being born on time."

"Same story. I was late getting born and haven't made up for it since," Taryn said, kissing the top of Rhea's head.

"Yet it worked. If you had been born when I predicted, you'd be Rosalind's age now, as is usually the case. But you refused and so are thirteen years younger. That allows the symbol to be in alignment with the original. The prince was younger than the priestess by that many years," Rhea said. She saw Rosalind flinch when this was mentioned.

"I know I was angry with you for the events that led to this," Rhea said to her.

Rosalind shook her head. "I would be, too. It was a ghastly thing."

"My rage at you kept me from seeing clearly. It was a ghastly thing Taryn did in her hurt pride. But only when I could look beyond that one event could I see the use for it. It allowed the age to come back into balance. It was terrible. I had no right to make you suffer for it this time. I was already gone when it happened. You had to live the remainder of your life with it."

Rosalind tried to speak, but found she couldn't around the lump in her throat. She felt the urge to sob with that remembered pain. She blinked furiously and looked away. When she could look back up, Rhea was speaking again, addressing the rest of the group. Rosalind looked over the witch's shoulder and saw Taryn looking back at her. They were both here now. It was time to let go of the past and try something new.

"What troubles me is the ending. We can enact the ritual as you've laid out, Rosalind. We can let Taryn take on the death. But I confess, my mind refuses to go on. I can't see what would come after," Rhea said, handing Taryn's blue glass mug back to her. There was a moment when their hands brushed in passing and held, the contact extended automatically. It was the reflex of a close-knit clan, to take affection and reassurance in whatever moments they could. The behavior of people who had to rely only on one another to face the world. Rosalind watched them together very carefully.

"We each have our roles. Egyptia, if you would, act as the satrap. Royalty needs to be symbolized by royalty," Rhea said. "Joe, Ellie, Laurel, and Goblin will be the soldiers."

"I have knives for us to wear. We need a weapon to indicate our profession." Joe started handing out the knives, a wicked collection. He handed Ellie a broad-bladed skinning knife with a bone handle.

It slashed the air convincingly when Ellie waved it about. "I feel like a killer with this thing."

"We will begin in a few minutes," said Rhea. "Change clothes, do what you need to prepare yourselves."

"I have some wine down in the basement that'd be perfect for the ending," said Joe. "Egyptia, Ellie, would you help me haul some of it up?"

The others abandoned the kitchen with unrehearsed speed, responding to the painfully intimate look that Taryn and Rosalind shared. It was as if Rhea could see the emotion coming and vanished first, unable or unwilling to witness the moment. Egyptia was still closing the basement door behind her when the gravity between the lovers exerted its force and they came together. With her arms wrapped tightly around Taryn's body Rosalind could almost believe in paradise. There, within her reach, was everything she hadn't known she desired. Pain, time, and circumstance would alter their bodies. Age would eventually bring them down.

Standing with her ear against her boy's drumming heart, Rosalind knew that it would one day cease. That earth would cradle what her arms now held. The name and memory of Taryn would wash away like a chalk painting in the rain. She knew that she might be alive to witness this. The only thing that let her bear that knowledge was the belief that the burning core that inhabited the body would not end.

Love is what lets us endure the knowledge that we must die, but love is also what makes death unbearable. New love balks at separation; what would a lifelong love feel at the final separation? The argument that cannot be won, the final reprove.

The night she met Taryn came back in a tidal wave, the recognition she'd felt when she first looked into Taryn's eyes. Desire had called her out, woken her body, made the urge to know her an ache. It was the surrender to that impulse, to follow desire where it led, that gave her back her soul. All things were connected forward and back; the golden snake formed an endless loop, a wheel.

"I know how to finish it," Rosalind said, her cheek resting against Taryn's chest.

"You breaking up with me already? Give me two weeks at least."

Rosalind took Taryn's left hand and kissed it. "The ritual. Rhea couldn't see what comes after completion. The only way to end it is in joy. We know that things begin, and end, and begin again. So all there is left to do is celebrate."

"You sure don't think like Rhea does. About ritual or anything else."

Rosalind looked up at her face and saw admiration, mingled with the desire that was never far from the surface between them. "I do about a few things. I think you are worth facing death."

Taryn closed her eyes, then opened them slowly as if gazing into the sun. "I've had enough of death. Screw it. Let's all live for a change."

❖

The middle room was cleared to the floorboards, swept by a cornhusk broom and prepared with sage and sweetgrass. Rosalind watched Joe carry the burning knot to each corner, speaking in his low, burring voice the household phrase. "Let all who come in peace be welcome here."

They'd all changed clothes. Joe wore his ceremonial robe—yards of simple white with a belt of braided leather. The robe fell open, exposing his powerful chest with the tattoo of intertwined snakes. In the belt he carried his knife to indicate his role as a soldier. He looked the part from the grim expression on his face, to his martial carriage. Laurel wore a robe of black with a crow embroidered on the back.

For a moment Rosalind felt like she should be wearing a more elaborate costume; then Goblin entered in jeans and a T-shirt. Egyptia glided in as only royalty may, gorgeous and strange, scintillating in gold and scarlet. In her arms was a black iron cauldron. She knelt in the center of the room and set it on a piece of slate. Laurel poured Epsom salts and a bottle of rubbing alcohol into it; Goblin lit a wooden match and tossed it. Fire danced in the pot, blue and yellow.

❖

Rhea came down the back stairs. She'd changed into a robe of shimmering black like crushed obsidian mingled with shards of beetles' carapace. The sleeves were sewn with spiders, and it closed at the front with buttons of carved bone. Her hair was free, standing out from her head. In her hands were a bouquet of wildflowers tied with a red ribbon and a knife with a curving blade and a hilt of brass. She set the flowers next to the cauldron and cut the air above it with the knife, before setting that down as well.

Ellie stood next to Rosalind, holding her hand. Whenever Rosalind felt the apprehension rise, Ellie would squeeze her hand and ground her. Everyone stood in a circle around the cauldron.

Taryn entered. She had changed into her black suit and strode the floor like a stage. The magic worked. Here was a beautiful young man, serious as an altar boy at his first Mass. Taryn offered her bandaged hand to her lover, almost apologetically.

Rosalind took it and drew it up to her lips. Rosalind watched Taryn and Rhea join hands, right hand palm down, left hand palm up, and imitated the motion with Ellie. She knew that Rhea would lead them in casting the circle; then the ritual would be under her guidance.

She tried to stay present, to listen to Joe, Laurel, Goblin, and Rhea call the directions, but all she could think about was the sweat gathering in her palms. Taryn called the center, spoke words of invitation, and everyone responded with a murmured, "Blessed Be."

The singing began. It took Rosalind a few moments to follow it; it was a chant, cycling around and around, names she recognized with a start as old goddesses. "Isis, Astarte, Diana, Hecate, Demeter, Kali, Inanna…"

Ellie picked up on it right away and joined in, winking at Rosalind. As soon as the list finished it began again. Rosalind joined in. It was the singing, or the anticipation, but Rosalind felt something gathering in the room. The chant ended, Rhea looked across Taryn, at Rosalind, and nodded.

This was it. Rosalind opened the paper bag and handed the arrow to Ellie. The bear-killing head caught the light from the cauldron and flared gold and red. Ellie and Joe, Laurel and Goblin moved to the doorway near the stairs, standing away from the center. Taryn squeezed Rosalind's hand, to get her lover's attention. Her eyes were as blue as steel in the witchlight of the cauldron. There was no question there, only a moment of connection that Rosalind felt rise in herself and meet Taryn. She felt the love she had for this splendid youth, this wounded warrior, and let her hand go.

Taryn walked to the center of the room and crouched next to the cauldron. She picked up the brass hilt knife with her right hand and cut away the bandages on her left. Perhaps it was a quality of the light, or of the mood in the room, but the wound looked savage when revealed, the damage greater than Rosalind remembered.

Taryn stretched out on the floor, flung her left arm out, and rested her dark head against the boards. Rhea walked into the circle, her hands full of white cloth, torn in strips. She knelt gracefully next to Taryn and took the mangled hand into her lap. She began binding the wound with the strips of cloth.

A shiver went through Rosalind. It was enough like her dream to give her pause—not just a symbol of something that happened long ago, but the thing itself, happening again. Taryn was really wounded, a product of her own anger, and Rhea was really caring for her. *Where does the symbol end and the event begin?* She looked at the scene, feeling the distance in time and place.

This was a window on the past. She saw the look Rhea gave Taryn and knew it wasn't re-creation. Rhea saw the angry youth in pain and took that pain on herself. Taryn opened her eyes and saw Rhea. Rhea spoke, but the words were incomprehensible to Rosalind, and perhaps to Taryn, but she appeared to understand the tone. She sat up, looking into Rhea's face, in wonder. Rhea cradled the dark head against her chest, tears streaming down her face.

The beautiful young man stood up, pushing away from Rhea's embrace. He stretched up toward the vault of the sky with his hands open, seeking, yearning. Rosalind knew that it was her time. She dropped Ellie's hand and stepped away. In the archway between the rooms she waited, lingering, looking out as if over vast distances. The young man strolled, walking around the room, a serpentine path that led to the archway.

In one eternal moment they saw one another and all else faded like smoke. The recognition was there; Rosalind nearly sobbed in gladness to see her. Her boy had come home, the other half of her soul. She held out her arms.

There was a crash from the doorway. She knew it was coming, she'd given everyone their parts, but Rosalind still jumped when Joe, Laurel, Ellie, and Goblin burst into the room. The soldiers came on them, seizing Taryn's arms. Rosalind went along willingly, unable to be separated from her lover.

In the west corner of the room they made Taryn kneel. Rosalind was kept in the south corner, her arms held by Joe and Goblin. Egyptia entered through the archway—cold, relentless, with the bearing of a ruler. As the satrap, Egyptia motioned to Ellie imperiously. Ellie drew forth the arrow from her belt. In the light of the cauldron the bear-killing head burned red and ghastly. She held it like a javelin, ready to throw.

There was a flash of yellow smoke; Rhea had hurled something into the cauldron. She appeared out of the earth, out of the smoke, standing between Taryn and Ellie. The choice she made was the choice she had always made, out of love, out of belief, out of sacrifice. Wordlessly, she pushed her body between the wounded Taryn and the presence of death.

Taryn got to her feet. She lay one hand on Rhea's shoulder, urging her out of the way. Rhea turned to her with horror in her face, unable to let this happen, even now. Taryn had to take her shoulders and move her, gently but firmly. With the witch behind her, she stood, the beautiful boy, and faced the soldier who held her death. She arched her head back, opened her hands, and in a moment of regal abandon took on the fate that was meant for her.

It was too real. Rosalind had coached everyone on the order of events, given them the sequence, but the reality was happening so fast. The soldiers attacked, the flames danced in the cauldron, Taryn offered herself as a sacrifice. Ellie threw the arrow.

It arched through the smoke-laden air, directly at Taryn's throat. Rhea collapsed with a sob, unable to face this. Rosalind cried out in horror. She had orchestrated these events; what if she'd been wrong?

The arrow took the beautiful boy in the neck, the bear-killing head gouging a bloody furrow across the front of the throat to lodge in the thick muscle of the shoulder. Taryn opened her eyes and saw the arrow sticking out of her flesh. She pulled it out. She had taken the death meant for her. The Wheel was free to turn.

Taryn held up the arrow in her fist, then, with a flexing of her hand, snapped it in half. She gave both halves to Rhea, her dark head bowed in reverence. Rhea took the pieces of the arrow, almost casually, then tossed them into the cauldron with a sideways flick of her left hand.

Taryn stood in front of Rhea, towering over the woman who had been her lover, protector, and friend. She took Rhea's hands in hers and held them. "Thank you. For taking care of me, every time around. I wouldn't have made it through without you. I'd like the chance to take care of you, now."

Rosalind watched them, the powerfully built girl cradling the slender form of Rhea, both of them with their eyes shut tight. There was something ending, and endings always bring a measure of grief. She watched as Taryn, with a gentleness she had never displayed in front of people, stroked Rhea's hair, murmured into her ear. Rhea had relaxed completely into Taryn's arms. For the first time, Rosalind saw Rhea's vulnerability. Taryn had taken on something beyond her angry youth—a seasoning of wisdom, a hint at the woman she would become. It gave Rhea room to be something other than unceasingly strong. The balance had shifted between them.

Joe took Goblin's hand and held his other out to Rosalind. She accepted. Egyptia gathered up Laurel and Ellie and joined them. They stood in a circle around Taryn and Rhea, holding one another in the light from the cauldron. A deep voice began singing, Joe's. It started out very low, a background to the scene before them, then rose, filling the room. He sang the song through once, then began again, this time with Laurel, Goblin, and Ellie joining in.

Rosalind looked at her lover, looked at the woman she held, and smiled. Something was ending, something was beginning. Rosalind joined in the singing.

"Amazing Grace,
how sweet the earth
that formed a witch like me—
I was once was burned

Now I survive
Was hanged, but now I sing.
'Twas grace that drew down the Moon,
'Twas grace that raised the sea—
The magic of the people's will
Will set our Rhea free."

The song ended, Rhea stepped back from Taryn. They took up position in the circle, Rhea to Rosalind's left, Taryn to her right. When Taryn took her hand, Rosalind felt a jolt of electricity sizzle up her arm. She looked down at their joined hands, expecting to see them glow. She glanced at her lover. Taryn's broad grin indicated that she had felt it, too.

"Would you do the honors?" Rhea asked her.

Rosalind cleared her throat before speaking. "I wanted to say something brilliant to complete the ritual, but all that came to me was the fragment of a prayer I read a long time ago, so I'm going with that.

"In beauty it is finished. In beauty it is finished. In beauty it is finished. Thanks."

❖

Sunday morning. Rosalind's eyes opened. She had been dreaming something and struggled to retain it. Nothing so earth-shattering as the battles she had seen. No, they were walking down a road. Two women, just having a conversation. She wished she could remember who they were, or what they were discussing, but the dream slipped through her fingers like smoke. Oh well, it was Sunday, and the ritual had gone well, and the handsomest boy in Buffalo was splayed out like a puppy at her side. Rosalind pulled the sheet down and stroked the bulldagger tattoo on Taryn's back, smiling like a satiated cat. It was a stroke to her ego, to have worn Taryn out.

"Didn't know I had it in me, did ya?" she whispered. "Neither did I."

Taryn slept like the dead. The mood after the ceremony had been joyous, celebratory. Joe had broken out a few bottles of wine he'd been hiding in the basement and even gotten Rhea to have a glass. Rosalind had a vague memory of Joe teaching them obscene drinking songs, after Goblin had gone to bed. At one point, while they both pried Taryn out of her suit so they could bandage her wound, Rhea had asked her something unbelievable.

Her eyes moved from the body of her lover to the room. Rosalind looked at the small circle of furniture, an oasis in the echoing space, and sighed. It had been sweet and generous of Joe and Taryn to move her stuff up to the third floor, to create a space for them. But it was still the third floor of 34 Mariner, Rhea's house. As much as she felt a part of the family, there was a part of Rosalind that still felt like a teenager sleeping over.

Rosalind slipped out of bed carefully, though Taryn was unlikely to wake up. She walked down the back stairs to the kitchen, half expecting to find Joe already cooking. The kitchen was empty, sunlight streaming in the windows. In one of the squares of light, the calico dozed. Rosalind put the coffee pot on the flame, then knelt next to her. She scratched between the calico's ears. The cat squinted in pleasure.

"Oh. I'm surprised to find someone else up." The voice came from the doorway, Rhea's. She had just come down the stairs, in the robe Rosalind remembered seeing the first morning she'd slept at the house.

Rosalind stood up, dusting her hands off on her pants. "I didn't mean to surprise you."

"Don't apologize. I think I'll get to like being surprised." Rhea sat down at the table.

"I was making coffee. Can I put on water for your tea?" Rosalind asked, filling the kettle.

"Coffee. I'll have a cup with you, if you don't mind," Rhea said, and smiled at Rosalind's surprised look.

Rosalind arched her eyebrow at Rhea, but set a coffee mug down in front of her.

"You do that as well as she does, you know."

"Do I? I think I picked it up just watching her. She got it from you."

"Or I from her. It's hard to tell, after a while," Rhea said.

Rosalind poured the coffee and sat back down at the table. "What a gorgeous morning," she said, looking at the cat dozing in the sun.

"Hmm. A time for change. We've done the clearing of the way. It's time to do everything the daylight world offers. I don't know what will happen with it, but it feels like there's a chance now for something different. You know, I owe you an apology," Rhea said, over the rim of her cup.

"You do?" Rosalind put her coffee mug down on the table.

"Yes. For trying to drive you out when you showed up. I was convinced that everything would happen the way it always had. I am very rarely wrong about anything. If I had to be wrong, I'm glad it was about you."

"Thank you. That means the world. You know I was scared to death of you when we met."

Rhea's eyes went wide. "Really?"

"Oh, yes. You were clear on your dislike."

"Well, you didn't let on. You were clear on your affection for Taryn. She made a good choice in you. You, however, will have your hands full," Rhea said, and smiled.

"That a prediction?"

"Observation," Rhea said mildly. "Have you thought about my offer?"

"To join the household? Yes, I have." Rosalind looked down into her coffee cup.

"Hmm." Rhea pushed away from the table. "Well, I think I could get a few more hours' sleep. Joe and his wine have that effect on me. I should know better than to let the man have me drink." She paused in the doorway, looking over her shoulder at Rosalind. "I circled something in the paper for you. You might find it interesting."

Rosalind pulled the paper toward her. It was open to the classifieds, and she scanned down the page. In the center was a red circle, done in Rhea's forceful hand. She read it, idly, until she reached the bottom of the ad. Her head snapped up, but Rhea was gone. A smile replaced her look of surprise. "You already knew," she said to the empty kitchen.

EPILOGUE

Taryn was sitting on the porch, blue glass mug in hand, squinting against the sunlight. It was afternoon. She'd slept through Rosalind's rising. Taryn had found Rhea and Joe in the kitchen, eating lunch. She'd asked after Rosalind. Rhea had smiled strangely and said that she'd be back. So she sat on the porch with her coffee and her sketchbook and waited.

She heard the leaves crunching; Rosalind was walking up Mariner, from Allen Street. She stopped every few steps and kicked a pile of leaves into the air, and grinned as they resettled themselves in her wake.

"You're in a good mood this morning," Taryn growled.

"And why not? The day is gorgeous, life begins anew, creation is loose on the world," Rosalind said, dropping down on the step next to her. She reached into her pocket. "I have something for you."

"Aspirin?"

"Not that. Close your eyes."

Taryn did so, reluctantly. Rosalind waited until she was sure her eyes were really shut. Then she took Taryn's right hand and gently pried it open. She dropped a small black box into the center.

"You can open your eyes."

"What is this?" Taryn said, her voice strange.

"Open it."

Taryn glanced at Rosalind with something that might have been apprehension. She creaked the box open and held up the contents. "A key? To what?"

"The house I rented this morning. I was thinking about Rhea's offer about moving in here, but it didn't seem right. This is her territory, and yours. You're a part of the family here, and I didn't want to take you away from that. But I wanted to have a place that's mine. And I wanted you to have a key to it."

"You scared the hell out of me. I thought you were…" Taryn said, lips quirking into a smile.

"Proposing?"

"Yeah."

"I may yet. Watch your back," Rosalind said, deadpan.

"Be careful of what you ask for. So, where is your new house?"

Rosalind stretched out her arm and pointed up the street. "41 Mariner. The brick one. Great porch, lovely backyard garden. The kitchen is a little smaller than here, but we can walk over and have coffee in the morning. You can belong to the family and still have a place to go. What do you think?"

Taryn put the coffee mug down and kissed the surprised Rosalind. "I think you're the best thing that ever happened to me. I think, if you did propose, I'd say yes."

"We'll test that theory one day." Rosalind slipped her arm around the drag king's waist and leaned back against her.

"I have something for you, too," Taryn said into her ear.

"Oh?"

"Yeah. An idea came to me while you were out. I just sketched it roughly, but you can see it." She picked up the notebook from the porch and opened it. It was the drawing of a dogwood tree in full flower. When she looked a little closer, she saw a serpent with golden scales wrapped around a branch, eyes as red as rubies.

"It's beautiful."

"For your first tattoo. Left shoulder blade, I think," Taryn said, moving her hair aside and kissing the spot.

"We'll see, baby. We'll see."

It was turning out to be a gorgeous day.

About the Author

Susan Smith is a handsome, brooding warrior king novelist. Smith was once described as a nice, small town boy educated well beyond necessary, but not nearly enough to please her. Smitty is in love with books—from reading them to writing them. She's been a writer, drag king, director, and librarian.

Perhaps by luck, or fate, Smitty has lived in Buffalo, New York and spends an inordinate amount of time in Toronto, Ontario. While old fashioned in a very modern way, Smitty still does not understand that coffee is never just coffee.

Her sequel to *Of Drag Kings & the Wheel of Fate* titled *Burning Dreams* will be available from Bold Strokes Books in December 2006.

Books Available From Bold Strokes Books

Forever Found by JLee Meyer. Can time, tragedy, and shattered trust destroy a love that seemed destined? When chance reunites two childhood friends separated by tragedy, the past resurfaces to determine the shape of their future. (1-933110-37-6)

Sword of the Guardian by Merry Shannon. Princess Shasta's bold new bodyguard has a secret that could change both of their lives. He is actually a she. A passionate romance filled with courtly intrigue, chivalry, and devotion. (-933110-36-8)

Chance by Grace Lennox. At twenty-six, Chance Delaney decides her life isn't working so she swaps it for a different one. What follows is the sexy, funny, touching story of two women who, in finding themselves, also find one another. (1-933110-31-7)

The Exile and the Sorcerer by Jane Fletcher. First in the Lyremouth Chronicles. Tevi, wounded and adrift, arrives in the courtyard of a shy young sorcerer. Together they face monsters, magic, and the challenge of loving despite their differences. (1-933110-32-5)

A Matter of Trust by Radclyffe. JT Sloan is a cybersleuth who doesn't like attachments. Michael Lassiter is leaving her husband, and she needs Sloan's expertise to safeguard her company. It should just be business—but it turns into much more. (1-933110-33-3)

Sweet Creek by Lee Lynch. A celebration of the enduring nature of love, friendship, and community in the quirky, heart-warming lesbian community of Waterfall Falls. (1-933110-29-5)

The Devil Inside by Ali Vali. Derby Cain Casey, head of a New Orleans crime organization, runs the family business with guts and grit, and no one crosses her. No one, that is, until Emma Verde claims her heart and turns her world upside down. (1-933110-30-9)

Grave Silence by Rose Beecham. Detective Jude Devine's investigation of a series of ritual murders is complicated by her torrid affair with the golden girl of Southwestern forensic pathology, Dr. Mercy Westmoreland. (1-933110-25-2)

Honor Reclaimed by Radclyffe. In the aftermath of 9/11, Secret Service Agent Cameron Roberts and Blair Powell close ranks with a trusted few to find the would-be assassins who nearly claimed Blair's life. (1-933110-18-X)

Honor Bound by Radclyffe. Secret Service Agent Cameron Roberts and Blair Powell face political intrigue, a clandestine threat to Blair's safety, and the seemingly irreconcilable personal differences that force them ever farther apart. (1-933110-20-1)

Protector of the Realm: Supreme Constellations Book One by Gun Brooke. A space adventure filled with suspense and a daring intergalactic romance featuring Commodore Rae Jacelon and a stunning, but decidedly lethal, Kellen O'Dal. (1-933110-26-0)

Innocent Hearts by Radclyffe. In a wild and unforgiving land, two women learn about love, passion, and the wonders of the heart. (1-933110-21-X)

The Temple at Landfall by Jane Fletcher. An imprinter, one of Celaeno's most revered servants of the Goddess, is also a prisoner to the faith—until a Ranger frees her by claiming her heart. The Celaeno series. (1-933110-27-9)

Force of Nature by Kim Baldwin. From tornados to forest fires, the forces of nature conspire to bring Gable McCoy and Erin Richards close to danger, and closer to each other. (1-933110-23-6)

In Too Deep by Ronica Black. Undercover homicide cop Erin McKenzie tracks a femme fatale who just might be a real killer...with love and danger hot on her heels. (1-933110-17-1)

Course of Action by Gun Brooke. Actress Carolyn Black desperately wants the starring role in an upcoming film produced by Annelie Peterson. Just how far will she go for the dream part of a lifetime? (1-933110-22-8)

Rangers at Roadsend by Jane Fletcher. Sergeant Chip Coppelli has learned to spot trouble coming, and that is exactly what she sees in her new recruit, Katryn Nagata. The Celaeno series. (1-933110-28-7)

Justice Served by Radclyffe. Lieutenant Rebecca Frye and her lover, Dr. Catherine Rawlings, embark on a deadly game of hide-and-seek with an underworld kingpin who traffics in human souls. (1-933110-15-5)

Distant Shores, Silent Thunder by Radclyffe. Doctor Tory King—and the women who love her—is forced to examine the boundaries of love, friendship, and the ties that transcend time. (1-933110-08-2)

Hunter's Pursuit by Kim Baldwin. A raging blizzard, a mountain hideaway, and a killer-for-hire set a scene for disaster—or desire—when Katarzyna Demetrious rescues a beautiful stranger. (1-933110-09-0)

The Walls of Westernfort by Jane Fletcher. All Temple Guard Natasha Ionadis wants is to serve the Goddess—until she falls in love with one of the rebels she is sworn to destroy. The Celaeno series. (1-933110-24-4)

Change Of Pace: *Erotic Interludes* by Radclyffe. Twenty-five hot-wired encounters guaranteed to spark more than just your imagination. Erotica as you've always dreamed of it. (1-933110-07-4)

Honor Guards by Radclyffe. In a wild flight for their lives, the president's daughter and those who are sworn to protect her wage a desperate struggle for survival. (1-933110-01-5)

Fated Love by Radclyffe. Amidst the chaos and drama of a busy emergency room, two women must contend not only with the fragile nature of life, but also with the irresistible forces of fate. (1-933110-05-8)

Justice in the Shadows by Radclyffe. In a shadow world of secrets and lies, Detective Sergeant Rebecca Frye and her lover, Dr. Catherine Rawlings, join forces in the elusive search for justice. (1-933110-03-1)

shadowland by Radclyffe. In a world on the far edge of desire, two women are drawn together by power, passion, and dark pleasures. An erotic romance. (1-933110-11-2)

Love's Masquerade by Radclyffe. Plunged into the indistinguishable realms of fiction, fantasy, and hidden desires, Auden Frost is forced to question all she believes about the nature of love. (1-933110-14-7)

Love & Honor by Radclyffe. The president's daughter and her lover are faced with difficult choices as they battle a tangled web of Washington intrigue for...love and honor. (1-933110-10-4)

Beyond the Breakwater by Radclyffe. One Provincetown summer three women learn the true meaning of love, friendship, and family. (1-933110-06-6)

Tomorrow's Promise by Radclyffe. One timeless summer, two very different women discover the power of passion to heal and the promise of hope that only love can bestow. (1-933110-12-0)

Love's Tender Warriors by Radclyffe. Two women who have accepted loneliness as a way of life learn that love is worth fighting for and a battle they cannot afford to lose. (1-933110-02-3)

Love's Melody Lost by Radclyffe. A secretive artist with a haunted past and a young woman escaping a life that has proved to be a lie find their destinies entwined. (1-933110-00-7)

Safe Harbor by Radclyffe. A mysterious newcomer, a reclusive doctor, and a troubled gay teenager learn about love, friendship, and trust during one tumultuous summer in Provincetown. (1-933110-13-9)

Above All, Honor by Radclyffe. Secret Service Agent Cameron Roberts fights her desire for the one woman she can't have—Blair Powell, the daughter of the president of the United States. (1-933110-04-X)